Testament

Brought up in west Wales, Alis Hawkins read English
at Oxford before training as a speech therapist. She lives
in Kent with her partner and teenage sons.

ALIS HAWKINS

Testament

First published 2008 by Macmillan New Writing

This edition published by Pan Books
an imprint of Pan Macmillan Ltd
Pan Macmillan, 20 New Wharf Road, London N1 9RR
Basingstoke and Oxford
Associated companies throughout the world
www.panmacmillan.com

ISBN 978-0-230-70638-5

For Edwina, Sam and Rob –

who fill my life with love and laughter

Acknowledgements

In acknowledging those who have helped in the writing of a book there's a tendency to thank everybody or nobody. But there are a few people without whom this book would, quite literally, not have been written. My family, Edwina, Sam and Rob, have watched our income go down and down as I have worked less and written more – I would not have been able to dedicate time to writing if they had once mentioned that they might like a foreign holiday or a designer . . . anything. Their emotional, financial and moral support and unswerving belief that one day I would 'make it' have enabled me to produce the book that *Testament* has become and not to lose my sanity in the process.

Years ago, when *Testament* was an idea, then an outline, and finally a tentative draft, my ex-husband, John, gave me enormous support of every kind for which I am truly and enduringly grateful.

And finally, very much in the here and now, I must thank my editor, Will Atkins, who has enabled me to make *Testament* the book I always wanted it to be.

Prologue

It was a small, almost insignificant fire, the smouldering consequence of wiring overdue for replacement a decade earlier; an irritating addition to the maintenance team's job-list rather than a major item of college news. But when the carpenters came to remove a small section of charred oak panelling they were confronted by an image that would change the history of Kineton and Dacre College.

There, on the newly uncovered patch of wall behind the Tudor panelwork, a soot-blackened face stared out, its mouth agape. And in that gaping mouth, a tiny figure writhed, an infant child, its arms outstretched.

The man nearest the wall jerked back with a muttered obscenity.

His companion peered into the space they had just created. 'Je – sus . . .' He half-turned. 'No one ever said anything about a painting, did they?'

The crude flesh-colours of the faces had been darkened and streaked by the fire, making the image even more hellish. The carpenter put out a hand to wipe away the soot.

'Better not, Will,' warned the other. 'You never know.'

The younger man, used to falling into line, dropped his hand. 'He's a stonemason,' he said instead. 'He's got those compasses.'

'The baby has too.' The other nodded at the infant's clutching hands. 'Come on, leave the bloody thing alone – we'd better go and tell 'em.'

After four and a half centuries of obscurity, the wall painting of Kineton and Dacre College was about to be restored to the light of day.

One

Salster, the week before Easter, 1385

In all the twenty years that Gwyneth of Kineton had waited to conceive a child, she had never imagined that giving birth might be the death of her. Though she had known others die in childbirth – had observed, bleakly, that her barrenness saved her from that, at least – she had not, in her bones, truly imagined that she would die bearing the child for which her very soul ached.

Yet here she lay, exhausted and almost beyond the reach of agony, sinking towards death. The child she had treasured all these months in her womb was killing her, stuck fast as he was.

She lay on a pallet, her knees drawn up, her damp shift twisted around her. Next to her stood the birthing stool from which she had fallen, vomiting, in an extremity of agony. Beside the stool, their eyes flicking nervously from one another to the semi-conscious woman at their feet, sat the midwives. Both had seen women die with their children unborn and both feared that Gwyneth of Kineton would make another.

They did not speak since neither had comfort to offer, but sat in resigned helplessness.

Worlds away from them, transported by narcotic pain into a delirium state, Gwyneth's mind raced through her life, stopping here and there momentarily, like a housewife anxious to reassure herself that everything is in order before she embarks on a long journey.

Her first certain memory: taking a wooden-headed mallet from her father's outstretched hand, feeling its weight and balance.

'They may not see you a master, Gwyneth, who can tell in these times? But the craft may be meat and drink to you.'

Thirty years ago and more. A long time to grow from a child to a woman dying of a child.

Her father again, Simon at his side. Simon as a young man, before he and Gwyneth married. Husband and father, mason and carpenter, burning energy and slow craft.

Years skipped by, their comings and goings ignored until her searching mind found him: Henry Ackland. Henry who lived under their roof and learned Simon's trade. Henry who had been all but a son to them.

He had visited, brought news – what was it? Important news. He had been away – too long! – but when he had come back to them he had brought news. What was it? Her mind searched restlessly, needing to know this last thing. Was it his love for Alysoun, her foster-daughter?

Again her unquiet mind shifted in its accounting. Alysoun: the child who had saved her from barren bitterness. That child had cost a death, and now her own child was demanding another. It was owed.

Alysoun's father had fallen to his death from a roof of Gwyneth's own design. The sound of his brief cry as he fell, the butcher's-club impact of flesh and bone on trodden-earth floor, came back to her now.

She had always said that it would be with her till her dying day.

Michael Icknield had lived for more than an hour, clinging to life with senseless desperation. All work suspended around him, he could not die in peace; they had not dared move him for fear of increasing his agony. They were all helpless, hushed, appalled. Masons fell to their knees, invoked saints; some for swift death, some for a miracle of healing.

A miracle. Simon had called this child's conception a miracle. Was it actually a curse? Would Simon lose both wife and unborn child in one death? Perhaps he would marry again and have the son he had prayed for so long.

Was she already halfway to another world, that she could look at her life as if it was already over?

Why did they not call a priest?

They had called a priest for Michael. He had done what he could, but Michael's wits had been shattered by the fall: he could voice neither confession nor repentance. Gwyneth had seen nothing in him but a beast-like will to cling to life.

The women, drawn by some change in the air, perhaps the sudden silence, had come from the workers' dwellings crowded around the site. Seeing the helpless shuffling of the still and silent men and the broken form on the floor, some turned back, forestalling the curious children and sending them away to their games.

Gwyneth knew that Icknield's child was motherless, and when his comrades had carried the mason's body away, she went, without indecent haste, to speak to the women.

And now, it seemed, she must answer for that and for everything else that her thirty-nine years had said and thought and done. But, in truth, it was only her greed for a child that she truly regretted – that hunger had robbed her of compassion.

And was it Simon's need for a son that was responsible for this double death now? Had her husband's passionate petitions, his prayer-broken knees, his refusal to bow – even to God's 'No' – brought her to this?

Was the Father Almighty so very just and so very unmerciful?

What little was left of her spirit rose up against such ingratitude. If God had given her a child, then he meant her to live.

'Oh God! Help me!' she groaned aloud, willing herself back into the startling brightness of full consciousness.

The midwives, shaken into motion by this evidence of a persistent will to live, took her under the arms and lifted her once more to the birthing stool. The heave and lunge that this required of her doubled body, straining against the tight-bound agony, forced a scream from Gwyneth. But as she heard the sound she also felt a twist of new, lurching pain and then fluid, copious and hot, flowing from her.

The elder midwife, ignoring her protests and pushing away her hands, felt inside. At her fingers' probing, the pain seized Gwyneth with fresh teeth, but through her own scream she heard the midwife shouting, 'The head is down! The head is down!'

Amidst her anguish at each new, widening pain, Gwyneth almost laughed with relief. The pain would soon be over and she would not die. She would see her child, hold it in her arms, feel its downy face against her own. Soon, soon . . .

❖

Simon of Kineton, unaware that the screams of childbirth, once begun, should be silenced only by the cries of an infant if news of the birth was to be happy, had no idea how close his wife had come, mere rooms away, to dying with his child unborn. The child's conception had restored his faith. All would be well; later that same day, Simon was confident, he would take his son to be baptised.

As Gwyneth struggled to keep a grip on both her wits and her life, her husband drew. Lines flowed from his hand's assured movements upon the sheet before him; bold lines, far from the meticulous, measured plans required of him as master mason. As his pen arced and scored, Simon of Kineton's mind was brimming over with ideas for this half-drawn building. Because the commission was his: to build a college at Salster for Richard Daker, one of the city of London's mightiest.

Only yesterday – *yesterday, the day his son began to be born!* – the news had finally come.

Simon, mallet and punch in hand, had been finishing the carving of a cross and horn – the personal emblem of the King's Bench judge for whom he had built a new, palatial London home – above its gatehouse arch. With his master mason's eye as always on the weather and the season's end, Simon had deliberately left all carving work until the building season was over.

'Master Kineton.'

As Simon turned on the scaffolding of withies, he was aware, from something in the man's tone, that he had worked on, oblivious, through several attempts to rouse him from his concentration.

'I'm sorry, friend,' he said. 'I didn't hear you.'

'No matter, master. I have a letter for you, from Master Ackland.'

Simon stuck his tools in his belt and strode down the steep ramp of swaying withies, dusting his hands palm against palm as he came.

Taking the letter, he broke the seal and opened it to be confronted with Henry's expansive hand. The boy had never lost that profligacy with ink and paper despite more than one thrashing at the hands of the monk who had made him literate.

From Master Henry Ackland to his fellow master and friend, Simon of Kineton, greetings and respect.

Sir, Master Daker now having given attention to all those plans and drawings presented to him for his college, he desires to see you in Salster at your earliest pleasure. I am in his confidence, and I know that he is best pleased with your designs. But he must meet with you. Please send word when you will come.

This fellow, Robin Yewell, is bid to business in London on my behalf, and will bring me any reply you are pleased to make.

I trust this finds you and all your household well, as I am, indeed.

Written this Tuesday fortnight before Easter.

Henry! The beggar's boy Simon had taught now looked set to more than repay the favour. Once his apprentice, now a

King's Mason; when they first met, Henry had been nothing but a rickety, palm-up brat.

All those years ago – how many was it? – eleven, twelve? – Simon had been at work on a new refectory at an abbey a day or so's ride from Westminster. Carving a saint's uplifted face on a stone for the pulpitum, he had suddenly known that he was being watched. Looking up, he had seen a small, dirty face in which darting, lapis lazuli eyes gazed warily at his work. He recognised the spy as one of the children who haunted the site, begging from the masons and hovering around the monks to be first in line when the leftover bread was distributed.

'Are you waiting for me to give you something?'

'No, Master. I was just watching. Watching you draw that face out of the stone.'

If he had said 'watching you carve that face' the whole course of his life would have been different. The fact that he could see what Simon felt, that he merely uncovered something in the stone which had been waiting to be revealed, turned Simon's heart over. He had worked with scores of masons, but not with a single one who had ever shared this feeling.

'Have you ever tried to work stone?'

If he frequented building sites, perhaps he had tried his hand with a nail and a pebble on a discarded piece of stone.

The boy shook his head. 'No. But I can carve wood.' And with the embarrassed pride of all creators he drew from some secret place within his tattered, inadequate clothing a small piece of wood that he offered to Simon.

Taking it, Simon looked at it carefully and, once again, his heart lurched. On the piece of wood, no bigger than the bowl of a ladle, was a copy, in miniature but faithful detail, of the Virgin Mary that Simon himself had carved for the abbey church.

In the Madonna, he had carved Gwyneth with an infant in her arms. He had transformed the sadness of his childless wife into tenderness for the newborn, the deftness of her craftswoman's hands into a sure and confident hold upon the child, the smooth softness of her body – his joy and delight – into a warm, womanly Mother of God. And this beggar child had recaptured it all.

'Did you really carve this?' he asked, hoarsely.

'Yes, Master.'

'Do you know who carved the Madonna in the church?'

'No, Master.'

It was true, Simon thought, now, as he drew. The child had not copied that particular statue to flatter its creator, but because he found it beautiful. Henry, he reflected, had never mastered guile.

From that day on, it had not been difficult to find the boy small tasks around the site. He had a quick mind and deft hands and soon Simon sought and was granted permission to take Henry as his apprentice, waiving the usual requirements of money.

Eight years a lodger in their house, Henry had learned, little by little, all Simon's love and mastery of stone. Master in his own right now, it was Henry who had first given Simon the news – months before – of Richard Daker's intention to build a college in Salster. While Simon was in London working at the judge's court inn, Henry was in Salster doing the king's work on the city's walls and gates. Salster was only half a day's ride from the coast and would need sturdy defences if the French carried their coastal harrying further inland.

Word of Daker's plans had been given to the two masons' lodges in Salster – one housing the masons at work on the abbey's cathedral church and the other those busy on the walls and Pilgrim's Gate bridge – and would, Daker knew, go out from there to every lodge, and every master mason, in England.

Once Simon knew of Richard Daker's ambitions, he began to find that he could leave work on the judge's residence to others. As if drawn by the promise of delight, he would sneak away from his sunlit buildings and make his way into the gloom of the lodge. Apprentices more accustomed to cleaning tools suddenly found themselves scraping sheets of parchment clean. But if they wondered what their master wanted with large drafting-sheets when there was no more falsework to be made, no more mouldings to be cut, they had enough sense not to ask.

Drawings began to appear at the desk where Simon worked, bold drawings quite unlike the buildings that had been his stock-in-trade. He drew walls that curved like a pilgrim-maze, pierced by vast, round windows; domed roofs beyond the skill of English craftsmen; stonework of banded colour like a striped garment. Simon had never worked outside England, had never travelled to study the ideas of Continental masons; these were designs drawn from the pattern-books of masons who had seen the countries of the south, the buildings, cheek-by-jowl, of infidel and crusader.

But, little by little, Simon began to see that such blatant foreignness would not take permanent root in Salster, home to the bones of Saxon saints.

As the days passed, the drawings piling up on his desk

became more assuredly English, more to the taste of a people inclined to favour their own after so many years at war with France.

So now, to dull the nervous ache of waiting for his son to be born, Simon drew. His attention to line and form was so complete that he did not hear the midwife enter the room. Perceiving her suddenly at his elbow, he started, marring his work with the unintentional movement.

Simon leaped to his feet. 'Is he born?'

The midwife sighed, her hands busy with the linen head-covering which she had neglected to tidy before coming to him. 'Your wife has borne a son, yes,' she said, 'and is alive—' her glance from beneath her twisting hands was sharp, '—though it seemed she might not survive the child.'

'But she is well?'

The midwife, tucking in the end of her coif, gave her whole attention to him. Was it really possible that he had not considered the danger to his wife of giving birth to her first child at an age when many women had grandchildren old enough to be a nuisance?

'Mistress Kineton will do well enough,' she said, watching him carefully.

'My thanks for the pains you have taken—' Simon blurted, oblivious to the shifting glance and uncomfortable air that would have moderated the thanks of a more observant man. 'I must go and see my wife.'

He pulled the door shut behind him without breaking stride, leaving the midwife stranded in the solar. Looking around, she stared at Simon's drawings and wondered, as her eyes puzzled at his designs, what this unpractised father would make of his new son.

Two

Kineton and Dacre College, present day

The fire, in itself, was not a remarkable event, and would have passed unnoticed by those waiting to be interviewed for the post of marketing manager had it not precipitated an urgent visit by two of the college's maintenance staff to the Regent Master's office.

Damia Miller, sitting outside this office in a comfortable waiting room, could not help overhearing the subdued conversation. 'Painting . . . on the wall behind the panels . . . weird, spooky . . . looks like there's more . . .'

What part in her subsequent successful interview did Damia Miller's prescience play? Prescience that led her to follow the Regent Master, at a discreet distance, across the yard to the college's magnificent Octagon and up its curving stone staircase to the Great Hall. Prescience that led her to snap several phone-camera shots of the terrible face revealed by a gap in the panelling; a face caught in the act of vomiting forth a child.

This painting, she told them, represented a mystery, an enigma, a story hidden for so long that its very existence had been forgotten. Who was this mason? What was the reality behind this grotesque birth metaphor?

This mystery, she swiftly pointed out, and the story it would yield, could become the college's USP – its unique selling point.

And she was the woman to do it.

Three

Kineton and Dacre College, present day

Later, when film was being edited to precise seconds, the videotape editor's first glimpse of Damia Miller was of a small, slight figure whose dark skin – too pale to be black, too dark to be white – and braided hair made her exotic in the surrounding gloom of a drizzly September morning.

In contrast, Damia's first impression of the camera crew was vague: a few individuals, their human outlines blurred in the damp grey air by cameras and cables. Her eyes were drawn to the focus of the camera crew's attention: men and women occupying the pavement outside Kineton and Dacre College, standing silently behind large, wooden-framed placards
stating 'KINETON AND DACRE COLLEGE TENANTS' (she noted the correct use of the apostrophe) RENT STRIKE' and, more emotive, '600 YEARS OF TRADITION UP FOR GRABS'.

Damia would have been happier had her walk down the Romangate been accompanied by chanting from the strikers, but they had been silent as she advanced steadily towards them and angled her path to enter the college through the nearest archway. The strikers would not have guessed, from the calmness of her manner, that their hostile stares and silent stance raised atavistic hackles on the vulnerable nape of Damia Miller's neck as she turned her gaze away from them.

But she could not escape the camera crew. They blocked her passage into Kineton and Dacre's central yard and crowded around her with deft choreography. A microphone thrust in her direction accompanied questions about her identity, her role, whether she was aware of the underhand way in which the tenants – 'these poor people' – had been treated.

Damia Miller's only answer was an arm uplifted, a pale palm raised to repel both questioners and their questions.

Edmund Norris, Regent Master of Kineton and Dacre College, found it considerably less easy to deflect Damia Miller's own questions.

'I'm sorry that this has all blown up on your first day here, Damia, but the rent strike is the result of a breakdown in communication, that's all. Once we sort out a few legal details, it'll all blow over.'

'What legal details?'

'Honestly, Damia, you don't need to get involved with this. It's just—'

'A little local difficulty?'

The Regent Master met her eye. Damia understood; both of them were feeling out the limits of their professional comfort zone. But she could not afford a comfort zone, not yet.

'Dr Norris—'

'Edmund.'

'Whatever. Edmund. If you're going to keep me out of the loop, then I might just as well leave now. I'm not here to send out begging letters and make sure we're fully booked with conferences and summer schools in the vacations. I thought I made that quite clear at interview.'

He inclined his head, once, acknowledging the truth of this.

'What you've signed up for with me is a whole new twenty-first-century image for the college.' She paused. 'Now, that little fiasco outside is impacting on our image in a way that I am very unhappy with. So, if you just fill me in on all the *legal details* we can talk about how we're going to deal with it.'

The composure that she had maintained as Norris reluctantly but succinctly provided the background to the rent strike dropped away as Damia closed the door to her new office.

Stupid! she raged silently, leaning back against the door. Stupid, stupid, *stupid!*

How could a man as brilliant as Norris – a classicist of international reputation – allow himself to be so crassly ignorant of the group he was dealing with as to send out a *standard letter* to all college tenants; a letter which requested, politely, that they sign the enclosed form stating that the college had always been their landlord and that neither they nor – to the best of their knowledge – the tenants from whom they had bought or inherited their holdings had ever paid rent to any other person or body for the said holding? *How* could he do such a thing when a cursory glance at the tenant list would have shown him, approximately one third of the way down the page, one Robert Hadstowe, graduate of the very college that was now so disingenuously asking for his co-operation?

Graduate in *law*.

Hadstowe had at once – and correctly – inferred that the college was preparing to sell land and that, for reasons that were not clear, it did not possess the necessary documentation to prove title. So it was asking those who farmed its estates to undermine their own position and prove it for them. He had immediately informed the other tenants of his suspicions and suggested that a rent strike would force Norris to the negotiating table. The silent vigil outside the college and the public embarrassment it was designed to cause was, obviously, the latest ratchet-notch of pressure.

'Why aren't you prepared to negotiate?'

Norris's discomfort had told her, with uncomfortable clarity, that he was still far from convinced that she needed to be included in any decisions to be made.

'Edmund?'

'We've put out an appeal to all traceable families of ex-Regent Masters for any documents relating to the college that they may still have in their possession.' He fell silent.

'And you're hoping that deeds or papers of endowment will turn up and make the statutory declarations you've asked the tenants to sign irrelevant?'

'Yes.'

She would have preferred negotiation, but at least the position was clear.

Four

Salster, four days' ride from London. A small city when compared with the king's capital but a thriving one. A city of monks and clerics, of monastery and colleges. Built on flat land at the meeting of two rivers, Salster was surrounded by meadows as fertile as its merchant life.

Simon, the last mile of his journey passing beneath the weary feet of his horse, smiled.

The city was fattened on pilgrimage. From the sellers of pewter pilgrim badges and those who hawked trinkets in the streets, to the smugly smiling keepers of the city's inns, money was drawn from purse to coffer with the speed and sureness of a petty thief's fingers. Simon, accustomed to brash and quick-tongued Londoners, was still amazed at the press of people suing for his attention and his money. With beggars imploring and ignored, and whores contracting ill-concealed business in narrow alleyways, he might as well have been walking through a preaching-friars' play. *The way of temptation – what vice, what beckoning sin will our pilgrim succumb to, what will empty his purse and fill him with shame?* Covetousness, lechery, gluttony, self-love: all could be fed and satisfied here.

Looking about him, Simon's London prejudices were astonished at what he saw. Surely Salster had more stone buildings than any city of its size had a right to? Sturdy three-storey rows from whose undercrofts spilled butchers, horn workers, leatherwrights, bakers, cutlers, silversmiths, candlestick makers, their doors thrown open to admit light and custom, the kennels at the sides of the street running with the offal and detritus of their trades. Stone-built churches, hardly two hundred yards apart, showed Salster's antiquity – new towns, in Simon's opinion, were no worse off with half as many. The defensive works which had brought Henry to Salster loomed massive and rawly new above the city, encasing it in stone armour, reinforcing the swagger of merchants' houses that stood everywhere, newly built and still a-building.

Simon was so accustomed to the freedom of his own building sites that at first he did not see the scowls directed at his appraising stare by working masons. Finally sensing their resentment, he realised that, dressed in good clothes without a trace of masonry dust upon them, with nothing more hanging from his belt than his wallet and knife, he was anonymous. He was just one more pilgrim, gawping through the city.

Tearing his eyes away from masons at their work, he let his feet be drawn, like those of every other visitor, towards the abbey's cathedral church, resting place of the bones of Dernstan, saint and miracle-worker.

The church, as ever in its five-hundred-year history, was in the process of improvement. Robert Copley, bishop of Salster, whose ambition and worldliness were notorious even to Simon, was determined that his cathedral church should overtop any in England. To that end he had managed to procure the services of Henry Yevele, the king's indispensable chief architect, a man of genius and some irascibility.

As he stepped into the abbey's precincts, Simon's eyes fell upon the great church's new nave, of which as yet only the outer walls were raised. Through the network of scaffolding he could see the Normandy stone shining white in the sunshine. In his mind's eye he saw how the walls would look when stripped bare of walkways, how they would rise from their surroundings, towering to an immense height. A creator to his fingertips, Simon exulted in a work of such genius.

Stretching long and clean from the older eastern apse, barely interrupted by the slenderest of buttresses, the walls opened, like parchment spreading its fine paleness around a jewel of illumination, into windows whose sheer area – as yet unglassed – astonished Simon. Gazing at their half-hidden beauty, he felt a surge of joy as he saw how the side-aisles of the cathedral church would be flooded with light for the laity who stood listening as the monks sang the Opus Dei.

That nave, Simon felt, would change the nature of worship. No longer straitened between massive, barely windowed walls and bulky piers, no longer oppressed by domed, overarching roofs that bore down upon the suppliant soul, the laity would be raised up into a light-filled prefiguration of the presence of God, their eyes and their souls led towards heaven by the vaults that genius had placed so high and sunlit above them.

Transfixed, he watched the masons and their labourers in their purposeful comings and goings, saw the apprentices running here and there with sharpened tools, staggering to barrow large stones newly squared on the workbench. The master mason's foreman strode about marking stones with his inspection-mark and issuing orders with the air of one to whom authority comes easily. Simon looked about, but could not identify who might be the site-master. With Yevele away so much on the king's commissions, there must be a master mason to whom he entrusted the day-to-day execution of his plans.

Suddenly, Simon saw him. Tall and full-bearded like Simon himself, he was easily distinguishable from masons of lesser caste. Unlike those who surrounded him on the building works he wore no cap or coif and his hair was long and curling. The man looked around and Simon turned away before he could be recognised. He knew the mason: Hugh of Lewes. So Hugh was finally back from his dallying over the king's business and goodness knows what else in France. Simon was intrigued to find him here. He was no great lover of churchmen and Simon had heard that he had fallen out with more than one French prelate. Still, men would swallow much to work with Yevele.

Simon turned away from the building work, running his fingers through his own uncapped hair. It might not be as luxuriant as that of Hugh of Lewes, he thought, catching himself, but I'm not an old man yet, and if I have my way, I'll build something that will rival this nave.

On meeting Richard Daker, Henry Ackland's keenness that Simon should build for him was explained; Henry had never altogether sloughed off his beggar-boy veneration of riches and nobility.

Standing half a hand taller than Simon, Daker was a man of olive complexion and a graceful, courteous manner that marked him – to Simon at least – as a man of the South, where the sea's waters were the fabled warm blue of the Mediterranean, not the chilly grey of his homeland.

But Daker's clothes were of fine English cloth and, though generously cut, they were the practical clothes of a man who disdains going about his affairs in court fashions that fit him for nothing but holding their trails out of the mud.

Having seen his guest seated and provided with wine and sweet cakes, Daker spoke directly.

'Your drawings astonished me, Master Kineton. I know from Henry Ackland that you have waited a long time to build something of significance, but even Henry – who gives you out as one of the finest masons in England – even he did not prepare me for what I saw in your drawings.'

He stopped suddenly. His elbow on the arm of his chair, his fist supported his chin as he appraised Simon. His eyes, Simon noticed, were of an extraordinary twilight blue, quite at odds with his southern complexion.

'Where have you travelled to see buildings like that?'

'I have not travelled outside England,' Simon began, slowly.

Daker raised a dark brow. 'Then you're rarer than even Henry was prepared to paint you. All the English masons I have ever met have been content to do very little different from that which has been done before.'

'That's the way we do things,' Simon replied, baldly. 'In building you cannot afford to do anything too different – it might not stand. You have to build on what has already been done.'

'But your drawings,' Daker picked up a sheaf of papers from the floor next to his chair and waved them at Simon, who recognised his work, 'they surely do not do that – they are completely new?'

'No. They merely use old techniques in a new way—'

'But this octagonal hall?'

'Have you not been to Ely, Master Daker? Not seen the octagonal lantern tower of the cathedral church?'

Daker shook his head, and Simon had to remind himself that a craftsman's marvel in his own profession might very well go unremarked by others.

'There is nothing new here but the use to which each element has been put,' he said carefully.

Daker gazed at him with penetrating eyes. Simon could feel himself being willed to say more, to state some sort of case. He remained silent.

'Master Ackland maintains that your skill has not been given ample scope,' Daker said suddenly. 'Why have you been denied royal employment all these years, Master Kineton? You were once a King's Mason, were you not?'

If he had expected prevarication and resentment, Daker was disappointed; this was a speech Simon had come prepared to make.

'I am an independent man, Master Daker, I bow to no one in the matter of how a building should be constructed, not even my patron. Once he has seen my drawings and commissioned me he must let me be. Even if he is the king.'

'But it was your father's similar opinions, was it not, which caused you both to be forbidden the style of King's Mason? And by the old king, not the new?'

Simon set his jaw, feeling his face flame with remembered shame under his beard. So, Daker would play cat and mouse with him. If he had already heard the tale from Henry, why tease after it again?

'My father was punished for not knowing the ways of gentlemen,' he said bluntly. 'He did not know that when the king expressed the opinion that a building should be built according to his whim and not in accordance with principles that would keep it standing, that its builder should say, "Excellent, your Majesty," and yet go on as before, once the king was gone. My father did him the courtesy of explaining why it was not possible to build as he had suggested.'

'Upon which the king sought a second opinion, and asked you?'

If you know, why ask?

'Yes.'

'And you agreed with your father?'

'Yes.'

'Why?'

Simon kneaded the flesh of his face with the blunt fingers of one hand, easing away the unaccustomed wariness of his expression.

He saw the scene again, details fixed vividly in his mind down twenty years: the disputed building, the shape of the towers which had cost him so dear, the burst blood vessels beneath the crimson of the old king's face as he stood to be instructed in building technique. Simon felt his blood surging hot and angry through him, rage shaking in the hands that held his wine cup. Twenty years was a long time measured on the scale of a man's life; measured on the rule of his journey towards forgiveness they were no more than the blink of an eye.

Why?

Because the king's simple question to him – 'And is this your opinion, also?' – had been a command: 'Take the shame of correction from me, or risk a king's displeasure.' Simon had been his father's apprentice and his journeyman; he was at that moment a fellow master, but he was first his son. No man should try to wrest a son's loyalty from his father.

'Yes, it is also my opinion.'

If he had been more conciliatory, honeyed his defiance a little with 'Your Majesty' and 'I regret', perhaps things would have been different. If he had not looked the king boldly in the eye as he stood shoulder to shoulder with his father, would he have been asked to design for the king, given licence to use the combination of knowledge and imagination which had produced the sketches so recently scattered about his desk in the lodge?

His mind shrugged off such profitless questions. No matter how he had champed at his enforced littleness for twenty years and more, he did not regret his loyalty.

Simon looked away from the dead king into Daker's eyes. 'If his patron had been any other man,' he said slowly 'my father would simply have told him that what he proposed was not possible. But for the king, he took time, explained why it could not be so, explained something of our craft to him.' He hesitated fractionally. 'The king did not understand the courtesy my father did him.'

'Kings are taught from an early age to expect common courtesy,' Daker said, mildly. 'The king's rearing could not possibly fit him for doing business with master masons. For men of your craft – you master builders, *ingéniateurs*—' he pronounced it in the French style, '—you believe yourselves beyond rank, don't you?' His tone was mild, but his eyes were acute beneath their dark brows.

Lost in Daker's maze of motives, Simon left subtlety to the vintner. 'Some will tell you our craft makes us proud,' he conceded, 'but doesn't your particular trade give you pride?'

Daker smiled, as if pleased to have the tables turned, and shifted his weight forward slightly, leaning on the worked arm of his chair. Gwyneth, Simon thought, would give her teeth for such deft intricacy.

'Yes, Master Kineton, but I may not turn my proud shoulder to a man's face as you may. Men cannot build without master masons. If we will have buildings fit for our purposes, we must take you on your own terms. Terms,' he continued, his eyes on Simon's, 'which say, "Take me as I am or not at all, I will not bend to please you."' He paused. 'Do you bend to please, Simon of Kineton?'

The question hung between them like the spider's drop at the web's beginning.

'No.'

'Not even where bending just so little' – Daker compressed the air between thumb and forefinger – 'might gain you all you ever dreamed of?'

Simon gripped the arms of his chair. This was too subtle. He breathed deeply, his eyes never leaving Daker's face, half afraid that if he took his eyes off the man his meaning would vanish completely.

'I have not wasted my time, thinking what might have been if I were different,' he said. 'I have simply waited my time.'

Half his life spent waiting; waiting for a son, for a chance like this. And now he could not see his way. This chance – come at last, like his child – was he to lose it because he could not see his way in the maze of the vintner's mind?

'And is this what you have been waiting for, Simon of Kineton?' Daker asked, lifting his eyes from the red glass of the cup he was cradling in his hands. 'Do you imagine that building this college in defiance of the power and authority of the Church will give you your revenge on the Crown?'

Simon stared at him. He was being tested, he knew that, but like a forgetful boy tested by his catechist, he was afraid of what might result if he gave the wrong answer.

'I *choose* to build,' he began slowly, feeling his way, 'I no longer must. Since Henry has obviously made you privy to the details of my life, you must be aware that I have other means to keep my family?'

'Your manors to the west, yes.'

Lands that had come to his father, Thomas Mason, in default of payment when the shroud of the Great Mortality had fallen upon his patron. Manors that, as well as unequalled sheep-turf, possessed deep beds of ripe, workable building stone.

'So, I build not from necessity, but because it fills me with delight to see my drawings take stone upon themselves and live. For me,' he continued, slowly, 'a building should be a living thing, formed for its purpose – as a tool is, as a man's body is.'

He halted, his eyes on Daker, his fingers feeling how he would carve the man, even as his mind strove for a more satisfactory way to say what he felt. How would he carve that grey-feathered black hair, shining with the deep lustre of polished Purbeck stone? How to capture the vigour of it which caused it to curl like a boy's past the high collar of his gown? The gown itself would be easy – Simon had a great facility for carving the hardness of stone into the soft likeness of cloth – but the curl and swathe of Daker's hair, the masculine fineness of feature that brought to Simon's mind a half-forgotten image of an old ascetic saint; those would require genius.

'Just as a man's character may be found in his face,' he continued, slowly, 'so the character of a building should be evident in its design. Take the plan for the nave of the abbey church – how many people will stand there while the choir sings the mass? Twenty score? Fifty? And yet fewer would not be enough for such a place, where the whole panoply of the church is present, where the voices of a hundred monks are raised in single worship. The scale allowed is only just – a more straitened space would not do. And yet if such a church enclosed but one priest, saying mass day by day for a draggle of parishioners, the sight would be ludicrous. God would not, then, be glorified by so vast a space of light and stone, he would be made a laughing stock by its emptiness. And yet—' Simon, though he noticed the smile that crooked Daker's lips, did not connect it with his own words '—the proportions that make the abbey church beautiful to the eye are the same as those that dictate the shape of the parish church. There is, in the mind of man, something that finds particular delight in certain combinations of length, height and breadth.'

Which combinations, from sheer force of the mason's habitual secrecy, he withheld.

There was a silence between them as each contemplated the mettle of the other. It was Simon who broke the silence.

'And you, Master Daker, what is your cause?'

Daker stared at him levelly, but did not reply.

Looking away, he poured more wine for each of them, then took a breath, as if to answer, only to lapse once more into silence. It was obvious to Simon that Daker did not know how far he might go with him.

'Learning,' the vintner said, finally, 'is, in England, kept within the Church's precincts. Here, to a far greater degree than in Italy and France, the Church broods over learning like a domineering mother, using her power to regulate every going out and coming in. And, as domineering mothers will, she has spawned a dependent and orthodox child.'

He stopped and gazed at Simon, who felt himself nodding slightly, as if in encouragement.

'To study, as you will know, a boy must take first orders. To be a scholar, a master, a doctor at a college, a man must gain preferment in the Church – a living – to keep himself. And those outside are told they may not, *must not,* think for themselves: that must be left to the college theologians.' He paused slightly. 'Heresy, disobedience, treason – these things, we are told, will be the result of untrained thinking.'

'But the Church's true dilemma comes when even trained theologians think too much and believe dogma too little,' said Simon, suddenly articulate. 'For that is what Wyclif has done and he has fallen into heresy. Has he not?'

Daker swiftly masked his surprise and asked calmly, 'You are familiar, then, with the writings of John Wyclif?'

Simon smiled, pleased to have wrong-footed him. 'I am familiar with his ideas, at least. I was in London when Wat Tyler and John Ball the priest and their followers came. They said John Ball preached Wyclif. It seemed to me that Wyclif must be worth hearing if he could inspire a man like John Ball, a common man, to rebellion.'

'Yes!' said Daker, the enthusiasm of the zealot suddenly raising his voice. 'And it is his writings – those which condemned the Church – which gave rise to Wyclif's persecution, not his heretical views on the eucharist!'

They stared at each other, both well aware that a point of no return had been reached. Daker, his hands folded in his lap, gazed with brief intensity at his wine beaker, then abruptly looked up, some kind of decision reached.

'You must know, Master Kineton,' he said, 'if you are to build for me, what manner of man I am. I too heard John Ball preach and went far to agreeing with all he said. I am a wealthy man but I do not therefore throw in my lot with all others who acquire and honour wealth. Wealth must be used wisely, and I see as well as John Ball did that it is not always so, in lordship or in the holy Church.' He stopped, stared at something Simon could not see.

'I share John Wyclif's opinion that each man must make his own way with God, free of corrupt and degenerate priests, and to that end I also agree that the Bible must be written in our own tongue. Furthermore,' he said, his eyes unwavering on Simon's, 'I believe that men should learn in their own native language, not in Latin. I have two native tongues, as you must know – English and Italian. I know that it is impossible to think in the same way in these languages, even for me.' He scanned Simon's face. 'In England, and English, I am more calculated, more measured. In Italy, speaking the tongue I learned on my mother's knee, I am freer—'

'And if Englishmen would learn in Latin, they must think with the convolutions of that language and not the natural order of English,' Simon finished for him. 'Do not look so malleted-about, Master Daker! I had not thought of these things before, but now I see them, it's not so different from working in stone. Different stones cannot be worked in exactly the same way. All have their beauty, but each demands a knowledge of its own possibilities. I can see how it might be the same with languages also.'

'There are those, in Oxford, who are persuaded by the

notions John Wyclif preached and who are ready to stand by them. Ready to come and teach in Salster, at my college. And to teach in English.'

'You are well advanced already, then?'

'There is no profit in building a college to specific ends, only to find those ends unattainable.'

They stared at each other, both waiting for the other to speak. Finally, Daker stood.

'Let us build together, Simon of Kineton, and I promise that I shall not interfere in your mastery.'

Simon stood too but, instead of offering his hand to Daker, said abruptly, 'And the Church? You think it will stand idly by and allow you to do this? Under the nose of one of the most powerful bishops in the land?'

'On the contrary. I know very well they will oppose me in every way they can. But I am determined.'

Simon offered his hand. 'Then I am satisfied.'

Five

Kineton and Dacre College, present day

From: Damia.Miller@kdc.sal.ac.uk
To: CatzCampbell@hotmail.com
Subject: How's New York?

Hey there! How are things? Did you manage to get that apartment? Hope so, it sounded fabulous. Things are interesting here in establishmentsville. Think I've walked into a bit of a hornet's nest.

Firstly, the college is in worse shape financially than I'd been led to believe. Apparently, there was an appeal to raise money for new student accommodation so that all undergraduates could be accommodated for their whole degree – the appeal was successful but the way the money and the building project was managed was, from what I can gather, a complete and utter disaster. Don't suppose they thought I'd take the job if they'd told me they were on the verge of bankruptcy. But still – it's a challenge. I'll be superhero No.1 if I can help them get out of this hole.

Secondly, the tenants on the college's estates are on strike because the Regent Master (head honcho) is trying to pull a fast one and sell the land (there must be more to this …) so income from tenants currently is nil (though we've got a couple of weeks before that becomes a problem, they do the old-fashioned thing of paying on the quarter days, so if we can sort this out by the end of the month, no harm done).

Thirdly, there seems to be some kind of internal battle going on in the governing body of the college (board of directors by any other name) – some kind of taking sides about the future of the college. I haven't quite sussed it yet but I keep expecting to be backed up against a stack of books in the library by a wild-eyed academic and forced to declare my allegiance … If you're suddenly informed of my sad demise you'll know what's happened …

On the good side, a complete medieval painting cycle has just been discovered behind the panelling on the walls of the Great Hall. One panel had to be removed when there was a fire and more and more painting kept emerging as they removed more and more panelling. Of the eight walls of the great hall four are pretty much taken up by windows and the other four are dominated by the painting – huge, oval-framed scenes, two to a wall. It's a pretty big deal but I suppose you'll know that …

Conservators are swarming all over it but from what I can gather they don't seem to have the faintest idea what it's actually about. It's a bit bizarre, some of it – I've attached pictures so you can have a look at it with your professional eye. Maybe you can tell us what we're looking at.

Damia took her fingers from the keyboard and covered her face with her hands. *Maybe you can tell us what we're looking at?* Desperate. Pathetic.

This was not, technically, a trial separation. They had not agreed that they could see other people; they had not talked about seeing how they felt when separated by three thousand miles of Atlantic. She and Catz had never lived under the same roof – though they had been together for four years they had never actually lived in the same city. Catz had been anchored by the artistic community to London and Damia's job had kept her in Salster. But there had been expectations of permanence. Until Damia had mentioned having children.

She deleted the last sentence . . .

Apparently, one of the reasons nobody knows anything about this painting is the fact that the college has no historical archive – nothing that dates back further than about 1850. There's some speculation that all college records were destroyed by Cromwell's soldiers in the Civil War – the college chose to side with the king, apparently – but that doesn't account for the missing two centuries.

As I mentioned, I'm looking to get a house of my own with the college's help. I've looked at the details now – they'll give me a whopping grant as a down payment, interest-free. With house prices in Salster, they need to do something. I'm looking at a little terraced house inside the city walls tomorrow, so I'll let you know how it goes. Hear from you soon.

All my love,

Mia

She hit Send and leaned back. She tried to imagine her lover in New York but her only images of the city came from car-skidding NYPD dramas and *Friends*: she had no visual shorthand for Greenwich Village, where Catz was currently living with an old friend from art school. Damia flicked to her saved messages and read the date on her last email from Catz. A week ago.

Clicking on the icon she had attached to her email, Damia stared at the first in the wall painting's cycle of oval-framed scenes. One of the conservators stood at the side of the shot, a human scale that measured the ovals at over eight feet high. Linked by vine-tracery, each was coupled to the next in what was assumed to be a narrative cycle: birth, sin, death and resurrection.

And what a birth! The face which had confronted the panel-removers after the fire was that of a child, screaming mouth stretched wide, head tilted back in agonized protest against a world of light and cold.

But it was the manner of this child's delivery that made the image so bizarre. The figure giving it life was not a woman but a man – tall and strong, his belt hung with the characteristic square and compasses of the stonemason. The child, like the fantastically begotten progeny of some pagan deity, was emerging from his gaping jaws.

The symbolism was entirely obscure, without any obvious parallel in medieval art. The same conservator who stood in the photograph had posited a possible interpretation in a twist on a phrase from the gospel of St John the Evangelist: 'Born, not of the flesh, nor of the will of man, but of the Spirit.' This child, he suggested, was born not of the Spirit but of the will of man; spoken forth, as it were, called into being as God did Adam at the beginning.

But, arresting as the photographs on her screen were, they were simply pictures. They conveyed none of the power and intensity that Damia had felt as she stood in front of the newly uncovered walls in the Great Hall. Transfixed by the painting's vivid images – even at the distance dictated by the conservators' anti-touch barriers – Damia had felt an inexplicable conviction that these scenes had not been painted simply to decorate the walls of the Great Hall. The way in which their newly uncovered presence utterly changed the character of the college's principal space suggested to Damia that, for some reason obscured by the passage of time, this extraordinary octagonal building with its lantern roof had been raised solely to display the eight ovals of what the conservators had nicknamed 'The Sin Cycle'.

As she gazed at the cycle her fingers itched for the surface of the painted wall, felt how the texture of the plaster would catch at the whorls and spirals of her fingerprints. Her body yearned over the barrier, straining to capture an echo of the wet, earthy, metallic notes which had filled the painter's nostrils as his brush imprisoned the sinner in his cage; delineated a violent, brutal death; washed the symbolic river of baptism in blues, greens and browns. How different did they smell – copper green, lamp black, lapis lazuli blue? Her nose was tuned to the fine differences in Catz's oils, but these were mineral colours, a different medium.

As both frame and setting for this work of art, the building could not have been bettered. Like the scenes of the cycle, the pattern on which the great Octagon of Kineton and Dacre College was built was unique. Of all British medieval college buildings, it was the only one to have an eight-sided hall; lantern roofs, though they appeared occasionally in ecclesiastical architecture, were unknown in academic buildings of the period.

Kineton and Dacre College resembled traditional Oxsterbridge colleges as much as the wall painting resembled traditional secular or religious art.

Damia began a new email.

From: Damia.Miller@kdc.sal.ac.uk
To: Mailing List (Alumni)
Subject: Fascinating Discovery at Toby

Dear Tobyite

As you will have read on the net or in the broadsheets, Toby has been the site of an amazing medieval find. Behind the panelling in the Great Hall, a complete medieval wall painting cycle has been discovered. [click here for images] So far, conservators and historians are baffled as to the meaning of this extraordinary work of art.

With the combined intellect and knowledge of Tobyites all over the globe, we cannot believe that this will remain a mystery for long. So, log on to the college site and register yourself as a participant in the Wall Painting Project. Registration entitles you to:

- an email bundle with a unique information summary available nowhere else on the web
- regular monthly updates on progress made in the painting's interpretation and conservation
- access to a members-only message board where you can post and read ideas
- access to exclusive Toby wall painting merchandise available only from the college site to registered members

So click on the link below to register, and pass this email on to any other Tobyites you are in contact with.

Best wishes and Good Luck!

Damia Miller
Director, Wall Painting Project

Norris had not been consulted about her additional title but, as sole instigator and administrator of the Wall Painting Project, it did not seem unreasonable that she should appoint herself its nominal director.

'Merchandise,' she wrote on a scribble pad. 'Mousemats, mugs, post-its, postcards, framed limited-edition photos.' Thoughts had already begun to crystallise – she was looking for an impression of the esoteric, a feeling of belonging to the only group that, with unashamed exclusivity, was entitled to engage with the enigma of the wall painting.

Not all the images in the painting's ovals would suit her purpose. The second oval, for instance – the one twinned with the child's grotesque birth – was too conventional. A mother-and-child communion: a Madonna figure in green and white, the linen-wrapped child cradled in her arms the focus of her adoring gaze. There was nothing here of mystery, of the arcane.

The third oval was more suited to her purpose. A group of clamouring demons clustered around the helpless, prostrate figure of a young child, stuffing its ears and poking at its goggling eyes with their skeletal fingers, swarming bodies the colour of old blood gloating over the flailing form like jackals on a twitching carcass.

'The Toby Enigma,' Damia wrote, on impulse, beneath her merchandise list, 'Can you solve it?'

It was, she decided, a good working hook-line. Using the cognomen 'Toby', rather than 'Kineton and Dacre College', implied a sense of shared understanding, of belonging. None but the initiate knew not only *what* but *who* Toby was.

Toby: in oral tradition the son of the college's mason, Simon of Kineton. His statue – or at least the statue called

Toby – stood on the east wall of the central yard, overlooking the Octagon. It was the statue of a young boy.

Why did the college have a statue of its architect's son in pride of place?

Oral tradition was silent.

Why was the college called Kineton and Dacre – the name of its mason displacing that of its benefactor?

On this subject, too, tradition remained mute.

The painting, Damia reflected, was far from the college's only mystery.

Six

Two women move quietly, purposefully, around a bed-chamber together. One takes clothes from the press at the bed's end and lays them out, to be folded or placed in a pile on the floor by the other. They speak little, and then in such half-phrases and single words as would be incomprehensible to any but themselves. The tone, the meeting of eyes, explains one to the other with the ease of long practice. Occasionally the older woman lifts a garment from the bed and holds it up for comment. A nod folds it, a shake of the head discards it to the poor-pile.

Such ease of understanding might be taken for that between mother and daughter, but for the unlikeness of the two women. The elder is tall and angular, gaunt in a way which suggests that, once, more ample flesh softened her; the younger is shapely with youth, a head shorter, her complexion dark where the other's is freckled and faded-fair. A long tendril of dark hair has escaped from the tucked linen that covers the girl's head, and now and again she pushes it absently behind her ear with a small, swift hand.

But in their silent movements the two women are alike: neat, precise, they share the assurance of those unacquainted with clumsiness. The older woman lifts and folds with large, practised movements; grasping hem and collar she folds a gown, pulling its length straight across her breast. The girl stoops and lifts, bends and straightens, with the lightness of one for whom creaking bones are another lifetime away.

The press empty, she closes the lid.

Alysoun motioned to the wall hangings. 'If you'll help me move the press,' she said quietly, her eyes flicking to the sleeping baby in the corner, 'I can take them down.'

Gwyneth's eyes followed her foster-daughter's. Tearing them away from Tobias, she said, 'I'll take them down – I fastened them, after all.'

Gwyneth grunted as they moved the chest. 'I trust these hangings will suit the house Master Daker provides for us,' she said. 'I've grown fond of them, painted linen though they are.' She stepped up on to the lid and began to twist out the first peg. 'If we were rich,' she said, 'we could commission you for a hanging, chick.' She looked at Alysoun, a half-smile on her face.

Alysoun's eyes were wide with mock horror. 'Do you know how long a hanging like that – a whole wall – would take with just one craftswoman working on it?'

'As long as it will take Simon to build Daker's college,' Gwyneth answered in all seriousness. 'Years.' Her eyes went back to the sleeping Toby. 'Time enough to see our boy grown.'

'Yes.'

'Daker's house was full of tapestried hangings,' Gwyneth said, 'if you believe Simon.'

'He doesn't generally overstate things.'

'No, but he does fail to notice things that don't interest him,' said his wife. 'His eye may have strayed from the masonry and woodwork onto one hanging . . .' she left the inference to be drawn.

'Yes, but Daker must be rich,' Alysoun pointed out reasonably, 'to build and endow a college.'

'True,' Gwyneth grinned, 'my little miracle worker.'

Alysoun smiled ruefully. 'The judge's wife will live to regret calling me that,' she said, 'now, all her friends are plaguing me to work for them too, if I am such a marvel.' She rolled her eyes at the thought of marvellousness, but Gwyneth was not fooled.

'Mistress Stowald, wife of a King's Bench judge or not, should have learned by now not to boast,' she said. 'People can't steal what they don't know about. She makes such a blether about your skill – a person would think that this was not London but some village and you were not a free craftswoman but some villein-wife who had no choice but to do her bidding.'

'Well,' Alysoun was blithe, 'she's suffering for it – once her press is filled and she is queening it in the judge's new house, I'll be done with her.' Taking her hands from her hips she bent to the press, lifting it with ease once Gwyneth had put her hand to the other end. 'She doesn't know,' she continued as her mother stepped onto the Welsh-work lid of the long chest, 'that I will be coming up from Salster to buy my silks.'

Gwyneth, speaking through the effort of twisting carefully worked pegs from their posts, asked, 'What difference does it make? She has no power over you, nor any of us. The judge's inn will be finished by then, finished and furnished for their moving in. Simon will be paid off and out of reach of her husband's wrath – even if he did want to take her part, which I doubt.'

Alysoun's sigh turned into a groan. 'It's not his wrath that worries me, nor hers either, it's her begging me. I cannot stand to be begged.'

Nor to beg, thought Gwyneth. Only once had she ever heard Alysoun beg.

'Please teach me! *Please*! I am a mason's daughter, now *your* daughter. *Please* teach me to be a mason.'

'I cannot.' Gwyneth had heard the finality in Simon's words; Alysoun, eleven years old and determined, had closed her ears to it.

'But you teach Henry.'

Simon's face clouded and Alysoun shrank slightly from him, yet Gwyneth knew that what had passed across his face was not anger but pain.

'I do not teach Henry, I guide him. He has a gift.'

'How do you know that I do not?'

'I cannot teach you, Alysoun, now or ever.'

'Why not?'

Simon had not answered, but later, the child's storm of enraged and frustrated weeping over, Gwyneth had. Having been mother to Alysoun for six years, she knew that nothing would answer the case but honesty, even if honesty cut to the quick and left no room for hope.

'Simon has taken on Henry because he must. It's just as he says, he does not teach Henry, but guides him as he learns for himself. Simon did not seek Henry out, the boy came to him – maybe God brought the child to him for his benefit, I don't know. But I do know that God brought you to me.

You're my daughter and I love you most dearly, and you're Simon's daughter too, which is why he cannot take you as his pupil. Men who teach their daughters admit that they have despaired of a son. Simon cannot admit that. Not to the world, not to himself.'

She had never asked him again. Gwyneth, recognising in her daughter the need to turn her hand to a craft, would gladly have taught her, but Alysoun had no inclination to work with wood. In truth, Gwyneth strongly suspected that she only wanted particularly to be a mason in order to keep up with Henry, whom she adored despite his habit of patronising her mercilessly.

Finally, Alysoun had turned the tables on her tormentor. Knowing Henry to be entranced by fine clothes, she had begged her mother to help her make a new tunic for him and, once it was made, had set about embroidering it with all the skill her tender years could master. To no one's lasting surprise she quickly showed that in eleven years she had mastered more skill than many women gained in a lifetime. Not only were her fingers nimble and neat, but she had an unerring eye for shape and colour which she translated into a whirling world of birds and animals, leaves and tracing vinery on the front and back of the tunic. Her joyous stitching made brocade-work look tired and before the garment was a quarter done Henry desired it more than he had ever desired anything. Alysoun, exulting in her advantage, made him teach her the rudiments of masonry.

The Sunday lessons she wrung out of him allowed her to master the theory and showed her how to carve (which is what she most desired) without allowing Henry the usual tutor's prerogative of having his pupil shape and smooth the stone first. Every week he vowed he would pander to her no more, and every Sunday afternoon saw him sitting with her, answering her imperious questions and looking longingly upon the tunic that she always brought with her in her linen bag, lest he should forget what he would lose if he did not bend to her determined will.

She proved no great shakes at carving. She had a sharp eye, but no real feel for stone. Carving demands that things must be seen and recreated in round, raised forms; Alysoun's carving tended to the flat, as if she was drawing on the stone's surface, rather than practising the true stone-carver's trick of drawing the likeness from the very heart of the stone.

The tunic finished, she gave it willingly to Henry and never asked for more instruction. She had found her craft.

'Don't fret. You'll be safe in Salster from Mistress Stowald's pleading.'

Stepping down from the press and stooping to lift one end, Gwyneth said, provocatively, 'Not that Mistress Stowald's absence is the only delight Salster will hold for you—'

Alysoun was not given to blushing and her colour did not change now.

'You know what you are taking on with Henry, Alysoun? A life of constant movement, never having one place to call home?'

Alysoun, keeping her eyes lowered to the floor as they moved the press from one corner to the other, said, 'I have not taken Henry on, Mother, nor been asked to do so.' Her eyes flicked up to Gwyneth's face, showing no surprise that her mother had read the situation so easily. 'Does Simon know?'

Gwyneth smiled thinly. 'He does, but only because I have

told him.' She straightened and looked at her daughter. 'You know him, Alysoun, he is a man.' She laughed in her nose, her eyes still on the girl. 'Simon is a master craftsman – in his craft there is no one to touch him. I would stake my life on his judgement as to how far stone might be worked, but his judgement in matters of feeling is as dull as a mallet.'

Involuntarily, her eyes went to the restlessly sleeping baby in the cradle.

Alysoun saw the direction of her gaze but would not let the subject of Henry drop. 'It doesn't need to be so bad for us,' she said. 'Henry's ambition is to leave building and work as a sculptor and image-maker. If he can do it – and if he cannot then nobody can; you know how skilled he is.'

'Yes, he always was,' said Gwyneth absently, her eyes still on the baby.

'He has persuaded the master at Salster castle to let him carve the saints for the new lady chapel. If they impress the king, who knows what may come of it?'

'Yes,' Gwyneth replied reflectively, her whole attention now regained. 'There is plenty of work in London for the king and his nobles. And sculptors may work at a distance from the building site.' Their eyes met. 'But the dust will still settle on his chest, my chick, his breathing will still come heavily as he grows older.'

'When he has made his name, he won't need to work so much.'

Her voice was the blithe confidence of youth. And the untarnished belief that her beloved will always do what she wants. Gwyneth had worried herself over Simon's health for years, had begged him to leave building and make their home at Kineton where he could trade his stone and farm sheep; his desire to create had always frustrated her. But now, finally, perhaps the end was in sight. Perhaps, when Daker's college was built, he would not need to cut stone any more. If this truly was to be his architect's masterpiece, then other men might see it and commission him to work for them. Building was a slow business, but drawing was speedy. Was it possible that Simon could follow the lead given by those masons of the first rank like Henry Yevele – supervising building at many sites left under the day-to-day authority of a site-master?

To live at Kineton and have Simon draw up his buildings in the tracing-house he would build for himself, where he would not have to breathe the perpetually dusty air of the common lodge: that was Gwyneth's dream. To sleep at night without the persistent dry cough which had begun to plague Simon this last year.

'*And where will my son learn his craft? If I am to put down my tools and become a wandering merchant, how will Tobias learn of me?*'

Simon had never spoken the words, but she could hear them as clearly as if he had. She looked at her son's cradle. Tobias's birth had determined their future.

Seven

Outside Kineton and Dacre College, present day

On Michaelmas, the day rent payments fell due, the rent strikers gathered outside the college, as usual, at 8 a.m. Though individual faces changed daily in deference to the needs of land and livestock, the strikers had become as much part of the landscape of the Romangate as the cars crawling along its patchworked tarmac in and out of Salster's congested centre.

The television crew – which had previously lost interest in the face of a unanimous, uncooperative silence from the college authorities – was back, drawn by the rumour of renewed conflict like kids to the yell of 'fight' in the playground. The college had not withdrawn its request for statutory declarations and the tenants remained resolute in their refusal to provide them; the stage was set for an 'ivory tower academics vs. honest sons of the soil' boost to ratings.

As the outside broadcast crew completed their electronic rituals, Damia and Norris reprised a conversation that was beginning to wear grooves in their working relationship.

'Damia, you must understand there's only so much I can

do in terms of damage limitation. I understand that this is a PR disaster, believe me, but I have no choice.'

'Yes, I know! The buck stops with you. All responsibility and no power.' Damia's frustration was caused, at least partly, by the knowledge that Norris was a victim of his own democratic instincts. Months before, a motion had been tabled by a member of the college's governing body to discuss the sale of parcels of college land. After reportedly robust debate, the vote had been in favour of going ahead.

'I'm not a great one for conspiracy theories,' Norris had said when he explained the situation, 'but I do wonder whether the motion was tabled precisely to provoke a crisis.'

'Run that one by me again?'

Norris's in-breath had been audible, as if he was preparing to say his piece all at once. 'Selling land is controversial, especially when it involves the issue of building on greenfield sites. I accept that we could generate a lot of capital—'

'*Building?*' Damia's excitement had been so aroused she had instantly forgotten about the tenants. 'Edmund, you could make a total *killing* if you're selling to developers—'

'But this kind of move also generates enormous amounts of bad feeling.' Norris had ignored her interruption and looked away. 'My argument – that we have a social contract with our tenants and that we can't arbitrarily decide to separate college and lands without consultation . . . well, it didn't carry the day.'

'What swung the vote?'

'Charles Northrop's persuasiveness. He's an economist, Damia, he knows what he's talking about at a business level.'

'And that's the whole issue, isn't it?' Damia's tone was neutral. 'The dean's hard economics versus tradition and the social contract.'

'It is when you're as near bankruptcy as Toby is currently, yes.'

The strikers' leader, Rob Hadstowe, initiated an ironic slow handclap as Norris and Damia walked through the north-western arch of the college. The clap, taken up by the rest of the strikers, was recorded as background noise by the over-sized boom-mic which was angled to follow the TV station's woman on the scene, Abbie Daniels.

'Dr Norris, Dr Norris!'

Norris held up a forestalling hand to silence her. 'Shall we do this with some kind of dignity?'

The journalist came to an abrupt halt, allowing the hand thrusting a microphone in his direction to fall to her side.

'Meaning?'

'A sensible interview, in my office, with Mr Hadstowe.'

A sudden grumble of disturbance ran through the shuffling rent strikers, drawing Damia's attention away from Abbie Daniels.

Stepping out of a car purring illegally on the parallel yellow lines at the side of the Romangate was a figure whom Damia recognised instantly. She put a hand on Norris's arm and chin-pointed at the new arrival. 'Trouble.'

Later, watching the resulting two-minute slot on local tele-vision news, Damia had to admire the editor's skill. Far more coherence emerged on screen than the chaotic to-and-fro of argument had actually possessed.

'No firm decisions have been made yet about selling land.' Norris spoke in the calm, reassuring tone of one talking down a suicide from a ledge. 'It's just one of the options the governing body is being forced to look at as we consider the future financial security of the college. But, whether we do finally put any of our lands on the market or not, it is simply unthinkable that the college should remain in a position where it cannot prove legal title to its holdings. We have to get the issue of documentation sorted out, whatever the future holds.'

The identity caption at the bottom of the screen blinked off as Norris was replaced in the camera's viewfinder and the voice of Abbie Daniels indicated that the tenants' leader, Robert Hadstowe, viewed things from a different perspective.

'It's all very well for Dr Norris to say that there are no final and definite plans to sell land,' Hadstowe was saying, an emotion he could not quite mask adding an edge to his voice, 'but if it's just a vague idea which might or might not come to fruition at some point in the future, why isn't the college prepared to negotiate with us on future terms for sale should that ever be exercised as an option?' His image flickered almost imperceptibly over a splice in the film. 'We feel it's only fair that if the college does take up the option to sell land, sitting tenants should be offered first refusal rather than simply selling to developers who will find a way to get rid of us.'

Hadstowe's face disappeared to the accompaniment of more words in Abbie Daniels' carefully flattened version of the regional accent and 'Sir Ian Baird – Principal, Northgate College' appeared. Ian Baird had, as far as Damia was aware, never played professional rugby, but his massive, brutal physique would have been well suited to the sport. His voice, pleasant and cultured, was a surprise.

'This unfortunate crisis is just further evidence that the small colleges we have here in Salster are going to find it increasingly difficult to survive in the current economic environment. If – as I and others believe we should – all the colleges entered into a formal university structure, whereby certain functions are delegated to university employees instead of each college duplicating staff, we would see a massive saving of financial resources. The only *efficient* way for the Salster colleges to meet the challenges of the twenty-first century is as a properly incorporated university. Much as I love Salster as it is, anything else is – unfortunately – a sentimental anachronism.'

Norris was allowed to interrupt, exactly as he had in real time, though his initial incredulous 'Oh, come off it Ian, you don't love Salster as it is *at all!*' had been cut, presumably as indicating too much humanity in Norris, a man the piece seemed determined to represent as an out-of-touch dinosaur.

'Northgate bears very little resemblance' – Norris faced the camera once more – 'to anything remotely resembling a traditional Salster college. It's nothing to do with when it was founded, or the age of the buildings,' he said, calmly, against an attempted interruption from Baird. 'It's entirely to do with the ethos. I believe that it's the job of Salster colleges to teach young people to think, to be critical, to question the society in which they live and to make it a better society to live in—'

Again, Baird attempted to interrupt off-camera.

'Yes, Ian, I own up to that, a liberal education *is* what I'm talking about. And I'm not ashamed of it. I know it's fashionable to talk about the relevance of education and the material taught but I believe that learning to think, to analyse and to be critical is independent of subject matter. And it should be independent of businesses who are brought in to bankroll particular subjects or fields of research.'

There was an audible but incomprehensible comment from Baird to which Norris replied, 'He who pays the piper calls the tune, Ian. And I believe our job in Salster should be to comment on the tunes and say "That tune stinks!" if it's true.'

Off-camera, the interviewer's voice, detouring around this diversion, remarked that Kineton and Dacre College's much-publicised financial difficulties must be embarrassing for Northgate as its associate college.

Baird contrived to give the impression of being simultaneously rueful and irritated.

'Yes, it is.' He paused momentarily. 'Nobody, least of all Dr Norris, can be unaware of my views,' he went on, with a glance to the side of the viewfinder as if assuring himself of Norris' level of awareness. 'I feel it's high time the colleges in Salster abandoned the archaic two-tier system of foundation colleges and associate colleges. It's demeaning to associate colleges – some of which have now been in existence for nearly two hundred years – to continue to insist that they can only award degrees and participate in the communal life of the colleges by tagging on to the coat-tails of an older – so called "foundation" – college. It's insulting, outmoded and stunting to the continued development of Salster as a world-class place of education and research. If all colleges belonged equally to a university – instead of each of the foundation colleges functioning as a totally independent entity, awarding its own degrees and selecting its students without reference to the other colleges – then we would be in a far stronger position when it came to negotiating government – and other – funding. It's clear that the colleges can work together effectively – if they couldn't we wouldn't have any science departments in Salster – but we must see this as a matter of urgency.'

Robert Hadstowe was asked whether he felt that the

current financial crisis at Kineton and Dacre College would have been avoided had the colleges entered into a species of federation where each took some responsibility for the financial well-being of the whole.

'Well, obviously, if there was some kind of central planning to decide how undergraduates should be housed in a city as small and as full of students as Salster, then perhaps Toby – that is, Kineton and Dacre College – might not have got into the tangle it has—'

'You're referring to the new undergraduate housing complex which has run so spectacularly over budget?'

'Yes. A wonderful design and something which – *as a university* – the colleges of Salster should be aspiring to. But to expect individual colleges, unless they are far better endowed than Kineton and Dacre College, to afford such developments seems absurd to me.'

Damia squeezed the rubbery off-button on the remote and replayed in her mind the scene which had occurred after the TV crew had gone. Baird, suave bonhomie discarded in favour of verbal pugilism, had assured Norris in no uncertain terms that if he did not vote for the abolition of the associate college system at the next college council meeting, and support Baird's proposal that the council form a working party to consider the development of a formal university structure, then 'I will buy you out, Ed. And don't think I haven't got the support from your own people. One way or another, I'm moving Northgate out from under your incompetent business practices – and sooner, rather than later.'

Eight

If Gwyneth had gazed at herself in a looking glass – had she possessed such a thing – she would have seen a woman much older than she felt. Though she had endured the painful weight of twenty years of fruitless marriage, though she had suffered the scorn and sympathy of other women, though she had embraced and loved a dead woman's child as her own, she would have been surprised to see how the sadness of these things had lined her face. For all she had endured, she felt herself still to be the girl who had married Simon two decades before.

Often, Gwyneth had regarded their marriage, like one who steps aside from life, and had shaken her head. Was tolerant love, however loyally given and steadfastly maintained in the face of royal disapproval, all that Simon deserved? Surely his passion deserved a wife who gave herself completely to him, cleaved to him with every ounce of her strength? Yet she could not do it. As much as Simon could not teach Alysoun her father's craft, so impossible was it for Gwyneth to give Simon that part of herself which waited for a child. Utter devotion had been dammed up in Gwyneth by her barrenness.

Simon, wanting a son to learn of him, had used the long and childless years in perfecting his skill, teaching Henry whilst storing up for his son all that might be learned of a lifetime's experience. Gwyneth, wanting a child for its own sake and having tasted, in her love for Alysoun, all that might await her, practised her father's craft to pass the waiting years, forcing the pain of barrenness to bring forth something of worth and beauty.

For twenty years she had been master carpenter to Simon's master mason, each deferring to the other in respect of what might be accomplished in their separate mysteries. Tobias's birth having coincided with the finishing of the judge's court inn, she had done no work since, content that her new status as mother set her apart from work that only a woman unmarried, widowed or barren would expect to do.

But Simon's view of the situation was quite different. He had made it clear that the time had now come for her to rouse herself from her preoccupation with Tobias and take up her tools once more. Her right and proper time of being as one with the child was, in Simon's eyes, now at an end and she must begin to take up her life alongside him as before.

With his mind firmly set on Toby's future as his apprentice, Simon did not see that *this* was the time for which Gwyneth had longed, this time with an infant born of her own body, an infant recognised as hers by his intimacy with her as she fed him from her own breasts, carried him close against her, felt his needs with her own being. Her love for Alysoun was a mother's love, but Alysoun had been a half-grown child when she came to Gwyneth's house, beyond such enthralling intimacy.

Simon needed her – she knew he did – as wife, master carpenter, friend. But the pent emotions which Toby's birth had released – grown more powerful, perhaps, by such long confinement – had overwhelmed her and left her in no condition to fulfil Simon's needs.

The days after his return from Richard Daker in Salster had been tense, for Simon had made it clear that his college had need of her skills.

Looking at his plans before Simon's first visit to Daker, she had been puzzled.

'Simon, show me what is within, here,' she had said, her finger at the centre of the building-plan, 'I cannot make sense of your lines.'

Simon smiled, gazed down at the plan. 'Very well. You have understood the blocks of living chambers here, here, here and here, with alleys between which give entrance to the central courtyard. In the courtyard is the hall – eight-sided.' His finger traced the octagonal shape. 'The hall itself will be here, reached by a stone staircase that will follow the outer wall of the building.' His finger traced one of the shapes that Gwyneth had failed to interpret. 'Under the hall will be a kitchen undercroft with cellars beneath.' Suddenly the massive piers and shallow, domed vaults of the cellar sprang out at Gwyneth from the plan. So much, now, she understood.

'Then what of this,' she asked, running her finger around the plan, 'above the hall? What is it?'

'Above the hall I have provided for the college's store of books.' He looked at her, delighted with himself. 'That is the library.' He pointed. 'See, here are windows which run around at the level of the library and, lower down within the belly of the hall, larger windows, here.'

'But there will be insufficient light for a library from such windows – even though the library rises above the level of the chamber-blocks.'

He looked at her intently. 'You have not considered the roof, Gwyneth.'

'No. You have not drawn it.'

'I have not, because you shall. The roof is to be your master work as the college is mine.' He looked into her eyes, pleading and demanding at the same time. 'We must have a lantern, to flood the place of learning with light.' He stretched out a hand and took one of hers. 'Gwyneth, I want you to build me a lantern roof.'

A lantern roof! Only one existed in England, in the cathedral church at Ely in the Fenlands. Gwyneth had never seen it, but had seen carpenters' drawings of it, as had any master carpenter who concerned himself with building. It was the crowning achievement of English roof work and Gwyneth knew that such a work was beyond her. Simon knew it too, she was convinced. His dual needs – to build Daker's college and to stretch the ties that bound her so close to Toby – had become fused in one desire: to have her with him in the work that he planned.

But she could not do it.

Simon's design was brilliant, she recognised it and would have rejoiced in it had he not sought to draw her in to the very fabric of it. A lantern roof would, indeed, be the answer to such a building's needs – an answer both practical and magnificent – but she did not know a master carpenter who would not pale at the thought of its intricate design. Gwyneth remembered her one glimpse of the pattern-book of the Ely carpenter, one uncomprehending glimpse which had left her thankful that she would never be required to attempt such workmanship. Looking upon it as a simple curiosity she had not exerted herself to understand the principles upon which the roof was constructed and now, casting her mind back, she found that the sketches and working drawings had not imprinted themselves upon her memory sufficiently even to have left a clear picture of the final result. Other innovations – like Master Herland's roof for the new Westminster Hall that covered the enormous width in one span by the use of so-called hammer beams – these she could compass. But a lantern roof – would even the skill of Hugh Herland, she wondered, be equal to such a thing?

Nine

From: Damia.Miller@kdc.sal.ac.uk
To: CatzCampbell@hotmail.com
Subject: Stop Press!

Just had to tell you! Against all the odds, Norris's appeal to
the families of ex-RMs for college documents has come up
with the goods! A trunkful of stuff (trunk, btw = wicker,
lined with calico, covered in what looks like tarpaper . . .)
arrived today from the descendant of a Victorian RM who
had removed the archive in order to write a college history
and then promptly died, leaving the entire college archive at
his summer residence! Hard to believe but true
nevertheless . . . All the medieval papers have disappeared
straight to the cathedral archivist because, apparently, they
belong there, not here. Will tell you when I find out why.

Why was she withholding from Catz the fact that the cathedral archivist was not a stranger? Why was she not dispelling
the image that she knew full well would spring to her lover's
mind of an elderly, stooped individual with thin white hair,
leather elbow-patches and strained 1950s RP vowels? Why
was she keeping to herself information about the cathedral

archivist that would send to New York the image of a man not yet thirty-five, a man with a head of dark curly hair and a gap-toothed smile?

Why was she not telling Catz that – even before his appearance at Toby in response to Norris's summons – she had known, from a few hastily emailed lines, that the cathedral archivist was her one-time boyfriend, Neil Gordon?

Ten

Salster, September 1385

Gwyneth's wall hangings did not come out of the press into which they had been folded as long as the Kinetons lived in Salster. The house with which Richard Daker provided them – a magnificent timber-framed house not two minutes' walk from his own grange – was filled with furniture, wall-hangings and all the luxuries in which the house they had rented from Judge Stowald had been echoingly deficient. Though neither Gwyneth nor Simon would have chosen blue and green striped worsted had they been given a free hand, a week in the house saw them adapting to its unaccustomed luxuries, its alien atmosphere settling around them as familiarity.

Salster seemed small and cramped after London's sprawling acreage; each hovel and town house known and knowable, the particular stench of each street and its wares identifiable, the city's beggars predictable in their haunts and supplications. And over the whole small, teeming city, wherever it was possible to walk within the walls, castle and abbey imposed themselves.

Simon, gazing with Daker at the proposed site for their college, felt the constraints imposed by his new home and voiced doubts.

'Master Daker, how many paces long do you count this row?'

Daker narrowed his eyes and looked from one end of the row of shops to the other.

It was plain to Simon that his patron had not gone into this on the ground at all. Daker's college had grown in his mind. But it had to be placed somewhere in the material world of roads and rows, shops and churches, and Simon was not convinced that this was the ideal place.

'From one end to the other, it cannot be more than fifty paces,' he said before Daker could hazard an inaccurate guess, 'and the depth of the tenement is exactly defined by the stream behind. I do not believe that it can be more than thirty-five paces deep – forty at the most—'

'We can measure it. Your paces or mine?'

'Mine.' Yours are over-long, thought Simon as he strode next to Daker down the alleyway which allowed access from the street, through the rows, to the tenements and gardens that ran down to the debris-fouled stream behind.

'Thirty-eight paces,' he said, turning to Daker a yard or so from the foul-smelling water.

'It's not enough.'

Simon was becoming used to Daker's trick of asking questions as if he were pronouncing judgement.

'Not if we are to build to the plans I have drawn up for you. I imagined a site of at least sixty yards square. We have not even fifty here. And we cannot make yardage we do not have. We are bound by the road in one direction and the stream in another.'

'Then we must adapt your plans.' Daker looked squarely at Simon. 'How long will your redrawing take?'

'When can we begin to clear the site?'

'Not for a month. Notices are served, but we must wait a month.'

'I don't need half that to redraw. A day would be enough – only proportions need to be changed.' He paused, knowing he was about to disappoint Daker. He was frustrated himself. 'But, in a month we will be in the second week of October. Too late to begin building.'

'Why?'

Daker, Simon reflected, must have seen buildings growing every day of his life in London. Had he never stopped to consider why the work went with the seasons?

'Stone is like wine – just as wine cannot be casked one day and drunk the next, so stone cannot be cut from the ground one day and laid the next. It needs warmth to dry it and harden it. Too much rain on unseasoned stone ruins it for ever – it will never harden as it should. And even if we had seasoned stone,' he said, forestalling Daker's next objection, 'mortar cracks and fails if frosts attack it.'

'So we can do nothing until spring.'

'No building. But the site must be cleared, these shops taken down – by the way, have you thought that we can sell the stone and timber?'

Daker shook his head slightly. 'No. Will you arrange it?'

Simon nodded, then continued, 'And then we may dig foundations – if the frosts hold off. Digging frozen earth is hard.' He looked at Daker. Like most men unaccustomed to building he had obviously never stopped to imagine the hows and whys of the trade. They had been mother's milk to Simon; he did not remember a time when the rhythms and constraints of his craft had not been clear to him. Now he must try to explain why things must be as they were. He hoped Daker had patience and forbearance enough to see that these things were necessarily so and not the result of intransigence on his part.

'Fortunately,' he began again, his eyes fixed on Daker in unaccustomed wariness, 'I have some partly seasoned stone at Kineton. It is too soon to order it yet, but once the period of notice is served and we begin to clear our site then I can have it sent. Once the shops are gone, we can put up a lodge and tracing-house and somewhere to store the stone and begin cutting. The winter will not be entirely wasted, Master Daker. We will make use of it.' He met his patron's intent gaze and said simply, 'I am as eager as you to see our building begun.'

But both men were to be frustrated. No sooner had Simon begun to adapt his ground-plan to squeeze his spacious vision into the constrained spaces of Salster, than the might of the Church began to engage the cogs of an engine designed to delay, frustrate and, in the mind of its wielder, Prior William, to crush Daker's plans.

It was Henry Ackland who brought the news. Henry, Simon reflected, seemed destined permanently to act the intermediary.

'What do you mean, Daker doesn't own the row?' Simon demanded, interrupting Henry before he could finish the sentence that would have explained precisely what he meant.

'Once Daker's plans for the row became known—'

'Known? How? He has hardly gone about the city trumpeting his intentions—'

'Simon, this is not London, this is Salster. There is no corner so dark here that the bishop and his minions don't see what is done in it. And they had no need of spies in this case – one of Daker's tenants did not like the terms of his notice—'

Simon snorted. 'His terms have been ridiculously generous!'

Precisely to avoid this turn of events.

'Evidently somebody thought less of them than you do. Or perhaps he has other irons in the fire. There are always sound reasons for keeping in good standing with the Church, Simon.'

Simon began pacing the room. 'So, the Church is laying claim to Daker's land?'

Henry ran his fingers through his hair and rested one ankle on his other knee for comfort.

'The land was granted to Master Daker's father. When he first came to Salster, he rented the row of shops which lay on it from the abbey but, as he became more wealthy' – and older, he thought to himself – 'he received permission to pull down the row and built a hospital. He had acquired land outside the city wall by that time, hard up against the southern gate, and the revenue from that – such as it was – fed and clothed the hospital's paupers. In recognition of his good work the abbey granted to him the land on which the hospital stood.'

'And now, grant or not, the positions are reversed.' Simon's tone was belligerent, as if Henry had arranged this transposition solely to confuse him. 'When did shops become hospital and vice versa?'

'Shortly after Daker's father died, a fire consumed the hospital,' Henry explained, 'and the fabric of the building – timber-framed – was destroyed. Master Daker decided that a bigger hospital could be maintained if the shops were restored to the original site and the hospital moved to the site outside the gates.'

'Fires happen.' Simon stated it baldly, making it quite clear to Henry that he neither cared not desired to know whether the destruction of the hospital had been entirely accidental.

'Indeed.' Henry could play that game too.

'And the shops have been in that row ever since, with never a squeak of protest from the Church?'

'Until now, yes.'

'And what is it that the Church finds to object to now? Apart from the fact of Daker's wish to build a college upon the land.'

Henry rubbed at a stain on his boot with a licked forefinger, not meeting Simon's eye. 'The prior's objection is given out as having to do with the hospital,' he said. 'It seems that whilst the land granted to Daker's father was being used, in some way at least, to support a hospital, then the Church had no objection. Now, of course, things are different—'

'If the Church granted the land to Daker's father with good title, then objections are neither here nor there!' Simon exploded.

'The prior questions whether the land was granted with good title,' Henry said, guardedly. 'If you believe him, the Church understood merely that it was waiving rent on the land to Daker and his heirs while there was a hospital upon it.'

'There has not been a hospital upon it for twenty years and more! If the Church has waited till this to enforce what it conceives of as its rights, then there is more to it than the mere letter of the law!'

Why, Henry wondered, am I taking the trouble to go softly on this when I am as outraged as he is? Because if I was the bearer of bad news in the past, it was usually the result of something I had done. Treading carefully could avoid a whipping. It's nothing more than habit.

'The prior's excuse' – Henry set tact aside – 'is that without revenue from the shops, he fears that the hospital will founder. Colleges, as he pointed out, do not make money.'

'Is he afraid he will have to dig into his own coffers?' Simon asked, withering Henry with his scorn for the prior.

'Look at it from the Church's point of view, Simon. This particular bird – a well-endowed hospital – is well worth having in their hand. If they stand by and watch Daker pull down the shops, they may well suspect that his next step will be to pull down the hospital too.'

'Henry, tell me truthfully, do you believe that this is anything more than an attempt to frustrate Daker's college? And that the Church would even tolerate that if he were not a Lollard dissenter?'

Henry was silent, his eyes on the man who had saved him from poverty, raised him up to his present stature as master mason, respected citizen. 'Simon,' he said finally, 'if Daker can prove good title to this land, he will build his college, Prior William and his bishop notwithstanding.'

'And if he cannot prove it?'

'Let's cross that bridge if we have to.'

Simon stared at him. 'I once stood against a king and lost. If I now stand against the church and lose too, I may never draw another building that comes to see stone.'

'You are not opposing the Church.'

'Not yet.'

Henry shook his head. 'You make too much of it, Simon. This is nothing more than the usual wrangle over land.'

❖

But land is money and money is power and power means getting what you want.

This was a creed familiar to Ralph Daker.

The existence of Ralph had been a surprise to William of Norwich, prior of the monastery of Christchurch and its cathedral. John, Daker's young son, was well known in Salster since he came to the city whenever his stepmother and father removed there; but Ralph had arrived in Salster, hot on the heels of his uncle's intentions, unannounced and unexplained.

Prior William knew, to his cost, that unknown quantities had a habit of springing unpleasant surprises whilst they were allowed to remain unknown. Making them yield up their secrets, on the other hand, often made them very useful.

By long-accustomed means the prior had learned all that was known or suspected about Ralph, in either Salster or London.

He found that Ralph was Richard Daker's nephew, his sister's son. This was the first surprise, since the prior had taken their shared family name as evidence that Ralph was a brother's son. It transpired that Ralph had quarrelled with his father and made his home with his uncle a dozen years before. Richard, at that time childless, had taken him into his own business and allowed him to adopt the Daker name, since Ralph's father, through rage or the simple desire to wash his hands of a troublesome younger son, had forsworn their relationship.

Ralph had worked for his uncle ever since and was, according to the general report, treated like a son in every respect but the obvious and inescapable one of inheritance.

A rumour that was not generally reported, but had, nevertheless, come to Prior William's ears, was that for the entire four years' length of Richard Daker's marriage to his second wife, Anne, he had been cuckolded by his nephew.

Anne, if hearsay was given weight, had chosen power and influence over youth for her marriage but, seeing that she might have both if she played her game discreetly, had taken Ralph to her bed on those many occasions when her husband was absent abroad.

The prior never made the mistake of believing everything he heard, but he did not discount this tale out of hand. If it were true, knowledge of it could prove extremely useful.

William of Norwich and Ralph Daker were unlikely allies, and yet no shop-tenant of Daker's would have complained at his terms of notice, had it not been made worth their while.

Eleven

Extract from the *Salster Times*

The prospects for next summer's Salster Colleges Fairings are hotting up as this year's victorious team, Kineton and Dacre College, have capped their win with another triumph, this time away from the cobbled streets and front quads in the financial world of corporate sponsorship.

Having been sponsored last year by bottled-water company Moorland Waters, Kineton and Dacre College has, this year, set its sights on bigger game. Their prize, announced this week, is Atoz, the international sportswear and equipment company.

'These were intense negotiations, as we needed to get a deal done quickly in order to support our athletes,' said Damia Miller, the college's recently appointed marketing and development manager. 'We needed the kind of deal which would enable us to retain last year's coach, Dean Epps, who could easily go on to more lucrative positions in college athletics in America.'

Mr Epps, a former Great Britain Olympic middle-distance runner, has made no secret of the fact that offers 'from overseas' had been made but he has always maintained that he would wait to see what Salster colleges could bring to the table first.

'The Fairings is unique,' he told the *Salster Times*. 'There is no athletics event like it in the world. It is the one truly amateur event left in athletics, but that doesn't stop the standard being extraordinary. It's highly likely that some of these college athletes could go on to run for their country if they chose to.'

And this determinedly amateur spirit has always been at the heart of the worldwide appeal of the Fairings. Unlike the Boat Race, in which young men studying for any kind of degree at Oxsterbridge are eligible to row, only undergraduates studying for their first degree are allowed to run in their college's Fairings team. Nobody can come to Salster, having done their undergraduate degree (and their previous running) elsewhere, specifically to run in the Fairings. It is a race for undergraduates who happen to be good runners and, despite a great deal of lobbying over the years from interested parties, it remains so. And, as running does not have the elitist connotations of rowing, Fairings teams tend to reflect the social diversity for which Salster, alone of the three Oxsterbridge universities, is justifiably applauded.

Atoz, who have previously been sponsors of the Boat Race teams and of Championship football clubs, announced their sponsorship of Kineton and Dacre at a press conference at the college.

'We are delighted to announce our partnership with the college's athletes,' their representative Kerry Kramer said, 'and hope that our backing of a non-professional sporting team will encourage other people to enjoy running at whatever level they feel comfortable with. Though our company is associated with sports of various kinds, running has always been our heart and soul and we have a reputation, which we are very proud of, for producing running equipment of the highest quality.

'Kineton and Dacre College runners will be attesting to this as they all run in their choice of Atoz running shoe next summer.'

Damia's hands shook as she put the paper down. It was all positive – no reference to either the rent strike or the college's financial position, thank God! Things could have been very different. From the outset, Damia had played the risky publicity card and used the college's current media focus as a draw – talking up the campaign to unravel the mystery of The Sin Cycle as a counterweight to the very visible rent strikers and their campaign. She had also, unashamedly, sold the good PR it would give the company to be seen to be supporting a college team which, in its alliance with Northgate, took more than the Salster average of state school pupils. If last year's team was taken as typical, ten out of the training squad of twelve runners would come from less privileged backgrounds.

The Fairings: the most famous footrace in the world after the Olympic marathon. Damia would, the following May, be included in scenes that she had only previously shared with tens of millions of other people via television coverage: the six teams in their college rigs; the traffic-free streets packed with people craning for a view of their favoured runners; interviews with team members glowing with youth, intelligence and the kind of fitness the human body was ideally designed for – the ability to run at a sustained pace in pursuit of quarry.

Strictly speaking there was no actual pursuit, since the quarry in the Fairings were roses, plucked by runners from specially erected trellises in each of the foundation colleges and, at the climax of the race, from the centuries-old rambler in the main quad at St Thomas' College.

The ancient rose of St Thomas' lay at the heart of the Fairings. Tradition maintained that the city's medieval apprentices, drunk on May Day festivity, would dare each other to scale the forbidding college walls and emerge with a sweet-smelling, pale pink bloom as a Fairing gift for their sweetheart. The precise origins of the modern intercollegiate race were obscure, though most historians of the event agreed in implicating the idleness of Victorian varsity youth.

In the twenty-first century, Damia reflected, neither those who ran in the race nor the colleges that nurtured them could afford to be idle. While the young people endured the dovetailing of training schedules with social and academic demands, the colleges' finance officers went through a no less gruelling procedure in order to secure big-name backing for their athletes. As government funding shrank and costs increased, Fairings sponsorship played a more and more significant role in sustaining a college's financial health.

Consequently, there was now far more at stake for the runners than the honour of simply taking part. Winning could make the difference between a household-name sponsor the following year and a less well known and consequently less lucrative one. And since top-flight coaches followed the money, here as elsewhere, success bred success.

The Toby runners – Damia hugged herself with the thought – would now be able to hold on to Dean Epps.

She could hardly wait to tell them.

Later the same day, Damia opened the door to the Toby junior common room and stepped from the warmth and brightness of a resolutely sunny October day into the muted cool of a largely empty room. As she took in her surroundings, she felt the confidence inspired by her position slipping away and was humiliated by the realisation that she was still capable of being impressed to the point of intimidation by age-stained panelling, battered leather furniture and a sideboard stacked with willow-patterned china teacups.

She grinned slightly sheepishly at the common room's mid-afternoon occupants – a young man with a lot of unruly russet hair sprawled on a sofa reading what looked like a large hardbacked notebook and an underweight girl sitting to the right of the doorway, playing solitaire on her laptop with a frown that Damia hoped denoted concentration rather than annoyance at being disturbed.

'Hi, sorry to invade your space – just here to meet the Fairings runners. I'm Damia Miller, the new marketing manager.'

'Cool!' the reader commented. Unexpectedly, he leaped to his feet and came to shake hands. 'Sam Kearns. The cheerful one over there is Lisa Gregory.'

Ms Gregory kept her eyes fixed balefully on her electronic cards and muttered a suggestion that Sam should attempt sex with himself.

Damia concentrated on the more appealing Mr Kearns. 'Work?' she asked, nodding at the book in his hand, suspecting it wasn't.

'Nah – just the Biz Book.' He proffered it to her.

'Sorry?' she queried, taking the book from him.

'Biz Book – Toby JCR institution. You can write anything in it for anybody else to read – get something off your chest, tell a joke, have a dig at somebody, monger a bit of gossip, suggest things to be discussed at next JCR meeting – anything.'

'So, Biz as in business?'

Sam lip-shrugged. 'Dunno – never thought about it. But probably, yeah. I suppose it might originally have been a suggestions book – or a kind of working agenda for JCR meetings. But we've all got a lot more frivolous since then.'

'Who's the cartoonist?' Damia asked, seeing what were evidently caricatures of college members as she flicked through the dog-eared book.

'Stephan Kingsley – third-year classicist. Fantastic mimic too. You should see his Tommy Thomas.'

Damia looked up and shook her head slightly, confessing ignorance.

'Tommy's one of the angels,' Sam explained, using the term by which Toby – in common with all other Salster colleges – referred to the domestic staff who looked after undergraduate rooms. Toby's angels worked one to a staircase, each angel taking responsibility for the cleanliness of twelve rooms; milk delivered daily and laundry done too, if any student had the means to enter into a private arrangement with their particular angel. Toby was one of the few remaining colleges to employ its angels directly rather than through an agency. That made them fixtures, known – and sometimes loved – by the students.

'I can't do him,' Sam continued, 'but if ever you meet Stephan, get him to do Tommy for you. It's perfect – even Tommy thinks so.'

First, Damia reflected, she would have to meet the original. It was high time she stepped aside from paperwork, websites, governing bodies and negotiations with sportswear manufacturers and became acquainted with the people who actually made the college work.

Sam's gaze moved to the window that overlooked the Octo yard. 'Here they are,' he said, 'at least the Toby runners – are you meeting the Northgate lot as well? That's them, by the way, if you want to see them in all last year's glory.' He nodded to a point on the wall over her shoulder and Damia turned to see a huge framed photograph of four laughing young people in the Toby rig, drenched in multicoloured silly-string, shaken champagne spurting over them from all directions. The photograph had obviously been taken in the yard outside, the Toby statue was poised like the ghost from a bad horror movie on the wall above the euphoric runners.

The door to the common room was thrust open and three people strode in, one male, two female, all dressed alike in tracksuit bottoms and zipped tops in claret and navy. A tastefully discreet logo indicated that this was last year's training kit.

'Hey Sam, hey Lisa,' one of the tracksuited girls said to an animated response from Sam Kearns and an eye-contact-less mutter from the solitaire enthusiast.

'Hi,' Damia greeted them, her hand outstretched ready to shake. 'I'm Damia Miller – marketing manager and,' she added, 'general find-me-money-wherever-you-can dogsbody to Dr Norris.'

One of the female runners grinned. 'Can't imagine Dr Ed getting so mercenary as to say anything like that.' She shook Damia's hand. 'Sally Mackle. And—' Releasing Damia's hand, she swept her own towards her companions in an invitation for them to introduce themselves.

'Ellen Ballantyne.'

'Duncan McTeer.'

As they finished shaking hands, Sally, in what looked to Damia like an attempt not to seem exclusive, asked, 'Are you going to try out for the team this year, Sam?'

'What, against you three? No chance!'

'You're a good runner' Duncan encouraged.

'Yeah, specially now you've given up the weed—' Ellen

joined in, immediately looking at Damia, who held her hands up, palms out.

'Don't look at me, I'm not your mother!'

Sally tried again. 'Why don't you try out, Sam?'

'Not against you.'

'But you might be better than anybody at Northgate.'

'Unlikely,' was Sam's opinion. 'But even if I was' – he shrugged – 'it's always two, and two isn't it – two from Toby, two from Northgate.'

'I don't know if it actually *says* that anywhere—' Sally began.

'Do you reckon it says *any* of that stuff anywhere?' Sam smiled, taking the sting from a remark which could have sounded superior. 'It's all just tradition.'

Damia's office, which all three runners had professed themselves eager to see, was in the fellows' quarters, the only block on the Octagon yard not to house undergraduates. A large first-floor room, its windows faced east, providing a bright welcome in the morning. This suited the early-rising Damia, who had no plans to spend her evenings in the office.

'This is much nicer than most of the fellows' rooms,' Ellen said, as Damia invited them to sit down on the low, cream-coloured sofas. 'How did you persuade them to strip the floors and give you new furniture? Most tutors have to put up with furniture older than they are!'

Damia grinned, catching her own expression reflected in the coffee machine she was in the process of priming. 'Well, the floor thing I swung because I have quite a severe dust-mite allergy – makes me wheeze and my eyes run – so carpets are out, especially venerable ones. I suppose I could have got the new furniture on that basis, too, but actually I told Dr

Norris that it was a matter of image – the faded glory look might impress academics but it doesn't impress potential donors and investors.'

She looked at the machine as if refreshing her memory as to what it was for, then asked, 'OK, espresso, cappuccino or latte?'

'Did that come as part of the "we are impressive" package too?' Duncan asked when they'd all made their choices.

'No such luck. I bought this as a congratulations present to myself.' Since anyone else who might have been inclined to buy me such a thing was three and a half thousand miles away, she thought sourly.

'What about the paintings?' Ellen asked, nodding at the one over the mantelpiece. 'Did you buy those yourself, too?'

Damia was pulled up short by this evidence of the gulf between their perception of her and the actual facts: that this was her first decently paid job, that, unlike these young people, she had never been to university and that, contrary to their obvious assumptions, she was virtually penniless, especially now that she had a mortgage to service.

'They were painted by my partner,' she said.

'Right,' Ellen said, admiringly. 'Talented guy.'

Damia didn't miss a beat; she was practised at not missing beats. 'Woman, actually.'

'Oh, sorry.'

Damia held up a relaxed hand, waving the apology away. She poured the coffee and the meeting began.

To Damia's chagrin, the runners were less enthusiastic about their new sponsors than she had anticipated. In fact they seemed surprised that a change of sponsor had been felt necessary, as the same company's name had appeared on Toby running rigs for the last five years, with obvious results.

'Don't forget you're the holders of the Fairings Rosebowl now. There were companies prepared to bid much higher sums in sponsorship this year.'

'But Moorland Water was a good sponsor – it was a good image for us – healthy water, healthy bodies, all of that.'

'Right, and in an ideal world, we'd have stayed with them. But, at this point, we can't afford to be too picky.'

The runners looked at each other and Damia saw an understanding flicker between them. 'We know Toby isn't exactly flush at the moment—'

'Guys,' Damia held up her hands, '"Isn't exactly flush" doesn't come close. You've seen the strikers out on the Romangate?'

Making conscious eye contact with each of them, she explained the situation, feeling uncomfortably like the representative of an older, wiser, sadder generation.

'We need sponsors like Atoz,' she said. 'Without the kind of big money they're offering, pretty soon there won't be a college to run for.'

'But what about their ethical and human rights record?' Ellen asked. 'They come pretty well bottom of the list in any league table of worker rights. Not to mention their use of child labour and that particularly delightful business practice of paying their workers in tokens that could only be used in the company's own store—'

'Which, to be fair, *is* ancient history now,' Sally interrupted.

'Only because of the boycott—'

Damia held up a hand. 'Look, guys, I have to be honest here and say that their human rights record wasn't something I looked into in much depth. Atoz is a household name, they came offering an extremely attractive package, I asked

Moorland Waters if they would match it – I was keen to keep them too – but they couldn't so we went with Atoz.'

She looked at their clouded faces.

'I'm sorry, but we've got to be realistic here.'

Wordless glances between the runners elected Ellen spokesperson. 'It's just that we did a lot of the work in keeping Moorland on board – we've never had somebody like you to do the negotiating before. It's kind of a new sensation for us not to be involved.' She glanced at the others. 'And Atoz's ethical stance does bother me.'

'To be honest,' said Damia, hoping she was right, 'the governments of the workers you're talking about aren't always known for their wonderful human rights either – chances are that Atoz is going to offer more than the government requires, actually.'

'But that's not the point, is it?' Ellen asked. 'Isn't it up to us who have the luxury of choice to demand what we'd want ourselves?'

Damia selected her words carefully, aware that she'd suddenly blundered into an ethical minefield where she'd thought to skip lightly through a good-news flower meadow. 'I hear what you're saying, and I agree, in principle. But, actually, I'm not sure we *do* have the luxury of choice. Right now, Toby is on the edge. We need all the financial support we can get.'

And, sorry guys, she added silently, but Toby's got a marketing manager now. And it's me. And the decision is made.

Twelve

While Piers Mottis, Daker's lawyer, took the long, slow and necessary steps to prove Daker's title to the land, Simon could do nothing but fret. With the case undecided, there could be no site to clear, no foundations to peg out. He could not even order stone up from Kineton for winter cutting in the lodge, so uncertain was the future.

He began to have the same nightmare night after night, one in which he was forced to watch whilst the parchments on which his plans were drawn were scraped clean and the palimpsests used in the abbey's scriptorium to write out the new deeds of title to the disputed land. As much as Simon had hated the thought of altering his original designs to fit a space more constrained than he had bargained for, such alteration now seemed an ideal when compared with the thought of his plans coming to nothing, their vision frustrated.

He looked over and over again at his amended drawings. Compressing the plan in an east–west direction to allow for a space of fifty paces instead of sixty, he had spared the fabric of the building entirely, choosing instead to narrow the bordering gardens considerably. The central structural block, deprived of so much of its setting, would lose in impressiveness but would accommodate no fewer masters and scholars.

Looking at his drawings, Simon knew that he had never felt such loss of heart. Through all the waiting years he had been patient, his eyes fixed upon his goal: a building worthy of his talents.

And finally, one man had put what he wanted into his outstretched hand. Richard Daker's need and his own had coincided in a way that must, surely, be providential. Many times Simon had been afraid that he had angered God by refusing to take No for an answer, for wearing out his prayers in endless repetition of 'Give me this one thing and I will show you that I have not wasted your gift.'

Except that he had not merely asked for this one thing, there had been the other matter between him and God. The matter of a son.

Simon had looked at Alysoun – and Henry in his turn – with deep suspicion lest he should be forced to accept in either of these fosterlings his answer from God.

But if Henry or Alysoun had been God's answer, Simon had not been prepared to listen. Still he held out against Heaven and nature for a son of his own body. And his obstinate prayer had been granted. In one miraculous year he had been given both a commission to match his ambition and a son.

But now, Simon was learning that things longed for, once held in the hand, do not always match the picture nurtured in the mind. His son had become a wall between him and Gwyneth and the masterpiece he had longed to build was still no more than lines upon parchment.

What did Gwyneth's reluctance to draw for him matter

now? If the college was not to be built, then whether the plans showed a lantern roof was neither here nor there.

So Simon said to himself a dozen times a day. And still it was not true. Still Gwyneth's refusal wrenched at him.

'Simon, it cannot be done. You must find yourself another master carpenter, I have not the skill to build the roof you need for your college.'

Gwyneth had been so desperate to have the words said that his hand had barely latched the solar door behind him before she had finished.

He had matched her passionate haste with aching silence. He could do nothing else, it was silence or rage and he would not answer for such rage as he felt. He could feel Gwyneth's desperation that he should say something, but it did not move him. Slowly, Simon walked to the chair which stood before the open-shuttered window, the chair she had made for him many years before. Standing with his back against the light he brought his violent anguish under control and said deliberately, 'Gwyneth, have you thought what you are saying?'

Her trembling tautness snapped. '*Thought*? Simon, I have thought of little else! I do not lightly cast such a request aside, but you must believe me when I say that *I do not possess the skill*.'

Her eyes were fixed upon him, willing him to believe her. He breathed deeply, controlling his voice with great effort. 'You are not wanting skill, Gwyneth, just confidence in your craft. Only *try*, and you will see that you may do more than you imagined.'

'Simon, a lantern roof cannot be built on trying! There is only one in England – do you think I am the equal of the man who built Ely's roof?'

'No, but you can learn from him!' Simon felt a sudden surge of hope. 'I have sent to Ely for a copy of the pattern-book. A carpenter is copying the drawings for that lantern.'

Gwyneth was struck dumb at this extravagance and Simon pressed home his perceived advantage.

'I want you for my master carpenter, Gwyn.'

She stared at him, and he felt the tautness which had held her lay its hold on him. She shook her head slightly, opened her mouth, but finding no words to fill it, closed it once more.

'You just want practice, Gwyneth,' Simon began again. 'These months you have been idle have made you a stranger to your craft.'

Gwyneth found her voice. 'Seven months do not make a stranger of one who has been twenty years and more at a craft.' She hesitated, then, her voice quavering, continued, 'I set aside my craft for *two years* once, Simon, only to take it up again as sweetly as yesterday's leaving.'

Simon felt her words like a blow. His jaw clenched on the retort he would have made and he strode to the window to breathe air not contaminated by the memory of old pain.

They had been married less than a handful of childless years when Simon, fearing that such unwomanly pursuits stopped up her womb, had explicitly requested that Gwyneth put aside her carpenter's tools. For two years she had confined herself to his accounts and her embroidery needle. Yet it had availed nothing. Her hands softened, but not her womb; still it had remained stubbornly closed to his seed. Quietly, without seeking Simon's permission or having it withheld, she had taken up her craft again.

His hands on the sill of the window, Simon said, 'Your craft meant something to you then. Does it mean nothing to you now?'

'It does, indeed, mean a great deal to me, Simon—'

He would not wait for the inevitable codicil, that though the work of her hands meant much, her child meant everything, that Tobias was her life's very blood. He plunged in where he saw a chink to his advantage.

'Then, Gwyneth, be true to the trade your father taught you! Study the sketches from Ely and try!'

She would not answer.

Finally, she raised her eyes to his face, but he forestalled anything she might say. 'Gwyneth, a master craftsman could wait a lifetime for such a commission as this, a commission that would make his name—'

Simon stopped. He knew that, through the vehemence of his words, she had finally understood.

Master craftsmen might very well wait for such work, but who would Simon of Kineton persuade to throw in their lot with him as he designed for a man who would take on the might of the Church? Without a carpenter of Simon's own rebellious cast of mind, his college might never be built.

The taut silence between them was broken by a weak cry. Held in the grip of Simon's intensity Gwyneth looked from the cradle to her husband.

'He needs me, Simon.'

Simon ignored the plea. 'We cannot hope to build until the new year – I will not need to see your drawings until then, and even then they need not be inch-perfect, it will be years before we come to roof the hall. His need will then be less—'

There was a silence between them, filled by Toby's cries.

'What must I do?' Simon asked. 'Must I cry, like him? Would your heart soften to me then?'

Gwyneth turned to the child in the cradle. 'It is not in you to cry, Simon, just as it is not in you to humble yourself.'

Did she defy him because she knew that if he did weep, she must respond? Simon had watched his wife with their son and had seen a woman he had never known before, a woman of tenderness and soft eagerness. If she felt it for one being she could surely feel it for another?

But she knew him and she was right, it was not in him to weep his need of her.

'I am a man, Gwyneth. With a man's needs.'

His wife looked up from their son. 'And he is a child, with his own needs.'

'Then you will not build my roof for me.'

She looked at him, Toby at her breast. 'Simon, you said yourself, it will be years before a roof is needed. Draw a lantern roof for Master Daker on your drawings and let what will come, come.'

Thirteen

From: Damia.Miller@kdc.sal.ac.uk
To: Mailing List (Wall Painting Project)
Subject: Toby archive discovered

Dear Wall Painting Project Member

Soon there will be an exciting addition to the information bundle which you received when you joined the project. The college archive, removed from the college many years ago and now restored, may provide the key that unlocks the mystery of the wall painting. Central to this hope is the bundle of medieval papers that represent the earliest Toby records. These are currently being curated and translated by the cathedral archivist as they are in the form of letters written by William of Norwich, prior of the cathedral, to Robert Copley, bishop of Salster during the period in which Toby was built. Quite how these letters came to be in the Toby archive we don't yet know. Watch this space!

Meanwhile, we have some questions that you may be able to help with. A cursory look through the Victorian part of the archive – which contains a detailed selection of oral history from Toby domestic staff and older Salster residents – has thrown up a few references which are obscure.

1   'Tobit Alms'. Aged residents of Salster, questioned in the
    1850s, said that within the memory of their
    grandparents a ceremony called 'Tobit Alms' was
    observed at Kineton and Dacre College, though in
    something of an irregular pattern. Can anybody shed
    any light on this?
2   A folk-memory of some doggerel is recorded in the
    college's recently recovered Victorian archive which
    makes reference to a curse of some kind falling on the
    college if a 'stick or a stone' should be removed from its
    fabric. Does anybody know the doggerel which is
    referred to, or what the alleged curse might be?

    If you can help with either of these, let us know here at
    the Wall Painting Project.

Kind regards

Damia Miller
Director, Wall Painting Project

No deeds. The trunk, its records of past generations lying like
inverted archaeological strata with the most recent Victorian
papers at the bottom, contained nothing that proved Toby's
title to the lands endowed to it by Richard Dacre, vintner of
the city of London.

So the daily personnel change behind the Romangate's
placards continued and the college moved ever closer to
bankruptcy and the humiliating prospect of being rescued –
or, to those less predisposed to believe Baird's propaganda,
taken over – by Northgate and its healthy investments.

When Damia and Norris had met with Neil Gordon in his
capacity as cathedral archivist, he had been upbeat about the

possibility of the letters revealing something to Toby's advantage. Norris, on the other hand, had been uncharacteristically subdued, apparently having put his faith completely in finding papers of endowment amongst the missing college archive.

The need to bolster Norris's failing confidence in a happy outcome had sustained Damia through what would, otherwise, have been an uncomfortable meeting. For days she had swung like a magnet suspended between shifting poles as she tried to decide whether to contact Neil ahead of any professional meeting or to pretend that she did not know he was in Salster. She had finally baulked at the thought of turning up at the cathedral and demanding that he explain what on earth he thought he was doing here. She did not, even tacitly, want to be seen to acknowledge that his coming to Salster at the very time when Catz was absent in New York might be anything other than a coincidence.

At the end of the business meeting, however, as she was signing him out of the college, Neil had asked if they could meet in a less formal way, 'to catch up'.

Time and place decided, Damia had pecked him nonchalantly on the cheek and headed for her office, acutely aware of his eyes on her back until she was on the stairs and out of sight.

From: Damia.Miller@kdc.sal.ac.uk
To: Mailing List Alumni
Subject: Exciting new addition to alumni pages on Toby website

Dear Tobyite

Hope you like the new-look website launched recently?

I owe a huge debt of gratitude to Nick Broom, a Toby undergraduate who has made real what I could only imagine and sketch on the proverbial backs of envelopes. He is credited as webmaster, do please contact him with congratulations, I hope you'll agree that he's done an exceptional job. And still produced two essays a week as well . . .

In the next few weeks a new page will be added to alumni's online experience. The Biz Book – a Toby institution for more than a century – is coming to the website. Each week a new page will be scanned in from a random year's Biz Book in a format in which you can add your own annotations. If you know who wrote the contributions (or if you wrote them yourself) stick on an electronic Post-it telling us. If you can introduce others to the people mentioned or shed light on a situation or event referred to, please do! It's an alternative way of doing Toby history – not the history of the buildings or Regent Masters and fellows, but of you, the heartbeat of the college.

We are particularly keen to give older Tobyites – those who matriculated before 1950 – access to the site. If you know any older members who may not have access to the web, or who do not routinely log on to the Toby site, please do tell them about this new page – they may see their own youthful comments immortalised!

Many thanks, and don't forget to sign up for the new Toby Forum where you can post your comments on this and any other aspect of Toby life,.

Kind regards

Damia Miller
Marketing Manager

Damia sat back and thrust her arms out in front of her as if preparing for a sitting dive. She scrutinised her hands. No shaking: the complicated anger she had felt at Neil, at his calculated re-entry into her life which made a mockery of all the times she had defended his intentions to Catz, had subsided. The fight-or-flight adrenalin – so weighted in favour of fight that it shocked her – had ebbed. The effort of grappling with a new idea, with the size and shape of it, of stabbing the evidence of inspiration into the keyboard, had calmed her.

A run to dissipate the tension stored in her muscles would ensure that she met Neil at seven thirty with equanimity.

Damia had run, for pleasure, fitness and the buzz of athletics meetings, ever since she had arrived in Salster with her system clean and her ambitions bright. As a member of the Saxon Harriers she had run on athletics tracks, on roads, fields and occasionally cross-country bicycle routes. Now that she lived within the city walls, she had several new circuits that she could run from her front door, none of which involved the toxic fumes and peace-shattering engine noise of main roads. Today, the darkening dusk of the Indian summer lured her towards what she mentally pigeonholed as the 'gardens run'. With judicious use of linking side streets and pedestrian alleyways it was possible to circle Salster through its public gardens, running in a distorted loop through green and ordered spaces.

Crunching along pea-gravel in the Pilgrims' Gate gardens she finally allowed herself to focus on the rendezvous with Neil.

'Mia, take your blinkers off and smell the bacon,' Catz had said with the crash-fusion of metaphors that her painting so often showed. 'Neil isn't just an old friend – he's an old boyfriend—'

'*The* old boyfriend. Singular. When I was fifteen and knew nothing.'

'OK, whatever! Doesn't make any difference to him, he was still there. He was still the boyfriend. He's got a *thing* about you, Mia – somewhere in his twisted little soul he wants you two to have a future together, just like your past together.'

Damia, her trainers spurting gravel, felt a chill at the thought of any future resembling the past she and Neil had shared. But, however bad it had been, the immovable fact remained that Neil had been there for her. When her mother had skidded their commune's VW bus into a lorry when Damia was twelve, killing herself and Damia's brother, Neil had been there. When her father died two years later of a broken heart (though the coroner, taking a more mechanical view, pronounced it to be a heroin overdose), Neil had been there. Neil and his family had sheltered her, taking her in when the commune's other adults had made only vague noises about 'making sure she was OK' and 'nurturing her like Maz and Tony would have wanted'.

Neil had been her protector at a school which had been deprived of its only other non-white student by her brother's death; her defender when she had missed lesson after lesson through simply not caring whether she lived or died, much less turned up to learn algebra; her passionate friend who played guitar for her, wrote poems for her, held her hand, kissed her gently and finally convinced her that what they felt was a deep and enduring love and took her to bed in his nest of sleeping bags and blankets.

The commune had shown not the slightest intention of stopping them or of putting any barriers in their way. Physical space was made for their relationship and contributory space was made for them as a couple within the decision-making apparatus of the community. It happened, on her part, without conscious thought and without the awareness of any momentous decision. Still dazed and confused by the renewed visitation of mortality, the wounds of her mother and brother's death torn viciously open again by the sight of her father's stiff grey body, Damia had insulated herself against life with marijuana, silence and a refusal to think or feel anything. She had sleep-walked through her days, dropping out of school on her sixteenth birthday and not returning to attempt any GCSEs.

When Neil left for university in London, there had been nothing to keep her at the commune. She had packed her mother's ancient hippy-trail rucksack a week after Neil's departure – taking his letter telling her that as long as they could get through the first year of his course apart, they could find somewhere together when he left halls – and hitched to Mickelwell, a small village ten miles or so from Salster, where an old friend of her father's ran an organic farm. There, she learned to loathe icy earth, hand-weeding and cutting leeks with fingers so cold they could barely grip the knife. She also gave up cannabis and endured the psychological cold-turkey of postponed grief and self-hatred for allowing herself to drop out. Before her parents' death she had been quite clear that their life-choices were not for her, that she would work hard, get a good education and get a job which enabled her to live in a house with hot water, central heating and carpets in every room. Thick, ankle-deep carpets.

Ironic, she thought as her even stride took her through Salster, that she had no carpets in her little house now. But, belatedly, she did have the education: GCSEs, A-levels and her marketing exams. All done while she worked, on the organic farm with other volunteers, as a *Big Issue* coordinator in Salster, as project worker and finally marketing manager and fundraiser for the Gardiner Foundation for Homeless and Roofless People.

She had not told Neil where she was going, simply sent him a letter saying that London – even with him in it – did not feel like her kind of place and she was going to find somewhere that did. She said she would be in touch and not to worry. She implied that she was going travelling but omitted the fact that the travelling would be limited strictly to getting her to Downs Farm, Mickelwell.

And she did stay in touch. She wrote to Neil after a couple of months to tell him that, though she did not want to hurt him, she had realised that she was gay. That she was in love with a girl called Anne. That she hoped he would find somebody to be happy with at university; somebody else he could move out of hall with.

Damia recalled her first love; the feelings – initial confusion, suppressed passion, final, wordless acknowledgement when the touch of a hand on a bare forearm had brought forth a gasp which had nothing to do with the cold of frozen earth.

If her relationship with Neil had been the comfort and familiarity of much-washed pyjamas, the passion she had briefly shared with Anne had been more akin to a hot, inflamed body being laid naked in deep beds of cool, scented rose-petals.

Although it was only Wednesday, the restaurant was crowded. Damia had arranged to meet Neil there: she was not ready to give him her address. Not yet. For the first time in her life she was experiencing the luxury of living alone, and each evening she mentally drew up the drawbridge. Even Catz did not yet know the address of the little house whose floorboards were being sanded, room by room, each weekend.

Neil was waiting for her. His dark curls, longer than when she had last seen him, stood out against the plain white walls of the restaurant she'd chosen.

Slowing her pace, she studied him before he became aware of her presence. He looked good – had he been a woman she might have said he was positively glowing. He did not look like a man traumatised by the loss of his partner of seven years. The brief email he had sent her six weeks or so previously had given no specifics about his separation from Angie, merely that he had taken up the job of chief archivist at the cathedral, was living in the city, and that he and Angie were no longer together.

Had he moved to Salster with Angie, Damia would not have thought twice about telling Catz that he was the cathedral archivist, that – what luck! – the man with the key to the college's medieval archive and therefore, potentially, to the enigmatic wall painting was her old friend.

Had he separated from Angie but remained in London, Damia would have told Catz. Almost without hesitation.

But Neil's sudden arrival in Salster without Angie had been too much for her to handle and now she was sitting on news that was going to look all the more suspicious for its late arrival.

Finally he felt her eyes on him and looked up. His face burst into a smile in which the emotion was so naked, so utterly undisguised, that she almost came to a halt. Leaving the table, he came towards her and, putting his hands on her waist, kissed her on either cheek, for all the world like a big brother.

Fourteen

Spring in the year of our lord 1387 was as bright in the eyes of Simon of Kineton and as full of promise as a new-struck penny. Though the weather was chancy at best and sunny days few, Simon's mood, after the final resolution of Daker's disputed title to the college lands, was soaring. He barely slept for weeks on end, spending hours before sunrise and after sunset at the site, working by candlelight in the tracing house next to the lodge, unable to bear separation from the works he had feared he would never see started.

As celandines in the hedgerows and aconites in the woods gave way to dog roses and stitchwort, Simon spent his days overseeing the final stages of demolition in the row of shops so long reprieved and looking to dig foundations as soon as maybe.

Gwyneth, whose eagerness to see the dispute ended and building begun had been tempered by the knowledge that, with such a resolution, Simon would attempt to bring her into the realm of his craft once more, found herself now on tenterhooks as she waited for him to bring up the subject of the lantern roof.

The pattern-book from Ely had shown Gwyneth that the work was, after all, within her scope – provided she could command the work of skilled journeymen and craftsmen on this building as she had on others – yet still she withheld the promise of her mastery to Simon.

The subject lay, like a dead dog which it is nobody's job to bury, slowly tainting the very air between them. But it was not the only subject upon which they were divided: Gwyneth admitted this to herself, if to no other living soul.

Wrapped up though she was in her tender care for Toby, she had not failed to notice Simon's loveless gaze at her and his son. She would look up at him over Toby's head when the child was at her breast and see in her husband's eyes a look that chilled her soul. As much as he had longed for the child, it was plain that Simon now loathed him. As long as the waiting years had been, the minutes when they three were in each other's company were longer and no less full of anguish.

Again and again Gwyneth strove to convince herself that Simon's failure to show love or acceptance towards his son held nothing more than a husband's jealousy and his resentment at her own insistence on keeping to the house and being a mother. The roof – the blasted lantern roof – was more important to him, she told herself, than his son. And so she fed her resentment against Simon and was able to resist him.

But now he stood before her once more, the pattern-book in his hand that had become the focus of all the enmity between them. 'Gwyneth, I will not beg! I cannot force you to do this for me. I had hoped that you would wish to do it for yourself. You know this is not beyond you!'

Gwyneth held her peace, knowing that he was not finished, that no response was yet required.

'You have said yourself that with these principles' – he waved the pattern book at her – 'you can design and build your own roof. This is not above your skill.'

'No.' She said it quietly, adding 'it is not' so that he would know that she was merely agreeing with him.

'Then there is nothing to keep you from the tracing house!' Simon shouted, visibly controlling his anger.

'Nothing except Toby.'

'For the love of God, woman! I am not asking you to build the roof today! I just wish you to show some consent, give me some ease about the completion of my work! You know I cannot roof this without you. How can I go on building, never knowing whether you will do me the service of roofing it for me!'

Gwyneth's eyes were drawn, in swift, involuntary movement to Toby's cradle, where he lay awake. Because she knew Simon had seen her, she began to try to placate him. 'Simon—'

But Simon was not disposed to be placated. He wanted her promise.

'In time the child will have less need of you,' he said, his voice almost pleading. 'When the time comes to roof the college, you will be free to leave him—'

Gwyneth covered her face with her hands, shutting out his insistence, garnering her courage.

'You know and I know, Simon,' she said finally, uncovering her face and focusing on her husband with eyes blurred from the press of her fingertips, 'that Toby will have need of me far longer than most children.' She stared intently at him, but he gave nothing. 'His sinews are loose,' she continued, 'so as to make his eyes wander from each other and his limbs difficult to order.' Still there was nothing from Simon and she had to force herself onwards. 'He needs me even to hold his head up, Simon, he will not cease needing me as other children do—'

'But Alysoun loves the child.' The words tore themselves from Simon. 'Cannot she be the one who looks after it?'

Choking through the pain of Simon's cold acceptance of her words, Gwyneth sobbed 'Simon, are you deaf to all that does not suit you? Alysoun loves Henry, they will be married – I do not know when. Alysoun will have children of her own! It will be for *me* to look after Toby! I know his needs.'

She got up and would have gone to the mewling Toby, but Simon roused himself and stepped between her and the cradle.

'No,' he said, 'you do not know his needs, Gwyneth, you know your own, and see them in him. Because you must always have him close to you, you think he needs to be held to you all the time. You want no other company, so you think he wants always to be with you, smotheringly close. You need and want to do things for him – you think he cannot do anything for himself.'

He spun around and tore the covers from his son. 'Look at him, Gwyneth, and see what you have made of him! His sinews are weak, you say, his limbs fall awry. If you had swaddled him, as you were advised, his sinews would have grown strong, but they have been stretched and weakened by allowing him to lie as he will or to loll upon your lap. And if you always hold him to yourself,' – he mimed the action with a crook of his arm, showing that he had watched Gwyneth a good deal more than she had supposed – 'how can he learn to hold up his own head? Your devotion has weakened him Gwyneth – it is not more of you he needs, but less!'

Gwyneth stood at the cradle's side, shock and pain making her unable to speak or even to move to pick up the crying child.

Finally finding her voice once more she said quietly, her gaze on Toby, 'And his eyes, how have I weakened his eyes, Simon?'

'It is often so with infants, his eyes will grow strong in time.'

'I have never seen a child so afflicted as to his eyes, Simon. And I have seen many children – many more than you. Believe me when I tell you that his eyes show us the truth – that something in him is not as it should be. He may grow to be as others are, in time – I cannot say – but he is not as he is because I have loved him.'

'I do not say because you have loved him, Gwyneth, but because your love has not been wise. You have not been advised. You have gone your own way—'

'And if I am like you in that,' she flared, 'who can blame me? For I have lived with you half my life, Simon of Kineton, I have been advised by you and learned of you!'

The silence of impasse fell between them once more, filled by Toby's cries. Simon watched as Gwyneth picked the child up and stroked him, then turned on his heel and left the room.

Fifteen

Kineton and Dacre College, present day

When Sam Kearns put his head around Damia's office door a few days later in response to her shouted invitation to come in, he was the first undergraduate to come, uninvited, to see her.

'Hi Sam – come to see the nicest office in Toby?'

He smiled awkwardly. 'Not exactly.' Crossing the room without meeting her eye, he perched his lanky frame on the sofa nearest to her work station and took an audible breath. 'This isn't exactly a social call actually, Ms Miller—'

'Damia,' she corrected automatically, her attention focused entirely on the seriousness he was making no attempt to mitigate.

'It's about – well – I thought you should know – an emergency meeting has been called in the JCR tonight.'

Damia narrowed her eyes and cocked her head slightly, inviting him to dispel her ignorance.

'It's the runners,' he explained, his expression an uneasy combination of sympathy for her and solidarity with his friends. 'They don't want to run for Atoz. They've called a meeting to see whether the college will back them to reject Atoz and go back to Moorland Waters.'

After making arrangements with Sam to get her into the meeting that evening, Damia found herself completely unable to settle to anything. The thought that, after the effort she had put in to securing the Atoz deal, the students who were supposed to benefit from it would simply bat it aside without a thought for the consequences incensed her. Did these kids think deals like this grew on trees? Had they no concept *at all* of the college's desperate need for this kind of high-profile, six-figure backing?

Decisively, she shut down her computer and headed for the records room behind the porter's lodge. Her time would be better spent beginning the trawl through a century's worth of Biz Books than fruitlessly cursing the callow ingratitude of undergraduates.

Having seen the total surviving archive of almost five Toby centuries contained in one wicker trunk she was unprepared for the sheer quantity of documentation that the twentieth century had not only produced but felt it necessary to retain. Ignoring box after labelled box of student records and financial documents, she made her way to the cabinet at the end of the long, windowless room. On the front was a small insert-window whose card read simply 'Biz Books'. Squatting on her haunches in the light of a single bulb, its scorching dust vying with the smell of ancient cardboard and stale air, she opened the cabinet. Rows of cloth-bound spines, mostly blue, some red and a few black, stood on close-fitted shelves. On each spine an academic year was recorded.

Selecting six volumes at roughly ten-year intervals, starting with 1939–40, she clasped them to her chest and made for the parquet-floored comfort of the Senior Common Room.

It had been her intention simply to open the books at random and locate six photogenic-looking pages. These she would scan into the computer in order to begin the Biz Book feature which, she hoped, would lure more alumni to the website and, consequently, to the campaign to recruit donors. But to open a Biz Book was immediately to be intrigued by it and Damia soon became lost in the day-to-day preoccupations of the Toby undergraduate community. Petty feuds over team selections, gossip about the sexual peccadilloes of dons, new ruses for smuggling young women into the college in the days when only men were educated at Toby, political jokes whose resonance or even referents had faded into obscurity – Damia devoured them all. Being from various decades, each book differed from the others in paper quality, handwriting and the kind of pen used. The book for 1967–68 was fatter than the others, its pages indented by the pressure of many ballpoints and lying less smoothly against their neighbours. A female Salster undergraduate referred to only as 'Izzy B' figured large; a young woman who had evidently embraced the summer of love and taken it forward with gusto into the following academic year, much to the delight of Toby's young men.

Damia imagined them all – long-haired, with flared jeans, duffle coats and CND symbols on their canvas satchels. Except, she reflected, that some of them would undoubtedly have kept up the tradition of flannels, sports jackets and ties. Salster had always been home simultaneously to the rearguard and the avant-garde.

Thinking of using a tradition or even a particularly memorable opener to launch the Biz Book section on the website, she flipped to the beginning of the 1967–8 volume to see how a new Biz Book was commonly begun, and a question on the first page caught her eye.

'*Does anyone know what's happened to the statue that used to be in the Lady's Walk Garden behind the large rhododendron in the corner? It seems to have disappeared along with the rhododendron. Peter D.*'

What statue? Toby's only present statue was the boy himself on his yard-side perch. She flipped the page over and found a contribution headed '*Peter, re Statue*'. '*Do you mean that horrible statue of the prisoner which – thank God – somebody had hidden behind the rhododendron? Charles.*'

A ballpointed line snaked around several subsequent contributions and arrowed the response. '*Yes. OK, not a thing of beauty but definitely part of the college. I assume you don't know where it is? Peter.*'

Charles had obviously had a heavy few days after that – Damia's eyes flicked through a couple of pages before she saw another contribution from him, confirming Peter's suspicion that he knew nothing about the statue's fate. But, as she searched for Charles's spiky hand, another word stopped her in her tracks. *Curse.*

She backtracked and read the whole comment.

'*What's the fuss about the statue? It was horrible. Good riddance. Or are you afraid of invoking the old "never move a stick or a stone" curse? Adrian.*'

So the tradition of a curse falling on the college should anything be removed had still been common knowledge in the 1960s.

Flicking pages Damia saw several comments headed 'Re Statue' but none of the contributors had any light to shed on where it might be.

She picked up her pile of books and headed back to the records room.

1968–69's Biz Book was entirely devoid of any reference to the statue, as were 1969–70 and 1970–71, at which point she stopped looking, on the basis that all the contributors to the original conversation would now have graduated. Picking up her pile of notebooks once more, she quit the cardboard-and-dust smell of the sepia record room for her office.

From: Damia.Miller@kdc.sal.ac.uk
To: Mailing List (Old Members)
Subject: Biz Book 1968

Dear Tobyite

If you log on to the Toby website now you will see that the first of our Biz Book features has been added in the alumni section. I hope you approve.

This page, from 1967, has an intriguing reference to a statue that seems to have disappeared in that year and never reappeared. If you are Peter D, the originator of the question, or if you know anything about this subject, please get in touch. It's not that we believe the old curse about disaster befalling the college if a stick or a stone were to be removed, but we'd like to recover lost property if we could!

Hoping you enjoy the Biz Book page – there will be a new one next week!

Kind regards

Damia Miller
Marketing Manager

Damia stared out of the window at the Toby statue. Dressed in a tunic that came to his knees, the boy had short, uncovered hair and ankle-boots in soft leather. How, she wondered, was it possible to carve such an unyielding substance as rock into folds that fell softly aside as if from long use or expensive material?

As she stared, her mind unfocused, for the first time she fully registered the boy's posture. Unlike most medieval decorative figures his hands were empty, his arms stiff at his sides, fingers pointing rigidly downwards. In fact, now that she truly looked at him, Damia realised that the boy was not simply standing but was on tiptoe, his arms held straight for balance. Apparently, he was peering over the Octagon as if looking for something. Or *at* something.

Damia skittered down the stairs and out into the yard. Backing away from her own building towards the Octagon she looked up.

There was nothing for the boy to see.

Just an empty statue niche.

As she waited in her office for Sam's text-message, Damia could see students converging from each of the college's alleys and blocks on the JCR, a floor below her and two staircases to the north. It was seven thirty and fully dark; the lamps that lit the Toby yard shone from each of the walls of the Octagon, 360 degrees of light casting consistent shadows. Damia watched the wind ruffle clothes and hair and felt gooseflesh crawl across her own arms.

There were still duffle coats – some things hadn't changed since Peter D wrote his message about the statue.

Her mobile phone beeped twice, making her jump.

OK – COME NOW. SAM.

She locked the door and hurried down the stairs.

The JCR was packed, most of the students standing,

though the backs and arms of sofas and armchairs were being used as perches, the feet of their occupants accommodated between the more conventional sitters.

As Damia pushed the door open a few heads turned, and the silence that nudged its way through the chattering crowd unnerved her.

'OK, no need for hostility.' Sam's voice cut through the staring stillness. 'I asked her to come.'

The uproar that broke out at his words seemed to leave Sam quite unmoved.

'Look, all we've heard the last couple of days is how un-democratic it was for the governing body just to decide who our sponsor was going to be and then just give it to the run-ners as a fait accompli,' he said, evenly. 'And then what do *we* do? We have a JCR meeting which excludes any of the governing body. We're being just as undemocratic.'

More shouting ensued, but Damia noticed that this time not all of it was hostile; Sam's matter-of-fact tone had made an impression on some.

'I think it's only fair that she hears what our objections are – then she can put her case. It doesn't affect our ability to vote, and it doesn't affect our autonomy in the end. We can still do whatever we decide.'

'Miss Miller,' said a slight, forceful-looking young man wearing rimless glasses. 'Would you like to come and intro-duce yourself?'

Damia made her way through the crowd, intensely aware of its antagonistic scrutiny.

The young man shook her hand, muttering, 'Dominic Walters-Russell, JCR president, pleased to meet you.' Nudg-ing a wooden box towards her with his toe and gesturing for her to stand on it, he raised his voice: 'Miss Miller has the floor.'

Damia cleared her throat nervously. 'I don't intend any offence by gatecrashing your meeting,' she began, 'but when Sam told me about it I agreed with him that it would be useful on both sides if I was here. I hope you'll allow me to stay.' She had one foot off the box when she suddenly remembered that she was supposed to be introducing herself and skipped back up to say, 'I'm Damia Miller, by the way, for those of you who don't know – college marketing manager.'

Dominic Walters-Russell took the floor. Had the box, Damia wondered slightly irrelevantly, become an institution for the benefit of a similarly diminutive JCR president?

'I propose the motion that Damia Miller be allowed to stay for the duration of this meeting,' he stated, his voice clear and strong. 'All those in favour raise your hand.' His gaze swept the room. 'All those against . . . I declare the motion carried.' He turned to Damia. 'You're welcome to stay but I can't rise to the promise of a seat.'

Damia experienced an increasing sense of unease as she listened to the debate's articulately expressed opinions. The young people of Toby stated their views with the kind of vehemence more usually reserved, in Damia's experience, for the deriding of reality show contestants, and she began to understand the depth of her error in not consulting with the students on a matter that was going to bear directly on them and how the world saw them.

'I think we need to distinguish between being pissed off that the governing body has made an undemocratic decision and the selection of Atoz as a sponsor,' was the opinion of a tall, good-looking boy who hardly needed the extra inches the box gave him. 'I mean, OK, can we accept that we all think they shouldn't have handed down an edict?'

General murmurs of agreement quickly turned to shouts of 'censure motion' and Dominic Walters-Russell held up a hand. 'All those in favour of a motion of censure being sent from this common room to the governing body raise your hands . . . Carried overwhelmingly.'

The track record of Atoz as a global brand and employer was discussed. Despite their apparent privilege, many of the young people present were passionate about the contribution they could – and felt they *should* – make to the welfare of those they would never meet. This was the gap-year generation, Damia reminded herself, many of them with months of voluntary work in the developing world behind them.

But not all agreed.

'I can't believe the idealistic naivety I'm listening to,' a girl with short blonde hair said belligerently. 'I mean, how old are we, twelve? You can't compare conditions in the Third World with those here! OK, nobody *here* is going to work for a dollar a day, but the cost of living is dramatically different. Take Atoz out of the equation and most of those workers' families will starve. It's not Atoz or some nice benevolent employer, you know! It's Atoz or nothing – famine in the countryside, starvation in the city. I mean, come on, face reality! Bring pressure to bear on Atoz now we've got leverage with them to offer better terms and conditions, but don't for Christ's sake just go "Sod off Atoz we don't like your attitude!" That gets nobody anywhere!'

Damia stood up at this point to agree with the blonde girl and to point out that their ethical stance, though laudable, could jeopardise the very future of the college. 'Toby is in dire financial straits – if we renege on this deal the college could very easily go under.'

After a moment's tense silence a quiet voice was raised. 'What do you mean by "the college"?'

It was Sam Kearns.

'I mean, what is Kineton and Dacre College?' he asked, coming to face her at the front of the room but declining her wordless offer of the box. At over six foot he was at least ten inches taller than Damia. 'What's the point of it?' He looked around, but the meeting was suddenly silent. The realisation seemed to have overtaken everybody that Sam's softly articulated question was actually at the heart of what was being discussed.

'Are *we* the college?' He looked around. 'Is the college here to support us, or do we – the undergraduates – just provide a revenue stream for the college? Are we the reason for the college's existence or just a moneyspinning sideline?

'Because if we're *it*, then saying that if we don't accept Atoz's sponsorship money there might not *be* a college is a bit arse-about-face, isn't it? If we *are* the college, we aren't making a decision on behalf of something that exists above and beyond us.'

Norris's liberal education, his aspiration to teach young people to think and be critical, seemed alarmingly alive and well in the junior common room.

Damia finally found her voice. 'Whatever the rights and wrongs of saving the college and who or what is or isn't the college, the unpleasant fact remains: we have a contract with Atoz – we can't just decide to reject them and swap sponsors back to Moorland Waters, however much anybody might want to.'

A furious clamour burst out at this, over which Ellen Ballantyne's voice was suddenly audible.

'But we aren't contracted to *run* for them, are we?'

'Well, yes,' Damia replied, weakly.

'No, *we're* not,' Ellen insisted. 'I haven't signed a contract to say I'm going to run under the Atoz name this year, nor has anyone else. We can just refuse to run, if push comes to shove. They may be contracted to sponsor the Fairings team, but if there's no team they can't sponsor it.'

Amidst the storm of appreciation that followed Ellen's words, Damia realised with a sudden skin-prickling dread that the momentum of the meeting was now accelerating away from her at a pace beyond her control.

A new figure excused its way to the front and Ellen gave up the box.

'I know I've got no real right to speak here, not belonging to Toby', said the young man, 'but I have to tell you, Ian Baird is about as likely to let us decide not to run as he is to go around main quad dishing out tenners. If we' – he motioned to his three companions who, Damia assumed, were the other Northgate athletes from the previous year's squad – 'decline to run, then I can just imagine *him* declining to have us in college any more. He could make things really unpleasant for us.'

'Obviously he could, but *would* he?' Dominic Walters-Russell asked, his voice commanding attention even though he had not moved from his stance at the mantelpiece.

'*Oh* yes,' said the runner who had spoken. 'He would.'

The JCR president looked at Damia then spoke again, moving forward as he did so.

'We need to be clear,' he said, authority effortlessly audible in his voice, 'what the declared wish of this meeting is.

May I ask not just Ellen, Duncan and Sally but any Toby runners who might have been thinking of trying out to come to the front and tell us their views on running with Atoz on their rig.'

After a little self-conscious shuffling, a handful of people moved to the front along with the three established runners.

'Are any of you prepared to run under the Atoz banner?' Dominic asked, his tone carefully neutral.

A moment's hesitation ensued as the runners looked at each other, unsure whether they should each give their answer or elect a spokesperson. After a moment or two of murmurings of 'Well I'm not' and 'Nor me' they began to answer more formally, their eyes on the room. 'No.' Ellen Ballantyne's response was a foregone conclusion. 'I am not prepared to run for a company that exploits its workers and ignores basic human rights.'

Duncan McTeer was similarly categorical. 'Absolutely not.'

But the response of Sally Mackle, the last member of the Toby triumvirate, was a surprise. 'I can't say I'm happy about Atoz in principle,' she began, 'but I think Stella's got a point.' Damia watched as Sally's eyes met those of the blonde girl who had spoken so forcefully earlier in the meeting. 'Maybe we have a chance to exert some influence over Atoz.' She paused, obviously not entirely happy about what she was about to say. 'So, with reservations, and providing we do everything we can to make our views known, then yes, I would be prepared to run with Atoz on my rig.'

Her response rekindled a shouting-match.

'Oh, come on that's like saying "I'm going to stay in the Nazi party and change from within—"'

'Finally, some sense!'

'We're not living in Enid Blyton land you know—'

'Oh just fuck off, will you?'

Dominic Walters-Russell ignored the renewed shouts of the meeting's pragmatists and looked expectantly at Damia. As she took the box again, the shouting died down.

'You need to be aware that if Atoz sue for breach of contract, the college could be bankrupt by the end of the academic year,' she warned.

'If they sue,' Sam Kearns spoke up, 'we go on the record and tell everybody why we reneged on the contract. I don't think they'd like the publicity.'

And then they'd sue us for slander or libel, Damia thought. Stella's accusation of adolescent idealism and naivety, though more dismissive than Damia would have dreamed of being, was in line with her own gut feeling about this. The meeting seemed to have little concept of the huge weight of financial resources which a company like Atoz could bring to any battle the college cared to join.

'Does anybody have anything new or different to say before we take a vote?' Dominic Walters-Russell asked after replacing Damia on the speaker's box.

'Yes.' Sam Kearns stood at his JCR president's side. 'I've decided to see if I can get into the squad this year. And, potential leverage or not, I'm not happy to run for Atoz.'

It was as if the final word had been spoken. The renewed shouting and jeering which Damia had expected did not materialise and Dominic spoke seriously into the resulting calm.

'OK then, let's vote. All those in favour of rejecting the proposal that Atoz be the sponsors for the college Fairings team raise your hand.'

The counting took place in tense silence. Dominic

Walters-Russell compared his total with the two other counters before asking, 'Would those against rejecting Atoz as the college sponsors raise their hands.'

This time the counting took considerably less time.

'The motion to reject the proposal that Atoz be the sponsors for the college Fairings team has been carried.'

There were cheers and jubilant air-punches, during which Damia sought Dominic's ear.

'I'll go and see Dr Norris tomorrow,' she said, heavily. 'Thank you for allowing me to be here.'

Sixteen

Salster, August 1388

'Does Henry not mind that you feed him yourself?' Gwyneth asked as Alysoun opened her gown to put her four-month son to her breast.

'You know Henry, mother. He still cannot look upon himself as a man who is served and waited upon. Cooks and kitchen boys he can allow, since he hardly sees them, but to have a woman sit with us and feed little Sim – his eyes pop out at the thought!'

'And you, chick? Are you content?'

Alysoun looked at her shyly. 'My friends laugh and shake their heads at me,' she confided, 'but since the minute he was born I have not been able to bear anybody else holding him.' She looked at her mother. 'It's how you felt with Toby.'

Toby, sitting on his mother's lap, started at his name and Gwyneth gentled him, stroking his hair and soothing his limbs into quiet once more. 'Yes, but I thought it was long waiting made me feel like that.'

'Whatever it is, you have passed it on to me.'

'Not through my blood, chick.'

'No.' Alysoun met her mother's eye. 'But through your love, perhaps.'

They smiled, enjoying the intimacy that being alone with their children allowed.

'Simon will miss his little namesake,' Gwyneth said with a small nod in the direction of the baby Alysoun cradled, 'while he's away.'

'Watching his church grow will make up for missing a month of Sim's growing.'

'Don't be so sure. He loves that child, and not just because you named Sim for him.' She took her eyes off Alysoun and bent to kiss the top of Toby's head. 'Besides, his patron in Norfolk is proving troublesome, which is why he has torn himself away from Salster yet again.'

Torn himself from Salster and Daker's college, she thought, but gone gladly from me and his son.

They had exchanged harsh words the night before Simon had ridden for Norfolk and he had gone unforgiven and unforgiving. Little Sim had provoked the quarrel but, as always, its real subject had been Toby.

Gwyneth had watched all afternoon as Simon played with Alysoun and Henry's baby son, dangling a key on a cord in front of him to watch him reach and grasp it; hiding his face in his hands and bobbing up; blowing on the child's face and watching him screw up his eyes and chuckle. Gwyneth felt all the passionate tenderness of a grandmother towards Sim, but Simon's besottedness was beginning to make her resentful of the child. She ached for Toby as his father ignored him and played delightedly with a child not his own. Having schooled herself long since to let Toby lie sometimes and watch what was going on about him, she had begun to carry him about with her once more. His taut, bony body – lighter than that of other three-years children – felt tense against her and she sought, by her gentling caresses, to make up for Simon's cruel lack of notice.

When she laid him on his pallet, all their old clothes wrapped up in a sheet to make a soft, supporting mattress for him, she could see him watching Simon with the baby. Toby's newborn squint had never straightened, his eyes could not work together and Gwyneth, feeling her son's frustration, had tied a swathe of cloth around his head, covering the eye that seemed to wander most. Though his one eye rolled each time he moved his head or raised an arm, Gwyneth knew that Tobias was watching his father with Sim. He watched, and he saw, and in his troubled way he understood something.

Gwyneth's heart bled for her damaged son and his pain caused her to rage against Simon.

'How can you drool so over little Sim when you never so much as look at Toby? Do you not see the pain you cause your son?'

Simon, keeping his eyes resolutely from Toby, asleep on his pallet, said, 'No. I do not see it. Because there is none. The child is incapable of pain – at least of that sort.' He stared coldly at Gwyneth. 'You will not believe me when I tell you that he cannot think and cannot feel, Gwyneth. But it is so. The child is an idiot – he has not the wit of a dog. At least a dog can come when it is called.'

'A dog has power over its limbs! Toby knows when you call, and he feels the cruelty of your calling because you know he cannot come!' She stared at the man before her. 'You have become like the stone you work, Simon. Hard and unyielding.'

'No. I have not.' Simon's tone was flat and unemotional. 'That is what you choose to see, Gwyneth. Just as you choose to see your child as whole in mind when it is as plain as a clod that he is nothing of the kind. The mind is written in the face Gwyneth, the slack-mouthed are idiots, those with intelligence have sharp eyes. His eyes roll despite your bandage, his features are slack, I see not one spark of wit in him.'

'You never look!'

'I have looked, Gwyneth. I – have – looked. And I have given up looking because there is nothing to see. The child is deformed in body and mind. Better it had never been born.' He fixed her with his implacable stare. 'I prayed for a son to continue my name and my skill and God has laughed in my face. This' – he flung out an arm in Toby's direction, though his eyes held tight to Gwyneth's, – 'is the son he gives me. This is the bag of twitching bones and wandering wits which is to inherit what I have.'

Gwyneth, unable to bear any more, had clamped her hands over her ears, her face contorting in pain as she tried to keep back her fierce and bitter tears.

For nearly three and a half years Gwyneth had poured out her love on Toby and had felt his love for her. She had wept her love over his inability to articulate any but the most broken sounds, over his difficulty in eating and drinking without most of what was put into his mouth escaping before he could swallow, over his pitiful, frustrated attempts to grasp and hold things.

It seemed that the harder he tried to do anything, the more it moved beyond his grasp. He could not stand, even if she held him; his arms flew up, causing his back to arch and his whole body to throw itself backwards. Neither could he crawl; placed prone upon their bed, Toby could not even raise his head and look about him, but merely gasped and snuffled into the cover.

But it was not Toby's condition which had caused Gwyneth's most acute pain, but Simon's hardness towards their son. Simon, it seemed, had come to see Toby as a being without hope, a being whose needs for food and shelter must be met out of simple Christian duty and the end of whose life would come, if God was merciful, as swiftly as possible.

Toby had driven a wedge between them that Gwyneth was powerless to strike away.

'When Simon gets back, the building season will be almost over,' Alysoun said, refolding her gown and holding a happy, bloated Sim on her knee.

'Yes. Barely a month more. Which is why he is so keen that all that can be done to further the work should be done.'

'Is it really true that he will pay his masons to work all day on the lesser feast days ?'

Gwyneth snorted a laugh. 'Yes. It's true.' She shifted Toby's weight slightly on her lap and, pointing to the window-ledge, said, 'Look Toby – a bird!' The bird disappeared in a flurry of wings as Toby, exerting himself to look where his mother pointed, agitated his ill-controlled limbs into flinging motion. Gwyneth, anticipating the action, had held his hands to prevent his arms flying upwards, but had not anticipated Toby's sudden spasm which almost jerked him off her lap. 'Steady, son,' she said, pulling him gently back, 'steady, now.' She transferred her attention back to Alysoun. 'You know what masons are, always grumbling about the loss of pay through feastdays coming around so often. Well Simon has given them the chance to earn the money they are so keen to complain over. And it seems most of them will.'

❖

But feastdays are holy days ordained by the Church, and it is rash to alter custom where the Church is concerned. As was his habit in the summer, Robert Copley, bishop of Salster, was resident in the city, and if Simon had expected to order his affairs as he chose while the bishop looked on, he was sadly mistaken.

Seventeen

Kineton and Dacre College, present day

Unable to face her office on arriving at work the day after the JCR meeting, Damia hurried across the yard through the tugging of a squally wind and scurried up the steps of the Octagon to the Great Hall. The silence within seemed absolute after the buffeting at her ears outside.

Though she had been at Toby a little less than two months, already the unique medieval architecture of the hall seemed familiar and welcoming. The buildings in which she had spent all her previous working life had remained alien to her. Daily, she had entered a world of engrained cigarette smoke, grimy vinyl and smeared metal-framed windows with a sense that this was not where she belonged, that sitting on the margins with the dispossessed, the unloved and the outcast was not her rightful place. Having endured a childhood throughout which she had unwillingly played the role of weird outsider, living 'with a bunch of hippies', her skin the wrong colour; an adolescence blurred and confused by death and drugs, the dream of her adulthood was to be welcomed into the fold of normality, of the accepted, of people who had not fallen through society's holed safety nets. Toby, with its unassailable air of permanence, of belonging, of having a rightful and deserved place in the world, had become a refuge into whose protective embrace she had gratefully allowed herself to be enfolded.

Six months ago naming all eleven Salster colleges would have been beyond her; they were part of another world. Superstitiously, as if reciting a litany which would confirm her right to be here, Damia ran through the colleges quickly now. Kineton and Dacre – always first, though not the oldest – the other foundation colleges: Kings, Prince Edward's, St Thomas's, St Dunstan's, Traherne; then the associates, Fakenham, Eversholt, John Wyclif, Dover and, of course, Northgate. Names as familiar now as the clients at the Gardiner Centre had been half a year ago.

She might not know whether she belonged more with the undergraduates of the JCR, the academics of the SCR or the administrators, functionaries and domestic staff who made the college work but, in such a short time, Toby had become home in a way nowhere else had ever been. And her little house within the city walls, bought with the help of money Toby could ill afford, was associated intimately with her life here. It was all of a piece. Toby, her house, this life – it was what she had always longed for but never named.

The work of conservation on the wall painting was in full, painstaking, particle-manipulating swing, and metal barriers of the kind Damia associated with royal-visit crowd control were still in place. Behind them, two conservators worked their arcane magic on the mineral pigments and lime plaster. Damia had gathered that an unexpectedly heated debate was in progress as to the dual exigencies of display and preservation. Since the sunlight admitted by the hall's enormous windows would inevitably fade and degrade colour and line, the conservative view maintained that the paintings should be protected from the light, disclosed only when tours came expressly to see the cycle. Opposing this, those who viewed the painting as an integral part of the Great Hall argued that the cycle had been intended for public display and that this should be respected.

Damia, with her instinct that the 'Sin Cycle' was far more than a conventional mural, gave her unsolicited support very firmly to the second view.

The silence in the air and the reverence with which the conservators carried out their work settled on Damia like a gentle caress and she found herself padding on quiet soles around the hall, exchanging muted smiles with the MP3-wired conservators and, finally, coming to rest on the edge of a dining-bench.

She gazed at the restoration work that was being carried out on the northwest wall. Whilst the first of its twin ovals with its helpless human form and goading demons was intact, the second was in a far from perfect state of preservation. Damp or impurities in the plaster had dissolved away much of the distinctness of the painting and the right-hand portion of the scene was severely damaged. All that remained was the suggestion of a human form standing, probably with its arms extended to the figure opposite. The demons of the previous oval were gone, but the Everyman figure's powerlessness in the face of evil's minions and the sins which they urged had not. His sinful condition no longer needed continual demonic prompting; now it had become hardened around him in the symbolic form of a cage.

The world as a cage filled with sin – a prison from which

the only escape was heaven or hell. Damia wondered whether the medieval view had really been so bleak. Had the cycle been painted to remind the college's students that there was nothing they could do to escape the rottenness of their nature – that they were condemned to sin and sin and sin? Surely not. If the point of learning was to increase understanding and to improve man's lot, surely such a fatalistic view would be anathema to an academic institution?

Peering at the badly eroded figure on the right-hand side of the wall, she wondered whether the putatively outstretched arms were those of Jesus, struggling to save the sinner, to draw him on to bliss, away from his state of sinful imprisonment.

A thought flashed, lightning-quick, across her brain; so fast that she missed its meaning and had to trail slowly after it to see what had made the impression. Imprisonment. The sinner was in a cage of sin. He was a prisoner.

'*Peter, re Statue*'. She could see the Biz Book entry clearly in her mind's eye, the unknown Charles's flamboyant handwriting fluidly expressing his opinion. '*Do you mean that horrible statue of the prisoner which – thank God – somebody had hidden behind the rhododendron?*'

'No,' Neil replied, when he picked up the phone in his office ten minutes later, 'there's nothing about any statues in the letters. Well, not up to where I've read, anyway. But you know that, I told you all about it.'

They had talked of little else but the prior's letters to his bishop when they had met for dinner the previous week.

'Yeah, I know, all about the Church trying to stop Dacre building the college. Have you found out why yet, by the way?'

Though she had asked the question as something to fill a silence rather than from any real expectation of a positive answer, Neil's enthusiasm suddenly burst down the line.

'Yes! I have!'

'And?'

'He was a Lollard.'

She said nothing, waiting for him to explain. His tendency to use technical terms as a way of aggrandising himself had always irritated her.

'An early form of Protestant. Part of an anticlerical movement that started during the Black Death and gathered momentum in all the chaos of the later fourteenth century. People felt things were slipping out of control, that the Church must be doing something wrong for God to allow all these catastrophes.'

'So he was a fundamentalist?'

Neil made an equivocating sound. 'Most of the upper-class Lollards were more anticlerical and radical than actually fundamentalist. They wanted root-and-branch political and social reform – a more equal society.'

'I don't get it – founding a college sounds more establishment than radical.'

'Yes, but it's the nature of the college he was setting up that's crucial. *Because* he was a radical, he wanted to set up a college which had *nothing to do with the Church*. That was ultra-radical in an age when – in England at least – all learning was *controlled* by the Church.'

'*Ultra*-radical?'

'According to the Church – especially the prior and the bishop – it amounted to heresy.'

Damia, still disappointed that he had no light to cast on the prisoner, forced herself to stop responding on automatic pilot and to think. 'So, if the Church was so against everything he was doing, how did he succeed? I mean, surely one man can't go against the whole monolithic power of the Church, can he?'

'Apparently so.'

'But how? Did he have some leverage against the bishop – know where the bodies were buried or something?'

'No idea. But he will have been amazingly wealthy. I mean "vintner of the city of London" doesn't mean he was a wine merchant. That's like saying Bill Gates runs a software shop. The vintners were one of the most powerful guilds in the City. They were fabulously rich. If Dacre didn't bankroll the king at one stage or another, there were certainly others exactly like him who did.'

Damia took this in. 'So the *king* might have protected him?'

'Unlikely. Although Richard II *was* quite pro-Lollard early in his reign, certainly while John of Gaunt was running things, later on, when most of Kineton and Dacre was actually built, Richard had been deposed and Henry IV was on the throne. And he was no lover of Lollards at all.'

'But he may have had influential friends? Dacre, I mean.'

'What I'm trying to tell you, you twit, is that he *was* the influential one. I'm not saying the Church couldn't touch him, but the bishop would have thought twice about going head to head with him.'

'Right.'

Her disappointment must still have been evident in her tone because he said, 'Sorry not to have any news on the statue thing.'

'Not to worry.'

'Shall I come over after work,' he said suddenly, 'and we

can have a look at the painting – see if I come up with anything you haven't?'

Damia hesitated. Apart from the unguarded look she had
caught as she entered the restaurant, Neil had not done or
said anything that remotely confirmed Catz's prejudices or
her own recent suspicions about his feelings. And she did not
want to give up any chance of solving 'the Toby Enigma' by
cutting herself off from Neil and the information held in the
prior's letters.

'Sure', she said with crisp decisiveness. 'Come on round.
I'll be finished about five thirty.'

From: Damia.Miller@kdc.sal.ac.uk
To: Peterdefries@dmlplc.co.uk
Subject: Biz Book 1968 / statue

Dear Peter

Many thanks for your email and for your description of the
statue. Attached is a photograph of one of the Toby wall
painting images. Though, unfortunately, this is the image
which has sustained some damage, you will see that the
'prisoner' appears on the left-hand side of the oval. Is this
anything like the statue that used to be in the Toby garden?

If so, what do you think we are to make of it?

Kind regards

Damia

Eighteen

From: Damiarainbow@hotmail.com
To: CatzCampbell@hotmail.com
Subject: Neil

I need to tell you something about Neil, Catz. He's turned up in Salster. Without Angie. They've split up. He's the new cathedral archivist. And if you've been taking any notice of my emails you'll know that that means he's got the college papers. Which may explain what the wall painting is about. Which may help us find the deeds or something else that might help us out of the financial black hole.

Which means I'm seeing quite a lot of him.

Obviously, he thinks there's something significant in the fact that you're in the US for a year.

But he's said nothing. About anything.

I need to see him, Catz. Not for him but for the college. To try and find something that will help us.

I know you'll understand.

Damia stared at the screen. It lit up her little sitting room, the only source of light now that the Saturday dusk had fallen.

She wanted to write, 'Come home, we're losing each other.'

She wanted to write, 'Have you thought about having a baby at all?'

She wanted to write, 'I miss you.'

She looked at the screen again and, slowly, she deleted the message.

Nineteen

Hard upon the heels of the first feastday working at the Daker site came the news that Hugh of Lewes, master mason to the abbey, had raised his masons' wages by a penny a day. Henceforth, all his journeymen would be paid seven pence a day instead of the six that all masons in Salster had earned before.

Since Gwyneth, in Simon's absence, was not prepared to match such an increase – was not, anyway, certain that she wished to violate a statute of Parliament to do so – the masons put down their tools and no building was done on the college site. Worse, as the week wore on, there was a steady flow of masons away from Simon's lodge to that of the abbey church.

'He cannot mean to sustain such payments,' Henry said, 'even if he considers himself beyond retribution, standing behind the abbey's walls. If he pays his journeymen seven pence then not a man on the site will work for the same as he did last week.'

Gwyneth looked up from her reckoning of accounts at the

chequerboard 'This is the prior's doing, not that of Hugh of Lewes. The prior is harrying us, Henry. If he can bankrupt Master Daker by forcing him to pay his masons more, he will stop the college being built in short order—'

'But,' Henry interrupted, 'he must know that Daker's fortune stretches beyond a mere penny-a-day increase!'

'He must suspect so,' Gwyneth agreed, folding her arms before her and giving her attention entirely to him. 'But his scheme will serve him equally well if he can frustrate our building by wheedling our masons away to work at the abbey church. I daresay he hopes that Daker, seeing insufficient progress and becoming disheartened' – she ignored Henry's scornful laugh – 'will leave off college building.'

'But the work on the abbey's church cannot employ all the masons who work for Simon?'

'No. But the prior will hope that enough will leave for work here to be slowed.' She looked squarely at Henry. 'And even if we pay seven pence,' she said slowly, 'it seems that some masons will be too frightened to work for Simon hereafter.'

'Too frightened?' Henry was perplexed. 'By what?'

'Richard Daker is already tarred with the brush of heretic,' Gwyneth said, deliberately, 'which is why he has left all to Simon and not appeared at the building site. While there is no cause for scandal, the men remain quiet, thinking they are building for Simon and not for his patron.'

She looked at Henry, and saw realisation dawn.

'And now Simon has turned heretic, too, and scorned feastday rest,' he said.

She nodded.

'It's not like him to be so ill advised,' Henry said, rubbing his scalp under his curls. 'He is hasty, but not usually so rash.'

'Ill advised, Henry, you are right. Or rather not advised at all—'

Henry looked at her steadily. 'Did you advise him against this action?' he asked speculatively.

Gwyneth hesitated then said, 'I would have.' She dropped her eyes to the board in front of her and continued, 'Simon goes his own way, now more than ever in his life.'

Henry moved uncertainly towards her. 'What is this coldness between you?' he asked, laying a tentative hand on her shoulder. 'I never saw it in all the years I lived with you. Hot words, yes. Plenty of those. And anger. And sadness—' he stopped and looked at her. 'But never this coldness. Where does it come from?'

Gwyneth looked up at him. He had been almost a son to her all these years; she owed him at least some of the truth.

'Simon cannot forgive me for bearing Toby so crippled into the world,' she said baldly, 'and I cannot forgive Simon for not loving Toby.' *For treating him worse than he would a dog*, she would have said, but held her peace.

She looked into Henry's eyes and might have been moved by his pity, had not all the tears in her been shed long since and dried on this rock of unforgiveness.

'He so wanted a son, you know that – to your own cost, I know.' She took his hand and held it against her face. 'But now that he has one, his prayers are answered in disappointment.'

Henry, one hand still held against her face, put his free hand on her shoulder, but did not speak. Gwyneth drawing strength from his comfort, said 'It does not make matters easier that Prior William speaks of Toby as God's judgement on Simon. And some believe him.'

She let go Henry's hand. Pushing back her chair, she stood

up and crossed to Toby's pallet, where the child was lifting himself up and down with bent legs, as he lay on his back. 'But Toby is God's judgement on nobody,' she said, picking him up and manoeuvring his stiff, rigid form into some kind of comfort on her hip. 'He is himself, loved by me and by God.' She kissed the child's head. 'Aren't you, my precious?'

Toby's head jerked back and his good eye looked at Gwyneth. He opened his mouth and issued a sound which Gwyneth had learned to interpret as a sign that her son understood her and would respond if he could.

'Some masons,' she said, pulling Toby tightly to her to control his spasms, 'are glad of the excuse to go. They did not need to be threatened with the wrath of God if they work on feastdays.' She looked at Henry. 'And if the abbey work is better paid and has not the threat of God's wrath hanging over it, why would they stay?'

'Simon is a good master,' Henry retorted. 'Some might say they should stay out of loyalty to him.'

'And some do,' Gwyneth answered, 'but there are others who are already uneasy' – with a free hand she pushed the hair back from Toby's pale forehead, showing Henry the source of their unease – 'and they are glad of the excuse.'

She would not say so, but she was aware that she had not helped this unease. She did not keep Toby within doors as Simon would have liked, but took him about with her, winding a strip of linen around them both to hold him to her as she had done since he was a baby, giving her at least the use of one hand. She had run the gamut of Salster's stares for the last three years, since Toby's growth away from the natural helplessness of babyhood had revealed that he was helpless still.

Now Salster had grown used to the child and averted its

eyes, all but the handful who were prepared to see what Gwyneth saw – a soul loved by God, to be pitied, not feared. Those familiar with 'the Kinetons' cripple' took care to hide their hands from Gwyneth as they made the sign against the evil eye, or surreptitiously crossed themselves, but pilgrims, seeing his face writhing and eyes mismatched as Gwyneth pointed at things in the street, would start back and cross themselves ostentatiously. Gwyneth could never accustom herself to it, could never stop the knife of hot anger finding her heart as they sprang back in panic.

'Henry,' she said abruptly, turning to him, 'we cannot let Simon return to this tangle. I do not even know who he has left as foreman in his absence – will you help me if I try to resolve all this strife?'

The boy she had known for more than half his life looked back at her from his slight, man's frame. 'Will they listen to you?' he asked.

She sighed. 'Who can say? But I am Simon's wife, a master in my own craft – if anyone can claim to know his mind on this, I can. If they do not listen to me, who will they listen to?' She paused fractionally. 'And who else will speak?' Then, not wishing to shame him after all, she said, 'Come, what am I thinking of? You are a King's Mason, you cannot be seen to embroil yourself in this mire.'

She made to open the door and let them both out but he called her back.

'Mother!'

She spun around. It was many, many years since Henry had used that word to her – it had never set easy on his tongue even as a child.

'I may be a King's Mason, but Simon has been a father to

me, and you a mother. I will help you.' He grinned. 'As best I may, God help you!'

Masons are never happy on their working site unless they are about their business, and there was a tenseness in the air as Gwyneth and Henry walked across the dusty, rutted ground from which knee-high walls rose, and into the masons' lodge. Gwyneth, having put prudence before pride, had walked with Henry the little distance to his house and left Toby with Alysoun and little Sim. She would fetch him when she and Henry were done.

Gwyneth was well known to every man on the site. Not only was she Simon's wife and putative master carpenter to the college, she was also clerk of the works and, as such, she paid them their wages. And as she sat at her trestle-table, wages and accounts set out before her, Toby would lie at her side on his pallet. Where Gwyneth went, Toby went, and if Simon's masons regarded her warily on that account, then she would have to pay the price for that wariness now.

She walked into the lodge and looked around until she found the man she was looking for.

'Good day to you, Edwin.'

The man she had addressed inclined his head, not quite lowering it enough to take his eyes off hers. 'Mistress Kineton.'

She endured his perfunctory courtesy, noticing, as he bowed, that his coif was thick with masonry dust, though no stone had been cut in the lodge for days. Edwin obviously did not regard his senior status on the site as requiring clean headgear too often. Did he have a wife, Gwyneth wondered, and if so had he brought her with him to the city? He had no son with him in his work, though he was of an age to have sons nearly grown.

'Edwin, who has my husband left as foreman here while he is in Norwich?'

'Myself, Mistress.'

Gwyneth had suspected as much. She nodded briefly. 'You know that I am charged with keeping accounts and paying wages, Edwin.' He nodded. 'I may be allowed to know my husband's mind in this and I am determined that this business of who will pay more and who will work when must be decided.' She stopped and allowed him to digest what she had said.

'So, if you will summon all to the lodge, I will see what must be done.'

As Edwin turned for the door, Henry took Gwyneth's arm and drew her aside from the bench where a few of the younger masons sat with dice and cups. 'Gwyneth, what do you mean to say to them?'

'I am going to ask them whether they will meet with the prior and the bishop. And the mayor. If we can get all the masons in Salster to agree to abide by city regulations, like the guild trades, then we may put an end to Copley's squabbling tactics.'

'And if they will not agree?'

'I must persuade them that it is not in their interests to stand against me.'

Twenty

From: CatzCampbell@hotmail.com
To: Damiarainbow@hotmail.com
Subject:

1.30 a.m. This city never sleeps. Somebody already said that.
Can't sleep either. Can't work. Have you thought about
Christmas?

Your Painter.

The phone on Damia's desk shrilled with the single-ring tone
that indicated an internal call. She picked it up, her hands
instantly sweaty. Finally, this must be Norris ringing to tell
her that he had received a letter from Atoz, issuing a writ for
breach of contract. It was more than a week since her letter
to the company had been acknowledged with the bland but
chilling statement that matters arising from the premature
termination of the contract were being considered by the
firm's legal department.

'Miss Miller – it's Bob.' The voice of the porter on the
other end of the line momentarily disorientated Damia, so

convinced had she been that she would hear Norris calmly telling her that they were being sued.

'Hi Bob,' she stammered, omitting, in her confusion, her habitual but ineffectual plea that he should call her Damia. 'What's up?'

'It's the local news – they said something about Toby. I think you'd better come and see.'

Ed Norris was already sitting alongside Bob in the porter's lodge, both their eyes fixed on the small television in the corner.

'You know they do that "Coming later in the pro-gramme" bit at the beginning?' Bob said.

Damia nodded, though she never watched local news, feeling she knew all she needed to know about back-alley stabbings, school closures and unknown local celebrities.

'They said something about how Toby'd been saved from being sued for breach of contract.'

Minutes later, Damia watched with a sick sense of the inevitability of his action, as Ian Baird effortlessly ascended what passed, on television, for the moral high ground.

'With the threat of Atoz suing Kineton and Dacre college for every penny they don't have, it seemed the natural thing to do for Northgate to step in and honour the contract,' he said, his eyes radiating the most authentic decency under the blaze of lights and the interviewer's respectful tone. 'So Northgate will be taking the unprecedented step of running its own team in the Fairings this year – it's the first time an associate college has done so.'

'Obviously,' the off-camera voice of the interviewer said, 'this goes against established precedent and tradition. Do you think there will be any backlash against your decision?'

Baird's serious gaze hid what Damia knew must be utter jubilation at having been handed – on a tinsel-draped plate – the opportunity not only to do exactly the thing he wanted to do, but to be praised for doing it.

'Given the circumstances, Abbie,' Baird replied, 'I would hope that there *won't* be a backlash. Without Northgate to honour the contract—' *that phrase again, as if Toby were somehow dishonourable in attempting to protect workers' rights* '—there's a serious prospect that Kineton and Dacre College would face bankruptcy. Compared with that tragedy, an associate college running its own team is a minor ripple.'

One minor ripple for local news, maybe; but a tidal wave was building in Baird's campaign for the obliteration of associate college status.

'So, will this be a one-off? Will you be rejoining the combined team next year?'

'No. We have entered into a binding five-year contract with Atoz, so we will be running our own team from now on.'

'And will that affect your status as an associate college?'

Had she, Damia wondered, been primed with these questions? If not, they were eerily apt to Baird's purpose.

'Inevitably, this whole affair will affect Northgate's position as an associate college. Regrettably, the fact that we have been put in this position is a symptom of the structural difficulties Kineton and Dacre College has fallen into. It will be impossible for Northgate to even consider retaining the kind of subsidiary role that associate status implies. I cannot allow the future of my college to be jeopardised.'

'So you'll be applying to the colleges council for foundation college status?'

'On the contrary. I will be putting a motion to the

colleges' council that the whole two-tier system of foundation and associate colleges is outmoded and divisive and should be scrapped. Salster colleges *do* need a structure, but it should be the federated structure of a properly incorporated university, not the old-fashioned and elitist structure imposed by the so-called foundation colleges.'

'So,' Norris said, tightly, as Bob muted the sound at the end of the interview, 'the campaign begins.'

Mere hours later, when she was, once again, called down to the lodge, Damia saw that her brief text to Sam Kearns had done its work.

A new, laser-printed poster had appeared on the JCR noticeboard in the Octagon's long, ground-floor corridor:

If you are a runner – TOBY NEEDS YOU!

The call was for a squad of eight to ten from which the four Fairings Day runners would be chosen. Not mentioned was the fact that the team had no coach, their victorious trainer – like Atoz – having been seduced by Ian Baird.

Behind her, the porter's door opened and she turned to see a sports-jacketed man of middle age and medium height being ushered in her direction by Bob.

'Hello,' he said, putting out a hand. 'Peter Defries.'

'Yes,' Defries said, as they stood in the deserted Hall. 'The statue was just like that – the cage enclosing all the lower body but not the head – and the hands in those manacle-rings.'

He stared at the imprisoned figure with an intensity that disturbed Damia.

'Most people,' she began, startling herself by the loudness of her voice in the rapt silence created by his gaze, 'seem to have felt that the statue's disappearance was good riddance. Can I ask – was there a particular reason why you felt so strongly about it?'

Defries did not turn around but his discomfort was obvious. 'It just struck a deep chord with me at the time. Its hopelessness . . .' Instead of finishing the sentence, he turned abruptly as if he had embarrassed himself and moved away. To cover the moment, Damia wandered in the direction of the final pair of ovals. Acutely aware of Defries's agitation as he swung from wall to wall, flinging brief attention at the painted surfaces, she wondered about the hopelessness that he had plainly shared with the imprisoned subject of the statue. Her eyes rested, barely registering what she was seeing, on the final scenes of the Sin Cycle: the prisoner, freed from his cage by the waters of baptism, kneeling before the saviour of the world to receive divine absolution and forgiveness.

'The sinner redeemed,' Defries remarked, his voice straining for a casual neutrality.

'Mmm.' Relieved, Damia colluded automatically in his retreat into the impersonal.

'Are they any nearer a clear interpretation of what it's about?'

'Have we solved the Toby Enigma?' she half-turned towards him, smiling in embarrassment at the obscurely shaming juxtaposition of blatant PR hook-line and medieval eschatology. 'No. But the cathedral archivist came up with an interesting idea recently.'

Neil's intriguing suggestion was that each pair of ovals represented the conflicting theologies of orthodox Catholicism and Lollardy. Seen in this light, the southwest wall's disturbing image portrayed the birth of a sinner as no more

143

and no less than a result of the will of man, whilst its twin, the familiar Madonna and Child image, represented a vision of handmaidenship and submission to the will of God.

Less obviously in opposition were the second two ovals, but Neil's theory had stretched to fit. In his analysis, the child-man who flailed and writhed beneath demonic goads on the northwest wall was Everyman, exerting himself to resist sins from without by the help of the Spirit within, whilst his unfortunate counterpart in the cage illustrated the belief that man was – from the very moment of conception – impelled to the pursuit of evil desires by Original Sin and could not escape this any more than the prisoner could escape his locked and barred cage.

'So then, these two,' Defries said, moving towards the northeastern wall's ovals, 'are presumably the effects of sin. Violent death here' – with the gesture of a bidder at an auction he signalled the oval the conservators had nicknamed 'Murder' – 'and the only remedy for it – baptism – here' – again, the decisive but unemphatic gesture to the second oval's half-submerged figure – 'in the river.'

Damia nodded. 'That's how the theory goes. With the cage of sin left on the bank as a symbol that the sinner is now washed clean.'

Her eyes were drawn again to the 'Murder' oval. Like all the others it was carefully composed; not in the way of later paintings, or modern photographs, with attention to balance, focal points and colour-weight, but in the way it conveyed the impact of its message. Crowded around a prostrate figure, the characters stood as in a tableau or carefully blocked-in stage scene, their shock and fear clearly visible. Face-on or in profile, their naked emotional response spoke directly down the centuries to the limbic system; the cortex did not need to process and evaluate this death with its half-squared rock and crushed head to know that the wide eyes and rigid stance of the witnesses bespoke a death of more than ordinary significance.

'And the final two?' Defries strolled back, apparently calmed by intellectual theory, towards the southeast walls. 'Man's submission and God's grace?'

Damia gazed at the figures which, in Neil's taxonomy, represented the archetypes of salvation by prescribed, measured-out penance on the one hand, and overflowing, freelyoffered grace on the other. The sinner, shrunk by penitence or terror to a diminutive stature, was on his knees, head bowed and hands clasped in the business of self-abasement; Jesus in glory, vastly more than life-sized, stood in profile to face the sinner, both hands raised in benediction or welcome.

'Could be.'

'You're not convinced by this theory?'

Damia smiled ruefully. 'Not really. It's clever. I wish it *was* true. But it just doesn't click for me.'

'Like the solution to a crossword clue that you can force to fit but doesn't have that "yes!" factor.'

Damia nodded, though she had never done a crossword in her life.

As they slowly descended the steps of the Great Hall, the early afternoon sun illuminated the entire eastern wing of the college, setting the distorted glass of the small-paned windows ablaze and picking out the intense colours of the winter pansies in the yardside bed.

'I wondered' – Damia chin-pointed up at the Toby statue – 'whether he was looking over the Octagon at the prisoner statue.'

Peter Defries looked over his shoulder. 'Yes,' he said. 'But what would that mean?'

Damia snorted in mirthless frustration. 'What does *he* mean? Why is he *here* – the *mason's son* if tradition is to be believed? There's not a single thing in the whole college that has to do with Richard Dacre – only his name, and *that* comes second! Where is he? And what is that statue all *about*?'

Defries looked up at the tiptoe boy, the expression on his face filling Damia with the conviction that he had looked at it in the same way many times before.

'He always reminded me,' he said, his eyes fixed on the boy, 'of that Laurence Binyon poem on the Fallen. You know the one.

> *They shall grow not old, as we that are left grow old:*
> *Age shall not weary them, nor the years contemn.*
> *At the going down of the sun and in the morning*
> *We will remember them.'*

He stopped, a crack in his voice. Looking away from Damia at the statue once more, he recovered himself enough to say, simply, 'He's for ever young. For ever there.'

'And always will be if anybody takes the curse seriously.' Damia smiled, made uncomfortable by this renewed change of mood.

Defries narrowed his eyes as he focused on the statue. 'There's a thought.'

Twenty-one

Salster, August 1388

In the event, far from masons standing against her, Gwyneth found that she had an audience whose ears were ready to listen to her call. There were too many masons in Salster now for the work that was being done, and even those who were enjoying their leisure could see that they must soon work for less than their fellows, or not work at all. They were keen to see matters regularised.

Bishop Copley was less cooperative. His grace could not see Gwyneth, his secretary reported; he was concerned with more important business.

Each day for a week Gwyneth solicited the bishop's attention and each day an audience – or even the promise of one – was denied. Robert Copley, it seemed, could not foresee a time when the affairs of his diocese would not take up his every waking minute.

Gwyneth fumed and her agitation at the sight of Simon's silent building site increased. Days' ride away in Norfolk, he must be smiling at the baking weather and imagining his walls rising course by steady course. His rage when he returned to the city and found that, with barely a month of reliable building season remaining, the college was hardly a stone further forward than when he had left, was not a vision Gwyneth wished to dwell upon. She knew he would find it in him to blame her – the more so since she had obviously assumed the responsibility for it – and another grievance would thus be added to the list against her.

Finally, her patience broke and she took herself to the home of Salster's mayor, Nicholas Brygge. Known to sympathise with Daker, he had already agreed to help resolve the dispute over masons' wages and employment. His was the responsibility for overseeing the upholding of all guild regulations within the city and he had seen at once that regulating building practice would work to the advantage of both patron and hired man.

'Those who would build will then know that they do not have to outbid all other employers to get their masons,' he had said, 'and masons will be content that the possibility of ever-higher wage bills will not prevent men from building. Even if it were not for the current dispute with the abbey, I would support you, Mistress Kineton.'

Not only had he supported her most civilly, Gwyneth blushed to remember, but he had paid her most flattering attentions. Now, as she stood waiting for admittance once more to his impressive house, she smoothed her gown and tucked away the wisps of greying hair that fell from her headcovering.

'Mistress Kineton!' Brygge hailed her as she was shown into his hall, where he sat with an amanuensis. After providing her with a chair and dismissing his secretary he said, 'I gather the Church is suffering you to knock on its door to no avail.'

'The bishop refuses to grant me an audience, yes. I think I could ask from now till Doomsday and he would not see

148

me.' She looked at him squarely. 'Will you speak to him, Master Brygge?'

Nicholas Brygge threw back his head and laughed, allowing Gwyneth to see that, although over forty years of age, he still possessed a full set of teeth. He looked at her with bright, blackbird's eyes. 'Mistress Kineton, Robert Copley would sooner admit the Devil to his presence than me. Old Nick at least recognises his authority.'

Gwyneth looked at him. Nicholas Brygge was elegant, urbane, the model of a guildsman made good. A grocer by trade, he commanded respect from everybody in the city and was enjoying his fourth term as Salster's mayor. And yet he was known to be no lover of the Church and churchmen. Those who disapproved of his unorthodox religious views were careful not to let this disapproval cloud their judgement of him as an excellent administrator and skilled politician. Brygge was a man whom nobody wished to cross and whom the ambitious cultivated.

He was not a man to be cowed by the bishop.

'Then if he will not speak to you and he will most definitely not speak to me, what shall I do?' Gwyneth asked, baldly.

'We must call our meeting without him,' said Brygge, leaning across the table towards her. 'While we sue for his attendance, he thinks to make us dance on the end of his string. If we exercise our rights within the city to regulate our own affairs without him, then it is he who will be forced to come to our pull of the string, and sue for attendance upon us.'

'And if he takes offence?'

'Robert Copley may take what he will as long as it is none of mine.'

And so, not without trepidation at challenging the bishop, as it were, in his own garden, Gwyneth let it be known in all three masons' lodges that a meeting would be held at the new guilds' hall the next day 'to end a dispute that brings the mystery of freemasonry into bad repute, and to show that we may regulate our own affairs and do not need to be at enmity with one another or hide behind other patronage'.

'Strong words,' Henry commented, sucking his teeth. 'Yours or the mayor's?'

'Mine,' Gwyneth said, jutting her chin in a way Henry remembered from childhood. Her professional competence was not to be questioned, and this touched upon her competence as a master fit to give instruction. 'I have lived amongst masons all my life, Henry. I know their pride and what is likely to move them to shift themselves. They do not sell their wares, like guildsmen, they sell their skill. And a man's skill is nearer his manhood than a mere chattel to be bought or sold could ever be. They would not be men if they did not wish to decide for themselves how they will dispose of their skill.'

Gwyneth saw Henry looking at her and saw, for the first time in many years, a look of admiration on his face. She had been able to inspire that admiration at her whim when they had first known each other and Henry had watched her work. Now that many years' observation had accustomed him to her mastery, his admiration was more difficult to arouse. And yet mere words had done it.

Gwyneth began to hope.

The new hall, built by the combined resources of the guilds of Salster, had been a surprise to Gwyneth. In a town where building in stone conferred status and gravitas, the guilds had chosen a timber-framed construction for their meeting place. But this was no modest building. An open-arched marketplace stood beneath, whilst the splendid hall was reached by a magnificent central staircase that swept up on to the screen passage alongside the hall.

Gwyneth stood outside for a moment admiring the fine, close-studded walls and carved jetty-timbers. The porch over the street-fronting gable-end she knew to be a repository of all the city's charters and licences, jealously guarded by Salster's guildsmen and the main weapon in their constant battles for independence from the abbey and its twin powers of bishop and prior.

The guildhall was not ten years old – as likely as not, the carpenter who had made the expensive, many-timbered frame was still alive and working. Gwyneth wondered idly what he would say if asked to produce a lantern roof. It was a scab she picked at often, and just as often she was surprised by the pain of an unhealed wound.

Climbing the wide sweep of the staircase with Henry at her side, she wondered what she would do if the masons of Salster ignored her call and did not come. To sit with Nicholas Brygge and the prior while every freemason in the city chose to stay away would be a humiliation she would not find it easy to bear.

Wordlessly, she preceded Henry along the narrow, painted-plaster passageway to the hall's central doorway and lifted the latch. She barely had time to notice the woodwork that she had come prepared to inspect and admire before realising that the hall was already occupied. Four men stood around the great recording table. The mayor and his secretary she had expected, though their early appearance was a surprise, but the presence of Piers Mottis, Richard Daker's lawyer, was totally unexpected.

Daker was obviously being kept closely abreast of events, despite his own carefully judged absence from the scene.

'Mistress Kineton.' Nicholas Brygge's words silenced the tense discussion that Gwyneth and Henry's entry had disturbed. 'And Master Ackland, welcome – though you, Master Ackland, are no stranger to the guildhall.' He smiled a welcome at Henry, who responded in kind, all ease and pride.

Gwyneth looked sideways at Henry. She would not have been surprised at this evidence of his participation in the upper echelons of Salster mercantile life, but for the fact that neither he nor Alysoun ever spoke about it. Were they afraid of offending herself and Simon, she wondered? If so, they should know by now that Simon had no patience for cultivating those who might be able to put business in his way, and she was not about to turn ambitious wife and push him towards the guilds and fraternities.

Brygge turned to the other men, still standing slightly awkwardly at the table. 'Master Daker's lawyer, Piers Mottis, I think you already know,' he said as Gwyneth and the smiling lawyer exchanged courtesies, 'but I believe you have not before met his nephew, Master Ralph Daker.'

So this was Ralph. Gwyneth had heard a great deal about this man, but never met him. As their eyes met, and his slid away with his courtesy, she thought that common report had not adequately summed him up. He had been presented to her as a giant of a man, even taller than his uncle, who was over six feet tall, but to Gwyneth, used to measuring length and height with her unaided eye, he was hardly gigantic, simply ill-proportioned. He might overtop his uncle by half a hand's-span but it was not that which made him appear to loom over those around him, but his large head and jutting jaw. His hair, like his uncle's, was thick and dark, though his was cut short, which seemed somehow to emphasise the length and bottom-heaviness of his face. Some Salster wag had called him Longshanks Daker and, though he wore a long robe which made it difficult to assess what proportion of his overall height was due to length of leg, judging by the uncommon length of his arms, Longshanks he was.

And was this the man whom the diminutive and delicately fair Anne Daker had chosen for a lover? Gwyneth raised a mental eyebrow. Based on their supposed relationship, Ralph was not at all what she had imagined. But though uncommon, his looks were far from unpleasant. His rare height did not stop him standing upright and his gaze, though it found Gwyneth's eyes difficult to meet, was as dark blue as Richard Daker's. A woman might find him easy to fancy if his devotion were directed towards her.

'Come, comrades,' Brygge interrupted her thoughts. 'We must agree our line before others arrive. It will not serve our cause if we disagree in front of everybody.'

As he spoke a sudden qualm sent a goose-pimpling shiver over Gwyneth. Had she done right in enlisting the mayor's help? Or had she given too little thought to what the outcome would imply for the independence of freemasons within the city? Whatever he might think of her, Nicholas Brygge was a shrewd politician and did nothing that could not ultimately be turned to his advantage. He had not now turned mediator out of the goodness of his heart. The best Gwyneth could hope was that he was motivated by the opportunity to thumb his nose at Robert Copley.

Prior William arrived with the subprior, the clerk to the abbey church's works, Master Mason Hugh of Lewes, and an excited-looking young secretary. Without a word to those whose arrival had preceded theirs, they walked to the table and took up places on the bench behind it. Nicholas Brygge grinned hugely at such brazen effrontery and motioned his secretary to help him erect one of the trestle tables that stood against the wall.

Brygge afterwards confided in Gwyneth that he had been sorely tempted to place the trestle table in front of that at which the prior sat, so as to be in front of him when he addressed the masons, but he resisted the temptation. 'I thought it best not to begin by humiliating the prior,' he said, 'though I had every intention of going on to do exactly that.'

No sooner had the trestle table been erected than Gwyneth's fears were allayed: the masons arrived. They came as three gangs, those from the abbey church first, the college's masons second and lastly the ragged army impressed upon the king's work. There were no stragglers; evidently they had met at their respective lodges before coming to the guildhall.

The men, some in their working clothes, some in dustless holiday garb, arranged themselves on the benches around the hall's remaining three sides and looked towards the opposing factions behind their tables.

What do they think all this is about? Gwyneth wondered as Nicholas Brygge rose to his feet and began to outline the purpose of the meeting.

He had been speaking for no more than a minute when there was the sound of many feet upon the staircase below, and the door was abruptly swung open. A man of middle height stood in the doorway, a furred robe and hood making significant a figure that would otherwise lack presence. Certainly, Gwyneth thought cynically, neither garment was being worn to ward off the cold of the warm August day. Robert Copley, bishop of Salster, had come escorted by the clerics of each of the city's dozen and a half parishes, to have his say.

Twenty-two

Kineton and Dacre College, present day

'You think there might be documents inside the statue?' Norris took off the reading glasses over which he had been regarding Damia's barely suppressed desire to climb a ladder and haul the statue down bodily; a desire she had been enduring with nerve-fizzing intensity since Peter Defries's suggestion.

'It makes sense – we found nothing in the rest of the archives relating to the college lands, so either they were destroyed or they were hidden somewhere.'

'But why would they be hidden?' Norris's tone, as much as his frown, betrayed an instinctive suspicion of anything that strayed towards the melodramatic. Damia took a breath and forced herself to adopt a calm, academic approach.

'Two reasons.' She held up a finger, rapidly digesting the mass of information Defries had given her into summary form. 'The Peasants' Revolt – Salster was occupied and one of the people's army's dearest wishes was to destroy all legal documents relating to land holdings – so as to erase the tradition of bondage and labour duties. That memory will have been pretty vivid in the memory when Toby was being built – when there was all the persecution of Lollards around the time Richard the Second was deposed and Henry took the throne. It may have seemed a sensible precaution.'

Norris nodded slowly, waiting for the second finger.

'Then there's the Civil War. Again, Salster was occupied. The parliamentarians wanted to teach the colleges a lesson for supporting the king – lots of college chapels were ransacked, but Toby didn't have one so they might have been inclined to wreak other havoc here.'

Again Norris nodded.

'*And* it makes sense of the so-called curse,' Damia said, playing the rationalist card. 'What better way to make sure that the statue containing all the important college documents was never removed than to threaten dire consequences to anybody who dared even think about it?'

'Fine.' Norris slapped his palms on to his knees as if his brain was signalling to his body that a decision had been reached and needed acting upon. 'Order scaffolding.' Rising from his seat he asked, 'What reason are you going to offer for this sudden interest in statuary? I don't want to give the media an excuse to start up the litany of our iniquities against the tenants again – it's bad enough still having the pickets outside.'

Damia was ahead of him. 'We'll say that the conservators want to look at the statue in detail to see if it casts any light on the wall painting. It's the only other piece of original decoration in Toby and the painting's supposed to be contemporaneous. I think it'd make sense.'

As Norris nodded, Damia caught the suspicion of a twinkle in his eye. 'Fine. But you'd better talk to the conservators first and swear them to secrecy.'

'It may turn out to be true, of course,' she pointed out.

'They really *might* like to get up close and personal with the statue.'

Norris acknowledged this with another nod and a slight raise of the eyebrows.

'No, don't go,' he forestalled her as she made to rise from her chair. 'I was wanting to speak to you anyway, as it happens.'

Damia sat back expectantly and watched him stroll over to the window, hands clasped, Windsor-style, behind his back. He stood, gazing out silently, for such a long time that Damia began to be apprehensive. Was he trying to find a palatable way to deliver devastating news?

Finally, he spoke. 'I'd like you to be present at the next governing body meeting.' His words were reflected towards her from the ancient window-panes, losing nothing of his clarity of diction but sounding strangely remote, as if Norris himself had not spoken them. 'Not as a member you understand, simply as an observer.'

'Fine, whatever you want.' Damia was at a loss. Was this a compliment to her enthusiasm – an invitation to see what life was like at the top table; or was it a subtle reprimand – an indication that she needed to be made aware of the constraints, financial and otherwise, under which his attempts to preserve the college must be conducted?

'Ian Baird is coming to present his proposals as to the dissolution of our articles of association,' he continued, his gaze firmly fixed on the window, as if he did not wish to see the look of commiseration with which she would inevitably greet such news. 'And I think Northgate's bid for independence bears sufficiently on our image as a college for your invitation to raise no eyebrows. Or at least' – his tone softened slightly towards joviality – or was it irony? – as he turned – 'not to raise to many or too far.'

Not a reprimand then. And, even better than a compliment, the Regent Master was taking her into his confidence.

Though she had left Norris's warm office with the specific intention of falling into conversation with the rent strikers around their newly acquired brazier on her way to buy a lunchtime sandwich, Damia actually found herself commiserating perfectly naturally with the huddled group on the sudden drop in temperature and she offered to bring hot drinks if anybody would like them. After a few moments of muttered wariness, the four men and lone woman who stood stamping and warming their hands at the fire followed the civil example of Robert Hadstowe, who was present for the first time in many days, and offered slightly embarrassed orders for coffees and teas. Not for the first time and, she was certain, not for the last, Damia wondered whether they had veered away from truculence or outright rudeness for fear of being thought racist. What the hell – there were enough disadvantages to having a foot in two racial camps to dispel any slight anxieties that she might be exploiting unconscious prejudices.

'This takes me back,' she said, sipping her coffee, sandwiches still in her shoulder-bag. Deliberately, she did not finish the sentence.

Inevitably, politeness prevailed and one of the pickets – a burly man in his fifties with a striped bobble hat that emphasised the roundness of his face in an unflattering way – asked, 'What, standing on a picket line in a freezing November?'

'Standing by a *brazier* in a freezing November. Once upon a time I was an outreach worker for a centre for homeless people – I spent a lot of time looking for freezing people and trying to persuade them that coming to the centre would be a better option.'

'Why wouldn't they?'

It was a common enough question. Why languish freezing, starving, fighting off disease and desperation on the streets or under a hedge when there was the offer of a warm centre with food and the possibility of a hot shower?

Damia sighed. 'Fear, shame, total loss of any sense that you deserve something better than what you've got on the streets,' she said, trying to keep the bitterness out of her voice; bitterness on behalf of all the people whom society had carelessly shut out – ex-cons; abused, neglected kids who'd been shuttled from one foster home to another; runaways too scared to look for any kind of help for fear they'd be shipped back to whatever they'd run away from; addicts; the mentally ill for whom care in the community had meant anything but.

'Did you get them to come in?'

'More than most outreach workers,' she said. 'I may have a middle-class accent, but the skin-tone's good for a lot of street-cred points. You can't be a middle-class do-gooder when you look like me.'

She was aware that she was making only fleeting eye contact as she spoke, afraid that one of them would see the hurt beneath the cynicism if she gave them her eyes for long.

'What did you do in between that and this?' asked Hadstowe. 'Or did you go from underclass to overprivilege in one giant leap?'

'Got into fundraising, then marketing and PR,' Damia replied, her eyeballs drying uncomfortably as she gazed, without blinking, at the brazier. She did not add that she had filled all those roles within the housing and homelessness sector; that she had, indeed, leapt from underclass to over-privilege.

And though she loved her new job, loved the college as she had never loved employment before, there was still a part of her that was uneasy at her abandonment of the desperate and the disillusioned. The part of her that wanted to embrace the hand which life had dealt, to accept as some kind of karmic destiny the fact that her early desires to live a life rooted in security and society had been washed away; that the death of those who could have given her security had left a lost and rootless soul who could – and therefore *should*? – reach out to the lost and rootless around her.

But by far the greater part of her – the part which had, from her earliest memories, felt profoundly uneasy in the pseudo-anarchic setting of her childhood – knew that to ally herself with loss and lostness would be to lose herself entirely, that the only way in which she could become whole and happy was to become part of something more vibrant, stronger and more securely rooted than she herself had ever been.

'How are you finding the job here?' Hadstowe obviously knew that she was recently appointed.

'Surprising.' She smiled around the group and they smiled back. 'I wasn't anticipating pickets on my doorstep at a Salster college, I can tell you that!'

'Maybe,' said the bobble-hatted man, 'you weren't expecting underhand behaviour from those in charge of this sort of place.'

Damia nodded slowly, the kind of nod that indicates cogitation rather than agreement. 'I think I had a lot of preconceptions before I came to Toby. It's been a big learning curve.'

'Shock to the system more like!' said one of the other picketers, the toe of his boot nudging moodily at a chip of tarmac flung from beneath the wheels of a car.

Damia half-smiled. He was quite young – possibly young enough to be Bobble-Hat's offspring.

'Have you spoken to Dr Norris recently?' she asked Hadstowe disingenuously, knowing that he had refused several invitations to meet and discuss a way forward.

'No need for me to speak. It's for him to withdraw his *polite request* that we all sign his statutory declarations. When he does that, then we can talk about how we resolve the situation.'

'It's not enough for him simply to withdraw the request?'

Hadstowe's eyes searched her face as if for evidence that Norris really would keep her this poorly informed. 'No. We're not prepared to go back to the status quo with this hanging over us. We want assurances that if the college does somehow manage to proceed with the sale of the land, then we – the tenants – will be given first refusal. To buy at agricultural rates,' he continued forcefully, as if heading off an interruption from her. 'We can't be expected to compete with the kind of money developers can stump up.'

A silence filled only with the low hiss and crackle of the brazier fell into place behind his words as if at the pull of a cord. All eyes fixed themselves on the flickering flames and red-hot charcoal, all hands offered themselves to the singeing heat.

Damia waited for Hadstowe to break the silence: for her to have done so would have looked like negotiation.

'So, where do you stand on this? Are you with Norris?'

Damia took a sip of her coffee, tasting the plastic taint of the lid. 'I think,' she said, choosing her words with immense care, 'that I'm prepared to stand with him – he's a man of integrity, who's prepared to take the rap for things that weren't his idea—'

'A man of integrity!' Hadstowe spat. 'I don't call selling our land from under us evidence of great integrity!'

Damia looked him full in the face. 'One of the things he's taken responsibility for,' she said quietly.

'What?' The voice of the only woman in the group pulled Damia's gaze away from Hadstowe. 'You mean selling the land wasn't Norris's idea?'

'That's right.'

'So whose was it?' Hadstowe's question caused Damia to switch focus once more.

'I don't know. But I do know that it was Charles Northrop's argument in its favour that pushed the motion through.'

'Northrop,' the woman said, sharply 'but isn't he—' she faltered, her eyes fixed over Damia's shoulder. When Damia turned, it was to see Hadstowe lowering an upraised hand.

'If Charles Northrop has been presenting himself to you as an honest broker,' she said, suspicion blooming, 'I think you need to be very wary. And of Ian Baird and any promises he's been making or implying.'

'What promises do you imagine he's been making?' Hadstowe asked, his voice even. Damia, because she was looking for it, saw the tension beneath.

'Well, I would guess that he's said that if Northgate takes over Toby – which would be easily done if Toby were to go bankrupt' – she quashed a rising desire to make explicit their complicity in that outcome – 'then Northgate will give written assurances that will secure your tenancies on a long-term basis.'

She saw in Hadstowe's unguarded expression all the confirmation she needed that she had read Baird correctly.

'It wasn't hard to work out what he would say to you,' she said gently, 'not when he'd already tried to woo me away too.'

Baird's attempt at recruiting Damia to his cause had come several weeks earlier, when, after a meeting with the principals of both colleges to finalise the sponsorship deal with Atoz, he had asked whether he could have a few minutes of her time.

'It's impressive,' he had said, once they were in the privacy of her office, 'the way you've played Atoz. Given the bad financial publicity there's been and the social issues with the tenants, I never thought you'd do it.'

Though Damia wanted desperately not to be charmed by this man, she found that his compliments generated an instinctive urge to preen herself.

Baird seated himself comfortably on the couch facing the door. His trouser-leg and sock parted company to reveal a narrow strip of pale, hairy calf as he crossed his legs. He was, the gesture indicated, totally at his ease here, totally in control.

'Damia, come and work for me.'

She did not reply, suppressing any reaction that her surprise might have betrayed her into.

'You're wasted here with this bunch of stuffed shirts and has-beens,' he continued, blithely insulting her colleagues in a manner that took it for granted that either she agreed with him or was suffering from illusions which needed to be shattered. 'Together, we could take Northgate to the top.'

Damia looked at him appraisingly. 'Top of what, exactly? I thought you were all for a federal college structure – a proper university.'

'Colleges will still function as separate institutions in most respects, they will simply cede functions which can be carried out more efficiently to a central administrative structure.'

'Don't you think it would be a bit disloyal of me?' she asked, unable to keep an edge of judgement out of her voice. 'Ed Norris has taken a gamble on me. I haven't any kind of track record in higher education but he still took me on. Coming to work for you would be a kick in the teeth.'

'That's how business is,' Baird stated, flatly. 'You can't be sentimental. You've got to know where you want to get to and be prepared to do everything you can to get there.'

Damia's eyes rested briefly on the dark-haired strip of shin beneath Baird's trouser-leg; its pale nakedness countering Baird's urbanity and consequent assumption of command.

'So you think I should hitch my wagon to Northgate's star?'

Baird raised his eyebrows slightly. He might just as well have said, 'That's a no-brainer, surely?'

'In due course, I expect to be chair of a federation of Salster colleges.' He looked at her, his eyes narrowing slightly in wary appraisal. 'I would be in a position to recommend you as marketing manager for the whole of the new university structure.'

When she did not respond immediately he said, evenly, 'It's not the kind of job that comes up every day.'

Damia could feel adrenalin coursing through her and was

disturbed to realise that she did not know whether it came from excitement or anger. She forced a sardonic smile.

'It's not the kind of decision that comes up every day, either, Ian. You'll have to give me a few days to mull it over.'

'Right you are.' He sprang up in a way which, two seconds earlier, she would have been prepared to bet good money was totally impossible for a man of his physique. 'Don't leave it too long,' he had said, heading for the door, 'or you'll get stuck in that mire of indecisiveness which Norris calls democracy.'

'I assume his wooing didn't work?' the woman asked from the other side of the brazier.

Damia smiled tightly, remembering with shame the list of pros and cons over which she had pored that evening. 'No.'

She hesitated and then, for reasons she would later sift through endlessly without coming to a satisfactory conclusion, she found herself saying, 'I used to think that one Salster college – one Oxsterbridge college – was much like another. Different architecture, different quaint little traditions, but basically the same idea. But over the few months since coming to Toby I've realised that I was wrong.

'If colleges *were* interchangeable I would have grabbed Baird's offer with both hands, thanks very much. Security over insecurity? *Please*, it's not even a question! But they're not interchangeable. Northgate is a base for the establishment of the Baird empire. He only cares about the college in so far as it serves his purposes and furthers his ambitions.

'But Ed Norris is a college man through and through. He *believes* in his position as first among equals. He takes it seriously.'

She felt the treacherous drooping of one corner of her

mouth as the deeply emotional part of herself threatened to weep with the intensity of what she was saying.

'That's why he takes the rap for decisions that the governing body makes – it's a collective decision. Even if he doesn't agree, he has to go with it. And that's why he's letting the students make this financially *disastrous* decision about the sponsors – because he respects their right not to have their integrity trampled over for purely financial reasons.' She gritted her teeth and looked across at them, all but Hadstowe, who stood at her shoulder.

'Toby is the sum of its parts,' she finished quietly. 'Its people, its traditions, its values. Northgate is just Baird. I'm going to fight for Toby. If I lose my job trying, at least I'll be able to live with myself.'

Twenty-three

Salster, August 1388

*On the walls of the guildhall birds strut and flap and voice
their particular sayings. From the mouth of the heron, poised
with wings bent to take flight, come the words, 'Bear no
malice'. The dove, settling on the roof of a cote like the holy
spirit on the head of Christ, issues forth, 'Deal justly'. A peacock, strutting away from its companions with tail-feathers
held magnificently aloft, has, inscribed around its haughtily
held head, 'Be not proud'.*

*The men sitting at two large tables under the eye of the
wall-painted birds would do well to remember their advice.
For there is malice here, and pride, and very little just dealing.*

Later, as she and Henry tried to stem the flow of Alysoun's
questions by describing all that had happened in the guildhall, Gwyneth's thoughts began to disjoint, the tenons of one
idea slipping from the mortice of another until the whole
framework loosened and fell. She found she could recall
snatches, vivid moments of seeing and understanding, but
could not reconstruct for her foster-daughter the way in

which loyalty and self-interest, collusion and opposition, hatred and resolution, had locked with one another as will met will. She left Henry to explain, and leaned her head against the wall, resting her overtired eyes as his voice faded in and out over her mind's dislocated attempts to impose order on events.

She felt like the crane in the guildhall's wall of birds. The crane that stands sentinel whilst its fellows sleep, holding a stone in one uplifted claw so that if it too falls asleep, the dropping of the stone will wake it. She held the stone for Simon and she had not slept. She had stood sentinel for him over his college and had not let it come to harm. She tried to conjure up Simon's face, but could see only a hard, unforgiving stare. Would her dutiful fidelity not soften him a little? If he could be convinced of her desire to champion his cause, even a little, would he turn towards her with love as he used to do?

If only she had the peacock's many eyes, to see into the future. But, as peacocks moult, so man loses foresight as he lives and comes to know nothing but his own mind. Once, she had known Simon's mind, but no more.

But she had declared to Edwin that she must be allowed to know Simon's mind on the dispute over wages. Had she claimed too much?

Edwin himself had been silent at the guildhall. She saw him now, in her mind's eye, his coif still defiantly dusty, watching, waiting and listening. Had he understood the battle being fought out between Nicholas Brygge and Robert Copley? For it had become apparent to Gwyneth that neither the mayor nor the bishop was there to discuss the wages paid to journeymen. Their concern was a larger and more personal one: who was to rule in Salster.

Both might have had as their emblem the hawk that stooped down the deep-windowed wall, claws outstretched.

Copley had marched in to the guildhall, pale with the effects of rage and exertion, his priests disregarded behind him. Ignoring every other being in the hall, his attention had focussed entirely on Nicholas Brygge. As he strode over to stand in front of the trestle table, the tension in his frame had been dangerously visible. Staring intently at the seated man, he had said nothing until the mayor rose slowly to his feet.

'Welcome . . . My Lord Bishop.'

Copley had not returned the greeting, but his eyes pierced into Brygge, every particle of his combustible energy focused upon the mayor.

'This meeting concerns abbey business, abbey labourers and abbey property.' His voice sliced through the tense air of the hall. 'And its proper place is the chapter house of the abbey, not here!'

Brygge, still standing and undiminished by his shortness of stature, did not so much as turn a hair. 'Had you invited us, My Lord, we would have come,' he said mildly. 'As it was, we could hardly march into the chapter house at our whim.'

Nicholas Brygge, thought Gwyneth, possessed, like the ostrich, extraordinary speed. Not speed of hoofed foot, like the ostrich caught in a manlike run on the guildhall wall, but speed of mind and tongue. And, like the bird's fabled ability to digest iron, nothing seemed to stick in the mayor's craw.

The bishop having no rejoinder immediately to hand, Brygge pressed his message home. 'Besides,' he said, 'it is not clear to me that the abbey's chapter house *would* be the proper place for a meeting that will seek to regulate the practice of a craft beyond your walls as well as within. *This* is where we conduct city business, particularly mercantile business, and since this is a matter of buying and selling, here we meet.'

'Do you suggest that it is not my right to employ men as I see fit?'

'I do,' Brygge maintained with a smile, 'if the reputation of my city is brought into disrepute as a result.' Their stares locked. Still no other presence in the room was acknowledged. 'For instance, I am sure you are aware, My Lord, of the statute that prohibits any master from poaching another's journeyman by offering him inducements. To say nothing of paying higher wages than those laid down by—'

'Are you accusing me of lawbreaking?' Though the bishop's tone was even, no one present could fail to detect the challenge.

The mayor's tone was definite and final. 'Without question, you overreach your authority.'

Gasps had greeted that suggestion, Gwyneth recalled, as she let out her own long breath in a sigh. Though masons might be used to audacity, the Salster clergy were not. Neither was Robert Copley. Leaning towards the mayor, he hissed through clenched teeth in a voice which, if he could, he would have forced solely into Brygge's ear but which, given their proximity, could not fail to reach Gwyneth's too.

'Do not try my authority or my patience too far, grocer, or you may find yourself the poorer for it.'

Brygge was not to be cowed. 'I can bring out the whole city against you, Copley. At my word, tithes will go unpaid, your priests here will starve unless you divert abbey funds to feed them, and you will be a laughing stock. Think on it. My Lord.'

'And if I throw you in gaol and let you rot?'

'That would not be wise.'

'Try me and I will do it.'

Their faces were less than a hand's span apart. Each had forgotten that they were observed. Or if they had not forgotten, their self-conceit was such that they did not care.

'Throw me in gaol and you will answer to Richard Daker. He is a city of London merchant and guildsman. He not only has the ear of the king, he has his balls too. Financially speaking, of course.'

The bishop's eyes grew narrow at the mention of royal patronage.

'Beware, grocer. You may suppose yourself too valuable.'

'Beware yourself, priest. For you may suppose yourself too powerful.'

Copley's face twisted into a vicious parody of a smile. 'Come then, let us put ourselves to the test.'

It was this reckless challenge and its tacit acceptance which had acted on Gwyneth like the crane's stone. As the implications of it filled her head, she knew that she must shake off her quietude.

'My Lord Bishop,' she said, rising to her feet at Brygge's side. 'I thank you most humbly for your attendance upon us. Will you be so good as to sit and allow us to begin? The freemasons of the city are gathered together and await the judgement of both abbey and city authorities upon the conduct of freemasonry in Salster.'

She stopped, her eyes flicking from one man to the other and back again. If she wounded a powerful pride now, she was well aware that it would be as catastrophic for Simon as his youthful refusal to mend the injured self-esteem of a king. She could not afford to make an enemy of Brygge, but his smiling belligerence, if given its head, would leave Copley nowhere to go but to the bitter end in his fight against Daker's college. She must give him some room to manoeuvre so that he would not have to back down.

Slowly, under her pleading gaze, Copley nodded and marched around the table. At a swift signal from Prior William, his young secretary leaped up and took himself off to an uncomfortable seat on the masons' benches and sat there looking as if he feared for his life, whilst Copley took his place without comment or thanks.

To everyone's surprise, Gwyneth remained standing. Trembling in every limb, she began to speak. 'Until now,' she said slowly, choosing her words with scrupulous care, 'any man with a vision to build has been at liberty to hire whomsoever he will and, as every man here knows, masons have come to Salster for generations to build at the abbey. But the city has prospered' – she looked at both men, including them both in the implied congratulation – 'and now, it appears, there is more work to be done than the masons of the city may well accomplish—'

Though she and everyone present knew this to be false, knew that in fact the abbey works were currently employing more men than could truly be justified, it would do no harm to aggrandise Salster and its wealth, for each soul present would feel in some small way a greater man for it.

'And, as is evident to all,' she continued, looking around and including the assembled masons in her conclusions, 'if there is more demand for labour than men to fill it, there is a temptation – in the teeth of law and statute' (the mayor and his bishop could both chew on their violations of wage-limiting statutes) 'to pay more to ensure that the job is finished.'

She stopped and looked down the table at Copley and at Brygge, both of whom had fixed her with a freak-show stare. Let them stare, she thought. I will not let them fly at each other and fight for dominance where it will injure me and mine.

But neither could she afford to let them feel hen-pecked; feathers must be stroked, not ruffled.

'Discontent leads to poor workmanship,' she said, 'which serves nobody's purpose. God is not glorified, man is not satisfied and our mystery is brought into disrepute. These matters sit on our shoulders, friends, and we must make them good.' She smiled upon both men. 'We are well placed to resolve matters, after all. As Master Brygge has reminded us, there are guild regulations in force in the city which regulate all makers and sellers. These regulations are respected and enforced to the great enhancement of Salster's reputation. And for this state of affairs we must look to the firm government of the mayor and his officers.'

Neither Brygge nor Copley had moved since she started speaking; the eyes of both men were fixed upon her.

'The abbey,' she continued, carefully, 'under My Lord Bishop's vision and authority, has grown in extent and splendour, and there is much experience there of masons and their employment. Those who have worked at the abbey' – she looked around at the packed benches – 'will testify to the just and equitable circumstances in which they have worked.'

If they defy me and tell out their grievances against the abbey works, she thought, all is lost. Copley must be presented as equal to Brygge to balance the scales of pride.

But not a mason moved; not a murmur was heard. Every man present seemed held in the spell of her words, the sheer extraordinariness of her daring to call two such hawks back to an ungauntleted fist.

Cautiously she proceeded, laying her words one against another with extreme care, like stones in a course. 'Possessing such skills and experience we are well placed to order our affairs in a way that will honour both builder and those who build and that will ensure that, in Salster, our craft is pursued with excellence, our mystery upheld as one which, of all others, may bring most glory to God.'

And if either man cared for his reputation as upholder of the good name of Salster or of the Almighty, he had little choice thereafter but to bend his mind to the drawing up of ordinances to regulate the craft of masonry within the city.

Bear no malice saith the heron. Why? Gwyneth wondered suddenly. Bird and saying were familiar to her in each other's company, but she had never stopped before to wonder why this should be the heron's particular saying. A plea perhaps, for man to bear no malice to the stewpond-thief who acted only after his nature?

Gwyneth stretched her hands towards the fire burning in the wall-grate as Henry talked on, and wondered whose malice she would bear as a consequence of her actions that day. Prior William's for one. Though he had come willingly enough to the meeting, his authority had been swept aside by the manner and conduct of Copley's dramatic arrival in the guildhall. Gwyneth had kept her attention firmly upon the bishop and the mayor while she attempted to turn them from conflict and bend their wills to resolution, but she had, nevertheless, been aware of the prior's eyes searing at her. His enmity had been almost palpable and Gwyneth had felt an irrational gratitude that the prior was sitting before her and not behind. Somehow, his smouldering at her back would have been too discomfiting to bear.

Was it simply her desire to thwart his purposes that stirred up such implacable opposition in him, she wondered, or was it compounded by her sex? That William regarded all women as mere conduits for the Devil was well known, and his revulsion at what he saw as their concupiscence had been amply demonstrated in the recent past by his treatment of an abbey laundress caught in the act of prostitution with one of the monks. William had had her flogged so severely that she had barely survived to live the purer life which was enjoined upon her, whilst the monk who accepted her was treated as one led astray and barely culpable since the act was judged so foreign to his nature.

Bear no malice. William of Norwich would bear malice to Gwyneth all her life, whether she opposed him or not. He would bear malice towards her for the simple fact that her existence in the world reminded him that, celibate though he was, his instincts beneath the clerical garb that covered and disguised them were those of any other man. William hated her because he had renounced the delights of her sex in favour of power, and had found that real power was denied him. Though William would have opposed Simon as implacably, it was she who had succeeded in making an enemy of the prior.

Gwyneth shivered slightly in the firelight as she remembered a favourite saying of her father's. 'Never lightly awake the wrath of a weak man.'

She stirred herself and made an effort of will to join Henry and Alysoun's conversation once more. She gazed at Toby, sitting quietly on Alysoun's lap as he had done since they got home and Alysoun had placed Gwyneth before the fire.

'I'm not cold,' she had protested through the shivers that shook her nerve-racked body. 'Only give me a few minutes' quiet and I shall be perfectly well.'

She had watched Toby strain, half-heartedly mewing, in

her direction but rested content without the child as Alysoun gentled him on her lap. 'There now, little brother, Mother is tired – tired – she needs a little rest – Toby rest too.' Her voice soothed as her hands stroked his head and held his writhing limbs.

'A minute, Toby,' she had said as she took her place by the fire, 'come to me in a minute, my chick.'

Now, Henry, having described the bishop's entrance and the ensuing clash with a true image-maker's eye, was giving Alysoun chapter and verse on Ralph Daker's eloquent silence.

'The man was like a lover whose sweetheart suddenly appears in his solar where he's sitting with his wife and children,' he said. 'There he was, standing for his uncle, when everybody knows he and William the prior are thick as thieves. No wonder he had little to say when the mayor asked him whether or not those terms would be agreeable to Richard Daker. Ralph can see the Daker fortune disappearing from under him. While there are lands, Ralph might very well expect to live on them and play lord of the manor once John takes over his father's business. But no lands, no future for Ralph. Except as his little cousin's right-hand man. Which Ralph could never take. One thing to serve a man like Richard Daker – quite another to serve a boy whose every growing year you've overseen.'

'Truthfully,' Gwyneth said suddenly, 'I think Piers Mottis spoke more for Richard Daker than his nephew did—'

'Ralph was bid to the meeting as much to remind him where his allegiance lies as to speak for Daker,' Henry put in. 'He said nothing. All was left to the lawyer. And a good fist he made of it, dry little stick though he appears.'

Gwyneth smiled. Piers Mottis might look like a dry stick but he was unfailingly courteous and never without a smile for Toby. Gwyneth had it on good authority that he and Daker had been young men together and that there existed between the lawyer and the vintner much more than the expected relationship between employer and employed. Though it was not unusual for a guildsman of Daker's eminence to include his lawyer in his own household, the provision for Mottis and his wife of palatial apartments within Daker's own grange had raised eyebrows in Salster. Either the man is a legal miracle-worker and must be kept in good humour, the theory ran, or he knows something to Daker's disadvantage and must at all costs be kept sweet. Such was the awe in which London merchants were held that the mere fact of close friendship existing between the two men was never considered. At the root of such apparent altruism advantage must lurk.

Gwyneth recalled the quiet but shrewd words that Mottis had slid in her direction several times during the meeting. Not wanting to appear to take part, present ostensibly as nothing more than a legal recorder, he nevertheless steered the agreements reached along a particular path. His face appeared before Gwyneth's inner eye, thin and pale, with the lines of concentration and much reading deeply drawn. But laughter lines were equally etched, and they turned the parchment-skin around his eyes into a spider's web of fine lines when he smiled.

'Mistress Kineton,' he had said in a low voice that carried no further than her ear, 'though wages are our matter here, it may be wise to regulate many things today, so that the masons may not have further cause for rebellion at a later date.'

Which had been sound advice, Gwyneth reflected. Advice which had sent the masons away convinced of their own importance and which had drawn the sting of defeat from

Copley, giving him credit, alongside Nicholas Brygge, for the conflict's resolution.

Gwyneth sighed. She was pleased with the regulations drawn up in Mottis's hand and signed by bishop, prior and mayor. She was very relieved that the freemasons of Salster had not defied her and stayed away. But, most of all, she was glad that Simon would not now have cause to be angry with her. He would return to Salster and find work in progress on his college. And he would have her to thank for it.

Her eyes moved involuntarily to Toby, still with Alysoun. Nothing was going to change Simon's anger towards her for Toby. She might have got his masons working once more, she might have rescued the college building from endless frustration and delay, but nothing would make a mason of their son. Nothing could mend that frustration.

'So what have the unruly masons of Salster bound themselves to?' asked Alysoun, attempting to calm an increasingly restless Toby. 'What regulations must they obey henceforth?'

Gwyneth, her attention on her squirming son and not on masons' ordinances, made to rise and take Toby, but Alysoun waved her back to her chair. 'Sit, Mother. He will do well enough with me for a while. Trust me and rest yourself while you can.' And she soothed Toby, her voice crooning to him as her hands imitated Gwyneth's practised movements over his troubled limbs.

'There were eight we agreed upon, as I recall,' said Henry, watching his wife. 'As to the present dispute it was agreed that work should not proceed on great feastdays and that it should carry on only until noon on lesser feastdays.'

'And the day-wages for lesser feasts?' asked Alysoun. 'Will Simon be free to pay more? Hush, little brother. Hush Toby.'

Though Toby was restive, Gwyneth was loath to take him lest she hurt Alysoun's feelings.

'No, he will not. Day wages are to be what they were before, and there is to be no extra payment for any day. And no master is to pay more than any other. In this much at least they came within the law of the land.'

Alysoun's attention was half on her husband, half on the writhing child on her lap. 'And the other ordinances?'

Her question was finished with a yelp as Toby almost threw himself off her lap. Gwyneth jumped up from her place, her hands held out to him as Alysoun caught the child's rigid form, holding him under his arms, her knees in his back. Toby, seeing his mother, threw up his arms as he reached towards her, causing another spasm that would have flung him over backwards had not Alysoun's legs supported him. He stood like that, arms upraised, his head tilted far back so that his one uncovered eye looked up at Gwyneth, and, for the space of two or three heartbeats, he looked like an ordinary child standing, wanting his mother. Reaching out, he made to move, lifting one foot as if to walk towards her. But as that foot left the ground, so his other leg crumpled beneath him and he would have fallen, had not Alysoun still had hold of him. Gwyneth stooped and swept him up into her arms, her heart galloping like the horse of a victory-messenger.

'Did you see?' she asked, her eyes fixed on Alysoun's, 'did you see how he stood and tried to walk?' Her eyes shone with joy and triumph. 'He tried to walk! Now Simon will have to see!' She stared at Alysoun, her arms fiercely holding the rigid Toby. 'Things will be different from now, mark my words.'

Twenty-four

Kineton and Dacre College, present day

Damia's suspicion that the conservators would metaphorically bite her hand off at the chance to study the Toby statue at close quarters proved well founded and, having agreed with both conservators and cathedral authorities that the statue would have all necessary conservation work done by the cathedral's own stonemasons, she was now waiting in the Toby yard for the winch and flatbed truck that would lift the statue from its niche and transport it to the cathedral.

Though advised against, Damia had been unable to resist the urge to climb up on to the scaffolding and take a closer look at the statue. She had stood in the yard below and studied it through a small pair of binoculars, but had abandoned that for the fingertip touch and bass-note smell of stone in close proximity.

The statue was, she estimated, a little more than life-sized. Though approximately her own diminutive height, its proportions were those of a young boy who had not yet reached adolescence. The face was round and the arms and legs lacked the length of bone that more years would give them.

Damia looked the boy up and down, taking in, for the hundredth time, his tiptoe posture and questing look. He radiated life and vitality, a mischievous sprite with no malice in him. Was he Toby Kineton? Had his father immortalised his son at the age he was when the college had been finished, just – in all probability – as he was about to begin his stone-mason's apprenticeship? Damia wondered whether he had been a willing worker or whether he had been keener to run off and play with his fellows; his stance indicated an aptitude for hide and seek.

Her own brother had not been a willing worker. The commune, whilst making Damia long for the everyday comforts of her schoolfriends' houses, had suited Jimi (named after Hendrix) like the patched and faded clothes he wore. A natural nonconformist, he had loved the freedom that their untrammelled life gave him, and during their primary school years he had attended school only as often as was necessary to keep the authorities from their parents' door. Maz and Tony had seen his truanting not as academic laziness but as an expression of his free spirit. 'Jimi's special,' Maz had been fond of saying. 'He's a wild untameable soul. School is not what he needs – he needs the woods and fields and the animals, not timetables and stupid baby stories.'

Though her mother's enthusiasm for Jimi's specialness and disdain of what conventional education could offer had not expressed itself in anything so bourgeois as a determination to teach him herself; Damia had always lived in fear of her brother's withdrawal from school, understanding that if Jimi no longer went, her parents would withdraw her too, on the basis of their version of fairness. School had always been Damia's refuge, a haven of normality and boundaried order in her otherwise chaotic life.

Jimi, her twin. As different from her as a fighting cock was from a starling. She had hated him and loved him, both with a fierce passion. Hated him because he was so clearly Maz's favourite, and she had loved him irrationally for the same reason that her mother had – he simply shone with the light of a chosen one. He could get any of the commune's children to do anything, not by threatening or cajoling but simply by implying that it would please and impress him if they did it. He was the kind of person, she reflected now, who could lead an army to hell and back. Or a cult to mass suicide.

His death had left her with no motive-force in life; their mother's death, followed, before Damia could recover fully, by their father's, had left her without reference points, however flawed, for her own growth towards maturity.

The one self-determining act of her whole adolescence – leaving the commune on Neil's departure for university – had set the course for the rest of her life and she had never regretted it. Though it had been a far more unorthodox journey than that which her childhood self had imagined, she had ultimately reached her destination. Her job at Toby and the little two up two down house with its kitchen extension and overgrown garden represented the realisation of her ambitions. The superlative medieval architecture of her workplace and the working-class Victorian craftsmanship of her red-brick terrace with its art deco glass door panels and miniature walled front garden gave her a feeling of being grounded in time and place in a way she had never been before.

Damia reached out to touch the pitted cheek of the stone boy. Toby – Tobias? She had always thought she would call a son David; Davie when he was little, then David as he grew. But never Dave.

Once, early in their relationship, Damia had caught

herself wondering what her children with Catz would look like until the utter stupidity of the thought crashed in on her. Clearly, the whole notion of bearing the children of one's beloved was hard-wired and could not easily be defused.

Catz. Damia had been shocked to realise how little the fulfilment of her dreams of security had relied on Catz's presence. Her delight in the furnishing of the little house had been untarnished by the fact that Catz had no hand in it; the successes of her job were sufficiently their own reward to leave her feeling no need of Catz's approval.

The divisive issue of motherhood had crept up on Damia in the unlikely setting of a funeral. One of her colleagues had died after a few short months of fighting a particularly aggressive cancer and the Gardiner Foundation had closed down for two hours while the whole staff attended his funeral.

It had been, like Frank himself, a deeply untraditional affair without hymns or religious readings. Rock tunes had played, family videos projected, and Frank's two grown-up sons had spoken movingly about their father and how much he had meant to them.

'They said they were so proud to have known their Dad,' she had told Catz later. 'So proud that they were his flesh and blood.'

'That's nice, don't you think?' Catz had asked, obviously puzzled at the concern in her lover's tone.

'Yes! Yes, it *is* nice! It's just that I've got nobody like that – nobody I'm related to by blood, not my parents – no siblings, no children—' She had stopped, then asked abruptly, 'Who'll sort out *our* funerals, Catz? Who's going to be there for *us*?'

'Well, whoever goes first gets done by the other one – or we could have a suicide pact—'

'I'm being serious!'

Catz met her eye. 'Yes, I'm sorry.'

'When we're old and grey, who's going to bury us? I mean, if we live until we're really old, the one who's left won't be capable of it. There's nobody!'

Catz had tried to draw her close. 'Hey – what's brought all this on?' But Damia had pulled herself out of her lover's embrace and looked into her eyes. 'I think we need to talk about when we're going to have a baby.'

Catz's response had been a bark of incredulous laughter. 'What – just because there's nobody to do our funerals?'

'No, of course not!'

'Then why?'

Damia stared at the statue. Because a need has been born in me, she thought. That's the only reason. There is no greater motive. I just feel a deep, yearning need to have a baby. Every day, more and more, it just feels like an utterly necessary part of my life.

The sudden low growl of an engine forced into low gear caused Damia to swing around.

The truck was here.

It took them a great deal longer than anticipated to raise the statue from its niche. Though expert advice had told them that there were likely to be stone pegs set into both niche and plinth, the fact that these might be mortared in had not been foreseen, and much twisting, heaving and rocking took place before the statue finally shifted a few millimetres. Damia watched in restless suspense, desperate that nothing should be broken but seething with impatience to find out whether Peter Defries's sudden inspiration was correct.

As the statue at last lifted free of its rounded embrasure, steadying hands attached guide-ropes and it was lowered down, the ropes pulling it over the flatbed of the truck. A conservator scurried down the ladder and continued to take digital photographs of every stage of its progress from niche to truck.

As the winch lowered the stone figure and the guide ropes pulled it into a horizontal position so that it could be transported in a coffin-like container full of polystyrene packing-curls, Damia could not contain her impatience any longer. Nipping between the conservator's camera and the statue, she stared at the base as it was pulled level with the head for the final half-metre or so of descent.

'There *is* something in there!' she shouted above the steady chug-chug of the winch's motor. 'Look!'

Swiftly, the conservator took her place and snapped several shots of the roughly circular hole in the base of the statue. Then he made a winding motion in the air with his hand to indicate that the winch should keep lowering the statue into the white curls.

'Hold on!' Damia's voice was a yelp. 'Aren't we going to see what's in there?'

'Not until we can get this back to the cathedral in the proper conditions.' He seemed unaware of the reason for Damia's haste and was obviously going to do whatever was necessary so as not to compromise any artefact inside the statue.

'Right.' Damia leapt up on to the flatbed and sat down firmly on the gritty floor. 'I'm coming too.'

Twenty-five

Sunlight fills a mason's tracing room, streaming in through wide doors. Evidence of builders' work is everywhere, from the trestle-board table with its huge pieces of parchment to the scraps of stone used for testing and demonstrating. Templates for windows yet unbuilt hang, half-done, on the walls; evidence of impatience, or optimism.

In the corner, surrounded by a halo of sunlit dust motes, a tall woman stoops over her rhythmically moving hands. With deft and practised strokes, she works and smooths small pieces of wood.

Two hoops of split and layered ash lie before her, each one composed of more than a dozen pieces, pegged and locked together. Other pieces lie about her, some whose thin suppleness is plainly made for a purpose (though that purpose is hard to guess at), some as yet uncut and rough.

Gwyneth of Kineton has seen how her son may stand, perhaps walk, if his disordered limbs and drooping head may be held as he cannot hold them. And so she has taken up her craft again, not for her husband's sake, but for her son's.

❖

When Simon returned home on a Sunday almost three weeks after the dispute's settlement in the guildhall, it was to find Henry Ackland sitting with Gwyneth in the solar. And it was Henry that Simon addressed, ignoring Gwyneth's stiffly offered welcome.

'What is this tattle about a dispute with the abbey?'

He flung his cloak on to the chest under the window and stood over Henry, who had jumped to his feet to welcome him.

'It's resolved,' Henry said, 'and all the masons at work again. Thanks to Gwyneth.'

Gwyneth heard the weight he laid on these last three words but Simon would not be steered in her direction. Henry continued to feel the lash of his tongue. 'Resolved? Open war has been declared! Copley now knows he has a fight on his hands. Before, he had nothing to complain of save Daker's religion and Daker did not flaunt it. Now that dunghill cock Nicholas Brygge has given him all the excuse he needs—'

'Simon—' Henry held up his open hands before his body, as if to push back Simon's onslaught. 'This was resolved a fortnight ago and more. Building has gone on. There has been no interruption. Copley has even left Salster—'

'Yes. To see what support he can get from his archbishop in bringing all work on Daker's college to a stop—'

'And how have we erred, Simon?' Gwyneth, a leaden lump of despair filling her soul, looked at the man she had once loved beyond anybody else in the world. 'What should we have done? Would you have thanked us for waiting until you got back?'

'I would have thanked you not to involve the mayor!' Simon's gaze snapped on to hers like the crack of a whip. 'Nicholas Brygge furthers no man's cause but his own. If he opposed Copley it was for his own gain.'

'He risked imprisonment, Simon. I heard Copley's threats with my own ears, as did Henry.'

Gwyneth looked to their foster-son, who murmured assent, though Simon's eyes did not leave his wife.

'To prove his own power, nothing more, nothing less. For he knew before he entered the hall that he could hide behind Daker's skirts—'

'Simon,' Henry interrupted, 'without the mayor we could not have held the meeting. We would have lost the rest of the building season—'

Simon turned on him. 'We? Why do you say "we", Henry Ackland? You are a King's Mason. Your place is at the king's castle, not at the side of my wife and the mayor. You presume too much if you think you may speak for me.'

Henry's complexion mottled to his hairline and collar-bones and he took a stride towards Simon.

'I did not speak for you, Simon of Kineton! I am a master mason in my own right, I do not need to speak *for* you, or *by your leave*. This dispute touched all of us. Every mason in Salster. I spoke for myself. I thought to support your cause, yes. But more than that, I wished to stand by Gwyneth.' He paused, his head tilted back slightly to meet Simon eye to eye. 'She risked humiliation and worse for you. And this is her repayment.' He held Simon's eye a moment longer then turned to Gwyneth. 'It has turned out a poor bargain in my judgement.'

Before Gwyneth could answer, or Simon find a retort, the door which opened on to the solar's courtyard staircase was pushed gently and Alysoun, who had taken Toby to the privy, stooped through the door, pushing the child before her.

Simon's reaction as he was confronted, for the first time in his life, with his son erect and straight, was one of complete revulsion.

The oath he uttered had, Gwyneth knew, come from his

lips without thought, but once said it could not be taken back. His reaction to Toby's new state was fixed at that moment, for her, for him and worst of all, for Toby.

'Dear God, what is this thing?'

Gwyneth saw with horror how her own joy and optimism had blinkered her to Simon's likely reaction. She should not have allowed him to come upon Toby in his frame unawares. His habitual distaste for the mere sight of their son should have shown her the need to tread more carefully, speak to him first, tell him how she had seen the way to help Toby, that now their boy might not need to be so crippled, might now have a way to use his disordered limbs.

But Providence had dictated that, by her carelessness, Toby should be brought into the room at the moment in his life least likely to find favour with his father. Simon saw nothing more than grotesquerie. For him, there was no rejoicing that, at last, Toby had the means to hold himself up like any other soul in the world, to see and be seen. There was no sudden joy at seeing him transformed from a pitiful bundle who lay, like an injured dog, simply watching day after day, into a boy. A small, scrawny and twisted boy, perhaps, but a boy nonetheless.

'Is it not enough that you must keep him always before me, Gwyneth? Must you hoist my shame erect and strap it to this . . . foul contraption? Look at him Gwyneth, he is like a hallows' even witch – like a bundle of rags tied to a pole the better to see it burning!'

The image hung in the air, snatching at them with its teeth. Gwyneth, as a desperate, agonised panic began to whirl the room around her, grasped the edge of the chair in which she had been sitting.

'Simon—'

'No more.' And with these final words Simon walked out of the room.

Twenty-six

Kineton and Dacre College, present day

'Tobias of Kineton, born this Thursday before Holy Week, thirteen hundred and eighty-five. Witnessed by me, Simon of Kineton, master mason, his father.

'Witnessed by me, Henry Ackland, master mason, god-father to Tobias.

'Witnessed by me, Alysoun Icknield, godmother to Tobias, embroiderer, and foster-daughter to Simon of Kineton, master mason, and his wife, Gwyneth, master carpenter.

'And Alysoun Icknield has appended a prayer, too,' Neil said, before reading it. 'Thanks be to God for such a blessed answer to twenty years of prayer.'

He looked up from the simultaneous translation of Middle English and the document's unfamiliar script.

'What does it mean?' Damia asked, 'Is it like a birth cer-tificate? No.' She answered the question before he could. 'They didn't have them then, did they?'

'No.'

Neil removed his reading-glasses and polished them with a bunched-up wad of his shirt. 'It's a proof of age document,' he said, laying his glasses down on the table between them. Damia did not speak, waiting for him to continue.

'They were used in disputes about inheritance – parents would get a proof of age sworn out by people who knew the young person well and who were in a position to say whether he was of an age to inherit. Getting one drafted in advance was less common and usually done only when there might be some kind of dispute over inheritance.'

'What kind of dispute?'

He pulled in a considering breath through his nose. 'Usually whether the child was a legitimate heir – if a child was born after the death of its father, for instance, and the widow wanted there to be no doubt as to his right to inherit.'

Damia looked at the stained and creased parchment. It had been wrapped inside a leather roll containing masonry tools and had lain, unopened, inside the Toby statue for six centuries. Had it not been carefully weighted to the baize cloth at each side, it would have curled itself into its lumpily cylindrical shape once more.

'So you think there might have been some dispute over Tobias's legitimacy?'

'That seems unlikely, given that Simon has signed the proof of age.'

'What then?'

Neil leaned back. 'Simon may have been elderly – there's this reference' he replaced his glasses and bent over the document again, putting his cotton-gloved finger on the relevant passage – 'to twenty years of prayer. This was obviously a child who'd been a long time coming. Simon of Kineton may have been worried that he'd die before his son could come of age.'

'And that somebody would dispute inheritance?'

Neil leaned back once more, removing his glasses and looking in her direction though clearly not focusing on her face. 'There's a lot of animosity in the prior's letters between Simon and the Church,' he said slowly, as if giving his thoughts time to catch up with his words. 'It may be that Simon was guarding against any future shenanigans on the Church's part – you know, like trying to impoverish Tobias by depriving him of his lands on a technicality and so bring him to heel—'

'Would the Church do that?'

'Would people who wield power and want to keep it do anything they need to?' He looked steadily at her. 'What do you think?'

When Damia got back to Toby, a group of tourists was passing through the first-floor doors of the Great Hall. Now that term was over and the majority of undergraduates had gone home for the Christmas vacation, tours were allowed into the Octagon.

On a whim, she decided to tag along. She bounded up the stone staircase and caught up with the tourists as they were making their way up the spiral staircase to the library.

Following them up the stairs that wound tightly inside their dark stone stairwell, Damia listened to the guide's words about the building of the new library in the nineteenth century. Only classics, history and early English studies, he told the listening ears, were catered for in the library above the hall these days. All other subjects were represented in the New Library on the other side of Lady's Walk.

Her mind floating free of the guide's raised voice, Damia wondered whether the child Tobias had run around the site as these winding stone stairs were constructed. Had he studied the work as riser-blocks were shaped and set, or had he been more fascinated by the planing and jointing of roof timbers, intrigued by the working of wood?

Damia wondered whether Tobias had been inclined to follow Gwyneth and become a carpenter instead of a mason like his father. She imagined working seasoned timber, so much more organic: warm to the touch, not hard and cold like stone. To be able to smooth away layers with fluid strokes of a plane rather than having to chip and crack at rock would surely be preferable.

She wondered at a the words on Tobias's proof of age. '*Simon of Kineton, master mason, and his wife, Gwyneth, master carpenter.*'

She looked up at the lantern roof for which Toby was justly famous. The thought that a woman might have built this roof – that a hitherto unknown female master craftsman could have designed and constructed one of the most famous works of wood in Europe – was almost as amazing to Damia as the unexpected discovery of the proof of age document and the carving tools.

Had those tools belonged in the hand that had written, '*Witnessed by me, Simon of Kineton, master mason, his father*'? The presence of the proof of age document seemed to confirm that the statue was, as tradition maintained, Toby Kineton, that the college really was nicknamed after him and had borne his name for more than six centuries. Had his image been carved by his father? Or had Henry Ackland, godfather to Tobias and Simon's fellow master, presented the statue as a gift to the Kinetons on the college's completion?

Why had the tools been left, with the document, inside the statue?

'Shall I tell you what I think?' Neil had asked.

Damia had nodded encouragement.

'I think it's like retiring a number in American football – you know, when a particularly famous player has worn a number, they retire it so nobody else can play in that number – it belongs to that player in perpetuity.'

Damia grasped the implication of his words immediately. 'You think he retired his tools? That once he'd carved that statue, he didn't want to use those tools again for some reason?'

'Yeah – as if to say, "That's the best these tools are ever going to do, I don't want them to produce something inferior after they've produced this."'

'It *is* an amazing statue,' Damia said, her inner eye fixed on the boy's eager stance and softly falling tunic.

'There is another explanation,' Neil said, cautiously. 'One that explains the proof of age document being in there as well.'

Damia sighed now, remembering Neil's all-too-plausible explanation, and looked up at the lantern roof, at the light that flooded into the library. If Neil was right, Gwyneth of Kineton might have produced that roof whilst mourning the death of her longed-for son.

'It's the neatest explanation. Proof of age no longer needed; doesn't want to use the tools he used for his son's memorial again. Stuff them both in the statue. QED.'

Damia looked up once more at the roof. She imagined Gwyneth standing on precarious scaffolding high above, overseeing the intricate joinery. Had there been a little boy at her side? Or had Gwyneth produced this roof alone, losing herself in her mystery as she tried to assuage her grief at the death of her only son, her only child?

Damia looked at the lantern, seeing its openness as a

joyful contrast to Gwyneth's long-closed womb; the light pouring in as a stubborn refusal to turn in on herself and mourn.

How different to her own father's response. Tony Miller had not sought consolation for his loss in a positive act of creativity; despite the fuzzily karmic beliefs prevalent amongst the communistes he had not tried to see the death of half his family as part of life's cycle of suffering and happiness. He had not found it in himself to celebrate their lives and give thanks for all that had been good about them. He had simply sunk – without, as far as Damia could see, offering any resistance – into depression and despair.

The thought of her listless father producing something as extraordinary as the Toby statue was enough to make Damia snort in derision, but she was sufficiently honest to ask herself how she might cope with the death of a much-loved child. Her instinct was to believe that she would fight the darkness, but she couldn't be sure. If she had waited twenty years for a child only to see him die in childhood, would she be able to find the strength of character to produce works of art like the statue and the roof above her?

Though she profoundly wished never to be tested on this point, Damia rejected the most obvious guard against such grief, realising, as she did so, that freely choosing to remain childless had already become unthinkable.

Twenty-seven

Salster, August 1388

Following his return from Norfolk, Simon refused to be in the same room as Toby, unless the child was lying on his pallet as he had always done. He could not bear to see his son in the frame that Gwyneth had made. For the first day or so after his return she was afraid that he might destroy it, but it seemed that he could not bring himself so much as to touch it, so great was his revulsion at seeing his son stand in its hoops and slats.

Worse, he extended his feelings of revulsion to Gwyneth. It seemed to her that he could hardly bear her presence, still less her conversation. Three days after Simon's return she saw Henry Ackland welcomed into the house and an unaccustomed apology torn from Simon, but there was none for her. She had to watch as Simon ignored her and listened to Henry's account of the guildhall meeting. But even Henry had been cut short.

'I do not need to know who kisses whose arse, Henry, just tell me what was decided. The rest I can guess for myself.'

So Henry laid out baldly what had been agreed upon.

Gwyneth had led the meeting by the nose, following the advice of Piers Mottis that this was the time to regulate the city's masons for the good of all lodges, and Simon could find little fault with what had been decided.

'With all the coming and going and need for men, some of the older journeymen were concerned for the apprentices,' Henry said. 'That they might just be used as labour and not taught as was their right.'

'And the decision of the meeting?' Simon's tone was still hostile.

'The decision – and it seems a sensible and practical one to me' – Henry glanced at Gwyneth – 'is that each apprentice shall be indentured to a master and that he shall have the sole right to instruct him, in return for the fee. If a master wants to be rid of his apprentice, he must find somebody else to teach him.'

Henry looked at Gwyneth again, for the rule that followed on from this had been hers in instigation.

'Journeymen are to be treated similarly, under the authority of one master, who must answer to the master builder.'

'So a master must agree to take them on? They cannot just take day-labour at the whim of the foreman as before?'

'No. To discourage men from roaming from one site to the other. If they have to answer to a master they will think twice about leaving one.'

Simon nodded. He could see the sense of such a rule. It would ensure continuity and consistent standards. He did not know how hard Gwyneth had fought, with Henry at her side, to ensure the passing of that particular regulation. The journeymen present, seeing their freedom curtailed without obvious advantage to themselves, were not slow to voice their complaints and it had been a long and arduous fight to convince them that they – masons already in Salster – would be at an advantage over those new to the city who would not find a responsible master so easily. It was only the addition of a further regulation, adding weight to the Salster advantage, that brought about their agreement.

It had been Gwyneth's suggestion.

'If journeymen coming new to the city may bind themselves to a master as easily as those already here,' she said, 'then there is room for complaint. It would be to everybody's advantage if masons new to the city were required to prove themselves first.'

And so it was agreed that journeymen or masters new to the city should at first be employed by the day until the quality of their workmanship should be established. Only then should they be employed at task, rather than for a daily wage.

'And if there are masons whose workmanship proves always poor,' Henry concluded, 'then their names must be circulated amongst the city's lodges and given to the mayor and aldermen.' He waited for Simon's objection to what he knew he would see as the usurpation of the lodge's authority.

'But there are already measures within each lodge for dealing with poor workmanship.'

'But they take time, Simon. If men are toing and froing they may shape up well at first and then lapse back into old ways with drink or idleness and then time is wasted getting the work done again. Small compensation to the builder to know that the mason who has cost him a day's work has lost that much pay.'

Simon sucked his teeth, but did not disagree. It occurred to Gwyneth, for the first time, that Simon might actually be out of his depth in Salster. Not as builder or mason, but as site-master, in charge of such a body of men. He had never worked anywhere before where there was such a glut of masons, and the problems of oversupply were new to him.

'Take courage,' she said to him, mustering her own, 'for in the end it will be clear who are the best masons. But because there are so many there must be sorting and grading to be done.'

Simon completely ignored her. She might as well not have spoken for all the reaction he gave.

'So,' he said, his eyes on Henry, 'who is to oversee all these new regulations? Who are to be our guildsmen?'

Henry's eyes met Gwyneth's. She nodded slightly, permitting him to ignore Simon's cruelty. He took a breath.

'Each lodge is to appoint three masters. Together they will make up the masons' council. It will make all necessary decisions and arbitrations.'

Simon nodded. 'So, it is all done and decided.'

His tone was difficult to read, and once more Henry looked questioningly at Gwyneth. But she had nothing to say.

'Yes,' Henry said. 'We have done as we thought fit, and it is done and decided.'

There was a silence as the two men faced each other. Abruptly, Simon held out his hand to Henry. 'I was unjust to you—'

'Simon, you—' Henry tried to interrupt but Simon waved his words away.

'I suggested that you had no right to act for me. That was unjust. If any man knows my mind, it is you.' He stopped, Henry's hand now clasped in his, and their eyes met, Henry having to look up slightly to meet Simon's gaze. 'You have shown the loyalty of a son to me Henry,' he said, 'and I will not forget it.'

Gwyneth looked away from Henry's proud smile. Simon's words had laid a cold hand around her heart. For the loyalty of a son to his father was sacred to Simon. He could not have paid Henry a higher compliment. But his words had also implicitly recognised that Henry stood in the place of a natural son, something Simon had refused to do all the years that the boy had lived in pupillage with them

Gwyneth could not bear to hear any more of what Simon might say. She turned and left the solar, unable to bring herself even to utter a goodbye to Henry, and went into her own chamber where Toby lay on the bed, his face turned to the window, his eyes closed in sleep. She stood looking at the child, his writhing limbs now relaxed, his eyes closed. He looked like any other three-year-old, as if he might wake up, jump off the bed and go running off to play.

But he never would. If his frame taught him to stand, and then to walk, he would never do so with ease. He might learn more control of his head, of the sounds he could make, but he would never jabber away nineteen to the dozen as other children did. If he found speech at all, it would always be as hard upon the ear as on his tongue.

'Oh Toby,' her voice came softly, 'I have failed you.'

She lay down on the bed next to him and fell into sleep while hopeless tears coursed silently down her face as she stroked her boy's damp and curling hair.

Twenty-eight

From: Damia.Miller@kdc.sal.ac.uk
To: CatzCampbell@hotmail.com
Subject: governing body meeting

Well, the battle lines are well and truly drawn now. Baird
came to address the governing body today, PowerPoint
presentation at the ready, and shot from the hip with figures
and trends, funding, fees, buildings, demographics and the
challenge of the East (i.e. China). He was supposed to be
telling us why he wants to dissolve the articles of
association and have Northgate function independently. But
what he'd really come to do was to ridicule Norris who – *he
thought* – would oppose him tooth and nail to maintain the
status quo. Baird's plan, evidently, was to say 'Look at your
leader – he's stuck in the past, defending the indefensible.
Abandon him and join me because I'm going somewhere
and the only place he's going is over the waterfall!'

But Norris turned the tables on him . . .

Baird had arrived at the governing body meeting looking like
a man who foresaw no plausible opposition to his arguments.

He had come, he made it abundantly clear, not to apologise for his actions in seceding from association, but to have them approved. Unstated, but nonetheless equally clear to all present, was his declaration of intent. As the principal of a combined college, his stock would be so high that to make anybody else chairman of the federated colleges of the University of Salster would be unthinkable.

'The world is changing,' he said, walking towards the head of the table having completed his PowerPoint presentation, 'and Salster has to change with it. We can't afford sentiment; we can't afford to hang on to traditions because we like them; we can't afford not to be at the very forefront of what we do and how we do it. Kineton and Dacre College has not been administered well and it is in deep trouble.'

He looked at the surrounding faces as if for signs of dissent or agreement. Norris, whose shoulder he was speaking over, was apparently engaged in the calm taking of notes, giving the impression that he was oblivious to Baird's simian display of status-assertion.

'That is why my college cannot afford to be associated with Kineton and Dacre any longer; and why it *will* not be associated with it any longer.

'If you feel that this college has let you down – or, more accurately, that the *leadership* has let you down – you need to give urgent thought to entering into a different kind of association with Northgate. An amalgamation of the two colleges into one entity – Northgate, Kineton and Dacre. NKD – I think that has a certain ring of the modern world.'

His vulpine smirk caused a churning of mixed apprehension and rage in Damia's stomach. Baird obviously had the sweatshirts printed already in his mind – grey cotton, blue embroidered capitals – a blocky 'NKD' forming the top half of a rectangle, a more discreet 'University of Salster' the bottom. Also available in navy and red.

What would he do for a college crest – insert the Toby tun with crossed square and compasses into his own college's stylised version of the old North Gate? Or had a graphic designer already been commissioned to produce a suitably twenty-first-century logo?

Without a word, Edmund Norris rose to his feet, pushing his chair back with an abruptness that forced Baird to back off smartly lest he be knocked over. Damia stifled a giggle of nervous amusement; Baird's overbearing posture had been toppled in half a second of fluid movement.

'Ladies and gentlemen of Toby,' Norris began, including them all in the sweep of his gaze. 'I feel that we have been presented with something of a false dichotomy.'

His tone, Damia thought, was that of a philosophy lecturer who, regretfully, found himself forced to criticise the remarks of a favoured but currently misguided student.

'Sir Ian presents us with a stark choice. On the one hand to embrace modernity and survive; on the other to maintain our traditions and endure a slow decline or, worse, bankruptcy and ignominy.'

He paused to allow these two futures to see-saw in the mental balance of his audience and then stated, with devastating calm, 'I do not believe that this is the choice before us.'

His eyes met those of his colleagues, one by one.

'I believe that what we are being asked to choose between is the ethos that prevails at Sir Ian Baird's college and what we have here at Toby. Sir Ian's philosophy is based on alliances with business, a corporate ethos and a finance-led philosophy that would deny the right to exist of subjects that have no obvious link with the world of employment.' He paused fractionally before continuing. 'The Toby ethos is to use our resources in order to provide an environment in which young adults can grow to maturity, learn to think for themselves, and become tolerant, compassionate people whose concern is not simply for their own prosperity but for the well-being of the whole of society.

'Sir Ian may say that this is a liberal tradition which, though admirable in its way, has no place in the modern world.' He paused slightly, apparently distracted by the contemplation of such an unpalatable thought . 'If that is true, it is our clear duty to rush to the aid of the modern world.'

The Regent Master looked around at the mingled smiles and frowns of the people sitting in front of him: friends, colleagues, allies and adversaries.

'Sir Ian's primary objective is to make Northgate financially sound, successful and expanding. A business empire.' He scanned their faces, the focused intensity of his gaze adding to his words. '*Our* primary objective *here*, I have always believed, is to contribute to the development of the whole person, not just our undergraduates but graduate students and faculty too. I do not consider myself to be a businessman – Sir Ian thinks that makes me weak, a failure. If this governing body agrees with him, then I shall, of course, step down—'

Several outraged voices protested at this, amongst them a woman whom Damia recognised as Lesley Cochrane, an ageing scientist who had sat on the interview panel for the Marketing Manager's post.

'Ed, for God's sake, don't be ridiculous!' Cochrane's high-coloured face was flushed as she spoke. 'There's no question of you stepping down. Just because Northgate chooses to plough a different furrow . . .' She tailed off, her eyes fixed on the Regent Master.

Baird chose this moment to rejoin the fray. 'Don't be so quick to assume that it's out of the question,' he said. 'I have it on good authority that three of your academics have resigned this week, wary of what will happen to their jobs if the college is declared bankrupt.'

This obviously came as a shock to some of the governing body, though Edmund Norris showed no reaction. Damia wondered where those academics had gone to ensure the safety of their jobs. Had Baird made the same kind of offer to them as he had to her?

'You're making a mistake,' he had said when she rang him to decline his offer to join the Northgate staff. 'When I pick up the pieces at Kineton and Dacre College – and, make no mistake, I *will* have to pick up those pieces – I shall be very selective in which I choose.'

Damia knew she had burned her boats before he started issuing bully-boy threats and she put the phone down on him. But academics lived or died by reputation, and to lose a Salster job would be disastrous for the CV.

'You need to think seriously about whether this is a confidence issue—' Baird tried to steamroller on.

'I don't think we've necessarily reached that state of affairs yet, Sir Ian,' Norris said, well in control of any emotions engendered by Baird's blatant attempt to destabilise his authority. 'Those of you who have known me for a number of years,' Norris continued, 'will know that I have always been a staunch supporter of the associate college system.' He paused. 'I have always believed that it provided a bulwark against pernicious forces that might wish to buy their way into Salster and use such questionable legitimacy to their own ends. For instance, a college established and funded by a billionaire of any fundamentalist religious persuasion could destroy centuries of interreligious tolerance and dialogue.' His gaze roved the faces before him, the tips of his fingers resting lightly on the notes he had made but was not, now, finding it necessary to consult.

'A college specialising in training businesspeople and entrepreneurs, which promulgated, uncritically, the philosophy of its founder rather than providing for the balanced study of many business models and economic theories, would represent the establishment of nothing more than a centre for indoctrination.'

Nods greeted this assertion, though Northrop, the economist, remained impassive.

'An establishment dedicated to bioresearch must find its scientific results at the very least called into question if it is funded entirely by large pharmaceutical companies. You may feel,' Norris said, his voice rising to quell a growing muttering, 'that I am taking an unduly pessimistic view, but one has only to look to the United States to see that I am not being fanciful. Fundamentalist notions which challenge empirical research are emerging from the kind of monolithic, monocultural and potentially unbalanced institution which I have always believed the requirements of association militated against.'

The room was pin-drop silent now. Even the muttering Baird seemed suddenly mesmerised by the fluency of Norris's case.

'But Sir Ian has shown me the error of that particular kind of thinking. Without anybody offering let or hindrance – least of all us, the governing body of Toby – Northgate College's focus has been diverted from broad intellectual pursuit and has been turned towards the pursuit of financial goals.'

'If that's supposed to be a problem—' Baird began but Norris stopped him.

'Please, Ian, if I could finish.' He paused and stared down at his notes, though Damia, who was sitting next to him, would have been prepared to bet that he did not focus on a word of what he had written.

'Northgate College,' he began again, abruptly, 'was founded by a successful entrepreneur who profoundly valued education as a social good; it has – in my opinion – been hijacked by those who view entrepreneurialism and the profit motive as the only valid foundations on which to build our society.'

Drawing himself up and squaring his shoulders, Norris met the collective gaze of his governing body once more.

'I therefore heartily endorse Ian Baird's proposal that the articles of association between our two colleges be dissolved. Our association has not influenced or tempered his philosophy – I encourage you all to approve his proposal.'

Twenty-Nine

Salster, August 1388

It was darkening when Gwyneth woke. Toby slept on. He had been hot and rheumy all day and she had suspected a cold in the head, so she was glad that he could sleep and find relief. Drawing the coverlet over him, she got up stiffly from the bed and rearranged her headcovering.

She looked at the door into the solar. Was Simon still there, or had he gone out? Taking a steadying breath, she smoothed her gown and lifted the latch. The room was being gathered into darkness, save for the embers in the grate and the pale grey of the window-lights. Cooling air butterfly-winged almost imperceptibly into the room and filled it with the smell of approaching night.

Looking about herself, her eyes found Simon. He sat at the table, his head in his hands, motionless. She would have returned to her chamber, gone back to bed, but found she could not move.

'Light the candles, will you?'

Simon did not lift his head, did not look at her, but the sound of his voice was one she remembered from a long time ago, before he became consumed with anger, before Toby's birth. Her heart shook her ribs with its beating as she took the taper and lit it from the embers, blowing gently to make it catch. Shielding it with a trembling hand, she lit the wall-mounted candles and then crossed hesitantly to the table where the remaining four-branched candle-tree stood.

As she held the shaking taper to the first candle, Simon put out his hand to steady hers. The touch of his warm fingers on her wrist was the first bodily contact she had had from Simon in many months. When the last candle was lit, he moved her hand towards his face and blew out the taper, drawing her down to sit beside him. Wordlessly, he laced his fingers in hers, his other hand stroking her forearm where her sleeve had fallen back.

Gwyneth shook in every limb and fought back the tears that caught at her throat. Harsh words had brought nothing but an answering hardness into her soul, but this tenderness of Simon's threatened to undo her completely. Simon opened his mouth as if to speak, but seemed unable to start, only clasping her fingers more tightly with his and stroking her, so lightly he must hardly have been able to feel the contact with his calloused fingers.

In silence, Gwyneth watched his hand move and wondered if he, too, was fighting back unaccustomed tears. She took his free hand in hers and brought it to her lips. Kissing each finger in turn, she then laid his hand against her face.

'Simon . . .'

He still would not look up but said, in a voice not his own, 'Henry shamed me. When you had gone, he shamed me.' Simon cleared his throat, but his voice wavered still. 'He looked me in the eye and said I had no right to speak of loyalty. He spoke of you—' Finally, Simon looked up at her and Gwyneth saw the man she had loved. All the hardness was gone from him, as if a charm had been reversed and his face turned back from stone to flesh once more. 'He said that his loyalty to me was nothing, compared to yours. He said that he would not have done as he did if you had not asked it of him. And asked it not for yourself, but for me.' His eyes searched hers, as if he would find the truth there. She nodded, holding his eyes with hers, but said nothing. 'He said that though I might deserve his loyalty – though I *have* his loyalty – I did not deserve yours, Gwyneth.' He stopped again, and dropped his eyes from hers, inclining his head until his forehead was resting on the boards of the table. 'And he is right.'

So softly was it said that Gwyneth hardly heard the words. But she knew what they had cost him. She put out the hand he had released and tentatively touched his hair.

'I am sorry Gwyneth. I am so sorry.'

'Simon, I have borne with you all the life I can remember.' She stopped, swallowing her tears and struggling to breathe so that she could say what must be said. 'And you with me. We have led each other a dance you and I.' She put her hand under his chin to raise his head. He lifted his eyes to hers.

Through the open windows Gwyneth could hear the sounds of a door being latched, a gate pulled to. The sounds of animals being closed up for the night, of people shutting their houses around themselves for sleep. She gazed at Simon, shaking once more. She must say it.

'Simon, it is not for me to forgive you. It is not me you have wronged. You and I have been stubborn and hard-faced, as always.' She stopped, unable to go on for fear of his reaction. Then, summoning all the courage she possessed she said softly, 'But you have wronged our child.'

Simon's response took her totally by surprise. He dropped

his eyes from her gaze and hung his head, his shoulders shaking with sobs. Gwyneth laid her arm across his shoulders and let him weep. She did not attempt to comfort him, nor to stem the flow of his tears. His grief – for himself, for his damaged son, for what he had done to their love – was not to be hushed away and belittled. Gwyneth heard in Simon's sobs and anguish all the pain she had endured in her own heart the last three and a half years. She heard atonement and repentance. She let him weep.

After a time measured more in the heat of heartbeats than in mere, cold, minutes, the candles began to gutter in the window-draught.

'I am going to shutter the windows, Simon,' Gwyneth said softly as she got up, so that he should know she was not leaving him.

Pulling the heavy wooden frames towards her, Gwyneth breathed deeply as a stirring wind swirled the night air around her face. Dimly, as the moon edged through a massing bank of cloud, she could see that the trees were beginning to blow, their leaves showing their undersides to the shifting sky. There was a change in the air. Tomorrow, things would be different. She latched the shutters and turned back to Simon.

Smearing tears from his eyes with the heels of his palms, Simon looked like a chided boy who has unexpectedly succumbed to tears and doesn't like this evidence that he is not yet quite grown up. As she watched him dragging at his tear-wet face with his sleeve, Gwyneth could bear the poignancy of his weeping no more. Sliding on to the bench next to him she took his hands from his face and smoothed his damp skin with her own fingers, feeling how his beard was wet and dripping still with tears.

He looked at her, and their eyes met without hostility or hardness.

'Is he still unwell?' Simon asked suddenly. Gwyneth found herself confused, didn't understand momentarily who Simon meant. He must have seen her confusion, for he laid a hand on hers and said gently, 'Tobias – he seemed unwell. Is he still?'

Words whirled in Gwyneth's mind, but she could not speak any of them. She could not remember Simon ever before having referred to Toby by name. And as to his well-being . . . Gwyneth did not know whether to be more amazed that Simon had noticed Toby's discomfort or that he should now ask after him.

'He is asleep,' she said.

'So perhaps he will wake up well.'

'Toby will never be well, Simon.'

Simon looked away and then brought his eyes back to hers. Swallowing visibly, he said, 'But he may be restored to what he was.'

Suddenly, Gwyneth was seized with desperation. 'Simon, come and look at him.'

He stared at her, wordlessly. Still his face was soft and willing, though now there was fear there too.

'He is asleep on our bed.' She stared into Simon's eyes, still reddened, and saw his need and his reluctance. 'Please, Simon, come with me and look at our son.'

They rose together and, Simon's hand in hers, Gwyneth raised the latch and let them into the bed chamber. It was dark and Gwyneth turned back to fetch the candle-tree off the table.

When she returned, it was to find Simon standing over their son, looking at him in the dim light of the unshuttered window. Holding the candles high so that their light fell on the sleeping boy, Gwyneth looked at Toby. His hair was slicked back from his face and forehead where she had stroked it, and he looked like a boy standing in the wind, his eyes closed to stop the stinging, his face still, held rapt by the buffeting.

'Now you see him as I see him,' she said, not taking her eyes off Toby.

Simon was silent. Then, in a voice still straitened by tears and pain, he said, 'I have always seen him as you see him Gwyneth. But you could bear it and I could not.'

She looked at him in confusion, shaking her head, quite unsure of what he meant.

'That frame you have made—' Now Simon shook his head, his eyes moving from her to Toby and back again. '—to you it makes him more like us – because he can stand and see – you think it gives him dignity.' Simon collapsed on to the chest at the end of the bed and looked up at Gwyneth, his eyes pleading with her for understanding. 'When I saw him strapped to it—' Simon stopped, his mouth still open, trying to find words for what he had felt. 'It was – I was appalled. Where you saw triumph and an ease for his disordered limbs, to me it was—' he stopped again. ' I saw the anguished eye of the tortured man, Gwyneth. That he must stand there, his every weakness shown forth for all to see. It was like an execution – as if a gibbet were erected in my own house for a man's final humiliation to be seen by all.'

Gwyneth slumped down next to him. 'But he makes no complaint. He does not cry out when we put him in his frame. If he did not like it, he would do so.'

It was as if he had not heard her.

'I looked into his one uncovered eye, Gwyneth, and I knew how I would feel if it were me in that thing. And I did not want him to feel that.'

Gwyneth's heart began its leaping in her chest once more. 'But you say he cannot feel like others, Simon. How do you explain his feeling like you?'

'You can be blithe, Gwyneth, about a sound mind living in such a crippled body. Somehow, you can rejoice that some part of our son is whole. But for me' – Simon's fists clenched upon his knees, – 'for me, the contemplation of a mind – a mind like mine or yours – being walled up in such a body – I cannot bear that thought. That he – one day – will have the thoughts, the desires, the vigours of a man – *like me,* Gwyneth – but that he will never be able to express them, have those desires satisfied . . .' He shook his head and came to a halt. But Gwyneth finally understood.

'And it is my fault,' he began again, startling Gwyneth out of her own thoughts. 'I prayed for a son in my own image. What have I condemned him to?'

Gwyneth stood, pulling Simon up with her. 'Come. Touch him. Stroke his head Simon, feel how soft it is. Feel the warmth of his little life.'

She watched as Simon's trembling hand gently touched and caressed Toby's head, his fingertips brushing the child's face. At a sudden impulse from somewhere in his disordered body, the child threw himself into a painfully tense spasm, his hips thrust out, his body bowed, his arms flung above his head as if in anguished surrender.

Simon started back and looked at Gwyneth in fear and confusion. She shook her head slightly. 'It's nothing. His sleep is always uneasy.'

Reassured but still wary of his son's uncontrolled reactions, Simon put out a tentative hand to take Toby's in his.

Suddenly, as he moved, the wind which had been rising all the while threw a gust into the room, guttering the candles and blowing one out.

Gwyneth stared at the smoking wick and tried to tell herself that she did not believe in omens.

Thirty

Damia arrived back from New York to find that, after only ten days, the English accents at Heathrow seemed foreign to her ears. New York over 'the holidays' had been fun with its competing Santas and menorahs, fairy-lights and oil-lamps, and it had been wonderful to be with Catz again, but Damia had come back to England with the impression that both she and her lover had felt suspended somewhere beyond the reach of everyday life, as if they were on holiday not simply from work but from the realities of their relationship.

As she boarded the Heathrow shuttle, a grey drizzle thickened the air and hid everything but the immediate foreground; vague shapes were visible beyond but nothing had form or substance. Her future, she reflected with some frustration, had the same lack of clarity. She had gone to New York ready to map everything out clearly with Catz, to say, 'I want to be with you but you need to understand that I want a child too, that I'm going to have one sooner or later; you need to know that's a given, a non-negotiable . . .'

It had remained unsaid; worse, she did not know why.

215

Opening the airport novel that she had been trying to read all week, Damia attempted to think of nothing but the characters whose lives were heading so clearly towards a happy resolution until she reached central London and the bus to Salster.

Her little house on Pound Street, unoccupied for ten days, seemed cold and neglected. For the first time, Damia felt the need for a cat. To have been greeted by a living thing would have been comforting, even had the greeting been confined to the languid stretch and vaguely reproachful stare that passed for feline welcome.

Dumping her bags at the foot of the stairs, she gathered the slew of mail from behind the door and quickly looked through it; mostly junk, a few late Christmas cards and a billet doux from the post office informing her that she had not been in when they called with a parcel.

She dumped it all on the telephone table and picked up the phone. Three messages. Sitting on the stairs, she leaned against the cold wall and keyed in the code. Catz, whom she must have missed by seconds before she left, checking the time of her incoming flight; her old colleagues at the Gardiner Foundation inviting her for Christmas Eve drinks; Neil welcoming her home and offering to cook dinner if she was too knackered that evening.

Sighing, she went to turn on the central heating then crawled into bed for a few hours in the hope of assuaging the greed of jet lag.

Neil fried onions and laughed at her descriptions of ice-skating on a crowded outdoor rink.

'Everybody else looked as if they'd skated virtually from

birth. Even Catz,' she complained. 'Apparently the ice rink was the place teenagers hung out where she grew up.'

'Not like us, eh?' he grinned, tipping the wok and stirring expertly. 'We didn't really hang out at all, as such, did we?'

'I barely hung *in*,' she mumbled, her mood slumping with an abruptness that brought home to her how exhausted and emotional she felt.

He looked up at her, surprised.

She turned away from his gaze. Strangely, though they had rebuilt their friendship over the years, they had never anatomised their time together, never compared the frayed ends of their relationship.

After watching him cook, silently, for several minutes she spoke, her voice dry and hesitant. 'I've never asked you what you thought when you got my letter . . .'

He glanced up at her, his face closed. 'The "I'm off on my travels, hope you find somebody else" one or the "Abandon hope, I'm gay" one?'

Damia winced at the old hurt beneath his forced levity.

'It was kind of difficult,' he confessed. 'I had a plan all worked out for us.'

'I'm sorry.'

He made a dismissive noise. 'I got over it.'

'Did you?'

He looked up, his expression caught midway between frown of incomprehension and smile of reassurance. "Course.'

'Only—'

His gaze invited her to continue.

'I just wondered whether . . .'

Neil allowed the silence to continue for a few beats longer than was comfortable. 'Whether I still held a torch for you?'

'Something like that,' Damia mumbled, feeling foolish.

Her eyes fixed on the table top, she heard the click as he turned off the gas. The chair next to her was pulled out and he sat down. There was a silence until she looked up briefly at him, then he laid a hand over hers.

'I'm not going to lie to you, Damia. There's a part of me that will *always* love you – whether it's the old thing about first love always staying with you or whether it's something more than that, but I think part of me belongs to you and part of you to me.' He paused, as if waiting for some kind of assent. 'But if you tell me you're gay and can't be happy in a relationship with a man, then I just have to accept that and respect it.' Again he paused, again she said nothing. 'I don't want anything from you that you're not happy to give, Damia. I never did.'

'Thanks' Damia's throat was constricted and the word came out as a croak.

'Correct me if I'm wrong, here, but I get the impression that things aren't going so well between you and Catz?'

'What's the worst thing that could happen?' he asked, when she'd finished explaining and he was cooking again.

'We'd have a baby, Catz would decide that it had been a bad idea after all, she'd leave and I'd be on my own with a child.'

'You don't fancy the single-parent bit?'

'I want a *family*, Neil.'

He nodded.

Abruptly, she changed the subject. 'Why did you and Angie break up?'

Neil made a rueful face as he restored the meat to the wok and tossed it with the vegetables. 'Faced with a straight choice between coming to Salster with me and staying in London without me she chose London.'

'Looked at the other way, you chose Salster over staying in London with her.'

He nodded slowly. 'I suppose we both found that when it came to the crunch, our careers meant more to us than each other.'

A sudden stab of panic pierced Damia; was that what was happening to her and Catz? Did Catz fear that parenthood, like the taboo of living together, might sap her creativity?

As if reading her mind, Neil asked, 'Why is Catz reluctant to have children?'

Damia stood up suddenly, needing to do something with the sudden surge of adrenalin her body was flooded with. She hadn't intended to drink any wine this evening but, whether from the need to excuse her abrupt rise from the table or from a subconscious craving for emotional analgesia, she reached for one of the bottles in the small rack on the work surface.

Neil eyed her without comment.

The cork emerged with a satisfyingly percussive pop, and from one of the wall cupboards Damia took two of the heavy recycled-glass goblets she had bought when she moved in. She had intended to buy cheap, easily replaced ones whose careless dropping she would not regret but had been seduced by the whirled and bubbled texture of the green-tinged glass.

She put a drink in Neil's hand and raised her own in rim-clinking salute.

'Catz says she's not ready,' she said abruptly. 'But I think it's more to do with fear. And love.' Damia had been on the receiving end of many hours of counselling and psychotherapy; she had what she considered to be a clear insight into her lover's procreation-avoidance.

'She's adopted, you know that, right?'

Neil nodded. 'I'd forgotten, but yeah.'

'Her parents – her adoptive parents – took her real mother in as a pregnant teenager. She lived with them until after Catz was born and then, one day when Catz was a few months old, she just disappeared, leaving a note saying she knew they'd look after the baby better than she would.'

He looked up from testing the rice. 'And she's never had any contact since?'

'No. Nothing.'

'And, as I recall, Catz doesn't get on with her adoptive mum and dad?'

Damia sighed. She had never met Catz's parents but had strong feelings about them nonetheless.

'They were fine while she was little – they had six children of their own, all older than Catz, so she grew up in this idyllic extended family. But by the time she was a teenager they'd all left home so there was no buffer zone between Catz and her parents and they clashed like hell. Then, when she came out, they just couldn't cope. They're very strong Catholics and they just can't see it as anything but a sin.'

'So does she still have contact with them?'

Damia took a gulp of her wine. 'Not really. Christmas cards, birthday cards, change of address. That's about it.'

'Grim.'

'Mmm.'

'Where are your plates? This is ready.'

'So you think Catz's baby issues are all to do with being adopted?' Neil resurrected the topic once they were well into the stir-fried chicken and vegetables.

'Well, if your natural mother abandons you when you're

a few months old and then your adoptive parents pretty well say "Change or leave", it's hard not to come away with the feeling that parents suck.'

'But *she* mightn't suck as a parent.' Neil pointed out, reasonably.

'It's a risk though, isn't it?'

'OK then, she lets *you* have the babies, then she's at one remove.'

'That's the position her adopted parents were in – looking after a child they'd taken on but who wasn't theirs genetically.' Damia poked a chunk of green pepper moodily, wondering why she didn't feel hungrier. 'And then there's the other thing.'

She felt Neil's gaze rest on her but she didn't look up from her food. What she was about to say had torn at her heart for months; she needed to see its effect through someone else's eyes.

'I think she'd rather not have me at all than share me.'

The attraction between Damia and Catz had been mutual and immediate.

'D'you know the artist?' the statuesque strawberry-blonde woman at Damia's side had asked as, together, they scrutinised a painting at the new Catriona M. Campbell exhibition.

'No, only that she's making a splash and being snapped up,' Damia confessed.

'What d'you think?' the tall woman asked in her liltingly curvaceous Liverpool accent.

'I quite like it, but then I don't really know much about contemporary art.'

'Because you don't have the time or you don't have the inclination?'

'Bit of both, I suppose.'

'If you had the inclination, you'd make the time.'

'OK,' Damia said, beginning to be annoyed by the woman's provocative attitude, 'if you want the honest truth, I think a lot of modern stuff is a rip-off. Piling up stuff off a tip into a "sculpture" that looks like something a kid from playgroup would produce, or flashing lights on and off while a rubbish video plays on a loop? Please! I can make rubbish videos and my bathroom light has never worked properly.'

The blonde tipped back her head and laughed uproariously. 'Jesus, tell it like it is, why don't you?'

'Sorry.' Damia apologised insincerely, feeling that the woman's laughter had given her permission not to be too contrite. 'It's just that I work in a sector which is perpetually strapped for cash and when I see people getting paid a fortune for rubbish when there are people literally dying because we can't get the grants, it makes me feel that we've got our priorities wrong somewhere.'

'So you don't think artists should be supported by the state.'

'No.'

'Just no. Never.'

'Just no, never. If nobody wants to buy what they produce, then it's obviously not good enough.'

'Ah, but if you're gonna go on that tack, don't you think that if people *do* want to buy what they produce, even if it is a flashing light and a dodgy video, that *does* mean it's good? Or good *enough*, anyway?'

Damia turned at her and grinned. 'I asked for that. But don't you think there has to be something that decides whether it's real art or not?' she asked. 'I mean, seriously, can *anything* be art?'

'Maybe it's like beauty – in the eye of the beholder.'

'Call it art and it's art?'

The blonde shrugged. 'It's a view.'

'Is it your view?'

The woman turned away, looked at the picture in front of them. '*I* think the defining feature of art is passion,' she said simply. 'If it's just an intellectual construct, then however technically well produced it is, for me it's not art.'

'And however badly it's done, if it's produced with passion, then it is?'

'If it's a passion to communicate an idea then yes.'

Damia blinked as this stranger's confident definition crashed into her own unformed opinion which conflated art and talent, or – at the very least – perceptible effort. 'So what about this then?' She nodded at the picture on the wall.

'You tell me. You're the one with the strong opinions. I'm hopelessly compromised by being into contemporary art in a pretty big way.'

Damia gazed at the painting, trying not to let any intellectual constructs she might have dictate the way she saw it. Generally she disliked portraits, preferring the freedom of response that abstract paintings allowed her. But this figure was as far from the stiff, self-satisfied court portraits of previous centuries or self-consciously iconoclastic modern portraiture as a child's drawing of a house was from an architect's blueprints.

The subject, a plump black woman in early middle age, was portrayed half-standing, half-sitting, a generous buttock on the corner of a kitchen table as she spoke into the telephone clasped to the side of her head. Her free hand was raised in emphasis, her face alight with animation as her wide mouth was caught in the act of exclamation.

That this woman's life was filled with communication was made clear in the background: kitchen cupboards stuck higgledy-piggledy with postcards, a fridge strewn with notes, message-magnets and children's drawings. A telephone/address book lay open and dog-eared on the table beside her and a mobile phone was plugged into its charger a few inches further away. Short of a thought-bubble emerging from the woman's close-cropped head saying 'I ♥ TALKING' nothing could have conveyed her enthusiasm for communication more clearly.

'I think it's fantastic,' she said simply. 'I'd love to know this woman.'

The tall blonde smiled, her eyes crinkling at the edges, the corners of her mouth drawn down slightly as if suppressing mirth. 'I could introduce you if you like. You'd get on. Marsha doesn't like modern art much either.'

Damia narrowed her eyes. 'You know her?'

'I should hope so, I don't tend to paint total strangers.'

In the years that had followed Catz had gone on from 'making a splash' to being described by one broadsheet art critic as 'the saviour of modern British figurative painting'. Her stock was high and the prices commanded by her work higher still. But that success, Damia reflected now, had not mitigated Catz's emotional insecurity. It had simply opened up an ever-widening gulf between her feted, successful public persona and the strained, conflicted, private reality.

Thirty-one

Salster, late summer 1388

Although, since Toby's birth, it had been Gwyneth's devout wish that Simon would pay him some fatherly attention, she found her husband's sudden, obsessional, interest in his child to be wearing. Much as she had wanted Simon to hold their son, she was reluctant to give him over entirely and, though Simon's hardness of heart had caused her long anguish, she had never had to share Toby as she did now. She found, whatever her joy, that it came hard. She was constantly having to bite her tongue as Simon handled the child clumsily, or did things in a cack-handed, distressing way.

At first, their son seemed bewildered by Simon's sudden attentiveness, rolling his uncovered eye at Gwyneth and mewing for her. It tore at Gwyneth's heart: all her instincts towards protection which had been honed and sharpened for the three and a half years of her child's life insisted that she should wrest him from Simon's grasp and hold him to her. But she knew she must not. She had wanted Simon to own him, and now she must bide her time patiently as Simon accustomed himself to the child.

But if she had thought that becoming familiar with Toby and his needs would entail Simon's learning to do things exactly as she did, Gwyneth soon knew better. For Simon had his own notions as to how their boy should be handled and taught. However harshly he had expressed his opinions as to her treatment of Tobias in the past, they had, it seemed, been his true feelings, born of an unease at Gwyneth's over-protection.

'Why do you carry him like that?' Gwyneth could not help herself asking one day as Simon hoisted Toby on to his hip, his forearm under the boy's bent knees as Toby tried to look out at the world. 'He cannot hold up his head to see.'

'Not all the time,' Simon agreed, 'but he and I together have found that if I hold him so, with his legs bent, he can pay attention to what he does with his shoulders and head.' He craned around to look at Toby and, with a visible effort, the child raised his head. As he did so, Simon surprised Gwyneth by swiftly bringing his other arm around Toby's body to control his outflinging arms. They looked at each other, father and son, Toby's face writhing uncontrollably as he tried to articulate sounds, and then Simon gently released the child's arms and put his hand on Toby's forehead, supporting it lest his head drop forward again.

'You see, Gwyneth,' he said, as if he was explaining some architectural principle to her. 'Because he cannot control his whole body at once, you have always carried him so that he did not need to work to control any part of himself. So he has remained as he is . . .' Gwyneth chewed her lip, but said nothing, watching Toby carefully. 'But we shall see whether he can learn mastery of one part if another is taken care of.' He swung Toby around so that the child was held against his chest, looking outwards. He gently pushed the boy's head back so that it was resting against him and then took his hand away. 'See?' he asked Gwyneth. 'I may be his frame for him.'

The frame. Simon still could hardly bear to see Toby in it, and preferred, when he had his son with him, to carry him about. It was as if he could not rid himself of his first appalled reaction to the contraption that Gwyneth had made.

But Gwyneth stood firm, and when she went to pay the weekly wages to masons on the college site Toby no longer lay on his pallet at her feet but moved laboriously about the lodge in his frame, his unpractised hands reaching for things while his eyes rolled in his restrained head, his face writhing uncontrollably in his ecstatic delight at such new freedom. Seeing his first attempts at grasping things fail as his over-eager arms flung themselves outwards, Gwyneth had added to the frame two small hoops placed upright in front of Toby. Restrained by these loops, his arms were prevented from flight and his hands were able to begin the long process of learning to reach, grasp, hold and turn things so that he could see them.

Determined that his son should see better, Simon had abandoned the bandage with which Gwyneth had covered Toby's more wandering eye and made him a leather patch on a thong which fitted snugly into his eye-socket and did not slip about, as the bandage had been wont to do.

'He looks as if a baby's clout has been thrown at his head,' Simon had complained to Gwyneth of her bandage. 'He must have something better.'

And so, with a patch on his eye, and the new clothes that Simon had asked Alysoun to make for him hiding the scrawniness of his under-exercised body, Toby was carried by his father on to the building site and his existence openly acknowledged for the first time.

Gwyneth knew what it cost Simon to hoist Toby on to his hip and walk with him amongst other masons. She knew how he would hate the pity, the fear, the superstitious warding of the evil eye. She knew how much it cost him to walk amongst men who had their growing sons apprenticed to them, his own crippled boy on his arm.

And yet Simon did it. Whether as penance or sudden, late-flowering affection for the child, Simon became his son's father overnight, as he had failed to do when Tobias was born. And being in the world with his father seemed to bring Toby on in a way that his mother's protective love and care had not.

It rankled with Gwyneth, whatever her joy at Toby's new life.

And yet she had not lost him to his father altogether. It became obvious to her that the one thing she could do for Toby which Simon could not was to give him the chance to walk. For all his father's ministrations, Toby's legs would not support his weight, and the more Simon held him beneath the arms and braced him as he tried, the harder Toby found it.

'He cannot bear to disappoint you,' Gwyneth said one day, her son's distress suddenly dawning on her. 'He knows you dearly want him to walk, and he wants to give it to you – but he cannot. And the more anxious he is, the more he cannot.'

And, though he was not a man to relish admitting defeat, Simon was forced to concede that this was true. There were many things that Toby learned over the next twelve months: during the long lay-off of winter; during the reawakening of the spring of 1389 (the year when the young King Richard took up the reins of power from his Lords Appellant); during the summer when, again, the walls of Daker's college began to rise. Whilst great things were afoot in matters of state, and smaller, though significant things were happening in his own city, Tobias Kineton learned to sit against a wall and not fall over, to push himself along on his back with braced legs and to look his father in the eye. They might be things that most children mastered well before their first year was out but they were minor miracles of perseverance for Toby and things which his mother had never thought to see him do.

But walking still remained beyond him – for that, he needed his frame.

Thirty-two

Salster, present day

From: Damia.Miller@kdc.sal.ac.uk
To: Mailing List (alumni)
Subject: Toby Fairings Team

Dear Tobyite

Whether you're an athlete or not, whether you ever ran in the Fairings or not, you're likely to have very fond memories of Fairings Day: Gathering in the Great Hall to watch the ceremonial presentation of rigs to runners, greeting the team as they appeared on the Octo's steps, following the race on foot or heading straight to St Thomas' through the cheering crowds for that final dash; not to mention hosting friends and family at a traditional Salster summer 'event'.

For many at Salster the Fairings is the high point of every year. For finalists it marks the end of their studies at Salster and the beginning of the gruelling round of exams that will allow them to write 'BA Sals.' after their name.

As you may well have read in the national media recently, Toby's sponsors for this year's Fairings, the sporting goods manufacturers Atoz, have been rejected by our runners who expressed grave concerns over Atoz's human rights and ethical trading record [click here for more information].

As a consequence, Sir Ian Baird, Principal of our associate college, Northgate, has seceded from association and is running an independent Northgate team for the first time in the college's history. Atoz will be its sponsor.

No longer having Atoz as our sponsor has left us with a significant shortfall. Financial backing is needed not only to cover the costs of training gear, running rigs, coaching and hospitality to old members and guests on race day; these costs, though significant to the runners, are minor in the scheme of college finances. But with ever-decreasing government support for higher education, Fairings sponsorship has become a more and more significant item on each year's balance sheet.

By now, you will not be surprised to read the words THIS IS WHERE YOU COME IN!

Toby is asking you – its worldwide members – to back our runners as this year's sponsors. To stand alongside the young people who took such a principled stance over the rights of workers whom they will never meet. To say 'We are proud of you and we will support you.'

Backing our runners will also send a very clear message of support to our Regent Master, Edmund Norris. If you value the spirit of democracy and self-determination which has always prevailed at Toby and which Ed Norris supports even when his reputation and future are on the line, I know you will want to stand alongside him and offer your wholehearted endorsement of his leadership.

Without your support, there is a very real chance that this Fairings will be the last to see Toby compete as an independent college. Please, support our runners and volunteer your sponsorship.

Finally, because we are aware that all our members are of very different means, we do not intend to offer a sliding scale of rewards for your generosity. The invitation-only champagne reception on race day will be open to every donor, be their donation large or small.

So, [click here] to if you'd like to register as a sponsor and ensure that Fairings Day next year sees a Toby team in good heart, supported by its own.

Whether you decide to become a sponsor or not, if you wish to show your support for our runners in a very visible way on race day [click this link] to see the range of Toby Fairings Day merchandise. Each item carries our specially designed logo representing the message BY, FOR AND WITH TOBY! This logo was designed by Stephan Kingsley, a third-year classicist here at Toby, and is his donation to the cause.

Kind regards

Damia Miller
Marketing Manager

Damia sat back and looked at the claret-and-navy T-shirt on her desk. Stephan Kingsley's cryptic logo

$$\left[\begin{array}{c} \text{X4\&}\overline{\text{C}} \\ \text{TOBY} \end{array} \right]$$

was designed to looked equally eye-catching on T-shirts, umbrellas (Fairings Day was not always seasonally sunny) and sweatshirts.

The self-sponsorship plan was one of the first steps taken by the College Action Plan Committee, a group appointed by the governing body and immediately rechristened by some of its members the Toby Rescue Committee.

Though Edmund Norris's surprising endorsement of Northgate's plans for secession had drawn the force from Ian Baird's full-frontal attack, in the wake of Baird's departure from the governing body meeting an uncomfortable number of voices had been raised, questioning whether this might be the time for Kineton and Dacre College to move forward proactively instead of waiting for the inevitable; to throw the weight of their tradition behind a new, twenty-first-century breed of hybrid college.

'It's the way colleges are going to have to go in the current financial climate,' Charles Northrop had insisted. 'We may as well get in now and reap the early-bird benefits.'

The majority of the governing body, however had been against such a course, preferring to maintain Toby's independence and find another way forward. This was the Rescue Committee's remit.

But, despite the presence of Rob Hadstowe as the tenants' representative at the committee's inaugural meeting, the rent strike dragged on. Hadstowe had remained unmoved by the concept of a college community coming together in a collaboration unique in the history of Salster, and made no further promises than to report on the substance of the meeting to his colleagues.

A similar lack of enthusiasm had come from the dean, Charles Northrop.

'I know he's the dean,' Damia had complained to Norris before the inaugural meeting, 'but does he have to be on the committee?'

Norris had regarded her gravely. 'Not to invite him to be

part of it would be tantamount to saying that I don't trust him.'

'Well, *do* you trust him?'

Norris had sighed and turned, in his habitual gesture, to look out of his office window. The building that Damia was learning to call the Octo seemed more than usually massive as it rose out of the gloom of a January dusk.

'I'm not sure I trust him to strain every sinew on Toby's behalf, no,' he admitted. 'I think he already fancies himself as dean of this combined college. NKD . . .' His voice had faded so much as he pronounced the last three syllables that Damia could not tell whether his words were scathing or despairing.

It was not simply Northrop's preference for a merger with Northgate that put him at odds with Damia – antagonism had flared between them as early as her interview for the marketing job.

'Your previous jobs seem to have had a greater emphasis on fundraising than on marketing,' he had observed after her presentation on 'Marketing Kineton and Dacre College in the Twenty-first Century'. 'How well do you think fundraising for the homeless will map on to maintaining us as a top-flight educational establishment in a world market?'

'The most effective marketing is always done by word of mouth – that's what viral marketing is trying to emulate in the global village,' she responded, engaging him on his chosen international ground. 'And word of mouth works best when you've created a really strong brand and a community that identifies with that brand. I would want to identify the stakeholders in the Toby brand' (she had caught a few exchanged glances at her deliberate use of the initiates' cognomen) 'and develop their sense of identity with it. Then marketing's half done and so is fundraising. Those who identify with the community will support it. We need brand loyalty. The more we can persuade people that they belong and that they count, the more loyal they will be.'

'That sounds very nice in theory, but in practice I think you may find we're fundraised out – that brand loyalty is suffering fatigue after our appeal—'

'Ah well, if you'll let me interrupt, this is where I think there's a huge difference between developing loyalty and tapping people for money on a one-off. Loyalty is all about give and take. My research into your appeal shows that all donors got was an honourable mention in the college magazine. That's not donor development. I hate to slag off fellow professionals but I do think you were let down pretty badly by your fundraising consultants there, actually.'

The short but glance-filled silence that followed was swiftly curtailed by a question from another interviewer; only later did Damia learn that there had been no consultants. Charles Northrop had coordinated the college appeal.

Northrop's challenge to her at the Rescue Committee's first meeting had been swift. The introductions were barely complete when he raised a point of order.

'Just on the composition of this committee, Regent Master,' he said, as if wearied by the mere fact of having to raise an obvious point. 'Is it really necessary that Ms Miller sits on this committee? Has she not already put into effect all her own ideas in her capacity as marketer for the college? It seems to me that while Ms Miller beavers away in her office doing her thing, this committee needs to adopt a very different approach. Perhaps we should vote on the committee's constitution?'

Those not used to working with Northrop as an equal looked down at their notepads and avoided eye contact. The dean's disciplinary reputation was as a steamroller of self-defence; miscreants prepared to profess abject repentance were generally regarded as wise.

The academics on the committee exchanged glances and rolled despairing eyes.

Damia, about to launch a robust defence of her role with facts and figures as to the success of her 'beavering' thus far, was pre-empted by Edmund Norris.

'Charles, everybody at this table is here at my personal invitation. This is not an officially constituted committee, demanded by college constitution. It can be disbanded, enlarged or shrunk at my whim.' A faint smile played in the crow's feet around Norris's eyes but his lips remained un-amused. 'If you feel you cannot work successfully with Damia and her approach, then you are free to withdraw your services. Personally, I would be sad were that to happen as I think your different contributions would both be valuable, but please, don't feel constrained to stay if you feel uncom-fortable.'

Northrop, from his seat at the end of the table opposite Ed Norris, glared at him. Norris's returning gaze indicated that he was waiting for Northrop's response.

'Very well. Underclass to overprivilege it is, then.'

Thirty-three

The summer of that year proved just as chancy as many before it, and dull days frequently turned to rain. Again and again building was suspended lest the mortar wash out and the stones themselves begin to take in water, which would weaken them.

Simon's patience was rubbed very thin by such constant interruptions and his masons began to avoid him.

Great quantities of stone were dressed in the shelter of the lodge and laid up ready to be set in place, but the setters, frustrated by rain, could make no inroads into the piles of precisely cut and marked blocks that rose every day. Ill-tempered with unreliable employment and the half-pay that was the agreed retainer for days on which less than four hours' work was done, the setters saw no reason why they should not do the work of hewers. Several tried, under the regulations for freemasonry drawn up the previous summer, to find masters who would recognise their skills and take them on for day-labour, but none succeeded, hewers always having considered themselves to be the more skilled of the craftsmen.

Resentments began to build which Simon, caught in the coils of his own desperation, did not exert himself to mediate. Several days saw blood drawn in sudden violence as tempers scraped raw by resentment were grazed once too often, and there began to be a steady drain of setters away to the king's works where they found masters' standards less demanding, roughstone castle walls being a different creature altogether from smooth ashlared facings.

Then – when it seemed that the miracle of a fine, cloudless day had finally been granted him – Simon strode out of the lodge, Toby on his hip, to be confronted by two of the mayor's officers.

'Good day, sirs.'

They responded in kind, one – a thin, lank figure of middle years – gazing about him like a clerk with an inventory, the other – younger and more wholesome-looking – keeping his eyes very firmly upon Simon. His reputation for unpredictable irascibility had spread beyond the building site.

'Well?' Simon prompted, shifting Toby's weight, automatically holding his son's wayward arms down as he did so. Both men's eyes moved involuntarily to the writhing face of the child and Simon felt the familiar surge of irritation that wanted to cover Toby's face, to tell him not to gurn so, to be still. He quelled it and snapped, 'I have work to do, I cannot be standing about. What is your business?'

'The weather being set fair,' the younger man blurted, startled into speech, 'the harvest is to be gathered this week while it may be.' He faltered to a halt.

Simon's eyes narrowed slightly as he looked at the men. 'What has harvest to do with me?'

The inventory-eyed man ceased his surveying and looked Simon in the eye. 'All journeymen and apprentices are required to lay aside their crafts and bring in the harvest.'

The hair on the back of Simon's neck began to prickle like the sting of tiny needles. 'Required by whom?' he asked, his eyes on the man's sallow, pockmarked face.

'The mayor—'

'It is a statute of Parliament,' the younger man interrupted quickly, 'which the mayor cannot but enforce.'

'Then he can enforce it elsewhere' – Simon dismissed them, turning away – 'amongst craftsmen who do not depend on the weather. I need this sun as much as the harvest does. Go and impress weavers and tanners – or the goldsmiths, let them blister their hands for once in their lives.'

The officers, forced to follow him, picked their way suspiciously over the lime-strewn site as if their shoes would rot beneath them if they trod unwarily.

'All journeymen and apprentices are to come,' the younger officer protested at Simon's retreating back. 'We cannot pick and choose. All must come.'

'Not today.' Simon's voice carried finality, though he did not look around at them. 'Today I have building to do and I need all my men.'

Before noon, by that peculiar method of travel which only news can accomplish, it had become known on the college site that, though Simon's journeymen and apprentices had been required to put down their tools and take up sickles, Salster's other masons had not. Masons on the king's business were to see it pursued as usual, whilst those at work in the abbey were apparently judged – by the bishop and prior at least – to be beyond the reach of city regulations.

Simon, enraged beyond endurance, stalked from abbey to castle lodge, demanding that masters at both sites bring their elected representatives to a meeting of the masons' council.

'It was Brygge's idea that this council of masons should exist,' Simon ground out between gritted teeth as Henry Ackland stood, not giving the advice that was plainly tickling the tip of his tongue. 'So now let us see how he likes the combined force of our opinion. He shall not make reapers out of my masons for his own benefit.'

Henry, who had watched Simon's impatience and frustration stretching him, fibre by fibre, to breaking point all summer, understood his feelings. Simon had waited so long for this chance that now to see delay piled upon delay was more than his nature could bear. The wet weather was beyond his control, but a stark order from the mayor that masons under Simon's jurisdiction should lay aside the tools they had been waiting for weeks to wield and ply themselves at some common task was too much. But Henry feared for Simon in his appeal to his fellow masons. For Simon's was seen as an unblessed cause, and no mason willingly courted ill luck.

The meeting had been set for that evening and Simon, not wanting to involve the mayor, had insisted that the council should be held in his own lodge. But when the abbey bell rang for Vespers, none appeared but one of the same mayor's officers who had come earlier in the day.

'You are bid to the guildhall,' he said, a gloating smirk revealing a mouth full of decay. 'This dispute is over city regulations and not your own craft—'

'So says Brygge,' said Simon, bitterly, seeing how he had allowed himself to be outflanked by the mayor.

'You can't stand against him, Master Mason,' the officer advised as he turned to accompany Simon to the guildhall. 'Others have tried. And all have failed.'

Silently, Simon stalked past him and strode, alone in his rage, to the guildhall.

Nicholas Brygge, having made his point by moving the council from Simon's domain to his own, was prepared to be conciliatory once the meeting began. He did not attempt to interfere but allowed Hugh of Lewes – agreed as senior master craftsman in Simon's absence the previous summer – to begin proceedings. Not looking at Simon, the abbey's master mason began.

'We are here to listen to the matter that Simon of Kineton, master mason to Richard Daker, wishes to put forward. He asks for the impressment of his journeymen and apprentices to be waived. Are we ready to hear him?'

Nods and assorted 'ayes' of varying degrees of enthusiasm were the response to this, and Simon looked around at the city's masons. Those from his own lodge – Edwin Gore, site foreman and master craftsman of long standing, and Alfred Mogge, a younger man who, like Simon, had a particular skill in image carving – were resolute behind him. They sat, their eyes upon him, waiting for him to begin. No other mason in the hall was as eager. Even Henry, the youngest master present, and one of the few who would meet his eye, did not look entirely at ease.

'The case is simple,' Simon began baldly. 'The mayor asserts that all journeymen and apprentices must lay aside their crafts and turn reaper. But if the king's masons do not and the abbey's masons do not, tell me – why should my masons do differently?'

Richard Oldman, master to the king's fortifications in Salster, stood wearily. 'We are exempt on ground of speed,' he said. 'There is no benefit in having the harvest safely gathered and the people fed through the winter if we cannot defend ourselves against the French, if they should come. All speed is needed to finish the walls and the new southern gate.' He stopped and looked Simon in the eye. 'I am controller of the king's works in Salster and I am given discretion. I am trusted by the king to decide wisely' – still he stared at Simon – 'and I have decided that while it is dry, we must build. It is nothing against you, Simon of Kineton, but my first loyalty must be to the king.'

The king. Though Simon's eyes were on Richard Oldman as he sat down, in his inner eye he saw the face of the young king's grandfather. A face with broken veins beneath the skin. The face which had kept him from royal works ever since. Masons were not slow to notice each other's preferment and common gossip had surely invented a dozen reasons for his lack of royal patronage. Well might Richard Oldman remind him – and everybody else – of it.

'Very well.' Simon stood and turned towards Hugh of Lewes. 'But there is not the same need for haste in the abbey works, surely? If my masons are needed more in the fields than on my building site, why are yours not needed equally?'

Hugh of Lewes rose to his feet with the look of a cat who has dined off stolen fish. 'The abbey masons are not subject to parliamentary statutes concerning labour—' he began, but Simon, full of outrage, interrupted.

'You cannot protest that the city's guild regulations do not hold good within the abbey walls—'

'I say no such thing,' said the abbey's mason complacently. 'We are exempted by a licence granted us by the king.'

He unbuckled the deep wallet that hung at his belt and took out a small roll of parchment. Without opening it, he waved it in Simon's direction. 'The king is keen to see the nave finished as soon as may be.' Simon felt the man's triumph as he thrust home the fatal shaft. 'His Majesty was pleased to be able to give our bishop special dispensation to see the building work speeded.'

Copley. Simon's inner voice groaned. This parliamentary statute had been promulgated the year before and Copley had obviously seen delays and frustrations ahead. The young king's love of beauty was well known, as was his childlike unworldliness; it must have seemed to Richard that he was giving Copley a well-deserved favour.

'So' – Simon stood wearily for one last assault upon inevitability – 'both your lodges plead a special need for haste. One to speed defence, the other to speed beauty.' He looked around at his fellow masters: only Henry and his own masons would meet his eye. 'Are my masons then to be treated differently because our patron is not the king? Does it sit easily with you that your journeymen and apprentices shall stay within the walls and speed the work through the dry days whilst mine shall take up sickles and bring home the harvest, leaving our works languishing for want of labour?'

There was no reply.

Nicholas Brygge, watchful and silent until now, addressed Simon. 'What question do you wish the council to decide, Master Kineton?'

Simon turned to face him. Their eyes locked, Simon sending out sparks like a poked fire in his frustration and humiliation, Brygge's self-contained stillness giving nothing away.

'The question I wish my fellow masons to decide,' Simon

said bitterly, taking each of them in with his gaze, 'is whether there shall be one rule for all masons in the city.' He paused and then laid his final card. 'I thought that to have been the purpose of the masons' ordinances laid down last summer.'

The mayor cast his gaze around the hall like a net. 'Well?'

Not a man stirred. Not a word was exchanged. Decisions, Simon realised, had been made before ever the council was convened.

Richard Oldman stood. 'This is not a matter of whether there shall be one rule for all masons, it is a matter of whether the king's writ runs in the city. There is a statute which says that, for a few days, journeymen and apprentices must – for the common good – help to bring in the harvest. For the king's own good reasons, which we have heard, two of the three masons' lodges in the city are exempt from this.' He looked around at the small band of men gathered in the carved magnificence of a hall that could hold hundreds. 'It is not our business to help you go against the king's interests, Simon. Our lodge will not stand with you if you defy the statute.'

'And you?' Simon directed his words roughly to Hugh of Lewes, knowing the substance of his answer but unwilling to allow the man the luxury of sitting in silence.

'My bishop is sworn to uphold the king's peace,' the master mason said smoothly. 'It would hardly befit him to begin encouraging rebellion against statutes within a stone's throw of his own abbey.'

Kings and bishops. Power and dominion. Authority and rule. The misuse of power for their own ends that Wyclif had preached against the princes of both Church and state. Never had Simon felt such common purpose with Richard Daker.

Nicholas Brygge stood. 'The council is decided. The

lodges of the abbey and the king's works are exempt from the need to provide reapers. The lodge of Simon of Kineton is not, and all journeymen and apprentices of that lodge must set aside their building tools until the harvest is gathered. Is that your decision?'

Nods and ayes assented.

'Then this council is ended.'

As the other masons left and Henry Ackland hesitated in the doorway for him, Simon approached Nicholas Brygge. 'And if I choose not to send my men?' he asked, bluntly.

'Then I would have all your shipments of stone and other necessaries stopped at the gates and turned away,' Brygge replied, evenly. 'As mayor of the city, I cannot afford to have my authority flouted. Neither will I tolerate guild meetings from which I am excluded,' he said, pointedly. When Simon made no response he said, 'I am no more a lover of the bishop than you are, man. But he is shrewd and has seen a way to get what he wants whilst pleasing the king and vexing you. But there is nothing to be done.' He stared at Simon, his eyes unwavering. 'I am not your enemy, whatever you may think. I want Daker's college built. He could not build it in Salster without my consent. But do not try to take on everybody at once. There is more than one way to kill a rabbit, Simon. But dropping a boulder on the creature is not to be advised.'

Thirty-four

From: Damiarainbow@hotmail.com
To: CatzCampbell@hotmail.com
Subject: art

. . . see, we need a big event, something that's going to grab
the attention of the media, so we can make a splash and
also get our message to old members out there that we've
lost touch with and need to reconnect to. So, I thought –
naturally! – art event. The whole concept of an auction
seems fun and also something the media might pay
attention to – a major artist (i.e. you) giving a work of art to
the college and having it as the centrepiece of an event
where we auction works of art by various people connected
with the college. Not that your profile needs raising, but it
couldn't do you any harm either?

I thought we'd have a theme – all works to be inspired by
the college: its history, architecture, current work, whatever.

So are you up for it?

I know this is going to sound cheesy but I'd really like it
if you were involved a bit in what I'm trying to do here.
Maybe you were right, it is too soon to be starting to think

about having a baby – maybe we need to do some other
things together first . . .

From: CatzCampbell@hotmail.com
To: Damiarainbow@hotmail.com
Subject: lots of things . . .

. . . You're right, we do need to do more together, be more
involved in each other's lives . . . we've made a mistake in
not living together. I can see that really clearly now. I seem
to be seeing things so much more clearly here . . . I want us
to live together.

Come to New York, Mia. Come to New York and live with
me . . .

Damia stared at the email she had forwarded to her office.
Opening the message at Toby, at her desk overlooking the
yard, positioned Catz's plea very firmly in the real world;
there was no possibility here, within sight of the Toby statue,
that the email was a manifestation of her own fantasy world,
the world in which she and Catz and two-point-four smiling,
crinkly-haired children lived in untroubled accord.

'Come to New York and live with me . . .'

Catz's vagueness as to time-frame made Damia profoundly
uneasy. Was the move to New York now becoming open-
ended, not limited by the notional 'year out'?

'I seem to be seeing things so much more clearly here . . .'

Did that include her work, still substantially stalled at
Christmas?

Damia, though she had longed for little else for the four
years of their relationship but to live with Catz, had never
questioned her lover's initial declaration that 'I don't do
living together, it's just not my thing.' To have Catz perform

247

a U-turn now, when geographical factors were disastrously inauspicious, was bitter.

And if Catz wanted her to go to New York, was this her oblique answer to the question of the art auction? Stop obsessing about that little Salster college and come and do something really important – live with me?

A sudden electronic 'plunk' startled her unreasonably: an email had arrived. Damia moved the cursor to her inbox.

> **From:** Peterdefries@dmlplc.co.uk
>
> **To:** Damia.Miller@kdc.sal.ac.uk
>
> **Subject:** Fw: Something alumni should know about Kineton and Dacre College
>
> Dear Damia,
>
> As you will see from this forwarded message, someone seems to have access to your mailing lists.
>
> I'm assuming there's no truth in the allegations and that the photograph at the head of the message is either a digital manipulation or more innocent than the writer implies?
>
> By the way, I tried responding to the email address on the original – my message just bounced back to me. It was obviously an address created just to send this message and then immediately closed.
>
> Is this a job for the police, do you think?
>
> Yours
>
> Peter.

The photograph that preceded the forwarded email's text was of Edmund Norris shaking hands with a man unknown to Damia. Made apprehensive both by the tone and content of

Peter's message, her eyes tracked down to the body of the email below.

Recently, you, in common with many other Kineton and Dacre College alumni, will have received an email message inviting you to contribute to the 'By, For and With' campaign. As will have been clear, though the campaign initially aims to support the Fairings team, 'By, For and With' is actually an appeal for regular tax-free giving to the college.

Before you consider giving money to what you may well consider to be a worthy cause, please take a few moments to consider the following facts about the finances of Kineton and Dacre College.

One: The tendering process for the contract to build the accommodation block which has sent the college into near-bankruptcy seems worthy of scrutiny. The successful company was Smith and Cowper, an interesting choice, given that this firm has never undertaken a project on anything like the scale of the accommodation block before. Admittedly, there is a long-established association between company and college – Smith and Cowper have done numerous, much smaller, building projects for Kineton and Dacre – but this seems a weak reason for taking a risk which has had disastrous results. Surely, the builders normally associated with the commissioned architects would have been a more logical choice?

This raises questions, at the very least, as to the judgement of the Regent Master, Dr Edmund Norris.

Two: Ms Damia Miller, new Marketing Manager of Kineton and Dacre College, has given it as her opinion that the college's recent appeal – launched to fund the building of the aforementioned accommodation block – was incompetently managed. Since she is in a junior position to all the college worthies who oversaw that appeal, it is difficult to see how the current 'By, For and With' appeal will fare any better. Perhaps, as a result of this appeal, too, there will be an overspend resulting in more financial difficulty?

Three: medieval documents were discovered before Christmas whilst the college was engaged in a search for deeds or endowment documents so that it could sell tenanted land to developers. These documents – including a rare 'proof of age' and other, unspecified, papers – were discovered inside the Kineton and Dacre statue together with a set of medieval masonry tools.

Without the approval of his governing body, or the knowledge of the rest of the college, Edmund Norris has sold these unique college artefacts in a private deal to an unnamed collector.

It is only possible to speculate on Norris's motives for acting in such an unorthodox way, especially when the minutes of a committee formed to rescue the college from financial ruin reveal that it was agreed that Sotheby's should be consulted on a valuation before any further decisions were taken.

These are all matters which **must** be clarified before any more money is made available to the college by its alumni.

The message ended abruptly. Damia sat motionless, her eyes fixed on the screen, her heart pulsing furiously with outrage and not a little fear. Her fingers shaking, she moved the mouse and reread the email, including Peter Defries's introduction.

Despite his suggestion, it seemed unlikely that the police would take an interest.

Not knowing what else to do, Damia quickly printed the message and left her office.

Finding that Ed Norris was scheduled to be out all morning, Damia had a brief conversation with his secretary about storage of email addresses and then went in search of Jason, the college's IT technician.

After an instructive thirty minutes, she made her way to the Great Hall, hoping that a change of scene would inspire a new train of thought.

The gloom of a damp cloudy day was dispelled, as she entered the Hall, by the conservators' working lights and Damia was immediately surrounded by vividly contrasting patches of brightness and shade. She was soothed by the careful, unhurried work of the conservators, whose small movements barely disturbed the resonant silence, and she came to rest on a bench facing the ovals on the Hall's southwestern wall.

As she gazed at the mother and child, cocooned in their mutual adoration, the image came into Damia's mind of a recently glimpsed print in a photographer's studio window: a woman holding her small, naked child to her own unclothed body. The black and white photography and entwined limbs of mother and child had made it difficult, at first glance, to tell where baby ended and woman began. Their gaze, intense, unsmiling, had further reinforced the impression that each was equally unsure of the boundaries that separated them. In the indefinable way such impressions are created, Damia had known that the baby was a girl. Mother and daughter, unsmiling, rapt. Wrapped in each other.

Now, with an eye trained by Catz to see intention as well as execution, Damia noted that the white-swaddled bundle clasped to the breast of the woman's green overtunic, found an echo in the white covering of her bent head. Had the upper lines of the woman's coif and the lower edge of the baby's swaddlings been extended to the point where they met, the shape formed would have been an ellipse, encircling mother and child in a visual unity.

Damia's eyes flicked back to the mason and the grotesquely emerging infant. Even without embracing Neil's interpretation of the wall painting, these two ovals clearly represented two ways of looking at the same reality: the horror, pain and danger of birth coupled with the deceptive serenity of new motherhood.

There were always two ways of looking at life, she reflected; sometimes simultaneously, sometimes consecutively. Orthodox Catholicism and Lollardy. Old beliefs, new ways of thinking. A time to weep and a time to laugh . . .

Damia believed that now was a time to fight; Charles Northrop believed that it was a time to capitulate, to bow to the inevitable and make the best of it. Could they both be right? Were fighting and capitulation morally equivalent in the case of Kineton and Dacre's future?

Her eyes fell on the printout she was still carrying.

There could be no moral equivalence if one viewpoint was trying to carry the day by using this kind of anonymous tactic.

Pondering her evidence and her suspicions, she separated a biro from the collected fluff in her knitted jacket pocket and turned over the printout.

'1.,' she wrote in her small spiky writing. 'Not possible to hack into email address lists.'

The central list of email addresses had never been used extensively until her arrival and it existed only in typed form in the Regent Master's office. Her own list was stored not on her computer but on a memory-stick so as to prevent virus-spread to all her college contacts in case of infection. She and Jason had agreed that there were three possible options: either somebody had collated their own address list by means – presumably – of a highly-cultivated network of contacts amongst Toby alumni; or the secretary's typed copy of the email list had been duplicated; or Damia's memory-stick had been taken without her knowledge and copied.

'2.,' she wrote again. 'Easy to access college day & night.'

Simon of Kineton had built a college without defensive walls or inward-looking quadrangle. The huge arches that gave on to the corners of the Octo Yard were like the welcoming arms of monumental largesse, thrown wide to admit all. Kineton and Dacre College might have been constructed outside the city walls but its architecture embraced the folk of the city who were, and always had been, welcome to walk through its precincts and observe the labours within.

Unfortunately, this freedom to come and go in the shadow of the Octo also meant that those with a more nefarious purpose than simple appreciation could enter without arousing suspicion and gain access to unoccupied offices as long as they strode into the Fellows Building with a convincingly authorised stride.

'3. Aim of email – to wreck By/For/With.'

Damia sat back and stared once more at the images on the wall in front of her. Tugging unconsciously at a flake of dry skin on her lip, she corralled the implications of her baldly stated facts into a somewhat shocking coherence.

Abruptly, she sprang up from the bench and found a release of tension in marching purposefully to the next pair of ovals. Her mind tangled with doubt and suspicion, she stared at the small, prostrate figure. Every limb and sense of the poor creature was being poked and goaded by demons whose very lack of humanity was somehow emphasised by their grotesquely enlarged human features – teeth, hands and eyes were all of unnatural size; like Little Red Riding Hood's wolf-granny, these demons were superficially human and fundamentally beastly.

Suspect – the word flashed in her brain – Robert Hadstowe. *Suspect* – Charles Northrop. *Suspect* – Ian Baird.

But . . . *surely not?*

Baird might be prepared to ignore the usual niceties of loyalty, fair play and gratitude, but would he resort to a smear campaign?

Apparently, she had been staring fixedly at the wall painting. The nearest conservator approached to share her absorption.

'Fascinating, that one, isn't it?'

Damia looked up, startled both at his approach and at the extent to which she had been oblivious to all but her own thoughts.

'Have you made any headway on finding the statue that might correspond to this one?' he asked, nodding at the prisoner in his cage.

Damia shook her head, guiltily aware that the putative 'other Toby statue' was something she had allowed to slide into the mental undergrowth.

'If it ever turns up, I'd be fascinated to see if the construction of this so-called cage is the same,' he said, eye-pointing at the prisoner.

Damia had not previously been alerted to anything particularly fascinating in the way the cage was made.

'Is it particularly interesting then?'

'Well, it's just that it's unusual to see a cage made out of wood. And if it's supposed to be a metaphor rather than a literal representation,' he continued, 'it's even more strange. You'd expect a metaphorical cage to be represented as the strongest it could be – or I would, anyway. Heavy wrought iron.'

Damia turned to look at the prisoner's cage. To her untutored eye it bore a strong resemblance to the gibbet-cages in which the bodies of hanged men had, in more brutal centuries, been left on public display. Like a gibbet-cage, that of the Sin Cycle's prisoner was birdcage-shaped, its vertical bars converging at the top while its round cross section was maintained by horizontal meridian-bars. But, unlike the cages in which felons were displayed, the Sin Cycle prisoner's cage did not enclose him completely; his head rose free from its confinement, the cage apparently hanging from his shoulders.

And she had to agree with the conservator – the bars of the cage were plainly not heavy, they were light and slender, though she had assumed that their dark brown colour was meant to imply aged metal.

'How do you know it's supposed to be wood?'

The conservator stepped toward the oval. 'These joints,' he said, his finger extended explicitly but stopping short of the pristine surface of the newly restored painting. 'They're woodworking joints. In fact, they're pretty heavy-duty woodworking joints, the kind you'd use if you wanted something to endure a lot of stresses and strains, rather than just look-ing good.'

'And . . . what? You wouldn't expect to see them on that kind of structure?' Damia was puzzled, as much by where this might lead as by the information he'd given.

'Well, put it this way, this kind of joint – a kind of adapted tusk tenon – was usually only used in building work or really heavy-duty stuff like ox-carts.' He looked up sheepishly. 'Sorry, medieval carpentry jargon – these pegs here, I think, go right through the wooden ring, which is probably com-posed of two layers of wooden strips, with the normal mortice and tenon joints, but then at crucial points these pegs have been put right through the structure and locked in with smaller pegs through a hole that butts right up against the rim and holds them in.' He looked up to see if Damia under-stood.

'OK,' she said slowly, 'so . . . what's going on here – why wood?'

The conservator rubbed his chin with his knuckles. 'Well, these wall painters just painted what they knew. They had a message in mind and the pictures reflected that, but they only had their own experience to go on. If this guy had more experience of woodworking than metalworking, then it's possible he just went right ahead and used what he knew.'

Damia looked at him with narrowed eyes. 'But you don't think that, do you?'

The conservator coloured slightly, embarrassed at being read so easily by a stranger. 'I don't know. But it doesn't ring quite true, no.'

Damia looked back at the oval with its struggling figure straining within the cage, the outstretched hands reaching towards him.

'What do you think it means?' she asked.

'I don't know, but it does strike me as strange that this cage stops at his shoulders – wouldn't it be more effective if he was peering out between the bars?'

'The spirit willing but the flesh weak?' she said, quoting an interpretation suggested to her by one of his colleagues.

He nodded with more encouragement than conviction. 'Maybe. But I really would like to see that statue.'

'Listening to myself say all this makes it sound fantastically lurid,' Damia admitted to Norris after he had read Peter Defries's forwarded email and listened in calm silence to her suspicions.

'Yes', he replied steadily, 'but, nevertheless, someone did send this email to all our online old members.'

Much as Damia would have liked Norris to rant, rave and tear his hair in outrage, his measured words were, on the whole, a greater reassurance of her own sanity.

'So,' Norris said, 'Baird recruits Northrop, Northrop recruits Hadstowe – all come at the problem with their own angles and their own potential for havoc.' He turned around to look at her from his position at the window, 'Do we have any actual evidence of collusion between them?'

'Only linguistic,' Damia mumbled.

Norris was a classicist, steeped in linguistic analysis; his eyebrows shot up questioningly.

'They both used the same phrase when commenting on my capacity to market Toby successfully' she said slowly. "Underclass to overprivilege." It has a ring to it.' Her mouth quirked in self-deprecation. 'Northrop used it as a put-down at the rescue committee meeting after you'd refused to dispense with my services. Hadstowe used it weeks ago, when we were talking at the brazier. He didn't mean it as an insult but he used it in the same context – to comment on how difficult it must be for me to adjust my working practices. And if Charles and Hadstowe are talking about *me*,' she pressed on, 'what else might they be talking about?'

'Yes, I see.'

Damia looked up at him. Norris was frowning, his jaw muscles working as if he was biting down on the idea and finding it unpalatable.

'Edmund?'

'The "unspecified" document,' he said, leaning both his hands on the back of the chair that stood between them.

Damia stared at him, alarmed at the sudden change in his tone.

'It exists. The cathedral archivist agreed to allow it to remain unspecified – undisclosed – at my request.'

'You mean there *is* another document?'

'Yes. Nobody, apart from Mr Gordon and myself, knew about the additional find. People' – he looked up at her with wry amusement – 'were either disappointed at the lack of documents proving title to college land or buoyed up by concrete evidence that the statue was, indeed, Tobias Kineton. It was easy to conceal what else had been found inside the statue.'

'And Neil Gordon knew all about it?'

Norris's eyes narrowed at the accusation in her voice. 'It was he who removed the documents from the statue. Yes.'

Damia's sense of betrayal at Neil's failure to tell her about the other document was tempered by a certain admiration for his refusal to buy his way into her good graces.

'So what was it, this unspecified document? Nothing to do with the college, obviously.'

Norris was silent for a beat, then he looked up to meet her eyes. 'If I tell you, it must go no further, Damia. You'll see why it has to remain anonymous.'

Damia nodded, not breaking eye-contact.

'Very well. It was a crudely executed copy of a few pages of Wyclif's English New Testament. The gospel of Mark, to be exact, chapters ten, eleven and twelve.'

Though this was hardly what Damia had expected, still the implications tightened her stomach muscles as if against a blow. 'Bloody hell.'

Norris's compressed lips and long indrawn breath signalled agreement. Then, into the silence, he said, 'The email was half-right. I did sell some of the papers found in the statue. I sold the Wyclif.'

Damia just looked at him, her mind a barging crowd of half-formed expressions of disbelief.

'But . . . didn't you . . . I mean – Edmund – that could have provided a revenue stream for us *for years*!'

He shook his head, but not in denial. 'I know. But a few thousand, year after year in entry fees, wouldn't solve our problems. We need the money now.'

Damia could not begin to express what she felt. Proof, almost 100 per cent positive proof, that Simon of Kineton had shared his patron's Lollard beliefs. Part of the Kinetons' story. Gone. Its existence, apparently, not even to be acknowledged.

'So, you see' – Norris was speaking once more, – 'the person who sent the email knew things nobody else in college knew. I *did* sell documents to a private collector. And I didn't get the permission of the governing body.'

'You didn't sell the proof of age?'

'No.'

She chewed her lip as she waited for him to continue, thinking of the three people who had put their hands to Toby's proof of age. How valuable would a document like that be to a collector of medieval papers? Much less valuable, she concluded, in monetary terms at least, than a fragment of the first translation of the Bible into English, rough and ready or not. Yet she was glad that it was Tobias of Kineton's proof of age that remained and the Wyclif that Norris had traded for the college's future.

'But,' Norris went on, 'I *did* get Sotheby's to value the Wyclif fragment. I made an appointment on the day of the rescue committee meeting, as we had agreed – to get the proof of age valued – and went down to London early in the New Year.'

'And they put you in touch with somebody there and then who they knew would want it?'

'No. Actually, we went through what I presume is the usual process. At the end they told me what they would suggest as a reserve, were we to allow them to handle the sale, and we agreed that once I'd spoken to the governing body we would schedule it for auction. The Wyclif – I'd already decided on the basis of its likely value that we should keep the proof of age in college.'

'So . . .?'

'That evening I received a phone call from a person claiming to act for someone he would only identify as "a noted collector of medieval biblical texts". This agent said that he understood that a fragment of Wyclif's New Testament was for sale and that his client would like to buy it. Privately. Without waiting for the "piece", as he called it, to go to auction. He said his client – whom he declined to name – would pay twice the Sotheby's valuation figure, but only if I would agree – there and then – to sell the Wyclif fragment to him.'

'What? And he was going to send round one of his men with a violin case in one hand and a briefcase full of money in the other?'

'Nothing so melodramatic!' Norris smiled, his eyes still wary. 'He said that his client was a well-known collector and that if the manuscript were to be auctioned, everyone would know that it was he who had bought it and he would come under constant pressure from other collectors to sell and from museums and collections to lend the piece. A private sale would avoid all of that and he was willing to pay for his anonymity. The agent made it clear that his client would want there to be no public announcement that the manuscript had come to light, much less that it was he who had bought it.'

Damia acknowledged that this seemed plausible. 'So somebody at Sotheby's tipped him off?'

'That's what I assume.'

'So who tipped off whoever sent that?' Damia nodded at the email printout on Norris's desk.

Norris drew in a long breath. 'I obviously explained my actions to the governing body as soon as I was able,' he said, uncomfortably.

'It all comes back to Northrop,' Damia said, almost unable to believe that it could really be so. 'Baird, Northrop, Hadstowe.'

Norris nodded, as if unwilling to utter the simple word 'Yes'.

Thirty-five

Salster, late summer 1389

Dew-fall signals an end to the day's labour for both masons and harvesters and a weary, stiff-backed draggle makes its way in through Salster's east gate as dusk deepens. But some mason–harvesters are already within the city walls, summoned in by rumour and outrage. Sickles thrown down, they are undoing the work that a cloudless day has seen others do. Stones are pulled from their courses and flung aside, mortar barrows upended, tools pulled from the safety of the lodge and scattered around the college site.

The setting sun, low behind the surrounding buildings, casts dark and towering shadows over the wreckers, touching them with the edge of night's concealment. A chill settles over the ravaged site as not just today's labours but those of many precious dry days past are undone. Stones begin to build haphazard heaps where half an hour before saw them laid with plumb-line precision one upon another, the mortar-gaps between barely visible. Now, scattered on their sides and ends, the chiselled grooves that channel binding mortar are

gashed open again and a thin limestone mud drips on to the
ground, hardening the rutted dust into sharp peaks.

'No! NO! Stop! I command you to stop!'

Simon's enraged bellows brought nothing from the rioting masons but black looks and a hail of still-wet mortar
flung at him. Even as he laid about him with a pickaxe
handle, reckless of his own safety, Simon knew his cause was
useless. His own masons, the only men likely to listen to his
yelled commands, were whipped up into a frenzy of righteous
anger before ever they set foot on the site. Men Simon did
not know had come twenty, thirty minutes ago, with sticks
and staves in their angry fists, demanding not an explanation
but retribution.

'You shall not put hewers to setters' work again,' one of
them shouted, pushing Simon from his path and setting to on
the day's building. 'You presume too much, Master Mason.
You are not God to give work ordained for one man to
another.'

'Setters may not do hewers' work,' another spat while his
comrades began their work of destruction, 'so why do you
think you can put hewers to setting?'

Simon flung himself, spreadeagled, against a wall. 'You
shall not do this! Leave this place! God damn you to hell –
go!'

The men he cursed barely hesitated before laying hands
on him and dragging him aside, pushing him into the dust
and half-dried mud. One thickset fellow held him there, a
boot in the middle of Simon's chest. 'Bide still, Master Mason
and you will not be hurt.' He had the calm of one who has
been assured that his act is just, that this act of retribution
will not be quashed by those with power to do so.

But Simon was beyond either fear or reason and struggled to throw the man off-balance and get to his feet. His captor lurched backwards but retained his balance and, coming forward, dealt Simon a blow over the head that felled him on the spot.

More and more men poured on to the site, oblivious of the senseless master mason; men with mayhem and blood-lust in their eyes and alehouse breath. Men who looked wildly about them, not knowing what to do but full of will for destruction. These were not masons but men who could be relied upon to join any fray which offered itself, so long as somebody made it worth their while. Add a palm-greased raggle-taggle to masons whose pride was easily worked upon, and a vengeful mob was the work of moments.

And now Simon's own masons, the journeymen who had set these courses, the apprentices who had barrowed the mortar and carried the stone, were flocking from the stubbled fields to cut down walls and stook the stones in hammer-smashed heaps.

The work of years, his masterwork, his long-awaited chance to prove his worth, fell before the wrath of men who, until today, had been his to command. Against sense, against reason, against Gwyneth's express advice, he had gone his own way. He had not been able to bear to see such perfect building weather squandered for lack of men to set stone.

Thwarted and humiliated by Brygge and the masons' council, Simon had blinkered himself to the likely consequences and chosen to believe that as the college's master mason he could do as he wished on his own site.

Someone had taken the opportunity he had thus afforded them to show him how wrong he was.

Richard Daker came, swift upon the heels of disaster, to remedy what could be remedied and to make the best of what remained. Upon the firm conviction being expressed by both Simon and Piers Mottis that the prior had had a hand in instigating the riot, Daker swiftly calculated in which ways his ultimate purpose would best be served and announced that he would make a gift of the land upon which the college stood to the Church and build, instead, outside the city walls.

'We fought for that land and won in court!' Simon was outraged. 'And now you give it to the Church without so much as a murmur when they have been coiled in the whole destruction of my work?'

'You said it yourself, man,' Daker rejoined. 'They have destroyed your work. And if we continue to build under the prior's eyes, the work may be destroyed again. But allow his pride to swell with this victory, allow him to take this gift and present it to Copley, and we may be out of sight and out of mind on the other side of the city wall.'

'And we may very well be in sight of the French when they come marauding up the river and sack the place!'

Daker laughed and laid a hand on Simon's shoulder. 'You are so English, my Simon! Never let it be a sunny day if there is so much as one small cloud in the sky!'

Simon made an irritable gesture. 'It sticks in my craw to give in to the bishop.'

'But we are not giving in. We are giving him a bribe to forget us. We have challenged him too closely and he has warned us off. If we stick out our chins and defy him, we may fail altogether. If we turn aside, and sail a different tack, we may still arrive at our destination.' His dark blue eyes held Simon in a powerful gaze. 'And my destination is a college which is free of Church interference. I may do that better out-side the walls than in, I suspect.'

Simon fretted still. 'But the rents from the shops where we wish to build were what supported the works within the walls! What will support the work when the shops are gone?'

Daker looked at him, amused. 'Do not be so hand-to-mouth mercantile, Master Kineton. You underestimate my resources.'

Simon felt the hot prickle of a deep blush under his beard. 'I did not mean to imply that you have not the means—'

Daker smiled and laid his hand on Simon's shoulder once more. 'Never fear, Simon, I am not one to take such easy offence. Sit down.'

Simon did as he was bid and Daker went to the door and called briefly. A servant came to his call and Daker asked him courteously to find Master Mottis and request that he attend upon them in the solar.

'You shall see, Simon,' Daker said as he poured wine for them both, 'that I have ordered everything so that my pur-pose will not be frustrated.'

As they waited in silence, Simon covertly observed Daker as his patron sat at ease in his carved oak chair. He reminded himself of what he had observed in Daker the first time they met: the intelligence of a subtle tactician. Daker was no mere merchant. Upon his word fortunes rose and fell, earls were advised and even kings paid heed.

The servant, returning, opened the door to admit the lawyer.

'Ah, Piers.' Daker smiled a small, confederate smile. 'You have brought the papers, I see. You are before me, as ever.'

Mottis returned the smile and inclined his head in recog-nition of the acknowledgement.

'Come, sit with us and reassure Master Kineton that our college will be well provided for, shops or no shops.'

Mottis drew up one of the heavy chairs and sat neatly at the table next to Simon.

'Master Daker,' he said, without preamble, 'being aware of the need for revenue for several years if you are to build securely, and being also aware of the vagaries of business, has seen to it that fortunes in the city will not affect the college's future.' He put one dry hand flat on his small sheaf of parchment leaves. 'I have here drawn up papers of endowment, ceding various lands to the college.'

Simon looked swiftly at Daker. To give lands to an institution was commonplace: to cede them in advance of its actual construction was not.

Daker nodded at him, slowly. 'You see, my friend? I may appear to concede, but I am as resolute as ever I was in my aim. We will build this college, Simon, never fear.'

Within weeks, all was settled and Daker was gone again from Salster, this time taking his wife with him and leaving his son, John, in the care of his tutor and of his cousin Ralph. John was thirteen and Daker evidently believed that it was time that the boy's studies were augmented by an understanding of his father's business.

Once the shops were vacated, winter was almost upon them and no building could be accomplished, but Simon was content to peg out the site to his original design, no longer constrained by street and river. Outside the city wall all was higgledy-piggledy and he could dig foundations in any way he wished.

The spring came and with it Daker and his wife returned from London to approve the beginnings of the work and to see to other Salster affairs. Daker departed again after a month or two, for London or the Continent, no one could say, leaving his wife once more in Salster with John and Ralph. But Ralph was less at his aunt's side than he had been previously, being constantly bidden here and there, hither and yon on his uncle's business. Tongues took up their wagging each time he returned to Salster and Anne's waistline was watched narrowly by suspicious female eyes, but while Ralph was away the gossips found others to slander and slaver over.

And so things continued for four years. Prior Robert, though not by any man's standards a friend to the building work, was at least scrupulous in his dealings with Simon. Daker kept to his word and neither interfered nor burdened his masons with a conflict of loyalties by too-regular appearances.

The college building prospered and, with the care of Toby shared between them, it was understood that Gwyneth would turn her mind to the challenge of giving the college a lantern roof. Scarcely a day went by but that she drew her brows together over the pattern book that Simon had had copied from Ely, and as she studied it, principles and practice became less obscure and she began to have faith that she might accomplish the task Simon had set her.

Thirty-six

The aerial view (facing page) of Kineton and Dacre College shows a college ground-plan which is almost an inch-perfect square. Set within this frame is an equal-armed cross, each projection of which is formed by a block of twenty-four rooms, arranged over three floors. Between each arm an arch wide enough to admit a carriage gives access to the irregular octagonal shape of the central yard in which stands the great Kineton and Dacre Octagon . . .

. . . Between the central cross and the boundary-corners of the square lie the college gardens, walled in knapped flint. Originally rendered to harmonize with the Wealden limestone of which the college buildings are constructed, the walls of local flint are now bare, showing the bones of their construction. Pierced by yard-high Gothic-arched windows which give sight of the gardens within, these walls hide a tranquillity which the original occupants would not have known, busy as they would have been with their garden duties of tending vegetables, herbs and fruits for the consumption of scholars and masters. As each garden is bisected by a path leading from pavement to Octagon, all eight resultant plots are triangular in shape.

Entry to the gardens (limited to vacations only) is via a

gated archway at the college end of each connecting passageway. A glimpse through the Gothic arch of window or door shows intimate, tranquil spaces much enjoyed by the young people of the college for both study and relaxation. Of particular note is the generally agreed convention that the north eastern garden is for quiet study only, with the Napes lawn being laid out, apart from ad hoc arrangements, in the southwestern corner . . .

– from Salster: A Bird's Eye View, pub. 1968

'And you're sure it was this garden it used to be in?' the college gardener, Johnny Newbiggin, asked Damia.

'Yes, the guy who told us about the statue said something about it hiding behind some rhododendrons. Then he came back in the autumn of 1967 and both the rhododendrons and the statue were gone.'

'Good God, yes!' Johnny exclaimed. 'Those bloody rhododendrons – sorry Miss.'

Damia waved his apology off, nodding for him to continue.

'God – forty years ago! Anyway,' he collected himself, 'I wasn't much more than a nipper then, but I'd left school and come here to work for about three shillings a week or something daft. I remember that summer – had a hell of a job getting those bloody rhododendrons up – roots on 'em like nobody's business. They had to go though,' he explained. 'Taking up the whole garden they were, slowly but surely. The students came to old Jack Robinson – his name wasn't really Jack, Alan I think it was, but everybody called him Jack 'cos of being Robinson. Anyway they came to Jack and said, "Mr Robinson, can you do something about these rhododendrons, they're getting beyond a joke." So Jack and muggins here had to spend half the bloomin' vacation digging the damn things out and then turfing over to hide the mess.'

Damia's eye followed his gaze to the corner. The sward was close-cropped and dense, with no indication of the havoc which had been wrought in the subsoil four decades ago. Would it show, she wondered, from the air, in the way that archaeological remains did?

'So you don't remember the statue?' she asked, for form's sake, inferring from his sweaty reminiscences that nothing but rhododendrons stuck in his mind from the garden's renovation.

'Yeah, course I do! Now you've said about the rhododendrons, I remember it clear as day.'

'So what happened to it?'

Johnny lifted his cap and scratched his head. 'Disappeared', he said simply, 'with Jack Robinson.'

Robinson, it appeared, had been rather too fond of a drink and had, on too many occasions, turned up for work the worse for wear.

'Tell you the truth,' Johnny said, 'I think that's why I got taken on – to keep an eye on him and to do the heavy stuff when he was off colour.'

But, Johnny's labours notwithstanding, the problems caused by Robinson's drinking had escalated and one day, during the period of returfing once the rhododendrons had been cleared, Robinson had started a belligerent argument with a PhD student about whether or not he – Robinson – was so drunk as to be incapable of work. This argument had resulted in an assault severe enough for the young man to need attention in the local casualty department. The college had agreed to persuade him not to press charges, if Robinson would go along with an immediate dismissal without notice.

'But why did the statue disappear with him?'

'He'd moved it out of the garden while we did the rho-dodendrons,' Johnny explained, idly plucking a seedling weed and shaking off loose earth from its capillary-like roots. 'Said he'd take it home and give it a bit of a clean – it was all over lichen. Jack reckoned it was a disgrace to hide it there, said nobody in the college cared about it. He did though – Johnny. He had a real soft spot for it.'

'And it was a statue of a prisoner – of somebody in a cage from the neck down?' Damia asked, finding it difficult to believe that a soft spot could be induced by a figure like the one in the wall painting.

'Yeah, more or less. Mind you, I did wonder whether it was some torture thing – the face on it wasn't pretty – looked in a lot of pain.'

Damia remembered Peter Defries's identification with the prisoner and wondered, again, what kind of pain the young undergraduate had been suffering.

'So when he got the sack, he just never returned the statue, is that how it went?'

'Something like that. Even if the college authorities knew it had gone – which I doubt, to be honest – I don't think they'd have wanted to go after Jack for it, not with all the fuss over the assault and trying to keep it quiet and all that. Jack wasn't the touch-your-forelock type. If they'd gone after him for the statue, he'd have made a stink, you can bet your life on that.'

Had she been a private investigator, Damia might have foot-slogged around asking after old neighbours of Robinson's and trawling records in the Family Record Office for birth, marriage and death certificates. But she was a marketer and, the college records having proved to be useless in her quest for Alan, alias Jack, Robinson, she took her problem straight to the media.

The resultant spot on the local news channel was brief but, she hoped, sufficiently intriguing to attract viewers and information from anybody who possessed it.

'And finally tonight,' announced the smiling, rigid-coiffed anchorwoman, 'we're making a return visit to Kineton and Dacre College in Salster. Not to speak to the rent strikers who are still there, campaigning against the proposed sale of their land' (Oops, Damia thought, Norris won't like that) 'but to report on a strange disappearance. Abbie Daniels has the story.'

The outside broadcast camera showed Abbie Daniels in the Great Hall, strolling, as if unobserved, towards the wall painting. Turning with studied nonchalance, she spoke.

'The authorities at Kineton and Dacre College, here in the heart of medieval Salster, would – like the rest of us – dearly love to find buried treasure. But when they did find a treasure which had been hidden away for more than four hundred years, it caused more controversy than celebration.'

Having drawn the viewers' attention to the three or four most arresting and enigmatic of the Sin Cycle's eight ovals to the accompaniment of artful camera-shake and screeching sound-effects, Abbie paved her way skilfully to the plea that Damia knew would come at the end of the item.

She interviewed the conservator who had spoken to Damia so animatedly about woodworking: 'Is it true that you don't really have a clue what it's about?' – 'What would you most like to know?' – 'Is the college going to be in a financial position to look after this unique work of art?'

And she spoke to Damia: 'Ms Miller, it seems the college has lost a statue. How did you make this startling discovery?'

Damia could not have written the script better herself. She was able to outline the college's vision of engaging its scattered alumni, of their participation in the ongoing life of the college, and the use of modern technology in pursuit of this ancient goal of securing the community of scholars at Kineton and Dacre College.

'One of the most cherished institutions amongst our undergraduates, now and throughout the previous century, was this.' Damia held up the 1967–68 Biz Book and explained its function.

'And it was this particular volume' – Abbie Daniels reinserted herself into the piece – 'which alerted you to the existence of the missing statue?'

Damia confirmed that it was and went on to explain – without mentioning his name – Peter Defries's involvement and her subsequent conversation with the current gardener.

'We think,' she concluded, 'that the head gardener at the time – Alan, also known as Jack, Robinson – took the statue away to clean and restore it, and for some reason it never returned.'

'It seems a little strange,' the primed Ms Daniels pointed out, 'that the college could simply not realise that it had lost something so significant as a medieval statue.'

Damia, as they had agreed, explained that the statue had, in all probability, been removed from its niche overlooking the central quad some considerable time earlier as a result of the disturbing effect of its medieval ghastliness on more modern sensibilities, and had subsequently been overgrown in its new, humbler station in the garden.

'So nobody apart from one sharp-eyed undergraduate in the Sixties knew it was there?'

'I think,' Damia corrected, 'other people knew it was there, but he was the only one who cared when it vanished.'

'Could it be so very awful?'

Damia turned to the prisoner oval, the incarcerated figure yearning towards the outstretched arms, head flung back, mouth wide as if groaning in despair.

'Not a pretty sight, certainly. So, how can people help to solve this mystery of the disappearing statue?'

Damia turned to the camera and made her well-rehearsed plea for any relatives of Mr Alan (or Jack) Robinson, former gardener at Kineton and Dacre College, to get in touch to see if the statue could, after all this time, be located and returned to its rightful place.

The following morning, Damia received a visit from Edmund Norris. She had been both surprised and gratified at his habit, when he wished to speak to her, of simply coming to her office and asking if he might take up a few minutes of her time. Had she been asked to predict the modus operandi of a Salster head of house she would unhesitatingly have put money on the 'PA rings minion with summons' model.

Pleasantries over, Norris's face assumed the pained look that Damia had come to associate with news he would prefer not to have to deliver.

'I'm afraid Mr Hadstowe was rather incensed by your appearance on the television last night.'

Damia felt a jolt in the pit of her stomach which accompanied a sudden acceleration of her pulse.

'Why?' she asked as calmly as she could.

Norris sat down on the low sofa and she, feeling awkward as she perched above him at her desk, moved to sit opposite.

'I think his exact words were "So you're still looking for those bloody deeds so you can shaft us."'

Damia bit down on the urge to swear offensively against Hadstowe. 'But that's *not* why we're looking for the statue!' She heard the plaintive note in her own voice, knew it was a futile thing to say.

'He didn't find the notion that we want to uncover the story of the wall painting at all convincing.'

'What, not even after the meeting where we talked about marketing the Kinetons' story? The statue, the tools, the prior's letters . . .' And the Wyclif fragment she added, silently, to herself thinking of the facsimile that lay – known only to her and Norris – in the college safe.

'I'm afraid he seems to think the Kinetons' story is some kind of elaborate blind to hide our real intentions.'

Damia stared at the coffee table between them, trying desperately to focus, to work out the implications of Hadstowe's suspicions.

'Damia?'

There was an edge to Norris's voice that made her look up sharply. 'Yes?'

Norris's gaze seemed suddenly speculative. 'You are playing this with a straight bat, aren't you? This isn't some kind of double bluff we're in here, where the ultimate aim *is* actually to find the deeds and persuade the governing body that Charles is right and we should sell the land?'

Damia froze. How could he think that? 'No!' she protested, hearing herself sound defensive and less than convincing. 'No, absolutely not.'

'I'm sorry.' Norris closed his eyes, as if to shut out the

scene and thus bring it to an end. 'I had to ask for my own sanity. Hadstowe was so convinced' – he stopped and looked at her – 'and you, I have to admit, seemed unusually keen to do this television appearance – to find the statue.'

He stopped, inviting her to fill the silence that suddenly descended as if subject to gravity.

Damia's heart was still pounding wildly, an atavistic response to the sensation of personal attack. She took a deep, steadying breath, but only succeeded in making her head swim. She closed her eyes and massaged her forehead with her fingertips.

'Sorry,' she muttered. 'Just give me a sec.'

Unbidden, he rose and fetched her some water from the small cooler next to her coffee maker.

'Here.'

Realising that he was simply giving her space to collect herself, Damia took it gratefully.

'Can you explain to me why there's such a desperate urgency to decipher the wall painting?' he said, evenly. 'It seems to me, though I'm no expert obviously, that from a marketing point of view, an unsolved mystery is more of a draw than a solved one?'

Damia laughed faintly in her nose. 'True,' she said. 'True.'

'So . . .?'

So . . . how could she explain the compulsion she felt to see this statue, to get to the bottom of the mysteries surrounding the college's earliest years – Dacre's demotion to second sponsor, the appearance of the mason's son in a place of high honour?

Instead she grounded her feelings in the college's current plight.

'If we're going to market "the Kineton story",' she said,

'we need to know exactly where the wall painting, the statue, the tools etc. fit in to it.'

Norris nodded slowly, his eyes on hers, and Damia realised that he knew she had short-changed him.

Thirty-seven

Simon's Salster is a city that nurtures crows as a dog's back breeds fleas. The kennels of the streets, overflowing with offal and the detritus of human and animal life, draw them like stinking magnets and their flapping discord is a menace to the townsfolk.

One of these crows, if it were to circle the city and look beneath it to spy on its human neighbours, would see, just outside the city's high wall, a building like a cross rising from the ground. Tiny, purposeful figures move around the skeleton of what will grow to be a college, their deliberate movements rendered slow and indistinct by the depth of air that separates them from the flying bird.

As the figures move steadily about their well-accustomed tasks, in ruts and paths worn by daily use, a party approaches the empty stone cross. Four people walk together, three led by another who turns this way and that, flinging out an arm here, bending his head there. They do no work, these four, do not turn their hands to building, but merely wander and look.

The crow, were it to fly lower and to have human thoughts and knowledge, might take the folk being led for a family – a tall, well-dressed man approaching middle years whose attentiveness to the dainty, diminutive woman at his side must surely mark him out as husband or suitor, and a boy well grown towards manhood. Whilst the man and woman move as if they are joined by invisible threads that which will stretch but so far before their ends pull together again, the boy wanders freely this way and that, observed narrowly by the man who leads them.

Flying lower still, low enough to breathe the air that the people beneath him breathe, the bird would understand why the woman flaps a hand before her face so frequently, and coughs delicately at her companion's shoulder. For the air is full of the masonry dust that is at once a smell in the nose, a taste upon the tongue and a sensation of settling upon the skin. Stone dust and the dust that churned-up mud becomes in weeks of sunshine – dust is everywhere and no one can help but breathe it. Those who work in it cease to notice it until it begins to line their chests and make them rack and cough.

Flapping up, unobserved in his ubiquity, the crow escapes from the profitless dust of the building site and his wings beat the hot and rising air as he flies back to the city's rich pickings. As he does so, he sees other figures moving this way and that about their business. One, a less than human figure to him, moves like an upright snail, sliding along inside a wooden body. A woman walks next to him, matching his slow progress. The crow is careless of them; he has seen them before – they are no more nor less significant to him than any of the other figures moving through the city's summer stench.

But all around them, the pressing crowds flinch and part as if they fear contagion.

The crow, taking advantage of this avoidance, swoops down to a severed chicken's head. It is still warm, the eyes are barely glazed. Leaping into ungainly flight again, the crow casts its own beady eye at the wooden-bodied boy. He looks back at the bird as well as he may and, as his face works itself into writhing ugliness with the effort of movement, the boy wonders what it must be like to fly.

John Daker was a youth as different from his powerful, charismatic father as Simon could possibly imagine. Fair where Richard was dark, short and stocky against his father's elegant height, John had a direct simpleness of speech and thought which was entirely unlike his father's intellectual subtlety.

Had Toby been whole and healthy, Simon wondered, could he have been such a conundrum as John must surely be to his father? Toby, for all his writhing disorder, wanted desperately to please Simon and would exert himself to that end until he dropped. And slowly, imperceptibly, Simon had found in himself a strange kind of pride in his damaged boy. Toby would never be a mason – his hands might hold a mallet and gouge, but he would never master the precision necessary to hit one with the other, still less with the exact degree of force required – Simon had accepted this, and yet he took pride in Toby's accomplishments. Henry and Alysoun he had urged on daily to master and excel in their chosen crafts, and yet he had never felt the pride in them that he took in Toby's commonplace yet hard-won achievements.

If Toby had been an ordinary boy, would he have shown as little enthusiasm for his father's profession as John Daker apparently did? Would he, instead, have turned scholar, monk, or priest?

John, feeling himself observed, turned. His eyes, when they met Simon's, were of just the same midnight blue as his father's, yet possessed none of his intensity. Would Daker willingly allow his son to leave vintnery to cousin Ralph?

'Would you do us the favour of explaining how the building is constructed?' John asked, holding Simon's gaze.

'Do you mean, what is the ground plan, or how does the building stay up?' Simon asked.

'Both.'

As he explained the building to them, taking care to include Ralph and Anne as well as the eager John, Simon could not help but let his eye dwell upon Anne Daker. Dainty, fragile-seeming, her hair caught up in a gilded net set with pearls, she seemed to glow amidst all the dust and debris of the building site. Ralph took pains to make sure that Anne understood all that was being said and tried to interpret mason's tools and language for her without any evidence of possessing great understanding himself.

Did he always treat her like a fool? Simon wondered. The woman was plainly able to follow all that was said without need for his interjections; Simon, long used to explaining both principles and practice, had an eye well tuned to gauge understanding. Ralph's behaviour would have irked Gwyneth to snapping point in five minutes, but Anne Daker seemed oblivious to it, taking it, perhaps, as no more meaningful than a compliment on her dress, which had all to do with her seamstress and her status, and nothing to do with her own essential beauty.

Ralph's questions were less to the point than his cousin's, but required more attention to answer them. Though not greatly acquainted with building, he thought he knew what a college should look like.

'Why do you build so open, here, Master Kineton?' Ralph asked. 'Why not in the style of William of Wykeham's new college at Oxford?'

William of Wykeham, bishop of Winchester, chancellor of the realm and patron to William Wynford, master mason. The college might be Wykeham's in instigation and patronage, but it was Wynford's in design.

'The bishop of Winchester sees a college as an enclosed order,' Simon replied, 'a small world within which its scholars can live, unmolested. And to be safe in Oxford, it is necessary to provide defences. So Wynford builds high walls.' Within which Wykeham's scholars cower, he would have added, but did not.

'But this—' Ralph indicated the growing college with a long, large-knuckled hand. Simon waited for him to finish, but Ralph had expressed his confusion eloquently enough, and said no more. Evidently, thought Simon, though his uncle was happy to depute Ralph to oversee the college's progress, he did not feel it prudent to discuss his plans with him over-much. So, where he might have told Ralph that the vision he shared with Daker was of a college open to the people of the city, a thoroughfare where they might see the scholars about their work, a building of which they might feel as proud as the guild hall, he said merely, 'There is no need for defences in Salster. The colleges have yet to see violence offered to them by the townsfolk.'

They walked on and Simon looked around as the masons on the site applied themselves with more than customary diligence in the presence of their patron's proxy. His feeling of alienation from them now was almost as strong as it had been when he had been forced to hire them for the rebuilding of Daker's college on its new site. They were no longer brother masons, they had cut themselves down to the rank of mere labourers by their willingness to destroy what had been made. They did not see the building as a being with a life of its own, but simply as courses of stone, one upon another, which made a particular shape; a lifeless form which might as easily be knocked down as put up.

Edwin Gore strode amongst the piles of stone and hammering masons, signing stones with his inspection-mark. Simon had never liked his foreman, though he respected his skills and his knowledge of the masons who worked under him. He had no firm evidence as to whether Edwin, like other masters, had joined with the rioting journeymen and apprentices, but he had made his own judgement. Edwin Gore was the one man who could have stopped the riot, and since it was inconceivable that he had not known of it, his failure to act condemned him.

His eyes met Simon's and then slid away, his head inclining just enough to indicate the required respect.

As they moved on, Simon saw out of the corner of his eye that John had drawn aside to watch one of the masons at work. In response to the brightness of the day, many of the hewers had abandoned the benches in the lodge and carried stones outside to work them on makeshift trestle-benches. It was not something Simon encouraged, as mistakes and misstrokes were more likely on these less reliable working surfaces, but when petitioned he had to agree that it was good for his masons to breathe in as little dust as possible and that dust hung less thickly in the stirring air outside than it did in the enclosed gloom of the lodge.

The young apprentice whom John stood next to was

plainly unnerved by the presence of his patron's son. His mallet and drag hung useless in his hands as he twitched and stammered answers to the boy's questions.

John turned and called to Simon.

'Master Daker, might I try my hand at this?'

'At cutting stone?' The boy was asking to do an apprentice's task. It was inconceivable and yet . . . Simon made his mind up. John was Daker's son after all.

'Walter,' Simon said, striding up to the stammering young mason, Anne and Ralph following his sudden turn. 'Go and fetch Master Daker a piece of stone, so that he may try himself.'

Walter looked at Simon uncomprehendingly. Only masons were allowed to cut stone, everybody knew that. How then could this boy be invited to do so?

'Only a piece of spall, Walter, or a marred stone if there is any such in our lodge.' He tried in vain to wring a smile out of Walter's confusion. 'Just for him to get the feel of the tools, nothing more.'

As Walter hurried off to do his master's bidding, Simon turned to explain how stone was worked from rough-cut stone to finished ashlared block.

'The stone is finished with a drag,' he concluded, holding up the wide tool with its many teeth. 'It's used like this.' He moved it in half-circles over an imaginary block of stone. 'It smooths out the groove-marks of the claw-tool.' Ralph and Anne nodded slightly, mildly interested, but John took the tool from him and examined it minutely.

'Does it not get damaged from so much work with the stone?'

'Of course. That's why we have a smith here. He makes tools, mends them and also sharpens them.'

Out of the corner of his eye, Simon saw the familiar, halting movement of Toby in his frame. With Gwyneth a little way behind him, the boy was coming to find his father. The masons on the site still regarded Toby with wariness and suspicion, and Simon had developed the habit of hailing his son as he came into view in order to signal his presence. The child was delighted that his father should greet him so publicly, and the masons, though they would still prefer not to have had him on the building site at all, were happier in the knowledge that his disturbing presence was unlikely to come upon them unawares.

'And what of these grooves here?' John asked, just as Simon had his mouth open to shout a greeting.

The youth had turned the block on to its back and was running his fingers along the joggles in the sides. Simon turned back to him, satisfied as he heard Gwyneth's carefully considered cry of, 'Master Mason, here is your son.'

'They are to carry the grout-mortar which binds each stone to the one on either side,' he said, slightly distracted by Toby's progress towards him. 'In ashlar facing, the blocks are so precisely cut that a man's eye can hardly see the gap that is left between them, so we must cut a gap for the mortar to sit in.'

John nodded. 'And the gap where one stone sits upon another? Are they not so narrow?'

Simon smiled. 'They are, yes. Less than the eighth part of an inch wide. So we use putty mortar – mortar made just from slaked lime with no sand in it. A thin layer is better than a thick one – limestone mortar dries and sets very slowly and a thick layer would make the wall unstable.'

'What is slaked lime?' John Daker displayed no resentment at not understanding Simon's words, just simple curiosity.

Simon shook his head slightly. He was so used to the techniques of his trade that he forgot others did not know lime from sand. He turned to face east and pointed. 'Do you see over there, on the bank of the river, great piles of pale rock?'

John nodded. 'Yes, I know that's limestone and I know that there are kilns there where the stone is burnt.'

'Yes. That burnt limestone is quicklime.'

Behind them, Ralph and Anne had begun a murmured conversation. Walter, returning from the lodge with a hod-full of spall on his shoulder for Simon to choose from, stood awaiting instruction.

'Quicklime is a treacherous matter,' Simon continued, ignoring both the whisperers and Walter. 'If it should come into contact with water, or any dampness, it will blow, producing an issue of heat. Sometimes it sets fire around it. So it must be transported carefully. They bring it here and we slake it ready to make into mortar.'

'Can I see?'

Simon hesitated, looking out of the corner of his eye at Toby.

'Very well. I will show you.'

Taking the boy by the shoulder he guided him over to the edge of the site, where the lime was slaked in tubs and then ladled out into pans to cool and to allow any unslaked lumps to blow. As they moved towards the cooling pits, Toby, seeing the direction his father was taking, changed tack and began pushing his frame along vigorously to meet him at the slaking tubs. Simon watched his son, noticing how, in the support of the frame, his movements were freer, less jerky. Toby gripped his hand-loops as if they, too, supported him, and now, with his back braced, he was able to move his legs in a jerky, jarring walk, pushing his cage along on its stabilising skids.

Simon was dimly aware that Ralph and Anne had not followed him towards the tubs but were still at the edge of the college walls. Walter trailed in his master's wake, waiting to be instructed how he should deal with the hod of stone on his shoulder. Simon was irritated – could the boy not see that he would do better to wait at the cutting-bench until John had been shown the slaking?

The labourer at the tubs, a day-labourer Simon did not recognise, had not heard them coming. His stooped shoulders moved rhythmically as he stirred the water in which the limestone bubbled and steamed, and as they approached he bent to pick up another shovelful of lime which he slid carefully into the tub.

Toby was labouring in his frame, his face writhing as he fought to be at the tubs before his father. Simon could see that this had become a race. Imperceptibly, he slowed his progress and John, slightly behind him, followed suit.

At that moment, the stoop-shouldered labourer, turning slightly in his stirring, caught sight of Toby's gurning form lunging towards him, mouth agape and unpatched eye rolling. Startled and terrified at this ghastly approach, the man swung around as if to flee, his stirring-ladle still in his hand. As he twisted, the ladle flung outwards, its steaming contents slashing through the air and catching John Daker full in the eyes. The boy screamed and staggered backwards, almost falling as his feet scrabbled on the stone-strewn ground. Walter, whose pace had not slowed with Simon's, was hard upon his heels and John, in his screaming agony, crashed into him, forcing the breath from his body. Walter gasped and doubled over, knocking John to the ground. As he fell, the hod full of stone on his shoulder tumbled forward.

Abruptly, John Daker's screams were silenced.

For a moment, horror held each person in its grip. Then, into the absolute quiet that follows upon disaster's heels, came the sound of Gwyneth running towards Toby.

Her action stirred Simon from his disbelief. He knelt and laid hands on the block of stone that lay across one side of John's head. He pulled it away and, seeing what lay beneath, he retched. The left side of the boy's head, from temple to crown, had been driven inwards. Blood, mixed with shattered shards of bone and a greyish pulpy mass, was too much for Simon's stomach.

Gwyneth, leaving a confused and mewing Toby, knelt next to John's head and put her fingers to his throat. She moved them around, pushed and probed and then put the flat of her palm upon his breast. Finally, she wet the back of her hand with her tongue and put it under the boy's nose. She left it there for half a minute or more and then withdrew it, wiping the moisture away with the palm of her other hand.

Still looking only at John, she reached up and took the linen covering from her head. Unwinding it and stretching it into some semblance of smoothness, she laid it gently over the ruin of the boy's head, covering his forehead.

Standing, she looked down at Simon and held out her hand. Not taking it, he got to his feet, wiping his mouth with the back of his hand.

'He is not dead, Simon. His heart is still beating.'

Simon was appalled. He had been convinced that such injuries must result in immediate death. He gazed at John's head, at the blood which was seeping slowly into the reforming folds of Gwyneth's kerchief.

'Dear God,' he said softly, 'what are we to do?'

'We cannot leave him here. We must take him to Daker's house.'

Where he can die decently, in peace. It hung, unspoken between them. Simon looked at his wife, knew she was remembering Alysoun's father and his agonizing death on a beaten-earth floor. But this death would have no happy issue. There would be no child to be taken in, no mother-love to be satisfied. This death – for Simon did not fool himself for a moment that John would live, with injuries such as these – this death would bring with it only anger, and pain and loss.

And the greatest loss would, most likely, fall on him.

Thirty-eight

Salster, present day

'Bob?' Damia leaned on the door jamb and swung her head and shoulders around the doorway to the porter's lodge to see Bob sitting in front of the computer. 'I'm just going out. If anybody wants me, I'm in a meeting with the archivist up at the cathedral.'

As Damia threaded her way between camera-toting tourists on Lady's Walk and hurried along the busy New Street she brooded over Neil's words on the phone.

'Damia, you're not going to believe this – you know the so-called murder scene in the wall painting?'

'Yes?'

'I know what happened – it's in the prior's letters. It wasn't a murder, it was an accident. And another thing – I don't know who your boy statue is but it's not Tobias Kineton – it can't be.'

He had refused to tell her any more on the phone, insisting that she come to the cathedral so that he could show her the letter in which he had made his startling discovery.

Obviously, she thought, this was an excuse to see her. Or

was it? Was it possible that the news contained in the 400-year-old letter he'd just read was so momentous that she really did need to see it first hand, even if he had to translate what she was seeing?

The fact that Neil had managed, apparently without difficulty, not to disclose the existence of the Wyclif fragment had complicated her view of their relationship in ways that Damia was yet to fully define.

Hurrying up Prince Edward Street, she glanced in through the huge college gate. The low winter sun shone on pale limestone buildings, making the walls glow almost with the intensity of the gilding on the clocktower's finials opposite the main entrance. The grass of the quad was an even green that spoke of obsessive tending and a prohibitive attitude towards shortcuts across it. Beautiful, but in Damia's view cold, without the intimacy and architectural uniqueness of Toby.

Dodging traffic on the Fairway rather than waste time going to the crossing, she slipped into the cathedral close, skirting around Henry Yevele's extraordinary nave to the north cloisters on which the door to Neil's dark office stood.

'A cripple,' she repeated.

'Yeah, OK, not very PC. But that's the literal translation of the Prior's Latin – the Kinetons' accursed cripple.'

'Cursed?'

'That's William's explanation for how John Dacre's death came about. Not a simple accident – and I may say accidents happened all the time on medieval building sites – but something sinister brought about by malign forces.'

'Does he say exactly what happened?'

'That "the Kineton cripple" "caused" a hod-load of stone to be dropped on to John Dacre's head.'

Exactly as shown in the 'murder' oval.

'What does it mean, "caused"?' Damia asked, her mind's eye still filled with the enormity of what she now knew the oval showed.

'No explanation given.' Neil scanned the text before him, his cotton-gloved finger finally coming to rest on the appropriate phrase. 'No, just that. Caused a load – actually the Latin word he uses is "bundle" but I'm guessing his Latin was just crap – a load of stone to fall on the head of John Dacre from a builder's hod.' He looked up, a small grin of derision creasing his cheek. 'William didn't have a Latin word for hod, so he just Latinises the English word.'

'Why did he use Latin at all?'

'Churchmen always did. And he wouldn't want the bishop to think his Latin wasn't up to it – though it obviously wasn't.'

'Not particularly bright?'

'Nasty toadying little toerag. But then what can you expect from somebody who's prepared to be a spy?'

Whoever the statue is, it isn't Tobias Kineton.

A small portion of Damia's conscious mind guided her back through the streets and traffic of Salster to Toby whilst the greater part focused on the implications of what Neil had told her. If the statue was not Tobias, then who was it? And why would the college, for so long, have been known as Toby?

It seemed unlikely, according to Neil, that the statue was a tribute to John Dacre, as the prior's letter referred to him as a 'young man' not a boy, whereas the statue was obviously the figure of a pre-pubescent child.

A representation of youth and innocence? Unlikely, given the medieval mindset.

And what was he looking at?

If he was peering over the Octo at the sinner in his cage, how did the sinner fit into this new scenario in which Toby Kineton – and not some Everyman sinner – was responsible for the specific death of John Dacre?

Toby Kineton. The Kinetons' cripple. Accursed cripple.

Tiny Tim Cratchit with his angelic attitude and his pathetic little crutch; Indian beggars dragging withered legs; wheelchair-bound amputees with tartan rugs. What kind of cripple was Tobias Kineton? Born or made?

If he had 'caused' a death, then, he was not likely to be sitting in a corner by the fire unable to move. Crutches, then?

Dating on the letter made calculations easy; at the time of John Dacre's death, Tobias would have been eight years old. How, she asked herself, does a disabled eight-year-old cause somebody's death?

'Dr Miller. Dr Miller!'

Damia swerved from the path to her office in response to Bob's call from the Octo.

'Hi Bob, what's up?'

'There was a telephone call for you. About Jack Robinson.'

Damia took the vivid yellow message sheet and made her way to her office, reading as she went. The rush of excitement she had felt at Bob's words turned to sick disappointment; the message left no room for hope. Jack Robinson, it told her, had died in the late seventies after (according to the person who had left the message) being hounded out by the college and never working again. Kineton and Dacre College was, in the anonymous informant's view, responsible for Robinson's death and had no right to be chasing statues after all this time when it hadn't been bothered back then. Even his daughter – Bob's unedited message rambled on – poor woman, had felt unable to come back to Salster and had moved away.

So, Jack Robinson had a daughter.

'How are you going to find her?' Neil asked, sipping at his pint. They had agreed to meet in the Unicorn, halfway between the cathedral and Toby, after work.

'Don't know yet. I'll give it a week, see if anything else turns up. If it doesn't, I'll think of something.'

Neil let the subject drop and they drank in silence, surrounded by the forced garrulousness of after-work drinkers.

'How's your wine?'

'It's quite nice, actually, thanks.'

She caught his eye and, feeling a flare of their old intimacy, said ruefully, 'It's my only drug these days.'

His smile transformed his face; the calm, responsible cathedral functionary slipped away and in his place beamed the ardent, intense boy she had supposed herself in love with half a lifetime ago.

'What kind of cripple do you think Tobias Kineton was?' Damia asked abruptly, before he could speak.

Neil blinked ostentatiously and shook his head, pantomiming sudden confusion. '*What?*'

'Crippled. What does it mean?'

'Shit, Mia, I don't know!'

Damia took another sip from her glass, her hand slightly

unsteady. 'Must have felt like God was against them,' she said, her eyes on his shirt collar, which was half in and half out of the crew-neck of his sweater, 'waiting all that time for a child and then . . .'

She could feel Neil's eyes on her as he grunted an agreement.

Twenty years! Twenty years ago – no, she corrected herself, twenty-two years ago – she had had a family; her father had not yet succumbed to heartbroken addiction, her mother had not rounded the fatal bend too fast for the failing brakes of the old bus, and Jimi . . .

'Did you know Dad had to switch off the life-support machine on Jimi?' she asked, almost conversationally.

This time, if Neil was thrown by the sudden dramatic dog-leg in her thoughts, he did not let it show. 'Jimi – your brother?'

She looked up, met his eyes. 'Yes. Jimi. He was in intensive care after the accident, remember? A week later the doctors told Dad he wasn't going to recover, that the damage to his brain was too massive. They could keep him alive on the machine but he'd never be anything but an unresponsive lump.'

'They didn't—' Neil began to protest at the harsh words but Damia interrupted.

'No, of course not. They didn't use those actual *words*, but it's what they meant.'

'And they made your dad . . .'

She took another gulp of wine, not tasting it, seeing again the face of her father, his dirty blond dreadlocks framing the ravages of grief and sleep deprivation. 'No, they didn't *make* him, it was his choice.'

Tony had not told her the truth at the time, simply coming

home from the hospital and announcing, starkly, that her brother was dead. It had been, she recalled now, with the familiar sense of heaviness, as if something in her father had also died, some vital spark gone out of him. It had never returned: he had passed the remainder of his life without any kind of animation.

Much later, a few months before his own death, in fact, though neither of them knew it at the time, Tony had told her what had happened at the hospital on the day Jimi died.

'It's killing me, Mia,' he had said, his fists twisted in his hair, 'the thought of him lying there and then . . .'

Damia had sat next to him, accustomed by now to his distress but still no closer to knowing how to help him than she had been at the beginning, on that first day when the policewoman had come with her world-shattering news.

'They kept saying there was no hope,' Tony said, his voice and face gripped by agony, 'that if he lived, he'd be paralysed from the neck down – he'd always need everything done for him, even breathing. And that's if he came out of the coma, which they didn't think he would – the brain damage was too bad . . .'

Damia remembered the hospital bed where her brother, still and silent for the first and only time in his life, had lain attached by wires and tubes to life. Jimi, who had been the definition of active, who had never come to rest until felled by absolute exhaustion, lay unresponsive and immobile, his face slack in deep unconsciousness.

'They said the kindest thing was to take him off the machine, end it there,' her father had said, grief constricting his voice to a strangled whisper that frightened Damia with the intensity of its anguish.

'They switched his life support off?' she wanted to yell.

'How dare they do that? How dare they kill my brother?' But she said nothing, simply sat frozen and mute at her father's side.

'I kept saying, "Where there's life there's hope!" But they just shook their heads.' Tony did likewise, his eyes fixed inward on their denials. '"No. No hope," they said. "He'll always be paralysed, probably never know what's going on around him, just a vegetable."'

'I couldn't bear it,' Tony sobbed. 'I couldn't bear it, not Jimi. Not my beautiful running boy. He was so full of life!'

Her father turned his bloodshot eyes on to her and Damia felt a shock of unidentified fear pass through her, earthing through her toes, flickering out into the air from trembling fingertips.

'I didn't want him to live like that – he couldn't live like that.' Tony forced the words out. 'They asked me if I wanted them to do it . . . but I couldn't. He was my boy—' His throat closed up and he could say no more.

Damia's eyes were held by the power of her father's stare. 'You . . . you switched the machine off?' she croaked.

Tony nodded, his thin frame trap-tense and shaking with dry sobs. 'I had to! I couldn't bear it . . . I just couldn't bear it!' Her father sobbed, tears streaming down his face now, and Damia, hardly knowing what she was doing, reached for his hand and gripped it tightly muttering, 'It's OK, Dad, it's OK . . .'

After what had seemed like hours, her father, calmer now that the worst had been said, began to speak once more.

'You know what the worst thing was – even worse than watching them take all the tubes and stuff out so I could hold him while he died?'

Damia shook her head slightly, feeling the tense muscles in her neck wince as she did so.

'Leaving him there, in the hospital, with them, after . . . I just wanted . . .' Tony faltered and his shoulders heaved. 'I just wanted to pick him up . . . and bring him back here . . . Bury him in the orchard . . . not leave him there, Mia. Not just leave him there for somebody else to . . .'

Damia recalled, with a numb bleakness, how her father's sobs had overwhelmed him, leaving him unable to speak for the rest of the day, consumed as he was by grief renewed. No wonder we deal with death so badly these days, she reflected, we've allowed it to become some kind of sanitary disposal operation. We don't lay out our own dead, we don't sit with them. No wonder we can't cope with them not being there any more, we've deprived ourselves of the opportunity to see that they've truly gone.

'He wanted to bury Jimi in the orchard,' she said to Neil, 'under the trees where he was always trying to build those stupid tree houses that invariably fell down.'

A faint smile ghosted Neil's features. 'Yeah, I remember. He was rubbish at building things.'

'He had no patience, always wanted things to happen in five minutes flat, that's why.'

'Where *was* he buried? I can't remember.'

'He wasn't. They were both cremated. Don't you remember scattering their ashes to the wind at the commune?'

Neil nodded slowly, though Damia could not be sure that he actually did remember.

She tipped the glass and emptied the last of the wine into her mouth. Feeling slightly lightheaded, from the wine or from the recollection of such anguish, she said, 'Funny now, with the whole Kinetons' cripple thing, to wonder what would have happened to Jimi if he had lived. Can't for the life of me imagine him as a quadriplegic, strapped into a chair with a respirator on the back. And that would have been the best-case scenario, according to the doctors.'

'Obviously, Tobias can't have been that bad. I mean, at the very least he must have been able to breathe for himself, or he wouldn't have survived five minutes.'

'Yeah, obviously.'

Neil reached out for her glass. 'Another one?'

'Why not? But I'll get them this time.'

Waiting at the bar to be noticed, Damia allowed herself to wonder how she would cope with a disabled child, a child who would never run across the playground to hug her as she came to school to meet him, a child who would not grow into normal independence, a child who might have other difficulties too. Had Tobias Kineton been mentally disabled as well as physically – was that what had led to the prior's description: 'accursed'?

If Catz fled the continent at the simple concept of *having* a child, what would be the consequence of Damia bearing a child less than perfect into the world?

When she returned with the drinks, Neil took up the subject of Jimi as if the gap in the conversation had not occurred.

'If things had been different – your mum hadn't died – do you think your dad would have done differently, wanted to keep Jimi alive no matter what?'

Damia gazed into the middle distance, seeing the ramshackle buildings and small plot of land where they had grown up.

'Wouldn't have been ideal for somebody in a wheelchair, the commune, would it?' she asked drily. 'Even if everybody had been motivated and up for it.'

'Which they weren't,' Neil confirmed.

'They weren't really up for anything were they?' Damia turned to him, her brow furrowed with a lifelong frustration. 'It was like they'd used up all their drive, their ambition, when they opted out – they knew what they *didn't* want, but they didn't really have much of an alternative to put in its place.'

'Which is why we left.' Neil toasted her sardonically with his glass. 'But have you found what *you* really want yet?' he asked, scraping froth from his upper lip with a pincer-movement of thumb and forefinger.

Damia looked at him sharply but saw only friendly interest.

'Yes', she said, unaccountably embarrassed by the fervour of what she felt. 'Yes, I have.'

'Catz?'

Damia was thrown utterly off balance, less by the ease with which he made the assumption than by the fact that it was incorrect.

'I thought you said *what*, not *who,*' she griped, her skin crawling with discomfort.

His hand reached out to hers. 'Sorry, Mia – I didn't mean – It's just, isn't that how it's supposed to be when you find "the one" – that everything else falls into place around them? Wherever they are, that's home and all that? Like it wasn't with me and Ange, evidently,' he said, deftly moving the focus away from her.

'Catz has asked me to go to New York – to live with her there,' Damia said, before she could stop herself.

He looked startled. 'Wow.'

'Yeah,' she replied, tonelessly. 'Wow.'

Thirty-nine

Salster, August 1393

A sad cortege walks through Salster's southern gate, over the bridge that crosses the Greling stream, and into the city. Four men, masonry dust thick upon their clothes, each supporting a corner of a scaffolder's withy-platform, are at the centre of this sombre group. They move slowly, not because their cloak-covered burden is heavy, but because the crowd presses around them, eager to know what disaster has befallen the Daker college now.

Ralph Daker walks before his cousin's makeshift bed, the injured boy's stepmother at his side. Both are pale and silent. Neither looks at the other, nor at any other living soul.

Behind the bearers walk Simon and Gwyneth, their son dangling his disordered limbs in Simon's arms. They, too, are silent and their thoughts may only be guessed at. For once, the signs of the cross being made all around them are not occasioned by the passing by of their deformed child, though many eyes turn to him once they have taken in the death-pale figure of John Daker. The crowd questions the masons bearing the boy.

'How did he come by his injuries?'
'Did the cripple have a hand in it?'
'Who is to pay?'

When Simon returned to the building site in the afternoon he found his men leaving their tasks and gathering around him.

Edwin Gore stood at their head, a palimpsested piece of parchment in his hand. He thrust it at Simon. 'We are all agreed on this.'

Simon took it. Written in a hand unused to the lightness of a pen, the words were, nevertheless, clear in both execution and meaning. Toby was to come to the building site no more. Fear, distaste and superstition finally had an ally in disaster. They were determined to endure him no longer.

'And if I do not agree?'

'A boy has near died here today. Because of him!' Edwin snapped. 'If you do not take heed of every man here present – for there is not one who has not put his mark to this—'

'I am master mason here,' Simon snapped in his turn. 'Do you threaten me, Edwin?'

'You are master mason, yes' Edwin's voice was level and his eyes held Simon's 'but your—' his tongue momentarily failed him – 'your *son* is cursed – that is now proved – and we will have no more of him here.'

A cursed child. A child from whom no good could come. So Simon had thought, once.

He did not wish to think it again, and yet, as he walked home through the dusk, he could not rid himself of the thought that if Toby had not come to him that day, John Daker would not be hovering at death's door. And he, Simon, would not be fearful for his future as Richard Daker's master mason.

The news came in the morning. John Daker was still alive, though he had not come to his senses and lay as if already dead, only his shallow breathing and faint heartbeat showing that life persisted.

The way from the Kinetons' house to the college was not long, but that day every step deepened Simon's sense of foreboding. Richard Daker was in France, tending to his business there, but Piers Mottis was in Salster and Simon knew very well that the lawyer was trusted to make Daker's most heartfelt decisions for him, without reference to Ralph.

Simon's boots kicked at shards of bone and gobbets of stinking flesh in the street outside the horn worker's shop. Immediately his stomach turned over as he remembered the pulpy mess of John Daker's head. Crossing himself swiftly and automatically he wondered how long the boy could survive. Surely he would fall into a fever as a result of his open wound? No one dared bandage or salve his head with that grey mass – at once precious and repellent – so horribly visible; the wound must fester, surely?

Yet while John lived, building would go on, as if no one dared admit that he must die. Simon tugged at his beard, trying to free his mind from the image of the boy lying on the ground next to the slaking tubs.

His curiosity killed him – Simon thought stubbornly – like the cat. If he had not asked to be shown how lime was slaked, he would not have been near the tubs and no amount of superstitious dread would have imperilled him.

Yet Simon knew that it was his own lack of foresight which had failed to see how the labourer at the tubs, who obviously had not heard Gwyneth's shout announcing Toby, would startle at the boy's appearance.

If it had not been for that blasted frame! If Gwyneth had been content to carry Toby, as he was himself, then the child could not have come upon them as he had done. If Gwyneth had not been so insistent that he must have his frame . . .

Without the frame, Simon was convinced, Toby would be walking now. It merely hindered his learning, lulled him into ways of moving that made him more dependent upon it. He would never walk while he had his frame.

Simon passed through the city's southern gate, offering muttered half-greetings to those loitering there. They simply gazed back at him in silence.

From the gate he could see the college, its pale stone white against the green of the fields that lay beyond. There was activity on the site, masons moved hither and thither about their daily tasks and Simon breathed again. Though his masons had delivered their ultimatum against Toby, he had been afraid that this would not satisfy them that they would abandon Daker's unchancy project altogether. The fact that they were here now and about their business was enough. Let tomorrow take care of itself.

But tomorrow, or the death that it would see, clouded today. Though Simon had long endured silent respect from his masons, the quiet that wrapped itself around him now was palpable. It stifled him like a heavy cloak on a sunny day and, wherever he went on the site, he could not rid himself of its oppressiveness.

That the masons blamed him for John Daker's mortal injury did not surprise him – indeed, he blamed himself – but their hostility set his nerves on edge. More than one man felt the lash of his tongue for slight or no cause, as Simon tried to brazen his way through the day.

Catching himself glancing around for Toby several times he found that he missed his son coming to look for him. Gwyneth sometimes carried him through the streets, though eight summers made even his scrawny body heavier than she could manage with ease. If only she had done so yesterday and left his frame at home, the accident would not have happened.

But Toby would come to the building site in his frame no longer.

The boy had wept loud and long when Simon had told him that he had decided the college site was too dangerous for him and that he must not come to the building any more.

'I had not thought he would be so distressed,' Simon said to Gwyneth once Toby was asleep.

'He has been distressed since the accident,' Gwyneth said. 'He knows a dreadful thing has happened, he knows that when bones are broken and blood spilled, something is amiss. And he understood the looks, the silence and the pestering of the crowds as we walked John back to his father's house.' She stopped and looked at Simon. 'He may not understand as fully as others of his age do,' she said. 'Nobody can know, since he cannot tell us. But I do know that he understands death and that once a thing is dead it is final and he will see it no more.'

'Master Mason!' The sharp-edged voice cut across Simon's thoughts and brought him back to the building site. Turning around to see the speaker, he noticed that dark clouds were beginning to gather in the south. They would have to stop work before the day was out, and stack withy-hurdles over the newly laid courses to keep out the worst of the wet.

He looked at the man who had addressed him. It was one of the journeymen – Alfred, Aldred? – Simon could not remember. 'Yes?'

'There is someone come to see you. Standing yonder.' He pointed to the north side of the site, where a slight figure stood. It was Piers Mottis.

Simon walked slowly over to where the lawyer waited for him, knowing with every step why he had come, and dreading to hear the words.

'Good day to you, Simon.' Mottis's eyes were sad, and his voice low.

'You give me good day?' asked Simon. 'Have you not come to tell me the boy is dead?'

The lawyer nodded, his eyes still fixed upon Simon, who shook his head silently, not knowing what to say.

'Simon, building must be suspended. There must at least be a period of mourning. It would not be fitting for work to continue as if nothing had happened.'

Simon knew that both convention and respect for Daker dictated that work on the site must stop. It had to be as Mottis said, and yet still he feared that, once stopped, the work would never be taken up again.

'And after the boy is buried?' he asked, his own fears making him brutal.

'We must await Richard's return—'

'So says Ralph!'

'Yes,' the lawyer agreed, evenly, 'but so says Piers Mottis, too. We must show decent respect, Simon. John was Richard's only son.'

His eyes bored into Simon's and Simon shifted uncomfortably. 'It was an accident, Piers! A brutal mischance!'

'I know that, Simon. No one has said otherwise. But it is

not the manner of John's death that we must consider, but his father's grief. We must suspend building until Richard returns.' He fell silent, looking at Simon with a look half of compassion, half of exasperation. 'Rain is coming,' he said. 'You would have to stop work in any event. Pay your masons if they will not stay otherwise. Pay them half-wages as you would if there was rain and wait for Richard's return.'

The two men looked each other in the eye for several seconds.

'Very well.'

Mottis nodded, then, with a small bow, took his leave.

When Simon announced John Daker's death, the masons' stubborn silence broke, like the heavy heat before thunder, into a storm of protest and question.

Half-pay was not enough – it was his choice they should be idle, not theirs – they should be paid as if they were working.

Respect was granted, but why could they not work after the funeral was over?

When was Master Daker expected back from France?

Would they work once he was back?

For all their frustration and resentment at being required to stop work and exist on half-pay indefinitely, the masons' real concern was for the future. Would Daker lose heart at the death of his only son? Would he, finally, take this as a sign that God was not pleased with the building? Would the college be abandoned?

Their questions echoed, without answer or end, in Simon's mind.

❖

By the time Simon returned home, he was half-mad with frustration and anger and grief.

Eight years! Eight years this college had been in his mind from the day Henry Ackland had given him notice that Richard Daker existed and wanted a master mason. A year of drawing and negotiating – the year in which Tobias had been born; years of frustration and thwarted desire as the Church and Daker's family tried to bring the college down – years when he had been unsupported by his own wife, when he had been friendless but for the absent Daker; years of compromise and beginning anew – years in which the college had been destroyed in the city and rebuilt outside the walls – years in which he and Gwyneth had been reconciled – years in which he had allowed himself to see Tobias as he was.

Had he been wrong to do so? If he had not allowed Toby on to the building site as he had allowed him into his heart, John Daker would be alive and building would be progressing, rain notwithstanding.

Even as things stood, all might have been well but for Toby's frame. If Gwyneth had not built his frame he would not have been able to race his father to the slaking tubs; no superstitious fears would have startled the labourer in his stirring.

Simon saw his son in his mind's eye, saw his face working and gurning with the sheer effort that movement cost him, saw him drawing nearer and nearer to himself, to the tubs. Simon could hear the scrape and slither of the skids on his frame as the boy pushed it forward, pace by halting pace. The slaker had not heard it because the hiss of the limestone blowing in the water had filled his ears, but Simon could hear it now – the scrape of smoothed wood on dust and stone, a sound which had become part of his life.

In his mind's eye he saw the slaker turn slightly as Toby neared him – had something caught the man's eye, his ear? – saw him turn and, seeing Toby, fling up his hands as if to ward off evil.

But evil had not been warded off. Burning, blowing lime had caught John Daker in the eyes and he, in his agony, had thrown himself into the young mason, Walter.

Why had Walter followed them? It was nothing but stupidity to follow them like that, with his hod of spall on his shoulder. A grain of common sense would have told him that the stone would be wanted on the bench, not at the slaking tubs! But if he – Simon of Kineton, master mason – had turned away from John's fascination, if he had so much as waved a hand at Walter to send him back, the boy would not be dead.

Simon saw again the image of Toby hurrying towards him; racing him. Small wonder the labourer had been terrified: the sight of Toby in his frame had turned Simon's own stomach once.

'Dear God, what is this thing?!'

Seeing Toby upright for the first time, he had spoken without thinking. Without stopping to consider that Toby, whatever his understanding, would think that 'this thing' meant him, and not his frame.

Arriving home, Simon threw himself up the staircase with a speed born of tight-wound nerves. He flung the door open to see Gwyneth emerging, startled, from the bedchamber.

'Simon!' The door stood open behind her as she approached him. Simon caught a glimpse of his son sitting, splay-legged, on the floor playing jerkily with a tray of wooden shapes of Gwyneth's making.

'He is dead. Did you know?'

'John? Yes.' She nodded, her eyes closing momentarily. 'Piers Mottis came, thinking you might be here.'

Yes, Mottis would not have found it fitting that he should be on the building site as if nothing had happened.

'Building is stopped.'

'Until after the funeral—'

'Stopped. Finished.'

'But when Richard Daker returns—'

'He will find his son dead. And me and mine to blame. I am finished here, Gwyn. We all are. John's death has finished us here.'

He turned away from her and looked through the window. The sky had darkened all around and rain was beginning to fall in heavy, thunderous drops.

'Simon—'

He did not turn. 'Years of work Gwyneth. All brought to an end in one minute! Less – the tenth part of a minute.'

'You cannot know Richard's mind! This college is dear to him—'

'And how dear is *a son?* Richard Daker's only son lies dead. How can he ever pardon that?'

He turned from her again. 'His son lies dead and mine – who caused his death – lives—'

'It was not Toby's fault!' Gwyneth half-turned to the bed-chamber. 'It was an accident—'

Simon swung around. 'An accident brought about by *my son.*'

'But Daker is not a vindictive man – he would not punish you for an accident!'

'The man has lost a *son,* Gwyneth. His *only* son. That is not a matter of vindictiveness or for forgiveness, it is a matter of the heart.' He looked at his wife, saw her desperation, but

311

was powerless to comfort her. 'How can I atone for the death of his son, Gwyneth? I cannot. There is nothing I can do.' He turned back to the window, to the battering rain.

'Richard Daker's return will see our departure, Gwyneth. We are finished here. I am finished with my college. I am finished.'

He gazed out at the sudden drumming deluge, watched the water pouring on to the ground, breathed in the smell of warm, drenched earth. If this continued long the stream would break its banks and flood the garden. The building site would be flooded too, but that would be no concern of his. Not now, not ever again.

Simon wheeled around, unable to contain his grief in his body's motionless quiet. 'Gwyneth! If you had not made that frame—'

His eyes followed hers to where Toby's frame, the third she had made as her boy grew, stood against the wall, its straps dangling, supple and soft with use.

It was the expression of his son's deformity. It was the scaffold upon which his shame was hung for all to see. It was the means by which John Daker had died.

Two paces took Simon to the frame. He took it up in his hands and looked at it. Scratched and dented from being constantly run against walls and piles of stone, its long, narrow skids were scored from being pushed over stony ground. Unslaked limestone crumbs still lodged in small cracks.

Simon's heard the labourer's cry, saw his fearful face as he saw Toby coming towards him.

'*Dear God, what is this thing?*'

With an animal sound that might have been of anguish or of effort, he smashed the frame on to the boards of the floor and brought his foot down upon it.

'Simon!' Gwyneth laid hold of him and tried to pull him away but he thrust her from him. 'Simon, what are you doing?'

He ignored her and brought his foot down on the frame again, catching it a glancing blow and sending it skidding across the floor. They raced to it but Simon shouldered Gwyneth aside. Holding the frame he began methodically to stamp it to pieces. His booted foot smashed down again and again, bending, breaking, as if Toby's frame were no more than recalcitrant firewood that must be broken into manageable pieces.

Gwyneth watched as wood splintered and cracked, joints sprang apart, hoops disintegrated into bowed strips in an act of violent, unwieldy destruction.

When he was done, Simon stood before her, racked with the dry cough that effort always cost him now. 'It will not happen again,' he gasped, his eyes livid. 'Never again.'

Forty

From: Damia.Miller@kdc.sal.ac.uk
To: Mailing List (old members)
Subject: Coming Soon: Toby Blog!

Dear Tobyite

In addition to the recently established forum which allows the Toby diaspora to keep in touch, a dedicated Toby blog will soon be up and running.

A blog will enable all Tobyites to keep up with the fast-changing situation at college, not to mention the views of the various bloggers and those who respond to it on life the universe and education.

So log on to www.Tobycollege.com/blog and become part of the Toby conversation!

Kind regards

Damia Miller
Marketing Manager

Toby Blog 15 February

The current preoccupation is rigs for the Fairings. We have
no choice but to commission a new style – with Northgate
out of the running (pun intended) we need a new-look rig
that reflects the unique Toby identity. The hive mind here
at college had thought of putting an embroidered copy of
the Toby statue on front and back, but since it's now
looking increasingly likely, as those of you who are part of
the Wall Painting Project know, that the statue is not Toby
Kineton after all we need another idea for a new-look rig.
(If you're not part of the WPP and want to know how this
was discovered and where thinking has got to so far, [click
here] to register for the Wall Painting Project and all the
information will be yours . . .)

So far, the favourite amongst the runners is traditional
knitted silk singlet, back half in navy, front half in claret,
embroidered on which, in silver, will be the X4&C logo.
We're also proposing, as soon as a design is approved, to
offer replica shirts, in silk, to any matriculated member of
college. These will be available – through the website –
exclusively to Tobyites. We thought this would be a good
way of allowing the Toby community to sponsor our
runners and get something in return – a unique running
singlet which doesn't shout 'I went to Salster' but allows
one to pound the streets with a certain quiet pride.

So if you are a latent sportswear designer, send us any
other ideas using the comment box at the bottom. We'll
have to make a decision in the next fortnight or so, so urge
inspiration to strike swiftly!

More anon

Tobyblogger#1

'Did the police ever come up with anything about the malicious email?' Sam Kearns asked Damia as the Toby runners prepared for a lunchtime training session. Given Damia's history with the Saxon Harriers, it had been inevitable that she would offer to coach the Fairings team in the absence of any other candidates or the financial backing to attract them. The team's unanimous enthusiasm for the offer had been less easy to predict and had come as a pleasant surprise.

Damia extended a leg, stretched her arms towards her ankle. 'No, nothing. It wasn't really a priority for them. Their internet security blokes came and gave us some advice but that was it, really.'

'Has it had a big effect, do you think?'

'Well, the damage-limitation exercise got the one-to-one email campaign going more quickly than we'd planned, so that helped.' The Rescue Committee's proposal that, over the next few months, student volunteers should make personal email contact with a small group of named contacts in order to welcome them to the new Toby online community – and, ultimately, encourage them to become donors – had been fast-tracked because of the need to show grass-roots college support for Ed Norris in response to the anonymous email. Undergraduates' messages had gone out the day after a strongly worded refutation of the allegations signed by both Damia and Edmund Norris.

Damia stretched her other leg. 'And, to be honest, I think some people were so outraged at the thought of sabotage that they gave money that they wouldn't have given otherwise.'

Sam grinned. 'The cynic in me says that'd be just such a brilliant double-bluff marketing ploy – get the sympathy vote by cooking up an apparently anonymous attack.'

'Hmm. Don't let Dr Norris hear you say that. I think he's

losing track of who's with us and who's against at the moment.'

Sam linked his hands behind his head and swung his shoulders rhythmically from side to side. 'Seriously?'

Damia shut the conversation down with a grimace and jogged briefly on the spot, but her mind was drawn back to the previous night's second meeting of the Rescue Committee.

'Mr Hadstowe,' Norris had prompted, in the quest for feedback from the tenants, 'any news from your colleagues on the estates?'

Rob Hadstowe looked up from the doodles which he had been embellishing throughout the reports from other groups and gazed at Norris, ignoring the rest of the committee entirely.

'Nothing's changed,' he said flatly. 'I made it quite clear at the last meeting that it was very unlikely that any of the tenants would want to work with the college until the governing body had given assurances that, if the land were to be put up for sale, we would have first refusal. That assurance has not been given, therefore none of us are likely to be rushing into business partnerships with the college.'

'And is that the view of *all* the tenants, or simply those you asked?' Lesley Cochrane's face was flushed; she obviously felt that Hadstowe was not playing fair.

'I'm the elected representative, that's the answer I've brought back.' Hadstowe looked her up and down.

'Did you even bother to canvass opinion?' asked Cochrane, her temper flaring.

'Lesley—' Norris tried to interject but Hadstowe ignored him.

'If I hadn't – and I did, *actually* – then I would only have been following the example of the governing body in not canvassing tenants' opinions prior to the decision being made to sell the college land.' Hadstowe spoke as if simply presenting an unpalatable precedent, but Damia detected a hint of triumph. He was relishing this act of revenge.

'Rob,' Norris began in placatory tones, 'it's in your interests to work with the college, you know. If we go bankrupt, the receivers will simply sell to the highest bidder – any assurances would be useless then.'

'Then give us our assurances now, withdraw your request that we sign statutory declarations and we can all work together.'

He made it sound so reasonable, Damia thought now, as the little group of runners began a warm-up jog, but he knew the truth as well as Norris did. The college needed the statutory declarations in order to put the estate holdings on a secure legal footing; and the governing body had voted – again – against giving the kind of assurances that Hadstowe was demanding. And it was Charles Northrop, Norris had confided, who had spoken most eloquently against giving in to the rent strikers' demands. 'He talked about not giving in to blackmail,' Norris said, 'and I have to say he was very persuasive.'

'But you think he was just trying to keep the rent strike going – to keep the college on the brink financially?

Norris had looked at her, shaking his head slowly. 'I no longer know what to think where Charles is concerned.'

Damia fell back to the middle of the group as it rounded the athletics track for the second time and looked around her at the Toby runners, wondering if there was the remotest chance that they could win this year. Without a trained coach and deprived of half of last year's victorious team, surely a win was too much to hope for? A creditable performance was, she suspected, all they could aspire to.

She had watched the Toby/Northgate win the previous year from a position on the Cobbles without the smallest inkling that she would be at the heart of the college's bid to retain the Rosebowl the following May. The Fairings – Oxsterbridge college life in general – had been located very firmly in a mental box marked 'happens to other people'. And yet here she was, in training gear paid for with the proceeds of an unorthodox sponsorship appeal she herself had initiated, running with the cream of a generation, young people who had given her their unhesitating support as coach. This, almost more than the worldwide appeal for the commitment and support of old members in Toby's hour of need, made Damia feel unequal to the job ahead of her.

In essence, the premise of the Fairings was simple: starting and finishing at St Thomas', six roses were to be collected by each team – one from each of the foundation colleges. The first team to gather all four of its members in St Thomas' quad, and thence to pluck a rose, was the winner. Refinements, however, complicated this simple idea.

The roses at Traherne, St Dunstan's, King's, Prince Edward and Toby were located on a trellis erected specifically for the occasion, only the lowest bloom being accessible from ground level. All other roses were fixed at a height that made it necessary – given the further refinement of a rule which stated that no runner could touch the rose trellises with hand or foot – for one runner to be lifted by another. The final rose's position demanded a pair whose combined metreage averaged out at well above the norm. To further complicate matters, runners did not leave the starting point at St Thomas' simultaneously; two runners from each team were sent off exactly one hundred seconds ahead of their team-mates, making it inevitable that each subsequent pair worked in tandem, as it had to be assumed that all roses accessible to single runners would already have been plucked.

The tactical possibilities that these conditions generated were legendary and occupied the greater part of the air time devoted to the Fairings on race day. There was much marking of aerial shots of Salster with on-screen routes as pundits described previously successful gambits and tried to second-guess each team's likely strategy based on information gleaned about its runners' strengths. Spying on the opposition's training sessions so as to predict their likely running pattern was an accepted feature of Fairings preparation, and each college had a company of 'observers' whose size was comfortably equal to that of its running squad.

As well as their lunchtime sorties to the Salster colleges' athletics stadium, Damia and her athletes braved the chilly streets of Salster in the dark of the early mornings, dressed in anonymous tracksuits and brow-hugging woolly hats. Sam Kearns had suggested paramilitary-style balaclavas to further obscure their identities but Damia had not taken this suggestion seriously.

'We need to talk tactics,' she said to her runners at the end of the session as they went through their warm-down.

'Makes a change from talking about finances,' said Tom, a promising freshman, to general nods and grins.

'We've got a strong team here,' Damia continued, contributing her own smile to Tom's tally. 'I think we need to make a big statement. The kind of thing which is going to see us come first or last. We need publicity and I'm prepared for that publicity to call us gutsy losers if need be. What do you reckon?'

Her athletes looked at each other, nobody wanting to be the first to speak.

'I suppose,' Ellen said at last, 'it depends what exactly you have in mind.'

Forty-one

Though the rain has stopped, as the clouds move aside the moon's thin, pale light still catches droplets falling from the leaves of the apple trees in the Kinetons' garden plot.

There is water everywhere. Its floodwater-brown reflects the fitful moon as it stands in puddles and sheets between the house and the swollen Greyling stream. The very air is wet, damp with half a day's rain, with standing water everywhere.

Toby Kineton's clothes are soaked and slimed with mud as he pushes and squirms over the sodden, slithering ground of the garden towards the stream. The small, shallow puddles gathered in the tread of each step of the solar's garden staircase had soaked his drawers and shirt before he reached the bottom, bruised and dazed from a long fall. He had attempted the descent wrongly, head down, but Toby will not need to learn from his mistake; he knows he will not do it again.

As he pushes with wet and shivering legs he can feel the grazing of stones and earth beneath him on his head and back. The cold of the groundwater numbs his flesh a little, but he still knows pain and the sudden sickness of impact as he thrusts his head against things he cannot see. The tears that start to his eyes mingle with floodwater as they run down his face and into his tangled, muddied hair.

His eye-patch lies with his outer clothes on the press at the end of his parents' bed, and both his eyes roll and stare at the moon which looks down, impassive, at his scraping progress. He knows that this light that he sees, imperfectly, is the moon, knows its name and knows that he will not see it again. For Toby Kineton knows what death is. He knows that when a thing has stopped moving, when it breathes no more, it is dead. A songbird stiff in its cage, a kitten caught by the hoof of a startled horse, a rat floating in the flood; they moved, they lived, caused smiles or frowns in those around, but now they move no more and will be the occasion of neither joy nor anger.

Toby has seen this come to pass with a boy and a hod full of stone, and so it will be with this boy.

As he nears the stream's bank, his task is eased; the ground drops away here and he need not keep the path away from the plantings on either side.

The noises he makes are loud to him in the still, windless night. He tries to keep silent, but can do no better now than ever before in his eight years of life. The contorting of his limbs forces sounds from his throat that he cannot suppress. Only lying still would silence them and he will not do that.

He pushes with his bare feet, his curled toes digging into the cold mud beneath them. Now, before he had expected it, water laps against the crown of his head, becoming deeper as he slithers backwards until he suddenly feels its coldness over his forehead. He pushes again and his head plunges down under the water. A moment later it jerks back above the *surface again and he coughs water from his lungs as his stiff and bloodied body falls finally from the flooded bank into the bed of the stream.*

Toby has seen boys swimming in the stream and in the bigger river on the other side of the city when his mother has carried him over to see Henry and Alysoun. He knows it is possible to stay afloat. But he has also seen a boy brought in, dead and grey and bloated, from the river. The river had killed him. Toby does not know how, but it is enough that the river has such power.

The water fills his ears with a rushing, gurgling noise and his eyes close as he sinks. Against his will, Toby's body is fighting the water, struggling to the surface. Making a last effort, he opens his eyes, sees light coming through the murky water. Moonlight. Toby has often wondered whether the fish that he could see could also see him. Now he knows.

He feels himself sinking back down, away from the light, feels cold invading him, his throat producing noises that the water steals away, his body trying to cough the water out. Briefly, his head breaks the surface again and he sees the moon.

Then he sinks down for the last time, hearing the rush and gurgle of the water soften as his movements become still, feeling the sting of water numb on his open wounds as the darkness claims him and he moves no more.

Forty-two

In the early morning of a grey and soon-wet day, the old cat dropped to the ground from the top of the fence and walked across the garden. Its tread was not the circumspect one of an invader but a proprietorial stalk; this garden, lacking a resident cat, was an uncontested part of its territory.

The garden provided good hunting, far better than the ruler-sharp edges and shaved grass surrounding the house that the cat entered by a magnet-controlled cat flap, the house where it ate food without fur or bones. Here, the straggling grass grew right up to the hedge and tangled with low-growing weeds; it stood in dead, damp clumps around the knobbly base of the flowering cherry tree in which fat birds sat; it ran in among the tangle of shrubs beneath which the cat sometimes insinuated itself. This garden offered the kind of cover beloved of the small, scurrying things that the cat, old though it was, hunted with the tenacity of instinct.

The cat made its way towards the house to see whether anything remained of the bread and butter scraps which had been thrown out for the birds the previous afternoon. The bread itself held no interest but the cat had been disturbed in its licking of the butter by the emergence from the house of a human figure. Since it had befriended no humans in this house yet, the cat had retreated.

Now, nothing remained of the fatty treat, scavenged no doubt by some other nocturnal forager. Disappointment did not break the cat's stride and it continued towards the unlit rooms.

It stopped outside the French doors of the kitchen and sat down, curling its tail around its front paws. In the penetrating, self-possessed way of cats it stared through the glass at the woman inside. She was not moving and therefore demanded little notice; indeed she was barely visible, sitting motionless at the table scrutinising something that lay on the table before her.

Had the cat been capable of reflection, or even comparison, it would have noted that this was the same woman who had disturbed it the previous evening when she had thrown open the door behind which she now sat so still, and had stood, water coming from her eyes, trickling down her face, looking, unseeing, into the garden. It would have noted that this was the same woman whom it had seen, later, pacing the lighted house restlessly, like the fruitless quartering of a tabby queen searching for her drowned kittens, while the world outside fell silent under the hunter's moon.

Finding the woman's current level of movement too low to merit observation, the cat disregarded her and began to wash its paws. Discovering a quantity of dried earth on its claw-sheaths it spread its pads wide and gnawed at the baked earth, occasionally licking with a pink and Velcro-surfaced tongue.

So consumed was it by this task that it did not notice the

*woman getting up and walking through the internal door,
leaving on the table the computer which had occupied her
attention so completely.*

*A cat's eyesight is designed for movement: static things do
not interest it. Even if it had cared to look, the typed message beneath the title* Coming to New York *would have held
no meaning for a creature whose vision was not designed for
two dimensions.*

Forty-three

Salster, August 1393

Gwyneth stared at the weighted pulley-line which she had attached to the solar's outer door. When the little weight was pulled, the thumb-latch was drawn up and the door swung open.

Toby had so loved to sit there, in a patch of sunshine, that she had given him the means to open the door himself, and find the sunshine whenever he liked.

If it were not for that length of hemp line, she thought numbly, he would not be dead, for he could never have opened the door without it.

They had brought back his body before the abbey bell rang for the third office. He had not gone far, despite the swollen stream. His shirt had snagged in alder roots at the bank side just before the Romangate bridge.

Hope had failed in the space of a heartbeat when they saw him. He was plainly dead. Though he had been in the water only a few hours and it had not marked him yet as drowned, he was ice-cold and stiff in the grip of death. Simon carried him, his eyes on the boy's face every step of the path home,

Gwyneth holding his arm lest he fall and throw them both down.

Bringing him within the house, they put him on their bed and he lay there, as he had done so often, but still, so still. Though sleep had often relaxed his tortured limbs into the semblance of wholeness, he had never long been without jerking movement, something in him compelled it, whether he willed it or not. And now he would move no more.

Gwyneth stroked the hair back from his pale forehead, wincing at the split skin that would never cause him pain. Gently, she removed his torn and bloodied garment and washed the mud from him with warm water, unable to bring herself to use cold on his broken skin, for all he could not feel it. Drying him gently with a linen towel, she composed his lifeless limbs as he had never been able to do for himself.

Straightening up, she heard Simon taking something from under the bed. He had been there all the while, pale and silent. He had not uttered a word since they found Toby in the river.

Drawing a clean sheet up to her boy's neck, Gwyneth turned to look at Simon. Everything in her was crying with pain and she could not tell whether moving made her pain worse. Every movement of mind or body was agony, and if she could have laid herself next to her wounded boy and joined him in death, she would gladly have done so.

Her eye, fixed on Simon, was caught by a movement in the solar and she looked up to find Alysoun coming to meet her. A servant had been sent to fetch her. The girl's face was streaked with tears which burst forth into wailing sobs as she saw her foster-brother lying beneath the sheet.

She and Gwyneth fell together into an embrace and, for

the first time since she had found Toby's pallet empty, Gwyneth's pain found relief in tears.

'Why? Why? How did it happen?' Alysoun asked as they released each other after many minutes had passed. She wiped her tears away with her finger-ends.

Gwyneth stood apart from her and held out her hand. 'Come.' Leading Alysoun into the solar she pointed to the heap of smashed wood which she had moved into the corner next to the window.

'There. That is why.'

Alysoun shook her head slightly and her reddened eyes looked their puzzlement at Gwyneth.

'Look at it,' said Gwyneth, her voice flat and dead. 'You know what it is.'

Alysoun went hesitantly towards the pile of broken staves and peered down at it. She reached out as if to pick up one of the runners then drew her hand back and spun around. 'It's his frame! What happened?'

'Simon.'

'*Simon* smashed it?'

Gwyneth nodded.

'*Why?*'

'Because he blamed Toby – for John Daker's death.'

Alysoun looked stricken. 'This was to punish Toby?'

Gwyneth's head drooped and she began weeping once again. 'I don't know,' Alysoun heard her say, indistinctly, 'but Toby saw that his freedom was gone—'

Alysoun suddenly became aware that Simon was standing in the doorway between them and the bedchamber. 'No,' he whispered, tears streaming down his face, 'no—'

With a cry of rage and anguish, Gwyneth flew at him. Simon grabbed her by the wrists and held her from him. 'It's your fault!' she yelled. 'It's your fault he's dead! Your cruelty has killed him!'

She tried to wrestle herself free of him, but he resisted her and shouted, 'No! No, Gwyneth! Come and I will show you!'

Gwyneth stopped and stood before him, her wrists still in his grasp, breathing hard. Simon, relinquishing his hold, began to cough but turned into the bedchamber, leaving them to follow.

As they went through the door, Simon crouched down on the floor where he had been, before the tray of wooden shapes that Gwyneth had made for Toby. It was long and wide, with a deep rim all around, so that Toby could push the shapes against the edge to help him pick them up. It also meant that he did not spill them if he knocked the tray awry.

Simon pushed the tray towards her. 'Look,' he whispered. Gwyneth and Alysoun looked down. All the shapes were thrust into the corners – six-sided shapes in one corner, four-sided in another and three-sided shapes in a third corner. Only the eight-sided shapes that Gwyneth had made for him had not been put together in a corner. Toby had built them into a clumsy tower, one stacked upon another, six-high.

'You see?' Simon asked, his voice barely audible.

Gwyneth looked up at him, loathing and confusion mixed in her face.

'Toby built the eight-sided shapes into a tower – *this is the college*. He did not throw himself into the stream out of despair at the limitations of his own life – he *gave* his life, deliberately, *of his own will*.'

The silence between them was filled with their breaths, still coming hard, and with Toby's utter silence.

'He gave his life, Gwyneth,' Simon said, his eyes full of

tears, '*for me*. For the college. *Toby gave his life to atone for the loss of John's.*'

Gwyneth looked at him, her brows furrowed with grief and confusion; at once desperate to believe him and desperate not to.

'Simon.' Alysoun's voice shook. 'What are you saying? A life for a life?'

Simon tore his eyes away from Gwyneth to look at his foster-daughter. 'Yes,' he said simply.

Alysoun looked to Gwyneth, her face full of doubt. 'Could he?'

Gwyneth rose and sat on the bed next to Toby. Reaching under the sheet she took one of his small, cold hands in hers and looked for a long time into her boy's face. Finally her lips moved and softly, so softly, she said, 'I failed you, Toby. I did not know. Did not know you understood so much, did not know you felt so much, my chick.'

Turning to Alysoun she said. 'He sat there, yesterday' – her eyes pointed to the position Simon occupied on the floor – 'while Simon and I talked' – she stumbled, bit her lip – ' of John Daker, and leaving Salster. And when Simon despaired of his college, despaired of atoning for John's death—' She looked at the ceiling, held a deep breath while the sobs subsided in her throat. 'I did not think to hush him. I did not think my boy would understand, still less—' Finally she could hold her tears no more. 'God have mercy on me, I loved him but I did not understand how whole his mind was—' And, as if in great pain, she lay slowly down next to the small, still form on the bed and wailed her anguished grief.

Alysoun turned to Simon, her face still clouded with doubt and suspicion. 'Is it possible? Could he truly understand?'

Simon motioned to the shapes on the tray. 'Do you see?

He has found how they fit together. Not all shapes will do it, but he has used the ones that will – look how he has locked them together.' He looked up at her. 'No one has taught him this, he has found it out for himself.'

When? Simon wondered. Only in the last month or two had their son been able to order his wayward hands and arms to such a task – the knowledge that these shapes would tessellate might have been inside his head long before then. Knowledge walled up, useless to anybody but him, inside the prison of his mind.

Alysoun was still staring at him. 'Did he love you this much Simon? Enough to forgive you all the years when you treated him worse than a dog – and *die for you?* For you to build your college?'

Simon did not reply but stared at his foster-daughter as if her face was strange to him.

'He thought I loved the college more than I loved him,' he said starkly, hearing the truth of it as he spoke the words.

'Poor Toby.' Alysoun's eyes did not leave Simon's face. 'To see so clearly and still to love you.' She shook her head in wonder and sorrow. 'He deserved better, Simon.'

His eyes met hers. 'And he shall get it.'

Forty-four

To: Damiarainbow@hotmail.com
From: CatzCampbell@hotmail.com
Subject:

What do you mean 'not yet'? Not yet as in not until you've decided how to tell me you don't really want to come to New York? Or until you've finished doing something more important than coming to live with me? Or is it until you've plucked up the courage to ditch somebody new and come back to me? What?!

Head bent over the keyboard as she typed furiously with four fingers, Damia's anger, finally ignited by Catz's egocentric petulance, blazed. Her heart racing as if from a panicked sprint, her skin clammy with tension, she neither thought about what she was writing, nor weighed her words. Part of her knew she would never send this incendiary response but still she needed to give vent to the feelings of betrayal and loss that she had suppressed since Catz's departure, to allow herself to acknowledge how profoundly she had been hurt.

To this day she did not know whether cowardice or loyalty had stopped her showing Catz how she truly felt when, almost a year ago, her lover had announced that she was taking a sabbatical in New York, that she would be gone in less than three months.

It had been the weekend following Damia's revelation of her desire for a child. As she did virtually every Friday, she had travelled up from Salster to London on the train, her bag on the floor at her feet giving her no leg room and causing difficulties when passengers on the window side of her wished to get out.

Unable to face the thought of the tube with its stale, tepid air and silent travellers in suspended animation between stops, she had opted to make the three-bus journey out to Catz's loft apartment.

When she arrived, hot and tired, she had seen at once that Catz was keyed up. Instead of finding her lover in the kitchen cooking or lounging on the sofa watching TV, Catz was spring cleaning.

'What's this, the sap rising?' Damia had asked, a sudden anxiety taking refuge in satire.

'Can't believe how much crap there is in these cupboards,' Catz had responded. 'Why do I keep all this stuff?' She backed away from the cupboard on her hands and knees, her hair sticking to her damp forehead.

Damia took in her lover's dishevelled appearance. 'You been at this long?'

'Couple of hours.'

In all the time they had been together, Damia had never known Catz to engage in housework. A cleaning lady descended on the apartment three times a week like the wrath of a particularly house-proud god, and prior to the current, unwonted outbreak of orderliness Catz had always been content to let things accumulate in cupboards.

As Damia made a pot of tea, Catz, allergic as ever to silence, announced abruptly, 'I've got a letting agent coming to see the place tomorrow.'

Adrenalin surged through Damia, her emotions responding before intellect could stir. As a vision coalesced in her mind of the two of them living together in a terraced house in Salster she did not speak, for fear that it was not true, that this was not what Catz intended.

Two seconds later her vision was obliterated, and Damia had never been more grateful for her own reticence.

'I'm going to New York for a year,' Catz clarified, her tone more suited to announcing an inescapable day with a financial adviser. 'I've been offered an artist-in-residence post. It's America,' she stated, as if this sealed the argument. 'It's too good an opportunity to miss.'

Catz's words sank, like heavy metal, into Damia's innermost core, chilling and numbing her and settling with the premonition of slow insidious poison.

'When?' she croaked.

'When what?'

'When were you offered it?'

The answer came without pause for recollection. 'Tuesday.'

'Why didn't you tell me?'

'I wanted to do it face to face.'

'Don't you think we should *discuss* it?' Damia protested.

Catz stopped what she was doing and sat back on her haunches, turning to face Damia. 'What?' she said, her attitude stopping just short of belligerence. 'Like we discussed having a baby? No discussion of *if* – just *when*.' She air-quoted. 'I think we need to talk about *when* we're going to have a baby.'

Damia was completely thrown by the hostility in her lover's words. 'I just assumed . . . I didn't think it was a case of *if*—' She faltered to a stop, her eyes locked on Catz's shuttered face.

'But what if it is?' Catz threw the words out like a challenge. 'If I don't want a child are you just going to go "Oh, OK then, we won't?"'

Damia lowered herself on to a stool at the island unit in the middle of the kitchen, her whole body trembling. If the argument had been about anything else she would have protested that Catz should slow down, that she had walked in through the door barely three minutes ago. But it wasn't. She stared blankly at Catz.

'Is this a punishment?' she finally asked, pain and incredulity raising her voice.

'No. But what you said showed me where you saw our life going. I need to work out where I see it going.'

'You're running away.'

'You're not listening to me, Damia. If I'm running, it's *towards*.'

Catz's stone-cold words had been less significant than her use of Damia's full name. Very soon after they met Catz had, unwittingly, adopted Damia's baby name for herself: Mia. Damia could not recall the last time her lover had used her given name. It had conveyed the impression, more effectively than any amount of raging, that Catz was removing herself quite deliberately from the inner circle of her life.

Damia leaned back from the computer keyboard and rolled her tensed-up shoulders, her eyes on the screen.

'You seem to think I don't exist outside my relationship with you,' she read. 'Well that's insulting and wrong. If you'd been listening to anything I've said in the last six months you'd realise that what I'm doing here is really important to me. You can't just ask me to drop it all and come to New York just because you've changed your mind about living together. I would never ask you to give up painting so we could be together – for crying out loud I've spent four years putting up with you telling me you can't live with me because your art will suffer if you're domesticated! This is the bottom line, Catz – I'm fed up with a part-time relationship but I'm not coming to New York. If you want us to live together, you can come and live here. You can paint wherever you are, my job is fixed. Oh and by the way, the baby issue has become non-negotiable.'

Leaning over and giving herself no chance to draw back from the act, Damia hit the return key and sent the message.

Forty-five

When Henry and Alysoun returned to Simon and Gwyneth's house later in the morning, matters had obviously been discussed and determined between them.

'Simon'. Alysoun faced him without gentleness. 'You must give out that it was an accident, that Toby fell in the water when he was playing in the garden.'

Simon looked at her dumbly, his mind pushing aside her words as a sick person fretfully pushes aside proffered food.

'Simon!'

Stubbornly, his mind refused to take in what she was saying, still less her reason for saying it. 'No,' he said. 'No, I will not.'

'You will, Simon! If you would have Toby given Christian burial, that is what you will do. And without delay, before the gossip hardens into fact.'

Simon stared at her as if at a resented stranger. 'I will not deny his sacrifice – the one perfect act of his poor life!'

'You must deny his *death by his own hand*, Simon! They will not bury one – even a child – who died in mortal sin!'

Simon did not meet her eye. 'You would have him buried by the church which rumoured him cursed around the town to frustrate our college?'

'I would have him rest in peace!' she flared, her voice cracking. 'And do you think my mother will bear his burial in unhallowed ground?' She stared at him. 'He died for you, Simon – or *because* of you, at any rate. Do not give her more grounds for grief by standing in the way of Toby's Christian burial.'

'So I am to do him the same disservice that everybody else has done him all his life,' Simon stated, baldly, his eyes on the smashed pieces of Toby's frame in the corner of the room. 'I am to deprive him of will and love and purpose in his actions. I am to say that he is dead because of his own dimwittedness.'

'If you say it, people may believe it and forget their talk of possession by demons—'

'Who says such things?' Simon's eyes blazed.

'Simon, open your eyes!' Alysoun raged. 'Your very servants are looking at the tracks in the garden and saying that he was dragged to his death by the demons who made their home in him! That they were commanded by the prince of lies because Toby frustrated his purpose in Daker's college! *Everybody* says such things!'

'Everybody says that Toby was cursed?'

'Yes! From the day he first went out with Gwyneth, wrapped in that binding cloth! And this only gives them fuel for their fire!'

'And if I say he sacrificed himself for me?' Simon whispered, as if the words were pulled from him against his will.

'Then they will say that he was driven to despair by his demons and that mortal sin was heaped upon possession!'

Simon sat heavily on the bench beneath the window, his head in his hands. 'So nobody will know his greatness of heart, his forgiveness—'

'Only those of us who knew him, Simon. And we the only ones he would have cared to know.'

Simon turned away, heartsick. It stopped up his very breath to think of denying his son's sacrifice.

'Henry,' he appealed, 'do you believe that those not buried in holy ground do not achieve bliss?'

Henry pinched the bridge of his nose, his gaze locked with his wife's as if their eye-beams were entangled. 'It is not what I think that matters, Simon, it is Gwyneth's opinion – her need and wish – that you must consider.'

Without meaning to, Simon turned his head to the door behind which Gwyneth lay silently with their son. He could see, though the door stood between them, how his wife lay, her hand on Toby's cold hand beneath the sheet, her eyes searching his poor face for a vestige of the boy he had been. Her beloved boy.

'Very well. I shall go and find our priest. I am surprised he hasn't come. The town must be alive with the news.' He looked up at them. 'Isn't it?'

They nodded, reluctantly.

'Will you stay here?'

'I will stay.' Alysoun turned to Henry. 'You go with Simon.'

'Do you not trust me, foster-daughter?'

'Henry may be heeded, where you are not,' she replied, coldly.

Simon turned, his hand on the latch of the solar. 'I shall make them know! I swear that people shall know what Toby was!'

'Simon—'

'Not now!' Simon shook his head. 'Not now. But in my college, I shall make them know. They will see Toby as we have seen him now.'

Though the priest's house of the parish in which Simon and Gwyneth lived was no more than three hundred paces from their door, every step reminded Simon that this was now a world without his son. The sun, shining merrily for once, was one that would never brown his boy's skin; these crows hopping and pecking as always in the detritus of the road would hop unseen by Toby; the scurrying hustle and bustle of the city in summer proceeded as it always had, pitiless, without recognition that a life was ended; a light barely recognised, extinguished.

Simon's feet dragged as, his arms free, he walked with a heaviness he had never felt with Toby on his hip. And though he was bereft of his boy, people still stared and muttered at his passing.

'Curse you!' he wanted to round on them. 'Curse you all for seeing only his deformity and not his heart! Curse you for your credulousness and your demons! Curse you for thinking him witless. As I did.'

The priest's maidservant opened the door to them and, as her eyes widened in shock, Simon observed her fearful hand whipped behind her to conceal the fingers already stabbing against the evil eye.

'We are here to see your master, girl,' Henry said, pleasantly. 'Tell him Master Kineton and Master Ackland would speak with him, if you please.'

The girl disappeared and the two men were left, standing

inside the door, to wait. Simon looked about him, noting, without conscious thought, the timber-frame construction of the house and its poorly kept interior. Girl servants who lived without a mistress could get away with slipshod standards unheard of in a house with a wife.

Abruptly the priest appeared, a small, corpulent man with an unhealthy complexion and uncertain eyes.

'Good day to you, Master Kineton, Master Ackland. Master Kineton, I weep for your loss, but I hope you have not come to ask me to bury your child within the cathedral's precincts.'

Immediately, Simon was stung to anger.

'And why do you hope such a thing?'

As the man faltered, Henry put a hand on his old friend's arm. 'Father, we come to ask you to give the final sacrament to a poor child who has died in the river through nobody's fault,' he said with quiet authority. 'He is a baptised Christian soul—'

'But there were the circumstances of his death!' the man blurted, his eyes on Henry as if willing him to see what an impossible position he was in.

'Circumstances?' Henry queried, his hand tightening on Simon's forearm in a warning to stay silent.

'The child was inhabited by demons—' the priest started.

'Demons?' Henry said, in a voice which Simon had never heard him use before, a voice at once disbelieving and full of confidence in his own judgement. 'I don't think so, friend. My foster-brother was no more inhabited by demons than you or I – he was a poor, slow-witted cripple' – again the warning tightened on Simon's flesh – 'who has sadly and pitifully fallen to his death in the river. We ask a Christian burial so

343

he can rest with his Lord, as we all hope to. You would not deny him that, would you?'

'Not I, Master Ackland! It is not for me and my like to decide when men of authority have laid down a decree. The prior says – on behalf of the bishop whom we have all sworn to obey – that this child must not be offered a burial by the Church.' He cringed slightly, as if to make himself a smaller target for violence. 'You may ask any other priest in the city and they will sing the same tune. I am sorry masters, truly I am, but I dare not go against authority.'

Much to Henry's surprise, Prior William did not refuse to see them but greeted them with appropriate solemnity when they were shown into the room where he was engaged with an amanuensis.

Henry and Simon were bidden to sit, though they were not offered refreshment.

Defying Henry's earlier request that he be allowed to speak to the prior, Simon began baldly and without preamble.

'As you know, my son lies dead in my house.'

The prior inclined his head to indicate that this fact, in common with all others of note within the city walls, was indeed known to him.

'I am told that you have issued an order that no priest is to offer my son a Christian burial within the common graveyard of the cathedral.'

The prior pursed his lips and brought his fingers together beneath his chin in a parody of prayer. 'Regrettably, that has been deemed necessary, yes.'

'So my son is not to be offered the burial of a Christian

soul,' Simon said, eschewing Henry's tone. 'Why? On what grounds is he denied this?'

'Sin had plainly entered into the child in bodily form many years past,' the prior replied, his voice, though full of pious regret, tinged with a fierce underlying triumph. 'Association with heresy and the works of darkness that seek to frustrate the truths of God's holy Church had plainly wrought a most terrible thing in this child. He lived and died not the master of his own mind or body—'

'What heresy and works of darkness is my son supposed guilty of?'

'Not he. But the sins of the fathers are visited upon the children, Simon of Kineton. You may not – yet – reap the rewards of rebellion in your own body but your son, an unformed child, was an easy victim for Satan and his hordes.'

'You are saying' – Simon's voice shook, as did his body, with rage compounded with terror at the consequences of his own actions – 'that because I build a college for a man who mistrusts a Church hand in glove with the princes of this world and believes we should have holy writ in our own language, my son was cursed and possessed by demons?'

Prior William, safe behind his writing table, looked impassively at Simon. 'Because of your association with a man who denies the *truth* of holy Church – the Church instituted and established through Peter *by our Lord* – a man who considers any peasant fit to read the words of our Lord and decide for himself what they mean – a man without learning or guidance! Because of your insistence that learning cannot be trusted to the Church and must be given to men who will look upon the word of God with eyes that have looked upon the nakedness of women and opened upon the sins of the flesh, because of these things your son has borne in his body the consequences of your presumption! He has suffered where you have not! He, the weaker vessel, has been cracked open and filled by the evil that you have welcomed into your house and your soul, Simon of Kineton! And while you persist in this evil, while you are puffed up with pride in your parading of ungodly deeds and intentions, then no, I cannot offer the burial of a Christian to your unfortunate son!'

Simon, hearing both the words and the implication, stared at him, appalled. Offer forgiveness to the son, eternal bliss to this boy, if the father will renounce his associations with heresy and abandon his ungodly work. Toby would be welcomed in death, as he never had been welcomed in life, if Simon would renounce Daker and his college and fall into line behind this fat, stupid man. This man who claimed to know the truth of God's will. This man who claimed that because he had never known a woman in love, never seen the miracle which was a child of his own body, he was fit to look upon holy writ in a way that Simon, and Henry and every husband and father, was not.

Simon took a deep, shuddering breath of air which had the taste upon his tongue of pus and putrefaction. 'You would condemn a child, an innocent, to the fires of hell, because I build for a man whose faith you do not recognise?'

The prior now stood, too. 'You do not simply build – you speak heresy with every breath, Simon of Kineton!' His voice rose till it took the tone of the ranting friars in the marketplace. 'For no one, no soul born into this world, is innocent – man is born of sin into corruption and it is only by turning to God and his mercy that we achieve grace! There is no *innocent* living! Only one was innocent and he was born not of sin but of a pure virgin who had never known a man in bodily lust!'

'And my son.' Simon barged his words in as the prior drew breath. 'How was he to speak the words which showed that he had turned to God? Who are you to judge that he had not so turned in his heart?'

The prior stared at Simon as if he had begun speaking in a foreign tongue.

'He could not speak the words because he was not in possession of himself – he had been given over to evil, as was plain for all to see. Therefore he could not incline his heart to God—'

'And yet you would give him burial if I ceased building for Richard Daker?'

The prior did not hesitate. Plainly this was an easy matter of cause and effect to him.

'If you renounce your sin and turn to the true path, you will break the bonds of sin that hold him in thrall. Your renunciation of evil will release him, too, and God will take him up into Purgatory to purge him of his years of possession and fit him for eternal bliss.'

Simon leaned forward over the table, putting his strong, work-thickened hands squarely upon the surface a finger's length away from the prior's protuberant stomach. 'No man needs to tell me that my sin was the death of my son. Not you, not any man. But no evil lived in Toby. His was a great and noble heart. I do not know the cause of his bodily disorder but no demons inhabited my boy. He knows forgiveness now because he has shown forgiveness to me. God will welcome him into his arms, be to him the father I never truly was. But you, with your—' Simon cut himself short, breathing hard. 'No. I will not speak of you. But look to your own sin, priest, before you presume to sit in

347

judgement on my son who never did harm in this world and could not do all the good that was in him.'

'Never tell Gwyneth what was said,' Simon instructed as they strode away from the cathedral precincts. 'Never – do you swear?' He looked sidelong at Henry.

'Simon—'

'Swear it!' Simon spun around and blocked Henry's path.

'No! I will not!' Henry exploded. 'Are you so certain you are right, Simon? Are you prepared to gamble Toby's entry into bliss – to swear on his hope of eternal salvation – that you are right and the prior – a man of learning and authority – is wrong?'

Simon's eyes held Henry's. He shook his head slightly, as if to clear it, as if realisation and grief were finally beginning to find a grip for their cold, pitiless fingers.

'It is not me or the prior. I would not trust my own judgement against him. But he is right, my association with Richard Daker has changed me. He has not uttered one word of Lollardy to me, and yet I feel its force. I have heard others speak, I heard John Ball all that time ago when the peasants went to London and met with the young king.' Almost involuntarily, Simon seized Henry's arm, begging him to listen. 'They spoke about God without the trappings of the Church. God and man in communion without priests. Each man reading the word of God – not in Latin, like the Church, but in good honest English, the English we speak and deal and swear in. They spoke of the false tricks of the Church – of the falseness of calling things holy just because a priest of the Church has declared them so. Things are things and men are men. Only men can be holy and only by the grace of God.'

'Simon—'

'You are afraid I am speaking heresy? That I will be taken up for a Lollard on the orders of the king?'

Henry stared at him dumbly, then pulled him aside and began walking, Simon following.

'Henry, I will say this then I will say no more. I believe that Toby will receive forgiveness for any sins he did because he showed great forgiveness to me. I do not believe that children are rotten with sin because I do not believe our Lord thought so. He said "let the children come to me. For the kingdom of heaven belongs to such as these." How could the kingdom of heaven belong to such people unless he meant that children were innocent of sin?'

Henry, astonishment written large on his features at hearing his erstwhile master not only quote but seek to interpret holy scripture, pointed a finger at Simon.

'You have some of Wyclif's writings, don't you? Some of his English Bible?'

Simon was silent, then admitted, 'I do not possess them, but I have seen them.'

He recalled, once again, the shiver of awe that had run through him as he read the words of God in his own tongue, as he read the sayings of the Saviour in the language of Englishmen. It had felt like a miracle, as if he had walked with the disciples and listened, with his own ears, to the Lord. Words that he had heard preachers speak came to him with new force, a tingling freshness, and he knew that these words were spoken for him, Simon of Kineton.

Henry, with a disbelieving shake of the head, turned from him and started walking.

Simon, dodging a knot of loiterers in order to reach Henry's side, tried once more. 'Henry, I do not believe that I am gambling with Toby's eternal soul. If the God of the

Church is the God who truly sits in heaven, then he is a God bound by unjust rules such as vengeful men would make. I would not have my Toby with such a God—'

'You would have him damned instead?'

'No!'

Henry plunged heavily to one side as a handcart suddenly thrust at him from an alleyway.

'What now, Simon?' he asked as he regained his balance. 'You do not believe the unrighteous shall be damned, is that to come next?'

'Damn the unrighteous if you will! My only concern in this is Toby.'

'So – what? Will you bury him with your own hands, say words over him of your own devising?'

Simon stared at his implacable foster-son. 'What words could I or anyone say that would speed a soul to bliss or damnation whom God has already consigned otherwise?'

Henry stopped once more, his rolling gait ceasing abruptly and his flushed face turning to Simon.

'So, you are a Lollard through and through, then?'

Simon batted Henry's words away with a wave of his hand. 'What does a name matter? I am done with the Church. It is rotten with power and wealth and its every action is designed to keep it so.'

'For God's sake, Simon, hold your tongue!'

'I will hold mine, if you will hold yours before Gwyneth.'

Forty-six

Kineton and Dacre College, present day

Action Points

✓ DW-R to approach Stephan Kingsley re. logo

    DM to form outline plan for marketing wall painting,
       tools, proof of age as 'the Kineton story'

✓ EN to contact Sotheby's re potential sale of proof
       of age

✓ DM to liaise with runners re coach

✓ DW-R to look into possibility of direct approaches from
       undergrads to old members

    DM to research feasibility of art auction

Damia had always made lists. They gave her a feeling of purpose. As a child she had made secret lists of things she would buy when she was grown up and rich; things that she longed for. *Lemonade*, her list would read, *biscuits out of a packet, fish fingers, my own bedroom, squashy carpets, radiators, a red hoover* (colour had been important to the young Damia, since so little of it was evident in the commune. Even their clothes, once bright, had a washed-out, greyish dinginess), *a tin of 100 colouring pencils, a TV, a cassette recorder, a pair of white trainers with rainbow laces, a fluffy red jumper, that stuff Emily's mum puts in the washing machine to make their clothes soft.* (Strangely, she had not wished for a washing machine. Perhaps it was because she, as a small child, had been exempt from the washing sessions at the huge sinks in the commune's erstwhile dairy.)

How different her list of life's prerequisites for happiness would be now. Damia's determination to let neither the unorthodoxy nor the tragedy of her childhood define her had moved her ever onwards and upwards away from her roots. Each time a little further from the commune, each time a little nearer to her goals. But her emotional life had not moved in parallel. Were she to write a list of her loves since leaving childhood and the commune behind, Anne would be at the top not only of a chronological list but of any list rating passion, self-abandonment, joy.

First love. Both its ecstasies and the hurt it inflicts, Damia reflected, are taken into all future loves. Does it match up, will it be different? She still had occasional dreams of Anne, dreams in which her first love was not a compulsive traveller. And still, after all these years, she would wake to the same feeling of loss.

Would future years, she wondered, see her dreams filled with memories of Catz? An image popped from nowhere into her mind – the frieze of cheering people that she had found her lover painting one day in the master bedroom of their apartment – a strange externalisation of the glee Catz had felt at their almost secret relationship. Would those cheering faces one day crowd into her dream and cheer at other triumphs? Or might they appear in a less joyful form, their smiles and whoops replaced by scowls and threats?

Would memories of Catz's sudden terndernesses – the gift of a beautiful, jewel-like canvas the size of a paperback on the anniversary of their first meeting; her ability to cook comfort-food when she knew Damia was coming to her weighed down by the sadness of a homeless person's death; the way she would shut the door of the apartment, take Damia's bag from her and say 'Welcome home', as if they had been separated for a year – would these things come back to haunt her, to accuse her of foolish haste in sending her email ultimatum?

Damia turned her attention back to her list and to the two unticked boxes.

Since Damia had heard nothing from Catz in response to her own explosive email she had started making plans that would allow the college to run a high-profile art event without the involvement of Catriona M. Campbell. Her idea was to inaugurate a bi- or triennial art prize, sponsored by a company with a suitable portfolio and a public image that would benefit from association with an Oxsterbridge college. Artists would enter their work to be judged by a panel of practitioners and cognoscenti with a national reputation, on the understanding that all entries with the exception of the ultimate winner of the prize would be auctioned at the award ceremony, the proceeds being divided between college and artist. Damia had yet to submit her plan to scrutiny by either of the relevant committees, but she was confident that it would be approved. It ticked all the right boxes – prestige, culture, money.

Marketing 'The Kineton Story' demanded more than efficient planning, however. She knew they were going to need luck, the kind of luck which had brought the discovery of the proof of age and mason's tools inside the Toby statue. Even without the fragment of Wyclif New Testament, the value of these unique, everyday items would only be known when The Kineton Story – part of the college rescue plan – became a reality.

'*Tobias of Kineton, born this Thursday before Holy Week, thirteen hundred and eighty-five. Witnessed by me, Simon of Kineton, master mason, his father.*'

Simon of Kineton, the same man who had wielded the tools found in the statue of the boy who was not – could not be – Toby. Why was the statue there? Who was he? The wall painting was beginning to give up its secrets, but would it finally tell them the identity of this whole, straight boy with his expectant stance? Or why he should be looking across at a grotesque statue of a caged man?

She sat back and closed her eyes. The familiar twin ovals appeared, wall by wall; savage birth and calm Madonna; demon-tormented child and the sinner—

Abruptly, she sat up, her chair rolling backwards slightly on its casters with the speed of her movement. The oval, with its writhing child and blood-red demons revelling in their game of stab and poke, was clear in her mind, despite her open eyes.

Her scalp prickled with eerie revelation.

She picked up the phone with a trembling hand and dialled Neil's direct-line number.

'It's Toby,' she said as they stood before the second pair of ovals in the sunless gloom of nearly noon. She stabbed a finger towards the tormented child.

'This is Toby—'

And then at the caged prisoner. 'And this is Toby. Which, presumably, means that all this' – she performed a pirouette, her arm outstretched to encompass each of the eight ovals in turn – 'is about Toby. The wall painting *is* the Kineton story.'

She looked at him, at his guarded, yet-to-be-convinced expression.

'I think you were right,' she said. 'I think they *are* different versions of the same truth.' She pointed at the demon-beset child. 'Tobias being attacked by evil spirits, which is the prior's version of his disability.' She took two sideways steps and pointed again. 'The cage is a metaphor' – she glanced at him, then back at the oval – 'for the physical state of a child who was imprisoned in his own body, a body he couldn't control. And,' she continued before Neil could interrupt, 'unlike the prior, Jesus – who we presume is behind this patch of mould – is reaching out to him as an innocent child.'

Neil shoved his hands in his pockets and narrowed his eyes, his focus repeatedly shifting between the two ovals. 'Well, it fits,' he said, finally. 'So you're guessing his disability, his crippledness was . . . what? Epilepsy?'

'Possibly. But that would come and go – the cage suggests something constant, always there. Like cerebral palsy.'

Neil made a 'maybe' face.

'But it fits! I mean, when you see a child with severe cerebral palsy trying to do something – even speak or reach out for something – it does look as if they're having to fight really hard against something that is trying to stop them doing it.'

Neil shifted. 'I'll take your word for it.'

Damia looked at the desperate, fixed face of the figure in the cage.

'Have you found out anything else about Toby – the boy – from the letters?'

'Don't worry, you'll be the first to know if I do.' He turned with her to leave the hall. 'Mia, you do know I'm not working full-time on the letters, don't you?'

'Yeah, 'course.'

'But I will try and get the lot read soon.'

'Thanks. I just . . . need to know.'

He looked at her quizzically as she pulled open the small access door let into the massive oak doors of the Great Hall. 'For you or for the college?'

She began descending the dished steps without looking around. 'Both.'

Forty-seven

Salster, August 1393

Gwyneth heard Simon come home from her place on the bed next to Toby. How long had her husband been gone? An hour? More?

She looked at the window, at the sunlit sky. It was well after noon. More than an hour then.

The sky, so blithe and blue, scraped at the rawness of Gwyneth's grief. Such happy sunshine was wrong, unkind. A day of still, grey clouds standing silent and motionless overhead, a pall for her boy lying over all the sodden city, would have been more fitting.

Her motionless vigil, stretched out next to Toby, would have accorded well with such grey stillness in the heavens; but this brightness, this sun that would lure people from their doors and make them linger in street and garden, was not fitting for a world in which her Toby no longer drew breath.

The door opened, slowly, and Simon entered. His eyes went straight to Toby and, for that, Gwyneth was obscurely glad.

Simon sat on the bed and took her free hand in his. She allowed him to hold it, though she did not return his grip.

For a long time Simon did not speak but kneaded the roughened skin of her hand, as if softening her heart to him and to the words he must speak. Gwyneth did not look at him but kept her gaze for her boy.

'When is his funeral to be?'

In truth, Gwyneth did not want to speed the funeral, did not want to give her boy up to the earth and live without any vestige of him near her, but she needed the comfort of hearing him speeded to God.

When Simon did not respond she turned her head slowly, with the sensation of fighting her own will, and looked at him.

'When?'

Simon's answer came in a whisper. 'They will not bury him, Gwyn. The prior forbids it.'

Gwyneth's head came up like that of a puppet jerked into readiness. Struggling to raise her torso to face Simon, she grabbed at his clothing. 'You told them! You told them that he took his own life!'

She felt him take her wrists, his hands gentle, though his grip fought her escape. 'No, Gwyn, I did not. Alysoun and Henry taught me wisdom in that. I did not tell them.'

Gwyneth, her breath coming in jerks, gasped, 'But they did not believe you!'

'The prior says he was accursed, that he was possessed by demons, that his demons drowned him in rage. It is for that reason that they will not bury him.'

Gwyneth felt sudden hopelessness smother her heart. She knew Simon was telling her the truth. She had seen the look on people's faces all her poor boy's life. Many believed him accursed, possessed by some evil force that stole the power of speech and movement from him, pulling at his limbs and twisting his face so that he would howl and gurn when he wished only to smile.

She dropped her tensed arms and Simon, his hands still on her wrists, tried to draw her to him. This she resisted and lay down at Toby's side once more, forcing Simon to let her go.

'You must make them,' she said.

'I cannot, Gwyneth! I cannot make priests go against their own bishop!'

'Tell them he did not drown himself. Tell them you killed him.'

Simon hesitated, as if he had not heard correctly. 'I?'

'Yes.' She did not mean to sound so cold but she had not the energy to force herself to be otherwise. 'Tell them you were in a rage at John's death and you killed Toby because of it.'

She felt Simon's stillness, felt his gaze upon her, but would not look up at him.

'How will it help Toby if I am put to death for killing him?'

Gwyneth put out a hand and stroked Toby's smooth-brushed hair, feeling his chill beneath her hand. A sob heaved within her.

'If you killed him, demons cannot have. If he was not killed by demons, he can be buried in holy ground.'

'Gwyneth . . . they do not just say that demons possessed him to kill him, they say he was possessed of demons from babyhood.'

Although Gwyneth knew this, knew that this was what he had meant to say, still she stubbornly held to her plan.

359

'Lie, Simon. Tell them that you procured a priest – a poor priest, one of those who wander – and he drove the demons out—'

'Gwyneth—'

Simon's patient voice caused a sudden rage to rise up in Gwyneth and she sat again and faced him, shaking with fury.

'You will do whatever you must to see my boy given Christian burial! I do not care whether you lie, cheat, bribe or threaten. But if you do not see this thing done then your college will never be built, I swear that on my life.'

She stared into his eyes, her whole will blazing in every word.

Simon's face seemed turned to stone beneath her gaze. His hair and beard were grey now and his face, this day at least, was a colour not dissimilar. She was suddenly filled with the memory of how gross his face had seemed when she looked at him after Toby's birth; how huge his features had seemed, how coarse his skin, how intrusive and ugly the hair that sprang from his face. Her eyes had, it seemed, been tuned to find only the fineness of her baby's skin lovely to her, only the soft downiness of his hair, the tiny perfection of his features.

She looked at her husband now, seeing him with a stranger's eyes. A man no longer young, though still in vigorous health. More than fifty summers had drained his skin of the smoothness of youth and deep lines scored the flesh between his eyes, pulling like purse-strings at the crows' feet that ran into his uncapped hair.

'There is someone who might help—' His voice was faint with unaccustomed hesitancy.

'Then find him.'

Simon's eyes searched her face, as if looking for a chink into which he could slip the lever of his argument.

'He would listen to you more readily—'

At once Gwyneth felt the stab of panic. She turned to her boy and gripped his cold and unresponsive hand. 'No! No, I will not leave him!'

'Gwyneth, Nicholas Brygge is no friend to me. But he would listen to you, he holds you in high regard.'

Gwyneth lay down, her hand still gripping Toby's. 'Then you must plead on my behalf and make him your friend. I will not leave my boy.'

As Simon walked the streets to Nicholas Brygge's door, he felt that every eye upon him must be hostile. Had this blasphemous lie about his son truly been believed all the years they had lived in Salster? Had Gwyneth truly run the gamut of a populace who saw her son as a thing not quite human every time she had defied them – and his own wishes – by carrying their son forth into the world?

He stepped out, cautious with his eyes as much as with his feet, keeping his gaze before him and not on those whose stare rested on his passing. In Simon's nostrils the scent of death and decay was everywhere, from the shit that his feet could not help but tread upon to the rotting meat that even the lowest butchers had despaired of passing off as wholesome and had thrown into the street for the dogs and crows.

The faint breeze brought the stench of the tanning vats to his nose from beyond the city wall. The devil alone knew what they put in those vats beyond piss and oak bark, but it stank worse than the scraped hides in the sun.

Two crows, flapping a beak-raised argument over a gobbet of flesh, banged against his shins as he walked past them and he lashed out with his booted foot, nearly losing his balance when the birds neatly avoided his kick.

'Master Kineton?'

He looked down as a staying hand was put on his arm and an old, dark-clad woman looked up at him. She spoke from a mouth that held few teeth he could see, and he would have pulled away but for her words, which came in a steady voice, though muffled by gum-sucked lips.

'I hear the talk is your poor dead boy was cursed and home to Satan's demons,' she began, 'but you should not think that all believe such things.' She looked up at him, compassion either for him or for Toby in her sunken face. 'He was a poor soul, but anybody who had eyes to see the way he looked at his mother knows that goodness and love lived in him, not the demons of the Devil.'

Simon stared at her, unable to find the words to express what he felt at such unlooked-for kindness.

'I have known what it is to bury children,' the old woman said. 'And grandchildren too.' She gazed at him with clear, blue eyes and Simon fleetingly wondered what she had looked like as a young girl, with those eyes, so blue.

'Thank you, mistress,' he finally said. 'You have cheered my heart.'

She nodded, her eyes still on him: accepting his gratitude, confirming that this had been her intention. 'I will pray for you. And for your boy.'

He bowed his head and she, releasing his forearm from her grip, turned away, her errand done.

When Simon was shown into the mayor's hall he was confounded once more, this time by the warmth and compassion with which Nicholas Brygge greeted him. Brygge dismissed the men – unknown to Simon – who had been in conversation with him over some business when Simon entered, and sent a servant for wine and sweet cakes.

The mayor sat, leaning towards Simon, who was seated in a sturdy oak chair opposite him. 'Today is a day on which any man with sons living feels himself ill at ease before you, Simon of Kineton. I am truly sorry for your loss.' He paused for a moment to allow Simon's bowed thanks and then said, 'I am sorry too to hear that the Church is barring the door to you in the matter of a burial with due rites.' Again he paused, his eyes on the mute Simon. 'Sorry, but hardly surprised.'

'Because I build for a heretic.'

'Because of *what* you build. They would not care a fart in the wind if you built him a house or a row of shops. But you build him the means with which to challenge them in their own pit. The pit where they have been undisputed cock of the walk. Now you introduce a new bird, a foreign bird, to the fight. Now they are at a disadvantage, they do not know the rules. If they begin to lose in such circumstances they have only two options – walk away poorer and listen to the laughter that pursues them or draw a knife and demand that you leave the contest on pain of your flesh.'

Simon kneaded the stiff and weary flesh of his face. 'The Church will never walk away poorer.'

'And its knives are sharp.'

Simon nodded and looked up as the servant returned.

'The prior calls him accursed, possessed,' he said when the man had gone, as if there had been no interruption in their conversation. He took a mouthful of wine, not looking at Brygge but wanting to hear from other man's lips the certainty that it was not so, that his son had not been cursed.

'The Church cannot admit to ignorance,' Brygge responded.

'It is afraid of ignorance, afraid that to say we do not know why something is so will allow people to come to their own conclusions.'

'And what conclusion do you come to about my son?' Simon looked up at the mayor, unable to mask the hint of challenge.

Brygge did not hesitate. 'I come to no conclusions, Master Mason. I did not know the child, barely saw him. But you knew him, lived in his company every day. What conclusion did you reach?'

Simon sat, silent, for a time. The mayor, unperturbed, waited for such answer as should come.

Finally, Simon spoke, his eyes fixed, unfocused, on the floor at Brygge's feet.

'I prayed for a son who would be like me. And God, in his wisdom, gave me what I asked. For I have been crippled in spirit by my own ambition. And because of that my son is dead.'

He bowed his head but would not weep before the mayor.

'How?' Brygge asked simply.

'By his own hand,' Simon said, indistinctly, his head still bowed. 'He dragged himself to the river and drowned himself so that the scales should be even between me and Daker. To atone. To persuade Daker to let me build his college.'

'You are certain this was the reason?'

Simon thought of the small stack of octagonal wooden pieces placed, with infinite patience, one on top of the other in the centre of the tray.

'Yes, I am certain.'

Brygge looked at his cup, his eye appraising, as if he was considering making an offer on it. 'The prior has not offered

you a bargain? Your son's burial for the cessation of building?'

Simon's eyes locked with those of the mayor and he knew
that the man had seen the truth, that there was nothing to be
gained by denial apart from Brygge's contempt.

'Yes, he put that offer before me.'

'But you were not minded to accept?'

Simon heaved a sigh. 'If he had been murdered, or died
in his sleep, or if it had been the accident that I have given
out, then yes, I would have accepted. But my son's life ended
because he was striking a bargain with Daker. A son for a
son, so that the college might be built. This was the one thing
of worth that he felt he could do for me, the only way in
which he would ever be able to be part of a building. I cannot
deny his wish.'

'Even if it means his entry into bliss?'

Simon stared at Brygge's unreadable face. This was the
sticking-point. The words he spoke now would put him in
the mayor's party, in the mayor's debt and power as long as
he lived.

'I do not believe that innocents are consigned to hell for
man's negligence,' he said, sealing his fate with a word.

'You do not believe that infants are born in a state of sin?'

Simon was unflinching. 'No.'

'Or that the Church can purchase entry to heaven by its
rites, deny such entry by the withholding of the same?'

'No.'

There was little reaction from Brygge beyond a single,
considering nod.

'Wait here,' he said, rising and leaving the hall.

Watching him out through the central door, Simon's eye
was caught by something on the end wall, the wall facing the

long table where Brygge had been doing business when Simon entered.

He got up and walked over to scrutinise it more closely. His eyes were ruined from too much close work in the gloom of the lodge and he no longer saw well at a distance. He knew it was only a matter of time before close work began to be difficult too.

As he came closer he could see that the thing which had caught his attention was a map, painted on to the plaster of the wall.

Simon was unaccustomed to maps and could not tell what he was looking at. Green and brown were the dominant colours, with some red and black. He went closer and made out twelve heads spaced at equal intervals around the oval perimeter of the map: what, he wondered, did they signify? Was this a pagan map, with deities watching over the world?

'Ah,' he heard Brygge say as he re-entered the hall, 'you have found my map.'

'Where does it come from?' Simon blurted, embarrassed at being caught peering.

'It is a copy of Ranulf Higden's map, from his *Poly-chronicon*,' the mayor said. 'I had it copied to remind me that although Salster may feel like the centre of the world, and all the goings-on here of the greatest significance, there are other places, other ways. That God has created a world of infinite strangeness. And,' he said with a smile, 'beings more out-landish and inexplicable than priors and bishops.'

'Or even kings,' muttered Simon.

'Or even kings,' Brygge confirmed, apparently amused.

'What do these heads signify?' Simon asked, suddenly unabashed at his ignorance.

'The twelve winds that blow across the surface of the world.'

Brygge went on to point out Jerusalem, in the east, at the top of the map; Santiago de Compostela, Rome and Babylon, each city drawn in magnificent size, cathedral-like structure writ large, crenellated buildings emphasising their importance.

'And this, here?'

'Africa.'

'A land of few cities, it seems.'

'A land of uncivilised savages who do not see fit to build like you or me, Master Mason.'

Brygge showed Simon the strange beasts who inhabited lands of which he had never heard, told him the names of the green mountains and traced the outline of a red area – 'the Red Sea'.

Simon scanned the map. 'The world is a wondrous place.'

'Yes, with more wonders than we, in our present time, can know of.'

Simon looked at him curiously. 'You speak more like a natural philosopher than a man of commerce.'

Brygge laughed delightedly. 'May a man of commerce not wonder about things unconnected with trade and the monetary value of objects, Master Kineton? Do you not lift your eyes occasionally from your stones and wonder about matters that have nothing to do with buildings and masonry? Matters of theology and religion, perhaps?'

Simon met his eye and, despite the dragging weight of grief and sadness, found himself answering with a smile.

'Do not be quick to do the Church's work for it, Simon,' the mayor counselled, lightly. 'It has influence enough to keep men's thoughts away from God and his works without you performing the work on its behalf.'

There was a silence while the two men regarded each other, aware that they had entered into territory where trust would be essential, both knowing things about the other that could send them to the scaffold.

Offering more wine, Brygge drew Simon back to the chairs and, as they sat, explained, 'I have sent for a man – a learned man and a priest – who will help you.'

'How soon may we expect him?'

'My servant will come back with him, or with word of him. We will not have to wait the hour out, my servant has taken a horse from the stables.'

Simon looked at him in amazement. A servant, given a horse of his master's to ride.

'When Adam delf, and Eve span,' chanted the mayor, a smile quirking his lips as he held Simon's eyes, 'who was then the gentleman?'

'Now we have a priest,' Brygge began after a period of silence between them, 'we must think where the ceremony will be carried out.'

The ceremony. The burial of his son. The interring of the mortal remains of Tobias Kineton, much desired, still more greatly mourned, son.

Simon looked at Brygge. 'The Church will not offer him room and I will not give the prior or Copley the satisfaction of discovering us furtive about the task after midnight lest any mortal see.'

'No.'

'I do not set store by the Church's notion of hallowed

ground,' Simon began, 'but I would like my son to lie somewhere proper.'

The mayor regarded him, his eyes level, his expression impassive. 'You are thinking of your college.'

Simon shrugged uncomfortably. 'It seems fitting—'

'I would counsel against.'

Simon looked up, stung by the mayor's directness.

'For what reason?'

Brygge narrowed his eyes. 'Your masons – however secret you think you are in the deed – will hear of it. And some will call the site haunted, cursed still. You have moved your college once, you and Daker, I would not wish to see it moved a second time.'

Simon kneaded his brows with a weary hand. 'My poor boy,' he mumbled.

'I have a chapel, here in my grange,' Brygge continued briskly, as if making a business deal. 'If you think it fitting, your son may lie there.'

Again, Simon looked up, astonished by the mayor's words.

'Why?' he asked, at a loss to understand the mayor's suggestion. 'Why would you offer such a thing?'

Brygge stared down, appearing to appraise his boots which were crossed, relaxed, at his ankles. 'Joseph of Arimathea gave up his own tomb for Christ,' he said, the lightness of his tone belying the seriousness of his words. 'Should I not offer a place in my chapel to your son, if I am able?'

'My son, God rest his soul, is hardly to be compared to Christ—'

'He who does so even for the least of these little ones, does it for me,' Brygge quoted, his eyes held fast on Simon.

'You quote the word of God?'

'Yes. And in our own tongue.'

The air between them was silent for the space of several heartbeats.

'How much do you have?'

'The four gospels, entire.'

Simon stared at him. 'So much?'

'And you?'

'A few pages.' Simon confessed the truth to Brygge as he had not to Henry. 'It started as a finger up Copley's arse,' he said, bluntly. 'Anything I could do that would vex him, I did. Procuring pages of Wyclif's Bible was a game to begin with, like a prentice seeing how much he can get away with behind the back of a hated master.'

'But then?'

'Then I read the words and it was as if no priest had ever spoken, as if I heard the words straight from the mouth of the Saviour. Straight to me.'

'The Church is corrupt and worldly. It preaches superstition and fear.'

Simon nodded.

'Christ said that no man should seek to be in authority until he could first be the servant of all,' Brygge continued. 'I do not see such humility in the Church.'

The two men looked at each other and Simon knew that, whether or not he ever called Brygge friend, they were allies now, for better or worse.

'Will Mistress Kineton be content with my chapel?'

Simon half-smiled. 'My wife holds you in high regard, Master Brygge. You stood friend and champion to her against the Church once before; she will be no less grateful on this occasion.'

Forty-eight

In a circle of dancing people a huge, wild-haired woman throws back her head and opens her red mouth in what seems a cosmic laugh, filled with the sheer joy of existence. She and her dancing, hand-clasped companions are draped in textiles of many colours – more rainbowed than Joseph's, less striped – gathered in voluptuous folds around them.

Inside the dancing ring, a profusion of small flowers spring up in a rich green sward, their petals starring the green with violet, vermilion and azure. The cool caress of lush young grass on the soles of naked feet is a palpable sensation.

Behind the backs of the ever-shifting dancers, outside the charmed and fruitful circle, all is desert, rock and sand. The water which has caused the grass and flowers to flourish is nowhere in sight: drought and the desiccated rasp of seasons-dead grass replace swelling life. The dried-out corpses of flowers, perhaps tossed with joyful abandon over the shoulders of those in the ring, lie here and there in the sand, their colours bleached almost to nothing by the sun, their sappy stems and succulent leaves scorched to brittleness.

Amongst the stones and the dust and the dead flowers sits a small child. She too is dressed in many colours – the vibrant

colours of the dancers – but her tunic is short and ragged and
appears to have been stitched together from off-cuts joined
this way and that, juxtaposed at any angle and quickly sewn.
The child's eyes are on the dancers, though she stands back
from them, unsure, unwelcomed. Her thumb in her mouth,
she dangles a rag doll from one hand.

It was Catz's vision of Damia's childhood, distilled – her lover
assured her – from all the things she had not said, all the joy
she had never expressed. Loneliness surrounded by other
children; a constant failure in her own eyes to be as interesting and exciting as her brother; a life lived on the ragged
edges of the commune in the overpowering presence of a
larger-than-life mother who had never quite been there for
her daughter, even before her death and subsequent translation to intangible perfection in Damia's mind.

Though the painting had been a present for their second
anniversary, the implied promise had never been fulfilled; her
life with Catz had not furnished the circle of joyful dancers
for which Damia's soul had cried out in the alienation of her
commune childhood. Eschewing connections with any other
living thing, they had formed a wilful cocoon about their relationship. And it had seemed, at the time, seductively natural.

Obviously they should spend weekends in London: the
whole of Damia's room in a shared house would fit into the
opulent guest bathroom of Catz's extensive loft-apartment.
Of course they would not wish to lavish time on cultivating
a group of friends when they had so little time for each other.
And there was absolutely no reason why Catz should introduce Damia to her family – they didn't get on.

But their geographical separation had left Damia in the
cold, lonely shadow of these decisions; a shared house that

did not feel like home, a town where she had no soul to confide in, a complete separation from Catz and her world.

Finally, staring at the painting that showed both how much and how little Catz had understood, Damia realised that she had not applied for the job at Kineton and Dacre College to while away Catz's sabbatical year, nor had she put her first foot on the property ladder as a sound investment. She had been building herself a new life. She had been aware, however subconsciously, that her old life with Catz was over.

As she walked back to Toby from the Salster athletics stadium later that afternoon, Damia felt her mood matching the sunniness of the day. A light breeze scented with the spring smells of warming earth and germination caressed her face and made her smile. She felt light, freed, as if the sunshine had evaporated a stifling opalescence which had separated her from the world. She smiled at those she passed, her smile broadening as it was returned by pleasantly surprised tourists or hurrying students. A beggar on Pilgrims' Gate bridge responded with the bleak statement that smiles were cheap but food cost money – did she have any change to go with the smile? She had no change but, reckless with her pinch-tight budget, gave him five pounds.

Looking down over the bridge into the turbid grey-brown waters of the Doutre as she walked on, she wondered whether she would go punting this summer; with the Fairings runners perhaps? The squad could take out a couple of punts and a picnic. Now that she was free at weekends, perhaps she could organise a social event for her athletes – a punting picnic and then back to her house for dinner and a DVD or something. She could invite Neil.

Suddenly, Damia was invaded by the heady sensation that

she could make plans without consulting anybody else's preference. The precarious mutability that she had sensed looming over everything that had come to be important to her – house, job, Toby – fell away with the realisation that they were no longer vulnerable in the face of a future need to re-establish the jerky rhythm of her life with Catz. Whatever Catz's eventual reply to her ruthless email, they could never pick up the threads of their former way of life.

A blackbird perched on a window-box caught her eye but, as she stopped to look at it, the bird flew off in sudden, vocal alarm. How wonderful to be able simply to take wing, Damia thought, to launch oneself into the air and know that one could resist the undertow of gravity, could rise above the terrors and constraints of the ground and simply fly.

Toby Kineton, imprisoned by his uncooperative body, must have looked at other boys and wondered at their ability simply to run, to escape those who despised them and to thumb their noses from a safe distance before running again, simply because they could.

Walking into the Octo Yard a few minutes later, Damia found an argument in progress.

The rent strikers had abandoned their brazier – unlit in the balmy weather – on the Romangate and were clustered around the bottom of the Great Hall's staircase. The argument was between Robert Hadstowe and a student Damia did not recognise.

As she approached, she saw Dominic Walters-Russell, whose room looked out on to the Octo, emerging into the yard. His eyes were on the fracas: presumably he had decided to intervene. She intercepted his course and, nodding towards Hadstowe said, 'Shall we form a united front?'

The slight JCR president inclined his head silently and they walked, matching strides, towards the staircase.

'I'm very sorry for you,' they heard the student say, in a tone that failed to convey either pity or sorrow, 'but I just don't see what it's got to do with me – this is between you and the college, isn't it?'

'But you *are* the college – isn't that what this new campaign is all about?' Hadstowe asked, his eyes flicking towards Damia and her companion, the suggestion of a smile twitching his lips as if he relished a confrontation.

'Fine, I've had enough now,' said the student, seeing salvation at hand. 'I've got to get an essay done this afternoon for a tutorial at six . . .' He turned and leapt up the Octo's stairs two at a time.

'Mr Hadstowe,' Walters-Russell said in his surprisingly commanding voice, 'I see you're stepping up your campaign.'

The full Hadstowe smile was now in place. 'I thought I'd take a leaf out of Ms Miller's book and rally the college membership to my cause.'

'It doesn't look as though you're having much success,' Damia put in.

'Oh ' – Hadstowe's expression implied that he knew more than she – 'I think you'll find that we've had some impact. I think you may have to call an emergency JCR meeting, Mr President.'

'If I am given a petition with the requisite number of signatures,' Walters-Russell said, equably, 'that is exactly what I will do.'

Hadstowe's easy assumption that things were beginning to turn in his favour unnerved Damia. 'If you are going to harass our young people,' she said, wishing she did not have to tip her head upwards to look him in the eye, 'we will have to ask the police to remove you.'

'We aren't harassing anybody, simply giving out our literature' – he proffered a pale yellow A5 sheet with the printed headline RENT STRIKE: THE FACTS – 'and asking "your young people" to read it. And I'm afraid,' he continued, 'that the police would not be within their rights to ask us to leave. This is not private property. By use and custom of several hundred years there is a public right of way through this yard. Richard Dacre, I believe, wanted the common folk to feel they had a stake in the place.'

For the next week the rent strikers convened daily at the bottom of the Great Hall's curving staircase. Some, who sat in folding chairs and were content to hand out their yellow sheets, became an accepted part of the college topography by means of that peculiar process that deals with novelty – even unwelcome novelty – by incorporating it as a tiresome normality. Others – those who refused to sit, who challenged the young people approaching the steps with questions as to their stance on justice and exploitation – were an irritant that chafed at nerves already fraying as finals and life after university loomed increasingly large.

Once or twice a scuffle broke out and, despite Hadstowe's assertion that the law was on their side, the police were called. However, without an injunction the strikers made it clear that they would not be kept away, and even those cautioned by the constabulary continued to picket the Octo.

'Norris is going to have to do something,' Sam Kearns remarked seriously to Damia as they jogged up Lady's Walk in the chill of one early morning. 'The only time we're free of picketers is when it's too dark to see their leaflets. People are getting really pissed off.'

'Do you think they're getting any support?'

'I don't know about support, but I know a lot of people just want them to go away. And if that means giving them their assurances then I don't suppose the people who are going to have to go up the Octo stairs to do their finals in a couple of months care much.'

Inevitably, the increasingly head-to-head nature of the tenants' protest drew the media. The *Salster Times* sent a journalist to interview anyone who would speak into his microphone and a photographer who was keen to get pretty young women in shot with the tall and – Damia was convinced – deliberately Heathcliffe-esque Hadstowe. Failing that, the photographer would have been happy with a punch-up and was not above egging students on with remarks like, 'I wouldn't let him talk to you like that, son – who does he think he is, eh?' or, 'Come on you strikers, say it like you mean it! Give these privileged arses something to think about.'

Damia, eager to state the governing body's position but well aware that anything she said would be taken down and used against her, wrote a press release that she hastily cleared with Norris before handing it over to the journalist who had obviously been hoping for personal contact from a more senior source.

'What's this?' he asked, glaring at her with an expression that seemed habitual; his long face fell in sneering folds that would narrow into mistrust far more readily than they would expand into delight. 'Who did you say you were?' he snapped.

Had he seriously not heard her introduce herself, Damia

wondered, or was this an attempt at a put-down? She was used to being taken for somebody ten years younger and her skin-colour, even in the first decade of the twenty-first century, was still unusual in the management of colleges.

'Damia Miller,' she repeated, trying to avoid speaking in any way that could be construed as antagonistic, 'Marketing Manager for the college. That' – she nodded towards the envelope in his hand – 'is a press release.'

'Ha! Writing my copy for me? How very kind.' His irony was a pretty blunt instrument, but the fact that he wielded it without apparent provocation made Damia ever more wary. She stood silently while he ripped open the envelope and swiftly scanned the single, word-processed sheet.

'Brief, to the point—'

'Thank you.'

'And a load of shit.' He crumpled the page theatrically, opened his fist and dropped it on the floor at Damia's feet, his eyes never leaving hers, waiting for a reaction. When she failed to oblige, he said, 'You're just trying to screw these people. You just want to sell their land to developers. Everybody knows there's five thousand new houses needed in that area in the next ten years. I bet you're just wetting yourselves thinking of all the money you could make.'

'Hmm, what an entertaining vision.' Damia threw caution to the winds. 'But no, as a matter of fact, we are not incontinent with joy at the fact that we may – under extreme financial pressure – be forced to sell college land at some time in the future. It is something we will do everything we can to avoid. But, if it becomes unavoidable, we cannot be dictated to as to how we sell that land and to whom.' She held up an imperious hand to forestall the interruption she could see forming on his indrawn breath. 'It would be like you being forced to sell your granny's house so that she could get good nursing home care and then discovering that you couldn't sell it for an amount that would see her comfortable in a good place because – years ago – she had agreed to sell it to her next-door neighbour at a pre-agreed price.' Again the hand went up as the journalist began to protest that her analogy was 'Bloody stupid'.

'No, it's not bloody stupid, as you so eloquently put it. The rent strikers want the college to enter a binding agreement that they will have first refusal to buy at agricultural rates. The *only* reason we might be induced to sell is so that we can maximise our returns, and that would mean selling the land in order to provide housing. Which – as you know – commands a premium.'

'So?' the journalist barked, raising his nose to the scent of victory. 'You *are* going to sell the land to developers.'

'No, not at the moment. Please, listen to me – we do not want to sell land. But if we are *forced* to – as land is our only asset: we don't have chapel plate like all the other foundation colleges – as I say, if we are *forced* to, then we want to maximise our returns, so that we can sell as little land as possible. Which would, obviously, mean that the vast majority of tenants could keep their land and continue to farm it as before.'

'Miss Miller,' the journalist said, holding his dictaphone almost under her chin to emphasise the fact that he was recording her answer, 'can you assure me in words of one syllable that the college does not have the current intention of selling any of its estate lands and that it is not negotiating with housing developers to do so?'

'Absolutely. No plans, no negotiations.'

Out of the corner of her eye, Damia saw Rob Hadstowe's twisted smile directed right at her.

Forty-nine

In the weeks after the death of John Daker and Toby, Simon awaited a decision from Richard Daker as to the future of the college.

'It has cost us our only sons,' Simon entreated. 'It cannot remain unbuilt, something good must come of it!'

'It has cost us our sons, is that not enough?' had been Richard's heavy reply.

A month went by during which no month-mind was observed, no paupers walked with candles through the streets, no chantry priests were paid to sing masses for the soul of either boy. Mutterings were heard about Lollard heresies but, despite the whispers of suspicion which had crept abroad since the King had taken control of his country and deprived John of Gaunt – a Wyclifite patron – of his power, no canon courts had been convened, no charges brought.

The same month saw Simon's masons – half-pay or not – begin to drift away to the other works in Salster. Those who remained did not know whether to continue to prepare the stones in anticipation of their laying or to sit in idle expectation.

Another month and the weather began to show more autumnal. Winds blew in with a breath of the north and of winter; the spate of pilgrims in the city dwindled towards its short-day trickle. Masonry began to be impossible as sharp and early frosts crept in and men drifted away from the college site: the rough and ready dwellings where they and their families had lived now all but deserted as people returned to their villages to sit out the winter and see what decision spring should bring from Richard Daker.

The darkening days shortened as Advent drew near and Daker, in an increasingly rare interview with Simon, told him that he would be in London for the Christmas festivities.

Standing before his patron, Simon allowed himself to acknowledge how grief and the death of future hopes had aged Daker, sapped him of that vitality which had made him younger than his years. His lean face was lined now and his mobile mouth no longer quirked constantly at the possibilities of life. His eyes, those intense dark blue eyes, had lost their fire.

'You shall have my answer with the new year, Simon,' he promised, his gaze meeting his master mason's fleetingly, as if merely to look upon Simon pained him. 'I shall take stock while I am away, and you shall have my answer.'

Simon had bowed and left, a feeling of judgement deferred hanging over him. He did not know whether it was better to live in hope against hope or to know, once and for all, that his dream was at an end, dead with his son.

Gwyneth and Simon observed the Christmas holy days at Henry and Alysoun's home and the presence of their foster-children's growing family diverted their sadness for a while.

But always, always at the root of everything, was a pain which would not ease, a pain that woke Gwyneth in the night, calling Toby's name; that took Simon almost daily to the college site outside the city wall.

Nicholas Brygge had asked him whether he wished to place a memorial stone over Toby's grave in his chapel, but Simon had replied that he would have a more visible and lasting memorial by and by, when the college was completed. In the meantime, needing something to stand sentinel for his son in this place, Simon had taken a young tree from his garden and planted it on the edge of the site, a hawthorn destined to be as bent and twisted as his poor boy but which would withstand the blasts and heats of life as well as he had done, and be generous in its sudden yield of pure white blossom in spring.

At the Christmas morning mass it was all Simon could do not to weep openly at the thought of a helpless child, born to live reviled and rejected by those around him and to give his life for those not worthy of his love. He was almost brought, in his grief and self-hatred, to believe that to be denied the chance to build the college would be a fitting penance for his son's death. But, in the depths of his soul, he rebelled against this. Toby and the college had come to him almost in the same breath, and Toby had died for its continued existence. It could not be right that he should give it up. Toby's willing death must not prove futile as so many attempted actions in his struggling life had been, it must be seen as the one perfect thing he had been able to do. The world must see him for what he was; all those who had flinched from him in life must marvel at him in death and think the poorer of themselves for seeing no further than disordered limbs and writhing face.

The hawthorn tree, though uprooted and made to grow in a place it had not chosen, did not wilt and sag, as Simon had feared it might, but grew cheerfully on, as if its new place suited it as well or better than the old. In truth it was a better place, for it had taken root in a shaded, stony part of Simon and Gwyneth's garden where it had held fast to life beyond the better-favoured apple trees and tilled earth of the kitchen garden. Here, in the sun of the city's southern edge, it was revelling in warmth and deep earth which were already nourishing it into a new, more vigorous life.

On the morning of Twelfth Night, after mass, Simon had sat in vigil with the tree and his son as the darkness of midwinter slowly, so slowly, seeped away and the sun rose for its few brief hours, low across the land. As the greyness gave way to light, Simon hung ribbons of green in the leafless twigs of the small tree.

'Spring will come,' he said softly, 'and I will build our college, my son.'

But the new year brought neither word nor sight of Daker. Simon fretted and paced but there was nobody he could take his frustration to – the whole household had removed to London, including Piers Mottis and his wife. There was nobody who might give him word of when Daker was expected back in Salster.

And then, abruptly, at the end of January when the weather had released its iron grip for a spell, Ralph Daker appeared in the city.

As soon as he heard the news, Simon presented himself at the Daker house and asked for audience with Ralph. To his surprise it was granted at once.

Ralph did not rise to greet him as Simon was shown into

the solar, barely looking up from the papers he was studying. Simon stifled the urge to ask where Richard was, but could not stifle wonder at Ralph's assumption of his uncle's place. He watched the tall man, noticing that he was moving now from youth to middle age – his frame thickening and jowls beginning to hang from his jawline. Did Anne still welcome him in her bed, or had the shine of youth and novelty gone off him?

'Master Kineton,' Ralph said, looking up at Simon with the suspicion of a smile playing about his heavy face, 'thank you for your prompt attendance.'

Simon's blood rose at the implication of Ralph's words but he held his peace; his business was with the uncle not the nephew.

'I am here not on my uncle's behalf,' Ralph said, as if Simon's thoughts were obvious, 'but on my own. I have to tell you that my uncle died this Christmas of a seizure and that his business is now become mine.'

Simon felt suddenly cold, despite the blood beating in his veins.

'My uncle had nothing to say about his further ambitions for the college he had proposed, before he died, and I am therefore free to take my own decision. As I do not have his interest in wresting learning from the Church and giving it to other men, I have no use for a college. There will be no more building.'

Rage coursed through Simon in a livid thrill. 'It is not your college to decide upon, Master Daker,' he said abruptly. 'It is its own entity, with endowments made to ensure its completion and continuance.'

'You forget, Master Kineton, that those endowments were put in doubt by John's death. My uncle's wishes as to the college were never made clear. But I am making mine quite clear. There will be no more building.'

Later that same day, Piers Mottis found his way to the Kinetons' house. He deflected Simon's frosty greeting by making it clear that he had come upon his own initiative, not Ralph's, and was admitted to the solar.

'Can he do this?' Simon demanded when the lawyer had been seated and furnished with food and drink.

'He could if I did not have, still, in my possession the papers of endowment that Master Daker drew up to ensure the college's building against the vagaries of his business.'

Simon waved an irritable hand. 'But surely Ralph will contest that, say that his uncle had changed his mind?'

Mottis smiled slightly. 'Forgive me for saying so, Master Kineton, but you are better versed in building than you are in the law. Ralph Daker may say what he likes, but what his uncle had written and put his name to is what stands in law until it is rescinded by another written statement. We must go to court, but I think that Ralph will find he has bitten off too big a lump if he tries to deny us these endowments.'

'Us?'

'Richard Daker was my friend as well as my employer.' Mottis said, evenly. 'Although his grief made it impossible for him – for many months – to think with pleasure of his college, he had planned it and dreamed of its influence for many years. I do not wish the fact that he died before he could finish mourning his son to thwart the ambition of half a lifetime.'

'You will fight for the college then?'

'I will.'

'And who will employ you when Ralph Daker throws you out of his employ?'

The little lawyer smiled a crooked, rueful smile. 'I have already been dismissed. Ralph is a new broom and he wishes to surround himself with young men like himself. Out with the old' – he smiled again, slightly – 'and in with the new.'

'Then will you work with us on the college? If my wife is to be master carpenter we shall need a new clerk to the works.' Simon stopped as suddenly as he had rushed in. 'I am sorry, I did not wish to insult you. I am sure there are many men who would employ you—'

'Doubtless there are,' Mottis said, with the unconcerned air of a man who knows his own worth and sits lightly upon it, 'but I would see the college built if I can. My house is mine – a gift from Richard to me and my wife many years ago – and we would rather live simply and honestly than go whoring around the court for riches.'

Simon looked at him steadily. 'So what must we do?'

'First I must make application to the court for the case to be heard. And then,' he said simply, 'the fight begins.'

Fifty

COLLEGE SPLIT ON SALE OF LAND

The Kineton and Dacre College tenants' rent strike has
taken a dramatic turn this week *writes Pete Darney*. The
strikers have upped the stakes and moved from the
pavement outside the college into the holy of holies, the
Octagon Yard of Kineton and Dacre College itself. Having
given up their silent protest, they are now employing more
vocal persuasions and are winning the hearts and minds of
the college's undergraduates with details of their shabby
treatment at the hands of Kineton and Dacre's mandarins.

One undergraduate, who did not wish to be named, told
the *Salster Times* 'There seems to be a developing
consensus amongst the students here that we need to do
something to help the tenants.'

The first step would be for twenty-four undergraduates
to sign a petition asking for an emergency meeting of the
Junior Common Room (JCR) which would then send a
censure motion to the governing body. This would put
pressure on Dr Edmund Norris, head of Kineton and Dacre

College, to perform a U-turn and to give the tenants assurances that their holdings are secure.

The tenants feel that such assurances are necessary because rumour has been rife for months that negotiations have begun with a construction firm to build high-end housing on land which forms part of one of the college's estates. Young professionals are being drawn to the area concerned by the booming development of Market Lenton – the fastest-growing town in the UK – causing a housing shortage and a need for premium building land.

Kineton and Dacre College has always maintained that no such negotiations are taking place.

On Tuesday of this week, this was the line taken by the college's Marketing Manager, Ms Damia Miller. Asked to confirm that no such negotiations were being entered into and that no plans to sell were being made, she stated, 'No plans. No negotiations.' But a source close to the Regent Master told the *Salster Times* this week that negotiations have been in progress for months with the construction firm NewtonKerry.

Sir Ian Baird, entrepreneur, businessman and, for the last five years, Principal of Northgate College, had this to say: 'When I took my college out of the archaic system of association which advantages tradition and disadvantages innovation, even I didn't know what a mess the leadership of Kineton and Dacre College had got itself into.'

Is there a conspiracy of silence and denial at Kineton and Dacre College, or does the left hand simply not know what the right is playing at? Either way, it doesn't look like good news for the long-suffering tenants.

(*Don't forget you can have your say on this matter on the* Salster Times *forum, just go to* www.salstertimes.org/yourviewsonthenews)

❖

Within two days the truth was known by the newest kitchen-staffer and the least networked undergraduate. Charles Northrop had, without the knowledge of the rest of the governing body, been pursuing negotiations with the construction company NewtonKerry.

Amongst those of the Toby Rescue Committee who had been able to attend a meeting called at short notice, Damia noted a distinct division of opinion. On one side, signs of fatalism were developing: a tendency to accept the negotiations and continue with them since they were clearly so well advanced. On the other, there was outrage at Northrop's high-handedness; the immediate cessation of all negotiations was demanded, along with Northrop's resignation as dean.

Northrop himself was unrepentant.

'For God's sake! I thought this committee wanted the college to survive – isn't that the whole point?'

When silence greeted this rhetorical question he continued. 'What the hell would have been the point of stopping negotiations with NewtonKerry? They'd have gone after land elsewhere and our one chance to save the college would have slipped from our grasp.'

'What do you mean "our one chance"?' The bursar, Keith McKie – as stalwart an advocate of the Rescue Committee as Northrop was a denigrator – was quick to challenge him.

'Just that! If you seriously imagine that all this touchy-feely stuff dreamed up by Miss Miller is going to provide the wherewithal to keep you busy, Keith, you're not the realist I always took you for. This college community idea is unprofessional and impractical – it's going to make a laughing stock of the college.' His tone slipped into a lisping, breathy parody of a young girl's: '*The good ship Toby, pushed along by all her friends!*'

Lesley Cochrane was rapidly heading for incandescence. 'So *you* took it upon your*self* to ignore the wishes not only of everybody else on this committee but the governing body too?'

'Yes!' Northrop exploded. 'In just the same way that Edmund did when he sold what we can only refer to as "an unspecified document". It's true, isn't it, Edmund? You did sell something none of us knew about? Something found in the statue?'

Where uproar might have been expected, an absolute hush prevailed, Northrop and Norris locked, as if alone, into the staring silence that followed the dean's accusation.

Then, in the split second before his failure to answer reached the tipping point that would force others to speak, Norris said, 'Yes.' He looked away from Northrop and around at the still faces. 'As those of you on the governing body are already aware, I did sell a document that was found in the statue. As those of you not on the governing body need to be assured, I submitted a full account of the transaction and was, I am gratified to say, supported in the decision I had taken by the majority of the governing body.'

The frozen silence was broken. Uneasy *sotto voce* murmurs combined with the shifting of bodies and the rearrangement of limbs. Glances that clearly didn't know what to think were exchanged between committee members.

Tommy Thomas, the domestic staff's representative on the committee, asked the obvious question. 'What was it?'

'I'm afraid I can't tell you, Tommy.' Norris turned to him with a look almost of relief. 'The terms of the sale were quite specific on that point. But I *can* assure you, all of you' – he looked around the table – 'that the documents, though contemporaneous with the building of the college, were neither college documents nor papers relating to any of the people involved in building the college.'

'What? And we're supposed to be happy with that?' Rob Hadstowe was incredulous.

'No, Mr Hadstowe, I neither ask nor expect you to be happy with it. But I am Regent Master of this college and – just occasionally – the buck not only stops with me, it starts with me too. You will just have to trust that I did what I thought was right for the college.'

There was a moment's absolute silence.

'That's it? "You'll just have to trust me"?' Hadstowe gave a thunderclap of mirthless laughter.

'Sometimes,' Dominic Walters-Russell said, without heat, 'we just have to let leaders lead, Mr Hadstowe.' Returning Hadstowe's dismissive glare with an unintimidated calm he continued, 'If we start bickering amongst ourselves we may just as well give up the effort to save the college now.' He smiled, lightly. 'United we stand, and all that.'

His gaze did not leave Hadstowe's face, but he was clearly addressing the whole meeting as he said, 'I, personally, am prepared to accept – without question – that the Regent Master has acted in good faith in this matter and with only the college's interests at heart.' Finally he broke eye contact with the tenants' leader and included others in his challenge. 'Is anybody here not prepared to accept that?'

Heads were shaken and mumbles of 'No, no, we accept that, of course' greeted Dominic's adroit invitation to declare unquestioning allegiance and avert the need for continued uncomfortable questioning.

Norris turned to the JCR president and inclined his head. 'Thank you, Mr Walters-Russell, for such an unequivocal vote of confidence.' He breathed deeply and looked around.

'All I think I *can* say is that the document concerned was an artefact very specifically associated with the latter half of the fourteenth century and that it has been bought by an anonymous collector who expressly wished, not only that the sale be kept out of the public domain but that the *nature* of the document, also, should not be revealed, as his well-known interest would mark him as the obvious buyer. The circumstances were such that I had to make decisions quickly. Given that my position enabled me to take unilateral actions on behalf of the college, I did so.'

His eyes scanned the meeting. When nobody spoke he said, 'Now, if we could just conclude the discussion concerning building development.'

The relief was almost a physical presence in the room's still air as the meeting moved away from the contentiousness of the unspecified documents.

'I have spoken to the CEO of NewtonKerry,' Norris continued, 'and clarified matters. He now understands that there is no proposal to sell and negotiations have been discontinued.'

Ignoring a muted show of exasperated despair from Northrop, Norris signalled with both voice and manner that the subject had been dropped.

'And now, I think, we need to discuss how to prevent our undergraduates feeling hassled by the justifiable concerns of the tenants.'

A public debate between Edmund Norris and Robert Hadstowe was held in the JCR the following evening.

The meeting was, if anything, even more crowded than that which had been convened to discuss the Atoz sponsorship deal. Every square foot of space on floor or furniture was occupied. The JCR was filled with the smell of clothing wet from the persistent drizzle that had fallen all day and given the city the atmospheric feeling of a film shot through a misty filter.

First-comers hung their jackets on the common room's two long radiators, leaving everybody else to eschew the coat-stand where coat would soak neighbouring coat and, instead, peel off their outer layers, turn them inside out and stow them at their feet.

'OK, thank you! If I could call this meeting to order!' Dominic Walters-Russell, from the box, shushed the assembled crowd and welcomed his guests formally. 'Miss Miller and I,' he said, 'will mediate as necessary.' His grin suggested that he relished the challenge of 'mediating' a robust debate.

Invited to state their case, both Edmund Norris and Rob Hadstowe did so with commendable brevity. The governing body wished to have its right to the land legally documented; the tenants wanted the college to enter into a binding agreement to give them first refusal to buy if the land was to be sold.

The first question from the floor was the obvious one. Why did the college not simply acquiesce to the tenants' request and then everybody would be happy?

Norris took an audible breath that he let out through his nose, his nostrils flaring slightly.

'Yes,' he smiled, 'wouldn't it be nice if everybody could be happy? Unfortunately, the net effect of giving the tenants the assurances they want – as Mr Hadstowe is, I am sure, only too well aware – is to fragment the ability to negotiate. It is inevitable that some tenants would decide to buy their farms, whereas others would feel unable to do so. And that would mean that anybody wanting to buy any of the estates as a whole, a parcel, so to speak, would be stymied.

'If we were ever to sell land – and I have to point out at this stage that it is unlikely that we ever would do so, despite the unauthorised negotiations which have been taking place – we would wish to sell as advantageously as possible, obviously, and that would mean selling whole estates.'

'Yes, to developers,' Hadstowe put in without invitation, to be asked, mildly, to wait in future until called upon.

Norris looked to the JCR president for permission to refute Hadstowe's point and was given the nod.

'Mr Hadstowe knows as well as I do that the estate with which he is particularly concerned is on green-belt land which is protected by law. There is no conceivable way we could sell it to developers or to anybody who would wish to use it for anything other than agriculture.'

Hadstowe played the game and was invited to retort.

'As the Regent Master knows equally well, green belt or no green belt, people who live in that area are going to have to be housed and houses are going to start going up on agricultural land sooner rather than later. I just want to make sure that it's not *my* agricultural land!'

As questions and answers were batted to and fro and the JCR became stuffier and more uncomfortable, Damia covertly scrutinised the gathered student body. The faces that followed argument and counter-argument, though no more nor less good-looking than the rest of the population, had that spark of attractiveness that more than average intelligence bestows. The academically gifted are not called bright for nothing, she reflected.

'Maybe I'm being thick,' a slight youth with vicious acne

said, 'but I'm not sure why the tenants are all over the Octo Yard and shoving pamphlets in our hands every five seconds when we're trying to go to the library. I mean' – he turned to Rob Hadstowe – 'what do you expect us to do? We've got no power over whether you get to buy your land or not!'

'Come on, Harry, 'course we do!' somebody else shouted. 'We get twenty-four names, take them to Dom, get a censure motion done and send it off to the governing body. Just like we did with Atoz. That's what they're trying to force us to do.'

'But there's no comparison!' Harry responded, blushing furiously at his implied ignorance of JCR politics. 'Nobody's denying the tenants human rights!'

'You don't think we should have the right to buy our own homes – farms where some of our families have lived for generations?' Hadstowe shot back.

'No,' another voice intervened, ignoring the fact that Dominic Walters-Russell was trying to rein contributions in and make them orderly. 'Why the hell should you? I think the whole "workers owning the means of production" model has got a bit old, don't you?'

'Yes, and if *you* don't think it's morally acceptable for the *college* to break centuries of tradition to sell the land,' one young man with a striped sweater and a grown-out crew-cut asked Rob Hadstowe, 'why do you think *you* have the moral right to buy your land *from* the college and then sell it on to whoever you feel like? Isn't it basically indefensible for either side to sell land that was meant to be joined to the college in perpetuity? A bit like a marriage.' He smiled, making dimples appear in his boyish cheeks, 'What Richard Dacre has joined together, let nobody else put asunder.'

This comment set the tone of the meeting thereafter as

both those who were inclined to favour the tenants' cause and those who saw the rationale for the authorities' intentions found a stance behind which they could unite. College and land should not be divided. No assurances should be given beyond the simple one that land would not be sold. The college should stand or fall as an entity, scattered lands and Salster college as one.

'There was a suggestion at the College Action Plan Committee' – Dominic Walters-Russell spoke up once the spate of questions and comments had run dry – 'that the college and the tenants should work more closely together, joint ventures where the college underwrote capital costs and shared profits with the tenants. That seems a much more constructive way of increasing revenue from college land.'

Enthusiastic agreement greeted his words and Damia could tell, by the look on Rob Hadstowe's face, that he knew he would not, now, have JCR backing for any action he tried to take against the governing body.

Walters-Russell spoke again. 'Though this was advertised as a debate, there was no formal motion for either side to speak to. I think it would be a good idea for this common room to make some kind of statement now that we've heard both sides.'

Muffled agreement rumbled back at him in the air of the overheated room.

'How about this.' He paused in brief mental composition. 'The JCR would like to see a closer working relationship, including – where possible – joint ventures, between the governing body of the college and its estate tenants. This to be undertaken as part of the new drive towards a greater sense of community amongst all those connected with the college.'

Damia felt her face break into the widest of cheek-stretching smiles as this motion was put forward to a unanimous show of undergraduate hands. This would be great material for the next blog.

Pavements and tarmac glinted with reflected streetlamp-light as she walked through the northeastern arch and on to the Romangate. The rain had stopped and Damia sniffed the air, relishing its cool freshness after the humid warmth of the JCR. Though the common room had been strictly non-smoking for years, the smell of ancient smoke seeped from carpets and cracked leather under the influence of so much moist heat and this, combined with wet clothes and the multitude of cosmetic fragrances released into the air by damp skin, had made for a slightly oppressive atmosphere.

Late-night shopping had been over for an hour and more but the streets were busy with pub-goers. The university library stayed open until ten thirty, a fact that students who needed the discipline of a quiet environment away from halls of residence or shared houses took advantage of. Individual college libraries, she had been told, could be too convivial for serious work late in the evening.

Another pang of envy: what had she been doing at eighteen? Suffering freezing extremities and learning more than she had ever wanted to know about vegetables at Mickelwell, not daring to move on in case Anne should try to contact her there from whichever remote part of the world she was currently experiencing.

Damia still carried a photo of Anne. Each time she bought a new purse she made sure that it contained a small, secure compartment where she could slip the passport-sized photo that was the only picture she had ever possessed of her first love. Was her dark hair still long and silky? Had she retained her slim, lithe shape, the body of a dancer? Damia recalled with a jolt in the solar plexus how their almost exactly equal height had meant that neither needed to bend into a kiss, how their arms had fitted naturally around each other's waists as they walked side by side. She and Catz had never been able to do that – with Catz almost a head taller, her arm had always been around Damia's shoulders.

Damia knew that if Anne were to walk back into her life she would give up everything to keep her there. She also knew, with equal certainty, that this would never happen. Damia did not doubt that Anne had genuinely loved her, but that love had not been enough to outweigh her need to keep moving.

Leaving with her had been a possibility right up until the moment when Anne made her plans and failed to ask Damia to be part of them. Damia had been too proud and too hurt to beg a place at her side.

A couple walked past, his arm around her shoulders, her hand slipped into the back pocket of his jeans. Damia smiled and they smiled back. She imagined them walking on trying to work out whether they knew her. With her unlined skin and petite figure, Damia knew she was easily mistaken for a student. For once, she thanked the genes her mother had passed on for her youthful looks. Maz – Marizella – had always told her children that mixing races produced people of true beauty. 'You get the best of both,' she had said, as if there could be no other opinion.

Damia had only one photograph of her mother, a proper studio portrait taken before she and Jimi had been born. In it her mother looked like an African queen, her mixed-spice West Indian skin darkened in half-lit profile and her chin tilted in pride or defiance. Her full lips were slightly parted as if she was about to speak or had just spoken and her nostrils were flared. Marizella had not been beautiful but she had been a striking woman, her personality clear in her face and the way she carried herself.

Damia knew that it had been she who led them to the commune. Tony would have gone anywhere for the woman who was not his wife but was his soul-mate and the mother of his children. Gone anywhere, but not, perhaps, done anything; Damia could not imagine him giving up his chemically enhanced life and getting a job.

Her melancholy train of thought was interrupted by the chirruping of her mobile phone. She dug into her coat pocket and flipped it open. Neil's name was on the caller ID.

'Hey, what's up?'

'Toby. He died *the day after John Dacre.*'

Damia arrived at Neil's cathedral office out of breath.

He drew her in and sat her down at the desk he had been occupying when she burst through the door. He opened a drawer and took out a pair of cotton gloves identical to the ones he was wearing and gave them to her.

While she was slipping them on, he leaned over her shoulder and put his own finger on the manuscript on the desk.

'Here.' Damia watched as his finger followed the line of illegible Latin script. 'The Kinetons' cripple lies dead, drowned in the flood. I have given orders that no priest of the city shall offer him burial according to Christian rites. It is not suitable. His father will repent of his heresy if he wishes to see his son given due ceremony.'

'What does it mean?'

'It means' – Neil's voice was a mixture of excitement and condemnation – 'that the prior was trying to bring Simon of Kineton to heel.'

'So Toby drowned,' she said, when he had read the passage again for her, 'and the prior doesn't say how that came to happen.'

'Correct.'

'Any clues?'

'None. But you've got to wonder about some kind of revenge attack from Dacre. Or maybe the masons thought Dacre might pull the plug so they evened the score up a bit. Masons were incredibly superstitious, they probably bought this whole thing about the kid being cursed. Even if it was an accident that killed young Dacre, the masons may have blamed Tobias's influence.'

Damia stared at him. 'And so they might have just killed him, thrown him into the river?'

'Doesn't have to be that dramatic, just a nudge at a crucial moment, nobody leaps in because they can't find anybody who could swim, river's in flood . . . Oh dear, Mr Kineton, there was nothing we could do, so sorry . . . wring hands, *exeunt omnes.*'

Damia shifted in her seat.

'And if not the masons, or Dacre?'

'You tell me.'

Damia was silent for a while, her gaze fixed on infinity in the table top. 'D'you think the Kinetons believed their son was cursed?' she asked, finally.

Neil tugged at an earlobe. 'Impossible to say, isn't it?' He stared at her, but she would not meet his eye. 'What? You think Simon and Gwyneth threw him in the river?'

She shrugged uneasily. 'I don't know, but what if Dacre said, "That's it, you're off the project, I can't see you without remembering your son killed mine" or something like that?'

'What? So Simon thought, OK, he's a cripple and he's

400

probably got demons, who's going to miss him – blessed relief actually – that kind of thing? Is that what you mean?'

'Does it seem credible to you?'

'I don't know. What do you think?'

Fifty-one

The months while they waited for the case to be heard at the Court of Common Pleas were cold and silent ones for Simon and Gwyneth. She, her grief jealously hidden from him beneath the smouldering pall of her anger, went about her tasks and mourned alone, a knotted, hurting weight growing inside her.

Simon, foundering beneath the heaviness of blame between them, abandoned the city. Despite the hardness of frost and icy air he struck alone across country to his manors at Kineton and the stone that was waiting for him there, the three days' ride a welcome penance.

'I may be gone a fortnight or three weeks,' he had said.

Gwyneth folded a clean shirt and put it in the top of a linen bag, jerking the drawstring tight before pushing it inside one of his saddle bags. 'Then I shall look for you no sooner,' she said, hefting the leather bag and holding it out to him.

He took it. 'Will you wish me Godspeed, Gwyneth?'

She looked at him, their eyes meeting briefly, painfully. 'Godspeed, Simon.'

The weather turned bitter after his departure and the snow lay thick on the ground beneath an icy, drifting wind; but if Gwyneth feared for her husband she did not voice her fears to a living soul.

When he returned on a waterlogged barge that lay deep in the water under its load, Simon was thinner, greyer in his features, and weighted down with clothing that had been nothing but damp for days.

Thereafter, every new day found him at his bench in the silent and deserted lodge, mallet and gouge in his hands. Though the mason in him cried out that he must finish his college, yet the father he had been did not know whether he merited such grace and was determined to endure the waiting. Judgement would come soon enough.

The day Piers Mottis told him that a date was set for their hearing, Simon approached Gwyneth with a plea.

'Will you come to the lodge with me, Gwyneth?' he asked. 'I have something to show you.'

Once, she would have flung down her work and come with him in moment; now she silently finished her assessment of the household's food stocks before answering him.

'What is it you would show me?'

'It is in the lodge.'

Gwyneth opened her mouth to complain but he forestalled her. 'Gwyneth, please. Please, do not deny me this one thing.'

His wife nodded and rose to her feet and Simon led the way from the house. In silence they walked through the cold and muddy streets of the city, enduring without comment or acknowledgement the glances – some of pity, some of curiosity, some of open hostility – that were directed at them from all sides.

Simon stopped outside the lodge and turned to face Gwyneth. 'Though I did not love our son as you did, Gwyneth, I did love him as I could – as a man and a mason could, deprived of the son he had sought.'

Gwyneth gazed at him but, even after all these years, he could not understand what the look on her face might mean.

'I had a dream after Richard Daker died where Toby appeared to me – not as we knew him here, but as he is now, in glory—'

'A vision?'

'I do not know. You know, better than anybody, Gwyneth, that I am not a man well versed in distinguishing dreams from visions.' Their eyes met and neither looked away. 'But I know that, from the moment I woke up, I understood what I must do.'

Gwyneth's eyes narrowed suspiciously, but Simon pushed open the door of the lodge and went in. 'Come,' he said. 'Come and see.'

Gwyneth followed him into the dim light of the lodge, holding the skirts of her gown up over the dust and fragments that Simon had not swept out. Did she, Simon wondered, thrill to the familiar smells of seasoned wood, masonry dust and oiled tools? She had been many months absent, did she feel any tug towards building, towards the creation that the last eight years of their life had been centred on?

He led her to a corner where a stone image stood, facing the shutters let into the wall. Walking past the statue, Simon threw open the shutters on to the cold, weak light outside and beckoned for Gwyneth to come and stand next to him.

Putting an arm tentatively around her shoulders he said quietly, 'This is Toby, as I saw him in my dream.'

Gwyneth stared at the statue before her. For a long minute

she was motionless, a lack of reaction sufficient for Simon to comprehend that she was battling with something in herself that he did not understand. He was desperate for her reaction; he had anticipated many responses, from tears to rejection, but not this silence.

'So,' she said finally, her voice flat and dead, 'he has become the boy you always wanted, Simon – a perfect boy.'

'So shall we all be in heaven!'

'But this is not *him!* This is not my Toby!'

And suddenly he understood – Gwyneth was jealous of him. Toby had abandoned her and given up his life for his unworthy father. This vision of Toby was a vision of the wholeness that had lived inside his writhing, contorted, confusing body, it was a vision of the largeness of soul that had found it in himself to forgive and to do the only thing he could, as a mason's son, to speed his father's building. Gwyneth wanted her crippled boy, the one she had loved despite his deformity, the boy she thought she had understood when nobody else would look at him.

'Gwyneth, you have not asked why he is standing as he is, what he is looking for.'

She looked from the image to Simon, her brows drawn together, her face closed.

'He is looking for his other self, his earthly self, trying to see himself as others saw him,' Simon said. Taking Gwyneth's arm, he led her to the other end of the lodge, unfastened the shutters and swung them open. A pool of light fell onto the ground, illuminating another statue. Gwyneth approached it slowly, her eyes fixed on the rounded form. Going down on her knees, she traced the carving with her fingers, following the curve of the frame, the stony hands, the patched eye.

Finally, finally, she turned a tear-streaked face to Simon. 'Where are you going to put them?'

'In the college, looking down on the courtyard in which the octagonal hall stands.'

'And if they will not grant you the endowments?'

'Then,' he said simply, 'I will find another way.'

Fifty-two

To: Damiarainbow@hotmail.com
From: CatzCampbell@hotmail.com
Subject: Neil Gordon

Damia, I feel I'm being kept in the dark here . . . Neil's in Salster, working on this wall painting with you? Talk to me, *please*.

Her eyes gritty from lack of sleep, Damia pulled her front door shut behind her and stepped out into the bright sun of what was undeniably a spring morning. A whole sleepless night had been too short to compose a satisfactory reply to Catz's email. Though she had initially been at a loss to understand how her lover had found out that Neil was in Salster, Damia had come to the conclusion that Catz must have logged on to the college website and read the new blog with its link to the wall painting project and Neil's revelations about Toby.

The implication – that Catz must have registered as a member of the project – provoked an unexpected response in Damia. Though, even a week before, she would have been overjoyed to see Catz involving herself in the work at Toby, now she felt that her territory was being invaded, her activities spied upon.

Evidently her decision not to rush to New York, though disappointing to Catz, had not signalled to her lover the effective end of their relationship.

Catz was not the only person who had been interested in the contents of Damia's blog. In the week following the debate, it had attracted considerable interest.

When she mused on the landlord–tenant relationship that existed between the college and those who farmed its estates and wondered whether this had anything to say about a change in perception from class struggle to joint enterprise, the message-board was inundated with contributions that ranged from hard-line Marxist-Leninism to warm and fuzzy notions of the brotherhood of man.

When she broke the news of Toby Kineton's death by drowning so close on the heels of John Dacre's's demise and speculated as to how a disabled eight-year-old came to drown in the flooded Greyling stream, responses varied from a long treatise on medieval deaths in childhood to conspiracy theories based on the Church as a hotbed of witch-hunters.

Now, a week after events in the JCR, she walked to college, secure in the knowledge that she no longer had to run a rent-striker gauntlet either on the Romangate or in the Toby Yard. The few days following the debate had seen their numbers shrink rapidly to zero.

Within sight of Toby, her phone suddenly took her by surprise. Digging into her bag she flipped it open.

'Hello?'

'Damia. Have you left home yet?' Norris's voice sounded flat, controlled.

'Yes, I'm at the top of the Romangate.'

'Well, prepare yourself. College has been vandalised.'

It was worse than the scene her imagination had conjured up in the seconds that it took to run the rest of the way to Toby. Though the red spray-painted obscenities on the flagstones of the Yard and the smashed and broken lights around the Octo were simply what she had expected, Damia had not prepared herself for the extent of the damage to the Octo itself.

The vast windows of the Great Hall, whose glass had, in a few small areas, survived Reformation, Commonwealth, Restoration and the aerial bombardments of the Second World War, had been destroyed. Torn and tangled strips of lead hung crookedly or bent inwards over sills and mouldings, tracing the trajectory of missiles which had punched through glass and metal, shattering and twisting.

Holding up a trembling hand to halt Norris's advance, Damia walked silently around the Octo, her mind blotting out everything in the Yard, her attention focused entirely on the ravaged building.

Each of the windows was in the same condition. A few small panes, some intact, most of them jaggedly broken, clung to the leaded frame at the windows' outer edges and the angles where mullions met decorative moulding; the rest were torn away. The great lead-veined expanses of greenish glass which had filled Simon of Kineton's huge windows were gone.

In the midst of the gathering crowd the Octo looked old and abandoned, its dignity torn away, like an octogenarian duchess's, her rigid decorum destroyed in a second by the violence of a stroke.

Norris approached and stood, mute, at her side.

Damia turned to him, touched by his consideration but aware that his devastation must be as great, if not greater, than her own.

'What's it like inside?' The question sounded shockingly banal, somehow, too prosaic.

Norris shook his head. 'I don't know. When I rang the police, they told me not to go inside and to stop anybody else going in.' He looked up, his face a picture of controlled rage and despair. 'I imagine it's carnage in there. Glass, bricks – I just hope to God the wall painting hasn't been damaged.'

His words made Damia's skin crawl with apprehension.

The facts, as established by the police, were simple.

At around 2.30 a.m. a gang of youths had entered college armed with shopping trolleys full of bricks. In what was clearly a well-thought-out and premeditated action, four of them had proceeded to hurl bricks through all eight of the Great Hall windows until each one – large and small – had been completely smashed. The windows' mullions and mouldings had also suffered considerable damage, along with the walls on either side of the windows. 'Looks like they weren't very good shots,' the sergeant in charge had said in a vain attempt to lighten the atmosphere.

Meanwhile, the two remaining youths had knocked out the Yard's halogen lights and spray-painted obscene graffiti on the ground. This had all taken less than two minutes, after which the youths – challenged and pursued by a couple of furious, half-clothed undergraduates – ran off, leaving the trolleys, still containing some unthrown bricks, behind.

A good deal of this had been caught on camera-phone: a student woken by the noise, instead of confronting the vandals, had shown the presence of mind to record the destruction from her first-floor window and the police had taken away her phone to analyse the pictures. They had also routinely dusted the trolleys for fingerprints, though all the youths had appeared – from the poor-quality images captured on the phone's camera – to be wearing heavy gloves.

In the Great Hall, the damage turned out to be less severe than anticipated. Two of the refectory tables were scored with deep track-marks from flying bricks and there was some denting and gouging of the floorboards but, fortunately, the braking effect of smashing through leaded glass had meant that none of the bricks had maintained enough momentum to get as far as the wall painting.

Despite the police's best efforts to keep people away from the crime scene, Toby students could not be deterred from gathering in small knots in the Octo Yard. The magnitude of the vandalism seemed to render mere work inappropriate, callous even, and all through the morning Tobyites drifted back from libraries and lectures to stand around the perimeter of the Yard, outside the police cordon.

Together, Damia and Dominic Walters-Russell organised this unfocused need to do something. Damia's office became an ad hoc operations room and all available laptops were imported to run off the admin building's wireless network. Teams of students were then given lists of old members' email addresses to contact with news of the vandalism and appeals for help.

'I'm not going to give you a standard message,' Damia told her volunteers. 'Just introduce yourself, tell them how to access the pictures on the website and say how you felt when you saw what had happened in college this morning. Personal feelings are always going to be more effective than some official pronouncement. And don't forget, point them in as tactful a way as possible to the donations page on the website. Oh, and tell them that you're doing this because you felt you wanted to do something, not because you were recruited. It has the benefit of being the truth and it might stir some people into wanting to do something themselves.' Like give us a lot of money, she added, silently.

As the kitchens, along with the rest of the Octo, had been put out of bounds by the police, Damia sent one of her volunteers off to collect a suitable number of mugs from students who lived on the Octo Yard and hoped that her machine would cope with the demand for an endless stream of coffee. Another willing undergraduate was dispatched to the nearest bakery.

Meanwhile, Damia updated the blog.

Toby blog.

This is not a good day for Toby. Those of you who are part of our online old members network may already know why – undergraduates have been volunteering to send out emails all day in response to last night's destruction.

For those of you who don't know, [click here] to see what saboteurs did to the Octo and the Yard last night.

But, having said that it's a terrible day, it's also proving to be a moving and extraordinary day too, a day that is bringing home to me more and more the fact that Toby is not just somewhere young people come for three or four years to study – for those years, Toby becomes home. Not just because this is where they eat, sleep and work but because they are made to feel that they belong here, that this is *their* college, that they are what makes it what it is. And not just for these few short years, but for always. Once a Tobyite, always a Tobyite.

And they have wanted to do something. Even with finals looming for some, work has taken a back seat to the desire to fight back against the systematic vandalising of the building at the heart of our college.

Because it wasn't just glass – however old and priceless – that was destroyed, it was the peaceful assumption of harmony between this place and the city in which it has always been the favoured college, home to Salster's own.

The action of six youths has asked hard questions about that relationship, and no one here at Toby quite knows what the answers are, because this does not have the feel of an opportunistic act. Bricks had to be acquired in quantity, shopping trolleys stolen and the two brought together under cover of darkness and transported down to the Octo Yard.

None of the graffiti sprayed on to the flagstones suggest motive or grievance but the police suspect a link with the college's financial troubles.

Who knows?

What I know is how it has affected me. The students are not the only ones who have come to regard Toby as their home. I have to admit to feeling a visceral sense of personal insult in what has been done to the Octo. The smashing of windows, the destruction of hundreds of years of history, is nothing compared to the sense of violation I feel, that people should come into this place, a place of open trust without doors or security staff, and betray that trust so utterly. It makes me sick at heart.

I have realised that I had come to regard Toby as a place of sanctuary not only for its scholars and teachers, not only for its staff, of which I am proud to be one, but also for the city. Academically elite it may be, but it has no huge excluding doors, it does not have 'Keep Off' signs, it is not a 'Members Only' enclosure. Anybody may come here without being looked at askance, may look, admire, wonder and aspire.

But six people came last night with bricks and spray paint. They looked, they despised, scorned and denigrated this place. And we are all – including them – left the poorer for it.

Blog posted, she drifted around the room reading emails.

So, apart from the shock, what does all this mean for Toby? Financially, it's a disaster. As a Grade 1 listed building, criminal damage insurance has always been prohibitively expensive so, with the peaceful town-gown history in Salster, it's never been seen as a priority. Replacing this quantity of glass and leading to Grade 1 standard is going to cost tens, if not hundreds of thousands of pounds …

Toby's current financial status makes this wanton destruction potentially disastrous and the college is obviously going to come under increasing pressure to adopt the Northgate supercollege plan. I, for one, think it would be a very sad day for Toby, and for Salster, if that were to happen.

Please, please, pledge your financial support now. With 72 graduating Tobyites per year, even if we only take the last 40 years' graduates, that's 2,880 people. If you all gave £10 a month that would net us £345,600 a year. If only half of you gave £10 a month that £172,800 would probably pay off most of the cost of the window repair.

They were, Damia reflected, prepared to be much more direct than she was. Even as the manager of an emergency appeal, she would find it unacceptable to be seen to beg; the young Tobyites had no such inhibitions.

Inevitably, the media lapped up the disaster. The press were hovering around looking for facts and soundbites almost as soon as the police got their scene-of-crime squad into the Toby Yard, and Damia made the most of the opportunity to present the attack as a crime not only against Toby but against the city itself and its reputation for harmonious town–gown relations.

Early in the afternoon, Bob rang from the porter's lodge to say that Abbie Daniels and her television crew had arrived. Glancing out of the window as she made her way out of the room, Damia swore softly.

Heads came up and Dominic Walters-Russell asked simply, 'What?'

'Surprise, surprise, Ian Baird has come to say what a terrible thing.' Damia nodded through the window to where the Northgate president was following the camera crew into the Yard.

She clattered down the stairs to the Yard, followed, after wordless glances, by the entire emergency email team.

Damia greeted Abbie Daniels with wary friendliness. Alienating the local station would not be a good PR move, but the fact that the reporter had arrived with Ian Baird in tow indicated an agenda that Damia was not at all happy with.

'Is Doctor Norris around?' Abbie Daniels looked about

as if expecting Norris to emerge from behind an undergraduate.

Damia's suspicions about Abbie's desire to orchestrate a head-to-head between Norris and Baird confirmed, she took the other woman's arm and tried to draw her aside.

'Look, Abbie, we really don't need this turning into another reason for Kineton and Dacre to draw stumps—'

Abbie Daniels coolly removed her elbow from Damia's grasp and gave her a look redolent of organ grinders and their monkeys. 'But that's exactly what it is, isn't it?' she asked. 'If the tenants are so incensed at the governing body's lack of willingness to negotiate that they resort to this sort of thing, then I think we need to question the judgement of the person in charge, don't you?'

'Wait a minute!' Damia held a hand up. 'There's no evidence – no suggestion even – that the tenants are responsible for this!'

'Who else would be pissed off enough at the college to do it?'

Damia looked nervously around at the video camera. 'Is that thing on?'

'Look, can you tell Norris I'm here please?'

'Abbie, I don't think this—'

Abbie Daniels turned crisply aside and beckoned to one of the undergraduates.

'Do you think you could go and tell Dr Norris that I'm here?'

Damia turned around and shook her head at the group of young people, not knowing which one of them had been singled out. Turning back to Abbie Daniels she took her phone out of her back pocket.

'I will tell Dr Norris you're here,' she said, 'though I can't guarantee that he'll be free right now. You can imagine he's pretty busy with the police and so forth.'

The other woman inclined her head stiffly then turned to look for Baird.

'Sir Ian,' Damia heard her say as Norris picked up his office phone at the other end of the line 'Perhaps, while we wait for a response from Dr Norris, you could give us your views on what has happened here?'

Damia, her attention on Norris's voice, was only half aware of what came next.

'No,' she heard a voice say authoritatively.

Stammering a few hurried phrases to the Regent Master, Damia finished the call and closed her phone to see Dominic Walters-Russell standing between the journalist and her headphoned entourage.

'Any interviews with Sir Ian will be conducted outside the walls of this college, if you don't mind.' His small stature in no way detracted from the young JCR president's natural authority. 'Sir Ian holds no office in this college, he has made it very clear that he does not wish to be associated with it in the accepted way, therefore he has no right to stand here and give his opinions. If you wish to interview him, I would like you to step out of the college on to the Romangate.'

Abbie Daniels tried to brush him aside. 'Don't be ridiculous. It's impossible to conduct an interview on the Romangate – there's far too much traffic noise.'

Dominic blocked her attempt to manoeuvre around him. 'Then I suggest,' he said, 'that you and Sir Ian go back to his college and conduct your interview there.'

Daniels, her lips compressed, turned to Damia. 'Are you going to allow him to dictate who I can and can't interview here?'

Damia did not hesitate. 'Yes.'

'But he has no authority to tell me what to do!'

'He has all the authority he needs. This is his college. Added to which, he's president of the junior common room and so speaks for all the undergraduates. But that's not the point.'

Daniels swung around, muttering, 'This is ridiculous.' Nodding curtly to her crew she lifted her microphone to her lips and said, 'Sir Ian, what do you make of the devastation we see here?'

Moving swiftly and decisively, Dominic stepped between Baird and the camera.

'No,' he said calmly. 'Not in this college.'

Baird, obviously furious at this move, put his hands on Dominic's shoulders as if to move him out of the way, but before he could do so the watching undergraduates moved as if impelled by a single neural impulse and surrounded Dominic, roughly detaching Sir Ian's hands from him and jostling the Northgate president.

'Are you getting all this?' Damia heard Daniels ask her cameraman, but before the man could respond, a hand had gone up over the camera's lens, barring any attempts to focus on the melee.

'I would like you to leave now,' Dominic said evenly, addressing Sir Ian Baird. 'Ms Daniels and her crew may accompany you or stay, but I would like you to leave.'

Baird glared at him with naked hostility but the JCR president was not to be stared down.

'Now, please.'

When Baird still showed no intention of doing as he was asked a voice in the crowd started a chant. 'Baird out! Baird out!'

It was swiftly taken up by all the undergraduates and, with 'Baird out, Baird out' ringing around the yard and Dominic Walters-Russell refusing to break eye contact, Sir Ian abruptly turned and strode out of the yard.

Fifty-three

Though courts had heard cases in English for thirty years and more, Simon might just as well have been listening to the proceedings in French for all he understood of Mottis's arguments.

Until he had seen the somewhat small and insignificant Mottis donning the white coif of the Serjeant at Law and watched him take his place with Ralph Daker's pleader, Simon had not realised how high Mottis stood in the legal world of London.

'Richard and I knew each other when I was a legal apprentice and he nothing more than his father's heir,' Mottis had explained after the first session, with the smile of a man long done with the need to prove himself. 'He promised me that when I was called to the order of the coif, he would employ me as his own man, to have oversight of all his legal affairs, both to plead for him in court and to ensure that his legal documents were as watertight as the barrels his wine came to England in.'

'Would not one of the apprentices have done as well?'

Simon asked, nodding towards the students of the law who sat in their 'crib' in the court, committing to memory everything said and noting techniques from facial gestures to past legal proceedings cited. 'I know not all are called to be a Serjeant at Law – is it not a matter of—'

He stopped, not wishing to imply that Mottis could not have afforded the lavish feast and present-giving that was customary amongst those called to the highest order of the law.

'Richard stood surety for my feast,' Mottis confirmed without a shred of shame. 'He wanted the best, and only a Serjeant at Law would do for him.'

Was Mottis living up to Richard Daker's expectations, Simon wondered. Only time would tell.

Law! It was all talk, talk, talk – so many words spinning and fighting each other like cocks in a pit that it made Simon's head whirl. There was no solid ground here, nothing a man could knock his fist against and call a certainty. All was opinion and precedent and judgement. He feared for the outcome of their case, and though he had been sure enough with Gwyneth, he doubted his ability to build the college any other way than by winning his suit and wresting the endowments back from Ralph. Or rather from Ralph and Anne, for Anne Daker, scarcely three months a widow, had been eager in allying herself with her husband's nephew in this bid to recover lands given away and alienated from the family.

The apprentices in their crib, having heard nothing like it, watched every facial tic and clearing of the throat that passed before them on the bench.

Mottis did not bluster or appeal like Ralph's pleader; he did not call on the judge's feelings as a father and a man of affairs, he merely took his stance, time and again, on Richard's unchanged papers of endowment.

Had his master wavered in his intention? The only evidence Mottis had as to his employer's intentions was his signal failure to instruct himself, Richard Daker's trusted lawyer and friend, to draw up new papers.

Was his master in his right mind after his only son's death? As far as the preparations for and execution of a highly proper funeral could give evidence, then his mind was as it ever had been.

Was there no suggestion that this death – Richard Daker's – was the result of despair, a mortal sin? Mottis surveyed the court with a cold and unblinking eye. His master had never despaired, of life, of faith, of the eternal mercy and love of God. Never. Never. Never.

'Simon, have you no care for your own safety? For Gwyneth's?'

Henry had been against the court case from the beginning.

'Do you not know that the king is come home from Ireland to rein in the Lollards in Parliament? To put an end to their influence?'

'And what has this to do with me and my college?' Simon had asked.

Henry had stared back at him in exasperation, no longer the apprentice boy seeking to placate his master but a husband and father now, a King's Mason and rising man of influence. Henry, Simon knew, must be fretting at his close association with the stain of religious unorthodoxy, of anticlericalism in the realm of a king as pious as he was capricious.

'Simon, Richard Daker may have stood between you and the Church when he was alive, but you pushed very close to the edge in burying Toby in the home of a known Wyclifite, at the hand of a Lollard priest.' He gazed at Simon intently, visibly willing him to come to his senses. 'They are watching you, Simon. Now that Daker no longer protects you, who will defend you when you are arrested and taken before the bishop, thrown in his dungeons?'

'As you say,' Simon answered levelly, 'Daker is dead. I will no longer build for a Lollard, I will build for myself. For Toby.'

'With the endowments of a Lollard, the college founded on the statutes of a Lollard! This court case will ruin you, Simon! You think it will ensure your college's future but it will not, it will simply seal your fate at the hands of the Church.'

'There are no statutes for the college. And land is land. It has no allegiance.'

Henry's fist had crashed down on to the arm of his chair in agitation. 'Simon, do not be so naïve! This is Daker's college and always will be. Or are you going to hand over teaching to the Church, once you have built your monument?'

Simon stared at him. Like a pregnant girl who looks no further than the birth of her child, not imagining him walking or talking, Simon had not imagined his college as anything other than a building. A perfect building, but simply that.

But a college was not simply a building. And that which Daker had taken responsibility for, the upkeep and philosophy of the institution, would now be his to decide.

'I will give nothing to the Church,' he had said flatly. 'Like

423

the Crown, the Church has done nothing but take away from me and mine. I will give it nothing. Beyond that, I do not know.'

'Simon?'

Mottis had been parleying with the Dakers' pleader and now appeared quietly at Simon's side.

'Yes?'

'An offer has been made.'

Simon looked at the lawyer. His face betrayed nothing but the desire to convey news.

'What offer?'

'Ralph's lawyer sees the way the wind is blowing and has suggested that we arrive at a compromise—'

'If he suggests that, then he must think we are going to win! Why compromise?'

Mottis drew Simon away from the ears of the apprentices and other court hangers-on. 'It is not so simple. In cases of land holdings, judges are loath to alienate an entire estate away from those who would, in normal circumstances, inherit the land. If we do not agree to their compromise, we may end up with less land than we need to build our college, as the judge tries to balance Richard's wishes whilst alive with what he would hope for his widow after his death.' Mottis's eyes were steady on Simon, maintaining calm.

Simon breathed heavily. 'Ach!' he protested. 'It is too much for me! What is it Ralph suggests?'

'It is Anne's suggestion.' Mottis' expression was half amusement, half surprised admiration.

In a voice that carried no further than Simon's ear, Mottis explained Anne's proposal. 'They suggest that since Anne has unexpectedly been left a widow, that Daker would not wish her to be unprovided for. They propose that one third of the lands endowed should revert to her in perpetuity—'

'Perpetual dowerage?'

Mottis flinched at Simon's volume but continued as if he had not spoken.

'Furthermore, since the college is not yet built, that a boundary of time be put on the endowments beyond which you may not stray. If the college is not completed within the appointed time, the lands would revert to Ralph.'

He held Simon carefully with his eyes. The master mason, taking his lead, remained silent until he should finish what he had to say.

'In effect, they are asking that the college be treated like an heir still in his minority. If the heir dies, the estate goes to the next nearest kin. If we fail to build the college during the prescribed period – the college's minority, if you will – the estate reverts in the same way.'

'And how long do they propose giving us to finish the college?'

'Five years.'

'Five years during which they will harry and harass us and try to frustrate us in any way they can!'

'Undoubtedly.'

Simon shook his head, at a loss as to how he should proceed in this mire of words and motives. 'How do you judge, Piers?'

The lawyer took a deep breath and was silent a moment, ordering his thoughts. Simon could feel curious eyes on his back but would not turn.

Mottis spoke. 'I think we should agree to the minority suggestion. It carries with it the risks you have named but we are resourceful men and neither of us easily swayed.' He paused, possibly waiting for an outburst. When none come he continued. 'As for the perpetual dowerage of a third of the lands, I judge a third to be too much. If Richard had wanted to make provision for his widow he would have done so, he was a man of caution and much older than she. I propose allowing Anne Daker to select any manor of her choosing for her dowerage.' He paused once more. 'Aside from that, I say let us take their compromise and build our college.'

Simon nodded and clasped Mottis's dry, cool hand in his. 'So be it,' he said. 'So be it.'

Fifty-four

From: dotdotdotdashdashdash@hotmail.com
To: EJCNorris@kdc.sal.ac.uk
Subject: the wall painting

Norris

The wall painting will be next if you don't see reason.

The email had been traced to a busy internet café where the prospect of tracking down the author of an individual message was negligible. Since it had arrived after Damia's blog had been posted and half of Salster had seen the state of the Octagon, the police had decided that it was nothing more than a malicious prank.

Neither Damia nor Norris saw the warning as anything but serious. But whereas Damia inclined to the opinion that Ian Baird must be behind it, Norris viewed the striking tenants as the more likely source. Following the failure of the rent strike and the public meeting to generate support in college, he argued, the tenants had a simple choice for their campaign – give up or step up.

'There's always your collusion theory,' he reminded

Damia. 'Hadstowe, Northrop and Baird as an unholy trinity, all working to the supercollege plan for their varying reasons.'

But Damia was less concerned with the provenance of the warning than with the college's response to it. As the police had dismissed the email as the work of a crank and therefore posing no threat, they had offered to do no more than divert patrol cars past college every hour or so during the night. Damia feared that this might be dangerously inadequate.

The undergraduates, alive to her concern and fired by their involvement in the email campaign, took action. They devised a rota for hourly guard duty on the steps of the Octo, each guard passing on to the next a gas-canister klaxon to be activated in case of emergency. The noise, demonstrated at lunchtime, was enough to wake every sleeper within a quarter of a mile's radius and was certain to bring students swarming into the Yard.

But Damia knew that this measure was time-limited. The end of term was only days away and even the most dedicated final-year student was bound to go home for a long weekend over Easter, leaving the college vulnerable to attack. She and Norris discussed security options, but all cost money that the college could ill afford.

Money was, however, starting to come in.

The email campaign had borne almost immediate fruit – both financial and in an avalanche of outraged email comment and support.

Nor was the response confined to the internet. A generous and unsolicited donation came in from the butcher who supplied the college with all its meat products and, as a very visible gesture of thanks, Damia placed a blackboard and easel on the Romangate with the message MANY THANKS

TO THOMAS GITTINGS AND SON, FAMILY BUTCH-
ERS, FOR THEIR MOST GENEROUS DONATION TO
THE RESTORATION FUND.

As she had anticipated, other local businesses followed
suit, their donations paying for a unique advertising opportunity on one of Salster's busiest thoroughfares.

But the most surprising response to the nocturnal vandalism came from an old Toby member:

Dear Ms Miller

As a Tobyite (1983) I was shocked by your blog on the
vandalism of the Octo. As CEO and sole owner of
WWWebads I am in a position to help. I would like to offer
to pay for the complete restoration of the Octagon's
windows which, I am fairly reliably assured, will run to a
cost of around £200k.

I would also like to make a further offer. I am prepared
to make up the gross value of my donation to college to
£500k if you can raise – from old members alone – an
equivalent £500k. This would net the college a million
pounds which should go some way to helping it out of its
current financial difficulties.

My offer to pay for the windows is entirely independent
of the second suggestion. The windows are a done deal. If
you can mobilise enough old members (a recent email
suggested that if each graduate for the last 40 years gave
£10 a month that would net the college £345,600 a year) the
college may benefit from this vandalism. It's not, after all, a
huge stretch from £345,600 to £500k.

It's not my business to tell you how to run yours, but
maybe you could call the campaign 'Max-a-Million'?

Looking forward to working with you

Jon Song
CEO WWWebads

As the final JCR meeting of term had already taken place, Damia put up a poster in the common room saying 'Emergency Emails on Vandalism Day Worked' and blu-tacked to it a photocopy of Jon Song's letter. Mobile phones picked up the message and within the day even those undergraduates who were packing to go home knew of the unknown Mr Song's massive donation.

Ed Norris was not acquainted with their benefactor. 'Before my time,' he said. 'Try somebody who's been here longer. Or the college records, of course.'

Jonathan Leong Song, the college records told her, had studied mathematics, in which he had obtained a second class honours degree, had rowed for the college at bow and played tennis, bringing home the Men's Singles Cup in 1985. He was not on the Toby Committee – the college's official graduate body – nor had he made donations to the college before. The appeal that Northrop had headed up had obviously left him unmoved.

After speaking to Mr Song on the phone, Damia sat down to include his donation and the Max-a-Million appeal in her blog.

'Will you be coming down for the Fairings?' she had asked him, experiencing an adrenalin lurch as she realised that the first of May was no longer on a distant horizon.

'Absolutely,' Song replied. 'I've already bought my "By, For and With" shirt. I'll be there.'

She was struggling to find the right tone to tell the Toby-affiliated world about the WWWebads offer when she was distracted by feet on the wooden staircase outside and unfamiliar voices. 'You stay here until you're called or there's going to be hell to pay. Right?'

The rumbled response was indecipherable but implied cowed acquiescence. Damia was halfway out of her seat before she heard the knock on the door.

Responding to the instruction to come in, a small woman in late middle age with improbably copper hair opened the door just enough to admit her slight frame. She hacked a rattling, sixty-a-day cough as Damia greeted her.

'Shirley! What can I do for you?'

The other woman, one of the under-chefs in the college kitchens, folded her arms protectively in front of her.

'You can try not judging me for what others have done, for a start.' Damia immediately understood that Shirley's attitude, caught between belligerence and apology, was connected with the person who stood on the other side of the door.

'I've got my grandson Danny outside. Told him he could either come here to you or I'd march him down to the police station. "You wouldn't do that, Gran," he said. I said, "I would, just you watch me. Might wake you up a bit, show you where you're heading if you carry on with that lot of yobs and wasters." So here he is.'

'Did he have something to do with the vandalism?' Damia sank on to one of the sofas, nodding to Shirley to do the same. The woman sat slightly stiffly.

'Yeah. Caught him red-handed I did. Literally red-handed 'cause they used red spray paint didn't they and it don't come off that easy. Only they were too stupid to know that, weren't they?'

Damia was about to ask what Danny knew about the

motive for the attack, but Shirley had not finished her disquisition on the stupidity of young men.

'I said to him, "You been spraying them tags of yours again, Danny Wiseman?" "No, Gran," he says, like he's a good boy. He'd've been better off saying yes, 'cause I got it out of him in the end. And I've brought him here to make amends.'

She rose as stiffly as she had sat down and went to the door, yanking it open as if daring it not to disclose her grandson on the other side.

'In. Now.'

A slightly overweight youth shuffled in, his head bent, though whether this was to obscure the dreadful acne that lurked beneath the hood of his top or to express contrition was not clear.

'Take your hands out of your pockets and take your hood off,' his grandmother snapped.

Short, home-bleached hair was revealed beneath the hood, along with more acne on the boy's forehead and mean-spirited grey eyes that glanced at Damia then slid away.

'Right. Say your piece,' Shirley instructed.

'Gran says I'm supposed—' the youth began, his eyes on the floor and his hands defiantly back in the pockets of his hoodie.

'No you don't! Take responsibility for your own actions,' his grandmother barked.

Danny's shoulders came up as he took a deep breath, then he squared up and looked Damia in the eye momentarily, before concentrating on somewhere in the vicinity of her ear. 'I was one of the people what did that,' he mumbled, his head indicating the Octo Yard. 'And I'm giving you this' – one of his hands emerged from the kangaroo-pouch holding an envelope – 'to say sorry.'

Damia took the proffered envelope, looking from Danny to his bristling grandmother.

'What is it?'

'It's his thirty pieces of silver,' Shirley spat before Danny could reply. 'After all this college has done for me and mine, all the times they've let me have time off without complaining, the time the old RM took me aside and told me about the staff hardship fund, after all that, this ungrateful piece took money off somebody to do the college down! Well that's it' – her head pecked towards the envelope in Damia's hand. 'Every penny. And if he'd had any other money to his name, that'd be in there too, but he never has got a penny. I suppose I should count my blessings and thank my lucky stars for that – least it means he's not thieving or dealing drugs!'

Shirley did not sound grateful. In fact, she looked as if she would prefer the entrepreneurship of drug-dealing to the gang mentality which had probably propelled Danny into spray-painting the Yard while his mates threw bricks through the Octo's windows.

'Who paid you?' she asked the boy abruptly.

'Dunno.' Danny, apology rehearsed, had returned to passive-aggressive surliness. His grandmother, however, had obviously extracted what information was to be had.

'Says his mate got paid to do the job,' she said. 'His mate had never seen the bloke who paid him before but he said he looked posh.'

'Would this mate be able to identify the man?'

'What? Grass him up?' The question's tone was such that Danny clearly wasn't looking for an answer.

'He might be a bit more forthcoming if the police got involved—'

Here, Danny looked wildly at his grandmother. 'You said—'

Shirley was shaking her head. 'You don't understand these lads,' she said. 'They think it's more than their life's worth to do the right thing and tell you who's behind it all. They'd rather go to jail than be a grass.'

Danny breathed a sigh of relief at this evidence of realism. 'Can I go now?' he asked his grandmother, ignoring Damia.

'Yeah, go on, clear off.'

The door closed and Shirley sat once more. 'What can I say, Damia?' she asked, all the hardness with which she had faced Danny gone with him. 'I'm so ashamed I could pack me job in here. If anybody else was to get to hear about this I'd never be able to hold my head up.'

Damia understood what was being asked of her and nodded. 'Don't worry, Shirley, your name won't pass my lips. I'll just tell Dr Norris that I've heard on the grapevine that it wasn't mindless vandalism – that the kids were paid to do it.' She looked at the other woman. 'I've got enough connections in the – what shall we say – slightly less law-abiding fraternity, from working at the Gardiner Centre, that he won't ask which grapevine I heard it on. And if I tell him there's no point involving the police, he'll take that as gospel too.'

'Thank you, Damia. That's more than I've got a right to ask.'

'It's not your fault, Shirley. You can't be blamed for what Danny does.'

'He's my flesh and blood. Done something wrong somewhere, haven't I, for him to turn out like he is doing?'

434

Damia shook her head. 'I'm not sure it works like that, Shirley.'

After meeting with Norris to bring him up to date with Shirley's revelations, Damia walked slowly up the Octo steps. She had not entered the Great Hall since she and Norris had stood at the door, accompanied by a police officer, and looked briefly inside. Now, the window-spaces had been filled with translucent plastic sheeting, filling the hall with a pearly light.

Walking into the quiet space – strangely empty without the silent concentration of the two conservators – Damia gazed about her. The damage to floor and tables was insignificant when weighed against the destruction of the windows, but the raw gouges and scratches gave the hall an unkempt, uncared-for feeling. The dim light, in a space normally so sunlit, added to the sense of down-at-heel ruination. Even the wall painting looked different in the unaccustomed half-light.

Carefully averting her eyes from the damage all around and fixing them on the painting, she crossed the hall to stand before the final two ovals. Looking up at the resurrected sinner, and the Christ in benediction, she tallied what she knew: Tobias Kineton, born latterly to ageing parents, imprisoned in a cripple's body, deemed cursed by Church and townsfolk, involved mysteriously in John Dacre's death, drowned in the river himself the following day.

How did he come to drown? As yet unknown.

Why were there two statues, one of Toby the cripple, another of a whole and hearty boy? As yet unknown.

Damia stared at the dimly lit figures. If, as seemed more and more likely, the wall painting represented the life of Tobias Kineton, then this kneeling sinner must be he, the figure's small stature accounted for by his age, rather than his lowly state. But how unlike the imprisoned Toby this individual was: his face still and rapt, eyes unpatched and true, limbs straight and pliant as he knelt in supplication. Was this the painter's idea of Heaven – all things perfected, healed, restored?

She stared at the perfect vision and then, without warning or process of thought, she saw it, in the fall of boyish hair, the soft boots, the tunic. She suddenly knew. This resurrected boy, gazing at the Saviour, and the Toby statue were one and the same.

Toby Kineton, whole in death as he never had been in life, had been set on the wall of his father's college, peering over the unique bulk of the Octagon at the pitiful vision of his earthly body.

Fifty-five

By the time Simon and Mottis returned to Salster the hours of daylight were becoming short and Simon knew he would have to wait for spring before he could reawaken his college site and bring back his masons to the building. To speed the time, he spent the weeks before and after Christmas travelling to the Daker lands, talking to stewards and bailiffs and settling affairs with them. Though one or two were wary, most were happy that tenants were to be allowed to continue as they had done under Daker and welcomed Simon's assurance that he or his representative, Piers Mottis, would attend at all quarter-days to settle disputes, answer claims and otherwise prove good landlords.

Simon made it clear that, although he would not be resident in the manors, he was interested in the good heart of the land upon which the college would depend and that Mottis, as a lawyer, would see justice done as fairly as his late friend Richard Daker had done.

'So if this college of yourn be not built in time,' stated one of the stewards, a bluff, brown man of Simon's own age or thereabouts, 'then we will be in the hands of Ralph, the nephew?'

'Yes. But I will not let that happen. I am not to be deterred. The college will be built, you have my word on it.'

The steward eyed him then turned and spat deliberately upon the ground, as if ridding himself of an evil taste. 'Let us hope your word be good, Master Kineton, for I do not wish to fall under Master Ralph Daker's yoke. He be a man not fit to be put over others.'

Simon returned the stolid gaze. 'I agree with you, friend. One day, perhaps men will not have ascendancy by birth but by right of fitness alone.'

'Aye, when the pigs sprout wings and fly from the woods, Master Mason. That be when that will come to pass!'

His words haunted Simon as he thought of those lands that would, following the judgement of the court, revert to Anne Daker's control and so – in Simon's mind – to Ralph. Although the college had not been forced to relinquish a third of its endowments as Daker's widow had wished, the court had seen fit to return to her more than the single manor that Mottis had proposed. Simon, knowing nothing of the finances necessary for an institution such as he was building, doubted the remaining lands' sufficiency, but he had no choice but to accept the court's ruling and build with what he was left.

Simon returned to Salster – following a detour to his own lands at Kineton – with several stone-laden barges in his wake and more ordered for the coming months. Finally able to see years of building ahead, he had ordered the quarries extended and taken on more men to cut stone, leaving instructions as to his needs with his steward.

Now that window-tracery for the hall would be needed, Simon determined to come back in the spring with moulds and masons to work *in situ*, so that his barges would carry less wasted cargo along the long waterway miles to Salster. It would also reduce the need for lodge-space on the college site if some of the cutting could be done at a distance and shipped in its final state.

He was planning the timing of his shipments as he passed into Salster through the Romangate and heard his name called out.

He turned in his saddle and scanned the crowds until he located the source of the cry. A figure was hurrying towards him.

'Master Kineton. You are welcome home!'

'My thanks, friend. What business do you have with me?'

The man caught his breath. 'I am bid to tell you that the mayor wishes to see you as soon as you may come to him.'

Simon was startled 'Before I go home to greet my wife?'

'Yes, master. My task is to bring you the moment you ride through the gate.'

'And if I had ridden through another gate into the city?'

The man looked at him gravely. 'Then another would have greeted you and given you the same message.'

When Simon was shown into the mayor's presence, Brygge greeted him as a friend, clasping hands with him warmly.

'Simon,' he said, after the greetings were done. 'It pains me to be the bearer of ill tidings, but I must tell you that Ralph Daker has been busy in your absence. He has got wind of your son's burial here and knows who performed it.'

'And is this so dreadful that I must come here before even kissing my wife?'

439

If Brygge was concerned at the brittle tone of Simon's answer, he did not show it. 'I am told, by one whom I trust, that the bishop intends to have you taken up for beliefs contrary to the Church's teaching and preaching discontent against him and therefore against the king.'

Simon's chin jerked up as he heard this news. 'Howso against the king?'

'Because the king would have his servants loyal to the Church and its anointed ministers and not questioning the foundations of its wealth and authority.' Brygge kept his voice dry and even, his eyes never wavering on Simon's. 'For if the authority of the Church is questioned, that of the king is also, anointed as he is by the Church in the name of God.'

Simon scrubbed at his beard with calloused finger-ends, his chipped, torn nails raising welts on the skin beneath.

'And this is Ralph, to stop me building the college?'

Brygge sat down, motioning Simon to do the same. 'Not solely. But Ralph Daker and Robert Copley have ever found each other come handy to their separate purposes. Ralph wants his lands back. Copley wants you slapped down. He wants no challengers to his fortune and influence. The Church is his power and he has no other. Your challenge – or Daker's challenge taken up by you – is a threat to the influence of Copley and those like him. They will do all they can to bring the king to see that a challenge to them is as good as treason against his own body.'

He looked at Simon. 'You cannot stand against the king, Simon.'

I did, once, long ago, Simon thought, seeing again the broken veins, feeling the old man's humiliated rage, and I have paid lifelong for it in littleness of name and work.

'Yes, I can.'

Copley narrowed his eyes at Simon, hearing certainty rather than defiance in the mason's voice.

'How?'

Simon leaned forward, putting his elbows on his knees. 'Copley knows me for a stiff-necked man,' he said bluntly, 'and I have proved to be such to Ralph.' He heaved a great sigh, feeling the weariness that had ridden with him from Kineton. 'But I can confound them by bending my will in a different direction.'

He stopped and half-smiled. 'Richard Daker once asked me if I would bend – even so little' – his finger and thumb, as Daker's had done, compressed a blade's thickness of air – 'to please another, if it would serve my purposes.'

'And you answered No.'

Simon laughed in his nose at Brygge's certainty and nodded. 'Because the bishop is right, I am a stiff-necked man and I do things as I would have them done.' He paused and, looking into the mayor's face, smiled again. 'But as another man also said to me, there is more than one way to kill a rabbit.'

A week after his conversation with Brygge, as Simon walked the streets to Henry and Alysoun's house, he felt the London air strange about him and reflected how different it was now to the city it had been when first he had heard word of Richard Daker's commission. Ten years before, the country had been under the control not of the young king but of nobles who ruled on their liege lord's behalf. The succeeding years had seen these advisers overthrown and Gloucester and Gaunt replace them at Richard's side, their hands upon the reins of power. But Gloucester and Gaunt, for all their ambition, had, in their turn, been put aside by Richard, when he took up the full mantle of kingship.

But now, Richard, second king of that name, was a man in mourning. His queen, whom he was said to have loved with a devotion unsurpassed between husband and wife, had died of plague the previous year. And with the death of his Anne, Richard, that lively boy, full of courage and love of beauty, had turned into a dark, scowling man whose judgement might be relied upon to be nothing but fickle and contrary.

Simon looked around and wondered, with a fancifulness that made him shake his head at himself, whether the volatile melancholy of the king had spread itself over the city and its people. For London did not feel as it had in the days when the king had been young and well. Its people seemed to strut less brazenly, their shouts were not so full-throated as before; the swagger of London had been subdued.

A country cannot thrive, Simon thought, when its king is not staunch to his own opinions.

The sky reflected his mood – dense grey clouds weighed down on the city, pressing the life out of the air, muting the spirits of its people and making them wary of storms and ill humours.

He was glad when, at last, he arrived at the Acklands' door.

Alysoun, still indisposed after the recent birth of their third child, did not come to join them. Simon, alone with Henry, wasted no time.

'Henry, I am here to ask you to stand my friend in the matter of the college.'

'If you are looking for another patron, Simon,' Henry smiled, 'you need a man with a longer purse than me.'

Simon smiled back, aware, despite Henry's levity, of the younger man's sudden uneasiness.

'Fear not, Henry! Daker continues to provide in that respect—'

'For five years,' Henry broke in. 'Five years!' He shook his head at the thought. 'Sim will be twelve years old – an apprentice to me – in five years' time. A new century will be almost upon us. Many things can happen in five years, Simon.'

'That I know, Henry. And that is why I am here to ask for your help.'

They stared at each other mutely and then Henry nodded, slowly, once, allowing Simon to begin.

When his foster-father had finished, Henry said, not looking at him, 'And you think, if you keep yourself away from Salster, they will let Gwyneth oversee the work? See it completed, without a murmur?'

'Scarcely that, but I am persuaded that if Gwyneth tells Copley she has said she will not live with me because of my heretical views, then her own love of the Church will not come under question. She attends mass daily and is suspected of nothing.'

'You do not think they will see it as a ploy?'

'You believe it to be a ploy, Henry?'

His head came up, sharply. 'What, do you tell me that this is so? That Gwyneth refuses to live with you? That she has said she will see the college finished by her own hand or not at all?'

Simon sighed deeply. 'She is pleased to have good reason not to live with me under the same roof, I think. And she has told me that she will see the college built, though for Toby's sake rather than my own.'

Henry rose agitatedly from his seat and paced towards the fireplace in the wall. Kicking a log off the fire-dogs and into the ashes, he turned and leaned against the chimney breast.

'Where will you go?'

'To Kineton. I will oversee the cutting of stone and, once Gwyneth has sent me the moulds for the hall windows, I can build a lodge and send the tracery down ready-cut.'

Henry scuffed ashes on the hearth with the toe of his boot, his face moody. Simon saw again the boy he had been, a boy who had never learned dissimulation. Set to a distasteful task, Henry had always protested silently, his face set and his whole body rigid with a defiance he had been too unsure of Simon's temper to express.

'And you will be content to stay at Kineton and leave the building to Gwyneth?'

His sceptical tone grated on Simon. 'No, of course I will not be content! How can I be content when this is the one building I have wished to put my hand and name to, life-long?'

Their eyes met and Henry looked away.

Simon moderated his manner. 'But if this will see my college built, then will I endure it. Seeing it built by another's hands, unwatched by me, shall be my penance for driving my boy to his death.'

'Penance?' Henry almost laughed the word. 'Surely you – the newly minted Lollard – do not believe in penance?'

Simon looked at him, something akin to loathing knifing into his guts. 'I do not believe it purges me of sin in God's sight,' he said, his jaw muscles so tight with sudden anger that his words ground out like sparks from a whetstone. 'But it soothes my guilt. And my grief.'

Henry pushed himself away from the chimney breast and stood, looking into the flames of the candles on their stand. 'Who will be site-master?'

'Edwin Gore.'

'He and Gwyneth are no friends.'

'They are not required to be friends, merely to give each other the necessary respect. I do not like Edwin myself, as a man, but he has remained loyal through all that has happened and I believe that he will see the work done well.'

'Then why do you ask this of me?'

'Because I may be wrong. And because those under Edwin will look to their work with more attention if they know that every four weeks a King's Mason will be on hand.'

Henry appeared to leave the question of his regular attendance at the college to one side. 'Has Gwyneth agreed to build the roof?'

'She has.'

'And what of the glass? I know Master Daker was to provide the glass himself, aside from the college's endowments.'

'I shall get work – making window-tracery will not take all my time – I may design buildings and carve images.'

'You could work from now till domesday and not do enough to provide glass for windows and roof!' Henry protested.

'But that would not be your concern,' Simon pointed out. 'It would be mine.'

Henry sat once more, his elbows on his knees, looking at Simon steadily.

'Simon, could you not build your college as a memorial to Toby and still give it to the Church?'

Simon narrowed his eyes. 'With Daker's endowments?'

'Let somebody else endow it! Let Ralph have his lands! Then everybody will be happy – the Church will not be mocked, charity is served by another man's money, Ralph has his lands and you have your college, your memorial to Toby.'

'But it would not be mine,' Simon said softly. 'It could not be my memorial to Toby if another man endowed it. No one who would endow a college would consent to see my son's image on the walls. He would want himself, his saint, the king, depending on whom he wanted to please most.'

Henry looked up to Heaven in exasperation. 'But what does it matter, Simon? If what you believe is true, then Toby gave his life so that the college would be built, not so that his image should appear there. He cared nothing for that!'

'No, but I do! This is to be his college! His and mine! And no other man will put his name to it and bid me do other than I will. Not some lord, not Robert Copley! Now, will you stand with me in this or not?'

Their eyes locked, as they had done so many times over the years when will was pitted against will.

'I will think on it' Henry said, finally, ' and I will give you my answer tomorrow.'

Fifty-six

After the vandalism, Damia began every working day by walking into the twilit Great Hall, in order to reassure herself that the wall painting had not somehow sustained mortal damage during the night.

On the morning after the end of term, when most of the undergraduates had gone home for the Easter vacation, she was heading across the Yard, having observed her new ritual, when she heard herself being hailed by Bob, one of his flurorescent telephone message sheets in his hand. 'Jack Robinson's daughter – Patricia Lean – that's her telephone number,' he said, striding to meet her. 'She said she was sorry she hadn't rung before, she's been in hospital.'

Damia's phone call to Patricia Lean revealed that the hospital stay which had prevented Jack Robinson's daughter from getting in touch earlier had not been the brief visit for a minor operation that Damia had assumed but a protracted period of treatment in a psychiatric hospital.

'It's depression,' Patricia Lean told her in the flat, half-apologetic tone of someone who, through years of attendance at self-help groups, had learned to pay lip-service to the proposition that her illness was nothing to be ashamed of.

She told Damia that she had seen the article in the Salster paper which, for sentimental reasons, she still had sent to her every week. 'I used to get it sent when Dad was still alive – it gave us something to talk about, the things I read about. And then when he died, I couldn't bring myself to cancel it. Silly, I know . . .'

Back numbers had piled up while Patricia had been in hospital.

'My neighbour very kindly comes in and feeds the cat and picks the post up,' she said, 'and she never throws any of it away, not even the papers and the junk mail.'

Which, Damia reflected, was lucky for her.

'Could I,' she ventured cautiously, drawing circles on the fake-wood surface of her work station, 'come and see you? Have a look at the statue?'

Patricia Lean had obviously anticipated this request and a date was agreed. 'Any day except Tuesday and Friday,' she said. 'I'm at the day centre on Tuesday and Friday.'

Neil was prevailed upon to chauffeur Damia to Dorset at the weekend.

'I can't believe you still haven't learned to drive,' he grumbled.

'There was never any need. Salster's small enough to walk around, the buses are good and I wouldn't want to drive to London even if I could.'

Neil's expression told Damia that, whatever her justifications, he had just remembered Maz and Jimi and a crumpled VW van.

Patricia Lean's address was a quaint-sounding cottage in an equally quaint-sounding rural village.

'Is this for real?' Neil had asked when she showed him the address. 'Apple Tree Cottage, St Martin Magna? It's like some American wet-dream of an English chocolate-box country-side.'

'It'll probably be a Seventies build next to an industrial estate,' Damia had responded drily.

They had been driving through the high-velocity tedium of motorway traffic for more than two hours when Neil suddenly pulled onto a slip road signposting places Damia had never heard of. She turned toward him, ready to ask where they were going.

'I know somewhere interesting to have lunch,' he said in explanation.

Less than five minutes away from the motorway, turnings to right and left into ever-smaller roads brought them into a vergeless track with sporadic passing places. Moss and an occasional hardy stem sprouted in the crumbling centreline of the ancient asphalt and the hedges on either side gave every sign that in high summer they would attempt to overgrow the tiny road altogether; tight-budded trees leaned over the car, their tall, sun-seeking limbs stark against a hazy spring sky.

'Where are we going – some gastro-pub in the middle of nowhere?'

'You'll see.'

After a few minutes they were forced to reverse in the face of oncoming traffic – a mud-spattered car whose sole occupant looked curiously at them, presumably wondering what tourists were doing here so early in the year, then nodded cursory thanks and sped off at reckless speed as if, having encountered one stranger on this back-road, his quota had been filled for the day and caution could be set aside.

A winding mile or so later, Neil pulled up on a patch of flattened, stony earth in front of a churchyard.

'We're having lunch here?'

'No, there's something I want to show you first.'

Damia followed him through a weathered wooden gate that had to be lifted slightly as it was opened. Evidently trodden by a dwindling number of feet as the years passed, the flagstoned path to the south door was slippery with algae and mossy at the edges.

To Damia's surprise, inside the porch the heavily ribbed door with its massive hinges and huge, pitted, iron latch-lifter opened to Neil's hand.

'How did you know it would be open?'

'Because I came last week and found the person who has the key. I rang and asked them if they could leave it open for us about now.'

'Why?'

'You'll see.'

The interior of the little church was cold and slightly clammy, mildew spores perceptible on each inbreath. Another, more dominant smell led Damia's eye to the centre aisle. The obviously new run of carpet that joined aisle and altar-step caused a momentary reconsideration of the vitality of the little church. But the red worsted was the only new thing here: plasterwork was flaky and speckled with fungal growth; hymn books were ancient and, when Damia picked one up, soft with damp. On a small table stood a modest pile of laminated information sheets which had obviously been produced on a manual typewriter.

Damia picked one up. 'Memorial Brasses.'

'Yup. That's what we're here for.'

Taking her hand, Neil led her to the north aisle. The plasterwork above the round-headed windows had fallen away in patches to reveal the stonework beneath. Damia wondered whether anybody ever sat here, in the coldest part of the church. Given the likely numbers Sunday by Sunday, she felt sure people were able to avoid the irritation of precipitating plaster.

Neil released her hand and knelt before a brass set low down in the wall. Damia followed suit and found herself looking at the etiolated figures of a couple depicted as if suspended in space, the woman on the left, the man on the right.

'Symbolic armour of a knight of the shire.' Neil indicated the male figure. 'And this is standard widow's garb.'

'Who are they?'

Neil's finger hovered above the unevenly sized letters – indecipherable to Damia – at the bottom of the incised surface.

'Pray for the souls of Ra. – for Ralph – Daker, knight, and his wife, Anne.'

Damia's scalp tingled.

'Ralph? As in Richard Dacre's nephew?'

'I can only assume so. It seems too much of a coincidence that there would be two Ralph Dacres at the right period, and that they should both be married to an Anne.'

'So they got married after Richard died.'

'Apparently.'

Neil's eyes were on the brass plate set into its stone surround. 'No mention of children,' he said.

'But they would have outlived Ralph and Anne, wouldn't they?'

'In the medieval period? Highly unlikely that every one of a couple's children would have survived them.'

'Perhaps they had no children.'

'Perhaps. We know Richard and Anne had no children – none that survived anyway.'

Damia leaned backwards away from the wall and sat crosslegged on the uneven stone floor, looking at the figures.

'So that's Ralph and Anne.'

'Don't get carried away. This is most likely a standard brass, not a likeness of the Dacres, just a representative well-to-do couple. They weren't big on portraiture in the fourteenth century.'

Damia felt obscurely cheated. Just for a few moments, she had felt that the brass provided a window through which she could look back six hundred years and see the faces of people who had known Toby Kineton. But no; these still, expressionless figures were simply a cipher that said, 'We were here.'

'D'you think they put it up because they didn't have children? So that there'd be somebody to pray for them, remember them?'

Neil shrugged. 'Maybe.'

A silence fell as they both stared at the memorial. Damia found herself wondering what Neil was thinking but, just as he might have spoken, she asked, 'Why did you and Angie never have kids?'

An emotion passed across his face too quickly for her to read, and when he spoke his voice was unchanged. 'I think we both kind of assumed we would one day, we certainly never ruled it out, but we just never got around to it.'

'I guess she had time on her side,' Damia said, softly. Angie had been several years younger than Neil, was – if Damia remembered correctly – not yet thirty.

'You're not exactly over the hill yourself.' Neil's heartiness jarred and Damia rose to her feet.

'Yes, but I've got to start all over again now. Even if I meet somebody tomorrow, having a baby is years off.'

'So is that it – with you and Catz? You've split up?'

Damia walked away from him. Catching her up he took her elbow. 'Damia?'

Damia shook him off, briefly hid her face with her hands. 'Nobody's said the words,' she muttered, 'but I can't see . . . yeah, I think it's over.'

He put a clumsy arm around her shoulder. 'Damia, I'm really sorry.'

She turned on her heel to face him, his arm still around her. 'Are you?'

Neil allowed his arm to slide from her shoulder. 'I'm sorry that you're in pain,' he said, 'that you've lost somebody who meant a lot to you, who you thought of as your future—' he stopped abruptly. 'But am I sorry Catz is out of your life?' He scanned her face intently. 'No, I'm not.'

Far from being a Seventies build, Apple Tree Cottage turned out to be just what it purported: a thatched cottage that stood a stone's throw away from the St Martin Magna village green. The apple trees, it transpired, were in the back garden.

'I've lived here nearly thirty years,' Patricia Lean said as they made polite exclamations about the beauty of the little house. 'I was fortunate not to lose it when my husband and I divorced. I think he realised that would be the last straw.'

Damia flinched inwardly at such naked honesty. Was that what mental illness did to a person, she wondered, made you so accustomed to having your vulnerability on display that no detail remained too personal for public consumption?

Neil, when she caught his eye, seemed no less ill at ease with Patricia's candour.

'It's very difficult living with somebody who has mental problems,' she continued as she ushered them into the kitchen extension at the back of the house, a large quarry-tiled room with a skylit sitting area at the garden end. 'I should know, I lived with my father's alcoholism long enough.'

'Did he always drink?' Damia asked, seizing on the chance to move the conversation on to less immediately personal matters.

'Yes. He'd been a POW in Burma during the war, but it was something he never spoke about. I think that's what started it. Now, of course, he'd have psychological help. But then . . . they just got on with it, the men who came back. No help, no real understanding, nothing. I don't suppose my mother encouraged him to talk about it. He was back and that was that.' She looked at them over her shoulder as the kettle boiled. 'Tea or coffee? Either's just as easy as the other.'

Jack Robinson's decline into alcoholism and despair had, Patricia told them, really been precipitated by her mother's death. 'I think the thing was, after she'd gone, there was nobody left who had known him before the war, before he went away. Nobody who expected him still to be that same man. All the men he'd joined up with were dead. His sister had married a GI and moved to America. So when Mum died he just lost the will to fight it, I think.'

Unlike the person who had rung the college after Damia's television appeal for information, Patricia did not blame the college authorities for dismissing her father.

'Really, they kept him on long after most employers would have given him his cards. They even took on an under-gardener, a boy who'd just left school, to help out. They didn't have to do that, really, did they?'

The assault had been the tipping point. 'They could have had him up in court, but the student very kindly didn't press charges. I suppose he realised Dad'd never get another job if he had a criminal record.' She stirred the tea in the pot. 'Not that he ever worked again, anyway, as it happened, but that wasn't anybody's fault but his own.'

'What I don't understand,' Neil said, carefully, 'is how he came to have the statue when he left?'

'You're being very kind' – Patricia said, her lips pulled into a sad smile – 'and not saying he pinched it. But he did; that's exactly what he did, he just pinched it from under their noses.'

The story was not long in the telling. Robinson had come across the statue of the boy in his cage hidden behind a luxuriant growth of rhododendron bushes and had felt an immediate affinity with it – 'for obvious reasons' said Patricia – and had always planned to clean and restore it before persuading the Regent Master to reinstate it in the vacant niche. 'But for years he never got around to doing anything. The under-gardener – Johnny was his name? – said Dad used to sit talking to it when he was in his cups, telling it that nobody understood what they suffered.

'When they started clearing the rhododendrons, he asked the Regent Master if he could take the statue away and clean it, now it was going to be more visible. Of course, when he got his marching orders, he didn't take it back. He managed to convince himself that they'd get rid of it if he did, that nobody at the college cared about it. You can see his point,' she said, mildly. 'It had been left to moulder in a damp, dark place.'

'So did he get around to cleaning it?' Neil asked.

'Oh yes. That was his life once he lost his job. He'd sit with a toothbrush and a bucket of water and just scrub a little patch every day. I saw it when it was about halfway through. The parts he hadn't touched were almost black, quite sinister really, you could tell why nobody wanted it around, it looked like some demon. But the bits he'd cleaned were perfect – a bit weathered, of course, but completely clean. It's amazing what a simple change of colour can do, isn't it?'

Damia felt her heart begin to beat perceptibly as she asked, 'Could we see it, do you think?'

Patricia led them through the patio doors into the little apple orchard which was her garden. The blustery wind which had alternated sunshine with showers all morning was twitching the apple twigs with their new pinky-white blossom. Damia looked around. To her left was a paved seating area, to her right a small rockery. And there, incongruous amongst alpine plants, was Toby.

Damia approached the statue, her legs trembling. Like the statue of the questing boy, Toby in his cage was rendered larger than life-sized, but still she felt the urge to kneel in front of him. Her hands hovered over the statue, not yet daring to touch the convex surface. Finally, she rested her fingertips on the clawed hands of the boy as they gripped their manacle-loops,. She traced the pitted limestone surface of the tortured face, the patched eye.

'Toby,' she mouthed silently. 'Toby.'

Tobias Kineton, born this Thursday before Holy Week, thirteen hundred and eighty-five . . . a blessed answer to twenty years of prayer.

Toby the cripple.

Son of a mason, son of a carpenter, master of nothing, not even his own body.

Dead in mysterious circumstances.

Commemorated, unknown, for six hundred years, in the form of a body he would not have recognised as himself.

And here he was, a small, twisted boy, staring out of his one unpatched eye, his face a mask of anguish. No wonder his father had wanted to carve his resurrected likeness too.

'I'll tell you something though.' Patricia's voice broke into her communion. 'That's not a cage he's in, Dad was wrong about that. It's a walking frame.'

Fifty-seven

Salster, July 1397

Gwyneth stood, her back to the wall of the northernmost living block, and looked at her college, its limestone bright in the haze of July's sun. The central, octagonal building had risen almost to the fullness of its height and the vast hall windows were completed, their tracery as yet enclosing nothing but warm, dust-filled air. Next season would see the lantern roof set in place, though Gwyneth still did not know how Simon would procure the vast number of sheets of glass they would need to see their light-filled building wind- and watertight.

It was her constant anxiety, this question of how the money would be found to buy the all-important glass. Simon, in his guarded communications, was blithe and certain. He would provide, she should not fear but simply raise the college and trust him for the glazing.

She had trusted him once and, in this, she trusted him now, though she did not know how he would hold good to his promise.

Henry strode across to her, his feet kicking up the dust of

a long dry spell. This time next year, Gwyneth reflected, paving slabs would be laid, sealing the dust from the tread of feet.

'How is she?' Gwyneth asked. Henry had come directly from the house she and Simon had once shared and where – since the Acklands' return to Salster two years before – Henry, Alysoun and their children now lived with her. Alysoun was waiting to give birth to their fourth child.

'She says nothing will happen till sunset at the earliest.'

'Well, she should know her own body's ways by now,' Gwyneth responded, her mind filled with pictures of Sim, a sturdy nine years lad, and his sisters, Meg and Beth. 'Are the children pestering her?'

'No. Sim has taken it upon himself to set up games for his little sisters in the garden to keep them amused. He told me, in quiet confidence, that he thought the girls were tiresome for his mother today.'

'He's quite the young man these days!'

'Not so much that he's not hoping for a little brother. He gets tired of the play of girls, he wants another man in the house.'

'He has you.'

Henry smiled at her. 'Yes, more so now than he ever did whilst I was at the king's beck and call.'

'And the king's clerk has not called into question your standing as a son to me in my need?' she asked, her eyebrows quirked.

'The king, if he knew, would be wistful, I think, at the thought of my loyalty to my foster-mother,' Henry mocked himself.

'Poor soul, he has known little enough of loyalty for himself.'

Henry snorted. 'I venture those lords whom he has lately arrested for trial would say he shows precious little on his own account.'

'He has suffered at their hands, too. They denied him lordship of his own kingdom, do not forget.'

'Perhaps they were wiser than we know,' Henry spat.

Gwyneth looked at him, surprised at his words. Henry had not used to be so free with his political opinions, if indeed he had any. 'You do not like his rule?'

Henry looked around, as if his words would carry to suspect ears. 'When the king and his nobles are at odds, how can the people prosper? We will always suffer at the hands of one or the other as they fight for dominance.'

Again, Gwyneth looked at him askance. Henry had always been such an uncritical admirer of nobility. 'You sound ever more like Simon, my boy.'

Henry pulled a face that tore at Gwyneth's heartstrings, sending her mind back to the raggedy boy presented to her that day, so many years ago, by her husband. 'When a man says that the laws of England proceed from his own mouth – whatever he may see fit to say – then I take issue,' he muttered fiercely. Gwyneth felt his heat – Henry was not a rebel by nature and it would tear at his loyal soul to admit that the king's insistence that his rule was by divinely ordained right did not sit well with Englishmen. Before the Conquest – how often had she heard it from her father! – lordship had been for the common good, and there were still some who remembered that 'lord' had been 'hlaford' in the old tongue – loaf-lord, provider for his people. Richard, with his lavish style of living supported by taxes, stood at the opposite pole to this English lordship; he saw his people as those who should provide for him.

Gwyneth did not respond to Henry but put a hand on his shoulder.

'Don't worry, mother,' he smiled wanly, turning his eyes to hers, 'I will be wise with my opinions before others. Never fear, they will not take me up for treason.'

'Or heresy?'

Henry did not respond directly, but from his face Gwyneth knew that he was thinking of Simon. 'Have you had word recently?' he asked.

'Not since his letter about the third quarry at Kineton.'

'Do you think he will work out *all* the stone on the estate for the college?'

Gwyneth shrugged. She had little interest in the stone of Kineton beyond seeing the college finished. Since Toby died she had been blind to the future, seeing only the task before her – that of building the college whose completion he had given his life for.

She had not seen Simon since Christmastide, when she had accompanied Henry, Alysoun and the children to Kineton to spend the twelve days with him there. He had been a subdued Simon, asking after the college only in general terms, as if unwilling to incur her displeasure and put in jeopardy the completion of the task. He had outlined his plans for the expansion of stone-digging on the Kineton estate and given Henry detailed instructions as to barges and men to be sent up at winter's end, but that had been all. Otherwise, he had played with the children and shown a dedication Gwyneth would have sworn he did not possess in ensuring that the manor house was comfortable for the family, complete with little chairs for the children, constructed – she had observed with a critical but approving eye – by his own hand.

Simon had been true to his word to her and to Brygge. He

had not set foot in Salster or even the countryside around it since the day the mayor had warned him of Copley's intentions.

'Does the little hawthorn still grow happily in its place?' he had asked, standing in the door of the chamber he had given over to her use, as she packed her clothes for the journey back to Salster.

She did not look at him, but her voice cracked as she answered. 'Yes, Simon, Toby's tree grows still.'

He had moved towards her then and they had come together in an awkward embrace. He stroked her hair and she was comforted, though she was glad that he made no move to extend his embrace. Though her body yearned for the comfort of another's touch, she could not endure the affections which had once brought a child to life within her. Now, such union would be cold and lifeless, and she had been unable to endure the thought of it.

When Nicholas Brygge walked on to the site later that day, apprehension rose within Gwyneth. Ever the politician, Brygge had kept his distance from the college for both their sakes, though, notwithstanding this precaution, he had taken pains to assure Gwyneth that he would stand protector to her in any way that he could whilst she was deprived of her husband. Until Henry had gladdened her heart by announcing his decision to return to Salster, Gwyneth had been very grateful to think that, should Ralph or anybody else prove troublesome, she had the authority of the mayor to call upon.

'Master Brygge!' she hailed him when he was still a score of paces off. 'Greetings and good day to you!'

He returned her greeting in kind and scrutinised the buildings beneath a shading hand. 'Soon you will be in need of a roof, will you not?'

Gwyneth shook her head. 'Not this year. I would not venture to set a roof such as the one I have planned on green walls like these. They need to settle and harden before I ask them to bear weight.' She sighed as she looked up at the empty space where her roof would rise. 'And as to the glazing . . .' she muttered to herself.

'The glazing?' Brygge queried.

Gwyneth turned to him, her mouth open to apologise for speaking her worries aloud, but seeing his expression she closed her mouth and sighed.

'The endowments will not allow us to glaze the college when the structure is finished,' she said baldly. 'We should have to wait several years for the revenues to be sufficient to afford the quantity of glass we need.' She met his eye briefly. 'Master Daker had undertaken to provide for this separately.'

Brygge nodded thoughtfully. 'And, should you be forced to wait, the five years allowed by the courts will expire, leaving Ralph Daker free to reappropriate his uncle's lands?'

Gwyneth nodded without speaking, her eyes fixed on the sunlit octagonal building.

'What does your husband intend?'

'He says I must trust him. That he will provide for the college.'

'But you fear that he will not?'

'I fear,' Gwyneth responded, all her anxieties about Simon's intentions welling to the surface in a sudden, fierce flow of emotion, 'that he will ally himself with those whom the king makes enemies of; those he pursues; those whose words and actions the Church proscribes and seeks to brand heretic.'

'Lollard sympathisers?'

Gwyneth did not answer directly. 'Since the Church has now condemned Wyclif's teachings, England is not safe for those who believe as he did—'

'It is never safe, Mistress Kineton, to believe something that stands contrary to beliefs commonly held. It is always seen as madness or threat.'

'But now it puts people outside the Church, under inter-dict – called heretic!'

Brygge looked full into her face, his eyes calm. 'Interdict? Heretic? We who believe as we do care nothing for the eucharist of the corrupt Church. Heretic? If it means that a man believes contrary to the Church's teaching, then yes, I am a heretic. These words neither shock me nor make me tremble.'

Gwyneth gave him the look of a mother whose child mouths adult phrases whose full implications it does not truly understand. 'So you will be neither shocked nor afraid if you are taken into the bishop's dungeons, Master Brygge? If your office is denied you as being no longer the will of the king and his ministers?' She continued to hold him with her level, challenging gaze. 'If you go against the Church, to its minis-ters you go against God, and if you go against God, then – to the king with his belief in God's ordination of himself – you go against the very crown of the land!'

Brygge, his face shadowed by an emotion Gwyneth could not name, looked past her shoulder, as if seeing another figure, as he spoke. 'The bishop will not touch me and mine unless he wants riots in the streets of his city.'

'But, friend to me though you are, it is not *you* I am con-cerned about but Simon! And myself.' She looked at him, squarely, her eyes measuring. 'The mob might riot for you but it would not take to the streets to protect my college.'

Brygge sucked his cheeks in and pursed his lips in thought. 'Do not underestimate our fellow citizens, Mistress Kineton. Remember the Great Rebellion. We in Salster were not found lacking in rebellious zeal. I believe we, as well as any city in the country, showed that we will not be kept in the place others have decreed for us if we think it unjust.'

Gwyneth waved a hand with a gesture more suited to dismissing improbable gossip. 'What has that to do with my college, Master Mayor?'

Brygge took her elbow and led her away, through the arch and out of the precincts of the college. Outside, the air was less dusty, the lines of the city wall and the buildings huddled at its base seemed clearer, brighter in the June air, as if drawn with a finer pen. She stood aside to allow passage to a boy struggling with an unwieldy handcart.

'Mistress Kineton, what are your intentions for the college once it is built?' Brygge asked, his voice low and soft, intended for her ears alone.

'My intentions?' Gwyneth's gaze travelled, unseeing, over the dusty street before them, her mind racing to formulate an answer that would satisfy him.

'Let me be more exact. Are you minded to follow Richard Daker's original purpose? That the endowments may pay for both teaching and boarding, so that not only the moneyed may learn?'

Receiving no answer, he pressed on.

'That the language of instruction shall be English, to make men who can both think and do in the world, not soft-handed men who sit outwith the commerce and muse on abstruse things?'

His gaze was insistent on the side of her head which she had turned to him; it seemed to burn into Gwyneth's neatly tucked coif, and abruptly she swung around to face him, furious that he should set so nakedly before her the dilemma from which she had, for so long, averted her eyes.

'And how *can* I follow those intentions? Where am I to find men who will challenge the authority of the Church? Any who will be licensed by the university must be approved by the chancellor!' Her eyes skewered his. 'By Copley!'

Brygge did not rise to her tone but kept his voice low and intense, as if it would wrap a weave of invisibility around them, so that the crowds would neither overhear nor even see them standing together in the warm, noisy air. 'Master Daker,' he informed her rapidly in his undertone, 'did not care to be a part of the university. He had determined that a new guild of scholars must be established outside such conventions. His college was to stand alone, needing no approval, not from Copley nor anyone else in authority.'

Gwyneth stared at him, speechless, as if he had grown a tail and commenced barking.

'Madness!' she finally declared and made to march back to her building. But Brygge grabbed her arm and held it as she turned, enraged at his grasp.

He held up forestalling hands in front of his face, as if warding off her angry words.

'Mistress Kineton, forgive me for laying ungentle hands on you!' He released her and stood, hands at his sides, plainly waiting to see whether she would stay or go.

Narrowing her eyes and folding her arms across her breast, Gwyneth stayed. Her silence bade him speak his piece.

'It is not madness, Mistress, it simply has not been done in England. But in Italy, where Master Daker's grandsire had his business, that is the common way. There, those who would learn hold the reins of those who would teach. It is the student who decides what he wishes to learn and how. It is he who pays the teachers and, as we all know, he who pays the piper—'

'—Calls the tune,' Gwyneth finished, slightly abstractedly, her hand again dismissing his words. 'But Master Brygge, we are not in Italy. We are in England. And here the Church pays the masters, and the Church calls the tune. And the Church in this city *is* Robert Copley. He will never abide such a notion! English elbowing its way in to the place that Latin holds?' She dropped her voice with her gaze and muttered, 'It has the taint of Wyclif and his Bible about it.'

'But what Copley does not see,' he said urgently, 'he may wink at! If this teaching in English is done inside the college, and not in the public gaze – if it takes place here, within the hall, instead of in the dean's hall as the Church's men do?'

She glared at him. 'Do you truly believe that he will shut his eyes and leave us be? For I do not!'

Brygge swallowed and his voice was flat and cold. 'So you will choose only teachers who will be acceptable to Copley?'

'It is not for me to choose! I will see the college raised, no more!'

'*But if you do not, then who will*?' Brygge begged, his voice tight with a passion she had never heard from him before. 'Richard Daker is dead, and his heir before him. Ralph is against the mere thought of the college and Anne – the widow – will follow Ralph in all things as it suits her to do. Simon cannot return to the city lest the bishop drag him into the ecclesiastical court and try him for heresy!' Brygge stared at her and Gwyneth wondered at this coming so close to his own heart. 'If you do not do it,' he said, 'nobody will.'

Fifty-eight

From: Damia.Miller@kdc.sal.ac.uk
To: Peterdefries@dmlplc.co.uk
Subject: Prisoner statue

Dear Peter

Thought you'd like to know we've found the prisoner statue. It's now in the care of the daughter of Jack Robinson, former college gardener. She is, for reasons connected to her father, very attached to the statue and has asked to retain possession of it during her lifetime. This has been agreed, though the statue is being brought back to the cathedral temporarily for conservation and examination. Would you like to come and see it for yourself?

Just let me know and I'll make the arrangements.

Kind regards

Damia

From: Peterdefries@dmlplc.co.uk
To: Damia.Miller@kdc.sal.ac.uk
Subject: Prisoner statue

Dear Damia

What wonderful news! Of course I would love to come and reacquaint myself with my old friend. I will ring and arrange something but I wanted to send you this brief note to give you time to think over a proposal. It seems sad, now you have rediscovered Toby as he truly was, that he is not to come back to college immediately. I understand and applaud your reasoning, obviously, but I would like to think that Toby could come home in some form. So, on that basis, I would like to finance the creation of a facsimile of the statue, accurate in every way, which could stand in the appropriate niche whilst the original is in this lady's keeping. When the original statue is returned to college, I would like, if I may, to take possession of the copy and bring it to my home. If you think this is a good idea, perhaps you could make the necessary arrangements?

I will ring in a couple of days' time to book a date to come and see you.

Yours,

Peter

Once again, Peter Defries's intervention on the 'prisoner' statue proved crucial. In order to create a plaster facsimile from which the immediately commissioned stonemason would work, the statue of the crippled Toby was coated in a layer of latex as the first step in making a mould. During the careful removal process, small amounts of limestone debris were dislodged, revealing an almost invisible joint in the statue's base.

By the time Damia reached the cathedral, summoned by Neil's call, the two halves of the base had been effortlessly slid apart and the documents contained in the well between them removed to a more appropriate environment.

'Got your endowments,' Neil greeted her. 'It's all here, papers drawn up and signed by Richard Dacre himself.' He waved a hand towards the single sheet of parchment on the table between them.

Damia bent over the pale brown document with its indecipherable writing. Only one thing could she read: the signature, 'R Daker', in a clear hand unconstrained by the conventions of legal script. Richard Daker: Lollard, heretic to some, founder of the college, original owner of the lands whose future control was now so hotly disputed. Richard Dacre had known Simon of Kineton, had – in all probability – known Tobias too. Damia put out her hand to touch the document but was stopped by a warning sound from Neil.

'Not without gloves, I'm afraid.'

Damia straightened up.

So now the college could prove title, could sell the land if it wished. The rent strike would be brought to an end. She wondered at her own lack of jubilation. But the truth was that the rancour provoked by Hadstowe's tactics meant that the legal regularisation of affairs would be only the beginning of a long period of bridge-building. Rents might begin to flow into the college coffers again soon but goodwill would be a long way behind.

'Interesting thing,' Neil said, putting his own gloves on. 'See here. Braddestowe – that's the village where I took you to see the brasses of Ralph and Anne. Bradstow. I don't think that's on your current estate list.'

Damia frowned. 'No.'

'So the question is, why is it on this one? If Ralph and

Anne lived and died there it must have passed out of college control fairly soon after Richard's death.'

Damia peered suspiciously at the document. 'Are there others on here that aren't college lands now?'

'I'll make you a list and you can check,' Neil said, his hand on the document, obviously keen to move her attention to something else.

'This wasn't all we found,' he said.

She looked at him, something in his tone suddenly causing her pulse to shake her slight frame.

Moving to a desk at the far end of the room, Neil picked up a rolled document and brought it over to the large table between them.

'You remember that reference to "Tobit Alms" you found in the Victorian records?'

Damia nodded.

'I think "Tobit" is a corruption of "Toby's Obit". The obit – obituary – was a ceremony marking the anniversary of someone's death. It was a common practice before the Reformation – usually involved prayers for the dead person.'

'Toby's Obit?'

'From what I've managed to read so far' – Neil nodded at the furled manuscript on the table between them – 'this looks like directions for the celebration of an obit ceremony for Tobias Kineton. In perpetuity.'

'This college, called Kineton and Daker College – founded by Richard Daker, vintner of the guild and merchant of the city of London, built by Simon of Kineton, master mason, and Gwyneth of Kineton, master carpenter – will be, as long as it stands and men look upon it, a memorial to Tobias Kineton, their son.

'Tobias Kineton, looked upon with scorn, called cursed and abomination, was great of heart. His life was a pattern of love and forgiveness, where he was shown hatred and neglect. He loved much and he gave much, as much as any of us is able to give, even unto his own life.

'For as John Daker, only son of Richard Daker, died in this place, cut short before manhood, so Tobias Kineton chose his own death as atonement for that other end.

'And to his memory, and in both their names, this college was completed.

'For each man has his own worth.

'Each man, though he be humble and crippled, is equal before God.

'Each man, though he follow not in his father's footsteps, will have his place in the world.

'And this college stands here to equip men, whoever they be, to take that place, to care for the poor and lowly and to remember love, faithfulness and forgiveness, even unto death.

'Those whose names will now be called, come forward and accept your alms, given in memory of Tobias Kineton, crippled in body, great of heart.

'You who are given these alms in remembrance of Tobias Kineton, will you pray for the continuance and good governance of this college, all the days of your life?

'Go in peace and remember your vow.'

Damia looked up as Neil's voice stopped intoning the words.

'Tobias Kineton chose his own death as *atonement* . . .?' Her voice sounded husky in her own ears. 'He committed *suicide*?'

Neil's eyes were fixed on hers. He moved his head from side to side, not in denial but in acknowledgement that there seemed no other way to construe the words he had read. He shrugged. 'That's the implication, isn't it?'

'But Neil – he was eight years old!'

Neil did not reply. There was nothing to say. Toby's age at his death was indisputable.

'Do you think . . . I mean, can he really have made that decision on his own?'

'Do I think somebody suggested to him that he might like to throw himself into the river as an atonement for John Dacre's death?'

Damia nodded.

'I've absolutely no idea, Damia. We don't even know the circumstances of John's death, only that it happened at the college site and appeared to be some kind of accident.'

Damia's mind, facts bouncing around inside it as pinballs ricochet around the walls and obstacles of the machine, suddenly flicked up the image of the river in the wall painting. A river in flood, its browns, blues and greens mingled in an impression of swift, uncontrolled water.

'He wouldn't have been able to get himself in and out of his frame, would he?' She reached out to Neil with her eyes. 'But in the oval where he's drowning, the frame is on the bank. Somebody must have helped him!'

Neil thrust his hands into the pockets of his chinos. 'The wall painting isn't a literal representation of what happened, Mia. Think of the first oval – that's not literally how Tobias was born, is it?'

When she did not reply he continued, 'Whoever did the wall painting probably put the frame on the bank to identify who it was that was in the water.'

'But Neil, he was a *little boy*.'

473

Damia's voice faltered as her throat constricted and sudden tears stung her eyes.

Neil put out an uncertain hand, laying it over her forearm.

'He was younger than Jimi.' Her voice tortured by the effort not to cry, Damia struggled against the overwhelming sorrow of a memory she had thought obliterated by the years, the memory of her twin lying attached to an artificial life by tubes and wires.

She had never cried for her brother. Her mother's death had taken all her tears and her own emotions had, anyway, swiftly been subsumed by Tony Miller's devouring grief. Now, stirred up by the shock of another little boy's death, a terrible sadness at the waste and futility of her brother's end swept through Damia and she broke down in tears. Sobs broke unwillingly from her as she cried for the times she had hated him, for the desperation surrounding his passing, for each of the years she had been alone, deprived of a brother's love and support. She cried for the loneliness of her own life and for the unfair brevity of his.

So absolute was the sudden grip of grief that she barely noticed Neil kneeling at her side and putting his arms around her, resting his head on her shoulder in mute sympathy.

Helplessly racked, Damia was lost in an uncharted wasteland of emotion in which weeping for what she had lost seemed the beginning of a life's work, as if now she had begun she would not be able to curb her mourning. The sobs, the memories of pain, the emptiness of a life without family seemed to possess her completely. But slowly, slowly, by infinite degrees, the sobs became less frequent, her tears ceased to flow and she became aware of Neil's embrace.

As she pushed herself into a sitting position, loosing the

hold of his arms upon her, Neil put out a hand and, with the edge of a finger, wiped the tears from her cheeks.

'They waited so long for him,' she croaked, feeling sobs well up once more, 'and when he came he was disabled and then he killed himself.'

Neil cleared his throat, the vocal rasp loud between them.

'Maybe,' he said hesitantly, 'it was a relief to him – Toby I mean. Maybe life was a burden, being as he was.'

Her mind jumped again from one little boy to the other and she heard her father's words as clearly as if he was standing between them. *'I couldn't let him live like that . . . I just couldn't bear it!'*

The thought of Jimi sitting, slack and unresponsive, strapped into a wheelchair, liquefied Damia's tears once more. She turned to Neil and buried her head in his shoulder.

Later, as they sat in Damia's kitchen drinking wine and eating bread and cheese, Neil asked, 'Do you think going through the obit ceremony helped the Kinetons, or did it just keep bringing it all back to them, stop them getting over Tobias's death?'

Damia rolled a pellet of bread between her thumb and forefinger, feeling the grittiness of the wheat's husk at the same time as the smoothness of the gluten-paste. 'I don't think you ever get over the death of a child,' she said, her eyes fixed on the rolling of her fingers. 'It's the death of part of you, part of your immortality, isn't it?' Her thumb and finger moved continuously against each other, the small chunk of bread kneaded and stretched. 'You've not just lost the child but all the things they would have done – become a teenager, become an adult, left home, fallen in love, had children of their own, grandchildren even. If your child dies before you, it kind of rips apart that cycle of birth and death and handing things on, dislocates you in time.'

'Especially if it's your only child,' Neil suggested, after a pause.

'I've never understood,' she continued as if he hadn't spoken, 'why my father just gave up after Mum and Jimi died. He still had me.'

Her eyes were fixed on her endlessly circling fingers, not meeting his gaze.

Her words, all the more poignant for never having been uttered before, were unanswerable. A silence fell between them, broken by nothing but the occasional sound of a car driving past the front of the house on some early-evening family errand. The hum of the fridge seemed unnaturally loud.

'He adored your mother, didn't he?' Neil asked, at last.

'Dad?' Damia's eyes did not focus, remained fixed on her fingers, seeing only the past. 'Yeah. Yeah he did. He couldn't live without her.' Finally she looked up, her face closed, her defences up. 'As events clearly demonstrated.'

'I think people tried,' Neil said, topping up their wine glasses, 'people at the commune. I don't think they just let him sink into despair without trying to rescue him.'

'Didn't succeed though, did they?' Her voice seemed matter-of-fact. 'Didn't try hard enough. Too much live-and-let-live, that was the trouble. There was never any sense that you could get it wrong. If it felt right you just got on and did it.' She suddenly threw the pellet of bread, dart-style, in the direction of the bin. 'Even if "it" was killing yourself slowly with fucking drugs.'

She saw his frown in her peripheral vision.

'You blame people at the commune for what happened?' he asked.

'Who else is there to blame?' Her calm was slipping towards belligerence.

'Does blame have to come into it?'

'Yes.' Something in her suddenly seemed to pull her to attention, as if all her sinews had suddenly lost their elasticity, jerking her into rigidity. 'Yes,' she said again, slapping her hands, palm down, on the table between them. 'It does have to be somebody's fault, because otherwise it's just a case of "Shit happens". And OK, shit like hurricanes and earthquakes and floods does just happen but shit like somebody dying of a heroin overdose doesn't just happen – somebody had to take the fucking heroin and somebody else had to fucking let him!'

'Damia.' Neil reached out to her but she pulled her hands away.

'*I* couldn't do it – I didn't know what day it was! Somebody should have looked after him, after us!'

'We tried—'

'Oh yeah, you tried! *You* looked after *me* didn't you?' Her tone was so bitter that he recoiled physically.

'I was so stoned most of the time I didn't know whether it was breakfast or Tuesday, but you were there, taking over—' She stopped abruptly.

Neil splayed a hand on to the table top, as if anchoring himself. 'Are you saying you think I took advantage of you, when you were vulnerable?'

She looked up at him, her face impassive. 'Well, did you?'

He raised both hands in the air in a gesture of incomprehension. 'I loved you – love you – was *in love* with you! My only aim was to support you, help you through it, take some of the pain away.'

Damia returned his wounded gaze with an expression of fixed dispassion.

'I thought you loved me, too,' he concluded in self-defence.

She dropped her eyes then and leaned forward, covering her face with her hands. 'I did love you.' Her words were obscured so much by the pressure of her palms that he had to strain to make out what she was saying. 'You were my best friend, of course I loved you.' She took a long, shuddering breath. 'We should have just stayed friends, Neil.'

Neil could hear the bitter smile in his voice as he replied, 'Blokes don't do having a lesbian as a best friend very well. Girls can have a gay bloke as a best friend but we're not very good at the other way around.'

Damia lowered her hands and looked at him. 'So how come we manage it now?'

Neil braced his elbow on the arm of the carver he was sitting in and rested his cheek on his fist. He said nothing as his gaze played around her face.

Just as Damia was about to say something, anything, to break the silence, he sucked in a deep breath and held it for a second or two before expelling it and saying, 'When I told Angie that I'd applied for the job here she said she'd move to Salster on one condition.'

He appeared to have stalled but, again, just as Damia tried to say something to prompt him to continue he picked up the thread. 'She said she'd come if I broke off all contact with you.'

Damia felt the cold adrenalin flood into her bloodstream. 'Why?'

'Why do you think?'

Damia looked at him. 'Are you telling me I'm to blame for you two splitting up?'

Neil put up a hand and rubbed one eyebrow with his fingers as if he was suffering from a persistent irritation somewhere beneath his skin. 'No, I'm telling you I was. I wouldn't put her needs first.' He leaned forward, resting his forearms on the table. 'To tell you the truth, if she'd asked me at the beginning of our relationship I'd probably have agreed. But things hadn't been right for a while. Nobody's fault really, it just wasn't working – not because of you.' He made a face and stared down at the table top as if he was deciding what to say next. 'In the end, our relationship – our friendship, whatever you want to call it – was more important to me than trying to salvage things with Angie.'

'Why?'

'There's no answer to that, is there?' He smiled a crooked smile. 'You could say you're my test. If I don't feel at least as much for a woman as I ever did for you, then I shouldn't bother.'

Damia glanced up at him, acknowledging his attempt at levity but not taking his invitation to leave the emotional mire. 'Are you saying you're still in love with me?' she asked, more abruptly than she had meant to.

His smile fading, Neil backtracked his mood to hers. 'No. I don't think that kind of romantic love can survive indefinitely without some kind of reciprocation.' He looked at her steadily.

'But—' she faltered, at a loss as to the implications of her instinctive conviction that feelings were not amenable to such logic.

He reached out and took one of her hands. 'Mia, I want you to think about something.'

Damia felt a jolt as if she had been punched over the heart. His words were so nearly the same as those he had spoken so many years ago.

'Mia, I want to ask you something.'

'Yes?'

'Will you come to bed with me?'

She had been fifteen to his seventeen. Her father had been dead less than a handful of pot-doped months during which Neil's family had become her family, Neil her refuge and protector. Had he asked her to go to the moon with him, she would have gone, having nowhere else to go.

It did not occur to her until after they had both left the commune behind to wonder where and with whom he had become such a practised lover, aware of what her woman's body would respond to. Nor did it occur to her until later to wonder why she had always preferred their foreplay, his stroking hands and tongue, to the joining of their bodies as he entered her. She had assumed it had something to do with the interruption enforced by condom-application, the unnatural, stingingly synthetic barrier to life awakening within her.

Now she knew better.

'Mia?'

'Sorry.'

'What do you think about us having a baby together?'

Fifty-nine

A straight, laughing boy, balanced on tiptoe, looking over the shoulder of a high building to spy his other self. Gwyneth looked at the soft folds of the boy's tunic, his calfskin boots – such as she and Simon could never have afforded for him in life – the enquiring lift of his eyebrows. It was like no image she had ever looked upon before. It was as unlike the stiff, unsmiling statues that adorned churches, colleges and chapels as it was unlike Toby himself in life.

The image was, as yet, unpainted and Gwyneth had a mind to ask Simon to leave it so. She could not bear the thought of the paint fading in the sun, flaking to motley, the eyes blinded by pelting winds and vicious frosts. Better to leave him like this, simple and lasting. Perfect.

'*So shall we all be in heaven*,' Simon had said. Was that true? When she met Toby again before the Saviour's majesty, would he resemble this lively boy rather than the twisted son her heart longed for? Gwyneth could not imagine how she would greet a Toby who looked so little like himself.

Turning herself slightly aside from the questing boy, she

stood before Toby as she remembered him. Simon felt he had done Toby justice in the image of his wholeness, but to Gwyneth's partial eye Toby was more justly rendered here, in the frame that had given him freedom and enabled him to face the world.

Must you hoist my shame erect and strap it to this . . . foul contraption?

Simon's horrified outburst on first seeing Toby in his frame had bitten deep and Gwyneth had never been able to cleanse her memory of it. Simon had done sufficient subsequent penance for his words and deeds to Toby – was doing penance still in his absence from the college – and Gwyneth might have forgiven him his harshness, but she could never forget it. Toby had been hers; the realisation of his needs had been hers; the means to provide for his needs had been of her devising.

And yet her son had sacrificed himself for his father. The father who had smashed his liberating frame and blamed him for shattered dreams. Almost four years . . . Toby had been dead a bare three weeks short of four years.

'Gwyneth?'

Henry's soft voice roused her from her reverie and she turned to him.

'Piers Mottis is here.'

'Did you tell him why I wanted to see him?'

'I think he can guess. He can see a building in need of a roof as well as the next man and he knows what manner of roof it is designed to be.'

When Gwyneth had explained her concerns about the cost of glazing the lantern, Piers Mottis's response made her wish she had confided in the little lawyer long before.

'I should have foreseen your concern, Mistress Kineton. Forgive me for not doing so.' He allowed Gwyneth silently to acknowledge his remorse and then continued. 'Richard Daker had many friends whose political and anticlerical views were similar to his own.'

'Birds of a feather flock together whether moneyed or poor, then,' Gwyneth muttered, beginning to hope.

'Indeed. When Richard died, more than one man of means approached me and gave me to understand that if the college building ran into financial difficulty they would provide funds discreetly and without the need for ostentatious acknowledgement.'

'By which you mean we would not need to erect statues of them or memorialise them in the name of the college?'

'That is exactly what I mean.'

'Who are these men?'

Mottis regarded her levelly, his pale, grey-blue eyes calm and unworried. 'I think it best that you do not know their names. It need be nobody's business but ours that the money for the necessary glass comes not from the endowments left by Richard Daker but from other purses. If such knowledge comes to the ears of Bishop Copley, it would be both to your advantage, and that of our patrons, if their names were unknown to all but me.'

'Are you not afraid of him, Master Mottis?'

A strange look passed over the grave set of the lawyer's features, one that Gwyneth could not readily name. 'It would be a foolish man,' he said, slowly, 'who said that he did not fear the wielder of such power as Robert Copley commands. But I do not think he would be unwise enough to use such power against me.' He gazed at her steadily. 'The Order of the Coif would not easily overlook threats or deeds of violence to one of its number.'

As Simon had done in different circumstances, Gwyneth abruptly revised her opinion of the unassuming man in front of her. Quiet humility might fit him like a well-worn cloak, but he was, quite obviously, not unaware of his own worth and influence.

He looked at her, a question in his eyes. 'Was there another matter you wished to speak about?'

Gwyneth sucked in a breath and began speaking abruptly. 'I fear what would become of our college if the bishop let it be known that he would consider any man who did it damage to be a friend to him and all right-thinking Christians.'

'You fear violence against the college?'

'It wouldn't be the first time.'

Mottis regarded her expressionlessly. 'But the incident to which you refer was occasioned by Simon contravening the laws and customs of masonry, was it not? When he set hewers to do setters' work?'

Gwyneth nodded reluctantly. The memory of Simon's bitterness in the face of his own masons' treachery was an unwelcome one, but she was forced to admit that the townsfolk, though they must have been aware of Copley's displeasure at the flouting of his authority, had never offered violence to the college's fabric. Indeed, they seemed to regard it with some of the superstitious dread they had shown towards Toby.

'But would they protect the college if it was threatened – fabric or future – by Copley?' she burst out.

Mottis, plainly seeing that this was her real fear, did her the courtesy of not reassuring her instantly that all would be well and that she should not fear.

'Master Daker wanted his college to belong to the people of Salster,' Gwyneth continued, an edge of desperation sharpening her voice, 'and I fear we have not made it so. Because of' – she faltered –'because of my son and people's mistrust of him, they see the college as something alien in their midst, not something of their own.'

'And yet it chimes very well with the tune of independence and dislike of overlordship that the city has always sung,' Mottis said gently. 'Though I am a London man born and bred, the fame of the Salster citizens, both before, during and after the Rebellion, was great.' He levelled his gaze at her agitation. 'The people of Salster have never been easy with any man's yoke, Mistress. They have stood against priors, bishops, kings and lords in defence of the rights of their city and their guilds. I do not think they would follow the wishes of the bishop—'

'Not unless his purpose was in step with their own!' Gwyneth's hands were restless in her lap, her fingers twining and chafing with the turmoil of her thoughts. 'They mistrust the college – almost as if the college itself were alive! They eschew it, walk past on the other side of the road.'

'Building sites are dangerous places, Mistress. Are people not being prudent by keeping their distance whilst building proceeds?'

'I have seen their faces,' she countered, 'full of fear and mistrust! Their eyes dart to the college as they pass, and then away, as if they fear contagion!'

Mottis leaned forward, his elbows on his knees as he looked up into her face. It was, she thought, an ungainly position more reminiscent of a working man resting his weight as he drank his ale than of an elevated, educated man like Mottis.

'Even to those who do not see demons lurking in every shadow, two untimely deaths within a week – deaths, moreover, of the only sons of the men who were united in their determination to build the college – seems ill-starred.'

'Yes!' Gwyneth cried, her own fears for the college apparently vindicated from his own mouth. 'And we must change that! The college can have no good future if it is always seen as a place of ill luck!'

Mottis leaned back again, apparently startled by her vehemence.

'How would you change people's minds, Mistress Kineton?'

Gwyneth felt herself harden as she took a breath to tell him. 'In the way that people's minds are usually changed, Master Mottis. By buying them.'

Sixty

Damia declined Neil's invitation to spend Easter with him at his parents' home in Brighton, telling him that she needed some time to herself to think. A troubling conviction was developing within her that she had no firm ground on which to stand. Toby, Catz, Neil – she no longer knew what place, if any, they would occupy in her future.

After a restless Good Friday night spent in the uncomfortable state between waking and sleeping, Damia was woken late on Saturday morning by a fist pounding on her front door. Quickly wrapping herself in a dressing gown she stumbled, half-seeing, downstairs and peered through the stained glass of her front door for some clue as to who needed her so precipitately. Seeing only the figure of a man in a shirt and trousers, she opened the door cautiously on the chain.

'Got a parcel for you, love,' the delivery man said, obviously indifferent to his reception. 'Can you sign here.'

Damia sat in the kitchen drinking tea and looking at the large, flat package leaning against the work surface. It stood as high as her shoulder and clearly contained a painting: Catz's New York address was on the delivery sticker in small letters above the larger print spelling out her own name and address in Salster, England, UK.

Damia had accepted the parcel and propped it up in the hall. Then she had returned upstairs and taken a shower. She had dressed carefully and come downstairs once more, bringing the unwieldy package into the kitchen with her.

Given the recent state of relations between herself and Catz, she was uncertain about what she would find on the canvas inside its corrugated cardboard sheath. Though Catz produced disturbing canvases only rarely, Damia did not relish revealing one intended specifically for her, alone in her own kitchen.

Her tea finished, she put her mug in the sink and allowed herself to be drawn towards the sound of bird song in the back garden. She opened the patio doors, admitting a blast of cold air along with the torrent of sexually boastful territorialism that humans find so appealing. For a minute or two she stood on the threshold trying to summon something resembling the clear perspective of the birds. Build a house, entice a mate, produce offspring, spread your genes.

Was that what her longing for a child was – just a primitive instinct to perpetuate her genes? But if it was that simple, Neil's proposal would instantly have presented itself as the obvious solution, instead of the cause of yet another round of self-doubt.

Turning away from the door, as if by doing so she could prevent a return to the endless internal debate, Damia strode over to the painting and hefted it into her arms. Whatever unpleasant surprise lurked beneath the corporate packaging, it would be easier to deal with in the garden, a space she hardly, yet, felt ownership of.

Staggering slightly beneath her unwieldy load, Damia made her way through unpruned shrubs and straggling grass towards the ancient arbour that some previous owner of the house had placed to catch the morning sun. She swept a hand across its slatted seat to remove dried bird droppings and sat down gingerly, sliding the parcel down until it rested, end-on, against her knees.

There had been no message alerting her to the arrival of a package from New York. Damia had heard nothing from her lover since her plaintive email about Neil and she worried that Catz had spent her time brooding on the apparent impasse in their relationship. Catz could represent emotional truth with devastating accuracy in her paintings; try as she might, Damia could not rid her mind's eye of the image of herself as a small, rainbow-clad child, perpetually excluded from the dancing circle.

She pulled tentatively at the top seal, opening the flat carton's short side, and then, with greater force, tore down the long edge. Pulling away the free corner, she saw an unframed canvas swathed in bubble-wrap. Her apprehension prolonged uncomfortably, she used both hands to pull the canvas out, turning it over to pick at the edges of the Sellotape binding.

There was a letter stuck to the bubblewrap with a simple address: *Mia*.

Her stomach clenched in a sudden knot, Damia detached the envelope and opened it. The letter was handwritten in Catz's over-fluent hand and the uncharacteristic evenness of the writing suggested to Damia that it had been composed and copied rather than simply written headlong in Catz's pre-ferred fashion.

As usual in her lover's correspondence, there was no salu-tation. It was as if Catz did not want to commit herself to a particular stance vis-a-vis her reader before she had said what she wanted to say. When they were first together, Damia had found it very hurtful to be addressed so peremptorily but she had become accustomed to it now and would have found anything else sinister in its abnormality.

New York, Thursday

Feel like I've been writing this all day. Still probably haven't got it right but anyway.

I'm sending you a painting. The one you wanted for your art auction. I know you've changed the idea to an Art Prize now (good move, you can have a prize every year but it'd look damn funny if you had an auction every year) but I thought if you had a painting by somebody who was already known then you could use that to encourage people to enter the prize. I know if I'd seen the name of somebody I knew associated with a new prize when I was an art student, it would've encouraged me to enter.

I wanted to do this even though you're not coming to New York and I'm staying here

In that line, Damia realised, was the unambiguous end of their relationship. She had been asked to join Catz and had declined. She had told Catz that if she wanted them to be together she would have to return to Britain, to Salster, and Catz was implicitly refusing to do so.

because I want to prove to you that you're wrong. That I _have_ been listening when you've talked about you, the college, the wall painting.

You were right not to come, Mia. I couldn't have painted this if you'd been here. I almost couldn't paint it anyway, it was hard to get into. I did 17 different sketches (you can see them if you like I've put them on the 'work in progress' page on my website, along with the photos you sent me of the wall painting) before I got what I wanted. Whoever painted the 'Sin Cycle' was a hell of an artist - he says so much in so little. I've tried to do the same.

The other reason you were right not to come is I need to prove to myself that I'm OK on my own - that I don't depend on exploitative relationships to produce work. (Yes, I am seeing a therapist before you ask. It's like going to the toilet here, people can't understand how you manage to function if you don't.) Making you keep away all week while I painted _is_ exploitative. But I don't know how far I can push myself. I might cope with living with someone but a kid too? A step too far. You know what I'm like, I'm obsessed when I'm painting. Not focused, not intent, obsessed. I'm in another world and if you drag me back into the real one the spell is shattered and I hate you. _Hate_. A child couldn't cope with that kind of thing, shouldn't have to. And it would come between you and me and you'd end up hating me and leaving and that wouldn't be good for the kid either. I'm not going to put myself in a position where any kid feels rejected by me.

So, there you go. That's the product of a day's sitting here and writing and rewriting. Not to mention weeks of therapy. I'm guessing you could have told me all that in about week three of our relationship. Except the bit about the kid, because you wouldn't want to see that. You'd be in denial as my therapist would say. He's called Joel by the way. I deliberately picked a bloke so I didn't have to fall in love with my therapist as per the cliché.

I don't want this to be the end for us, Mia. I know it has to be the end of us being together because of the baby. I couldn't give up painting and I'm guessing you feel the same about having a baby so that isn't going to work. But I don't want you not to be in my life. Can we work out something which is a bit more equal – a friendship where I'm not calling the shots? If I don't have to be paranoid about protecting space for my work, I think we might be good friends.

Anyway, that's it.
I love you.

Catz

Toby Blog 9 April

Where would any of us be without friends? I ran a marathon last year for charity and my friends, even those who didn't necessarily support the charity themselves, gave generously because they wanted to help me.

Now a dear friend of mine who has no connection to the college except through me has made a most generous and moving donation.

Catriona M. Campbell – a young British artist twice shortlisted for the Turner prize – has donated a work to be auctioned at the award ceremony for the Art Prize announced by the college on this website last term.

If you [click here] you can see the painting in all its glory. For those of you who like to know these things it stands 28 inches high and is 56 inches wide, the medium is oil and the surface canvas.

The canvas showed, at first sight, a straightforward representation of the Toby Yard, in which three people were placed at various points in relation to the viewer. However, more diligent examination revealed that the yard had been foreshortened in the manner of pre-Renaissance painting to allow the symbolic juxtaposition of buildings. Had Kineton and Dacre College's great Octagon actually stood as close to the western range as it did in the painting, two men could not have lain end to end between them, whereas in reality the space was three times as great.

The left foreground of the canvas was occupied entirely by the head and shoulders of a woman standing with her back to the viewer so that one was, as it were, obliged to look over her shoulder into the sunlit Yard beyond. The green dress and neatly wound white coif identified her as the woman who cradled her swaddled child so tenderly in the wall painting's second oval.

Sitting on the Yard's flagstones in the uncluttered centre

of the canvas was the cross-legged figure of a boy-child, gazing up at the 'prisoner' statue in its niche on the western wall. In this rapt little boy, Catz had brought to life the lithe, tiptoe figure of the Toby statue. His blond hair fell into waves around his ears, as if pushed back the better to see; his tunic, over a linen undershirt visible at neckline and cuff, looked worn and soft from a thousand boyish expeditions, muddied and scrubbed clean so often that its azure colour – which drew the eye immediately to this, the focus of the painting – was muted from the blue of heaven to a more earthy tone.

Though Catz had stayed faithful to the statue and reproduced his soft-leather boots in stained and dusty tan, she had chosen to paint him bare-legged, with knees as scabbed and brown as those of boys everywhere.

Further away, though not in anything that could be called the background of this painting with its medieval perspective, stood a bearded man of average height. Though his clothes were more vibrantly coloured, his stance more naturalistic, his face animated by a skilled portraitist's touch, this was clearly the mason who occupied the wall painting's first oval. Simon of Kineton stood, his face in shadow, his gaze fixed on the sunlit son he had wished for, half turned away from the shadowed western wall and the son he had been given.

Only on a more critical examination of the painting did Damia notice the almost disembodied hand that stretched out from the figure of Gwyneth of Kineton towards her child. The trajectory of the outstretched fingers could be extended to either boy – flesh and blood or stone resemblance – so the longing expressed by the gesture could have been occasioned by her yearning for either vision of her son.

The ring on the hand's third finger was less ambiguous.

With its green stone and white gold, it was an exact copy of the one Catz had given Damia for her thirtieth birthday.

From: Damiarainbow@hotmail.com
To: CatzCampbell@hotmail.com
Subject: the painting

Well, you did it – you said so much in so little, just like the wall painting. It's amazing Catz, a truly remarkable painting – so medieval and so modern. It's just what Toby – the college – is trying to be. Thank you.

Your letter made me cry, but not in a totally sad way. I feel we've let one another go but only just so far. I don't want to not have you in my life either . . .

I'm glad you're in therapy, not because I think you're screwed up but because I think you're scared of yourself and what you might do or become if x, y or z happened. So keep at it – it'd be amazing to see what a fearless Catz would look like.

On a totally different subject, I'm sorry I didn't explain to you about Neil having come to Salster. I think I didn't want to admit that you might have been right about him and, at the same time, I knew that you *weren't* right, if that makes any sense. No, probably not. Him being here has been amazingly cathartic – I've managed to face up to some of the stuff around Dad's and Jimi's deaths – and I don't think I could have done that without both the wall painting and Neil. Funny how different bits of your life come together, isn't it?

Anyway, the somewhat mind-blowing upshot of all this is that Neil has suggested that he and I have a baby together.

Don't worry, I was just as gobsmacked as you're feeling

now – it just came out of nowhere. Admittedly, we were both a bit drunk but he definitely meant it. I just babbled something about having to think about it, about how it was too big a question to just say yes or no straightaway . . . we haven't talked about it since. Well, we haven't actually seen each other – he's gone down to see his parents for Easter and I'm here by my lonesome after turning down an offer to go with him. It would've been nice to see his Mum and Dad again but in the circumstances . . .

Catz, I am actually considering doing this – having a child with Neil. We never really discussed it, you and I, so I've never really told you about the reservations I have about AID – I mean, even though the child has the right to know who their father is now, you're still proposing bringing them up without any sniff of a Dad – they can't get hold of the records until they're 18. And I don't know whether I could do that.

Since Neil suggested it, I've been thinking of all the advantages to having him as the father of my child. I've always wanted a family but I don't know if I'm brave enough to bring a child up without a father in sight. I think that two lesbians bringing up a kid is a very different proposition – for the kid especially – if he or she can say 'I see my Dad whenever I like' or 'my Dad lives in London' or that kind of thing – it basically says to the other kids 'I'm just like you, only I have two women at home instead of one.'

I don't want to live with Neil, so for the child it would be no different from what millions of other kids cope with – living with Mum most of the time and Dad some of the time. Except that there wouldn't be a history of bitterness between me and Neil. We'd be able to be together as a family sometimes without any of that tension . . .

But then maybe I'm kidding myself. Maybe things would get difficult – one of us wouldn't like the way the other was bringing the child up, or there would be arguments about holidays, or Neil would want to see the child more than I wanted him to . . . and what happens if one of us needs to move away from Salster for a new job – how would that work?

As you can see, I'm far from having got to the end of thinking about it, never mind making a decision. I need to talk to Neil about it – about the nitty-gritties – but I'm afraid of making him think it's going to happen and then deciding against. Perhaps I'm afraid he'll talk me into it too . . .

Sixty-one

From: Damia.Miller@kdc.sal.ac.uk
To: Old members email list
Subject: Extraordinary Meeting of Governing Body

On Friday afternoon at 5 p.m. there is to be an extraordinary
meeting of the governing body of Kineton and Dacre
College. This has been called as a result of a formal takeover
bid, made to the governing body and fellows of the college,
by Sir Ian Baird, president of Northgate College.
To have launched such a bid, Sir Ian must feel that he has a
good deal of support within the college; therefore if you
oppose it (as I sincerely hope you do) please take a few
minutes to register your support for our Regent Master,
Edmund Norris. If sufficient numbers of emails, letters and
phone calls of support are received and logged, Dr Norris
will go into the meeting with a greater degree of
confidence that he speaks for the whole college community
in rejecting Northgate's bid.

It seems no coincidence that, just as the college
launches the 'Max-a-Million' campaign in response to Jon
Song's incredible gesture of financial support, Northgate

wade in with an offer based on our financial position. It is entirely probable that they are aware that the results of the Max-a-Million campaign are likely to go a long way towards resolving our immediate financial difficulties and that other schemes under way but yet to come to fruition could, once more, put the college on a sound financial footing.

I am sorry to have to ask you for your support yet again this year but, as you will appreciate, the future of the college does, genuinely, depend on those associated with the college standing up for Toby.

With many thanks for your support

Kind regards

Damia Miller

PS Don't forget to come and support our runners on Fairings Day or, at least, tune in and cheer them on. Whether they win or lose, I can promise you a Toby performance you will never forget!

Toby blog

Thanks to some amazing detective work by our *de facto* curator of medieval documents, Neil Gordon, we now know that extraordinary events surrounded the continued existence of Toby after the shocking deaths of John Dacre and Tobias Kineton. John's father, Richard, the man whose conviction that learning should not be the unique privilege of the Church, and that all men should learn in their own language; the man whose Lollard faith inspired him to see all men as equal and deserving of advancement; the man who proposed to found the college and endow it with his own lands; this same Richard Dacre died only months after his only son. Who can say that he did not die of a broken heart?

Richard's death put the whole college building plan in jeopardy with Richard's widow and his nephew suing to regain the lands endowed to the unfinished college. Fortunately for us, Simon's lawyer, Piers Mottis (who had been Richard Dacre's lawyer during his lifetime), was a wily one and suggested a ploy that would gain Simon the necessary time to finish his college whilst throwing a bone to the disinherited nephew ...

Toby needs time again now. And, as ever, time is money ...

From: JSTodd15@hotmail.com
To: Damia.Miller@kdc.sal.ac.uk
Subject: Re: Extraordinary Meeting of Governing Body
Attachment: A modest proposal ...

Dear Ms Miller

I wonder if you would be kind enough to read the attached document and, if you think it is suitable, send it to all Tobyites who have committed themselves to standing orders to college? I think it would make the Governing Body sit up and take notice, don't you?

Julia Todd (Toby 1985)

Sixty-two

Salster, late summer 1397

If some force of alchemy had so arranged nature that certain, particular, words were to be visible in the sultry August air, those same words would have been seen to trace a swift path through the rows and streets of the city. Their origin would be seen as the house of the mayor, Nicholas Brygge; the first stopping point the chandler's shop in Jewry Lane; their congregation into a susurrating mob, the site of Richard Daker's strange, mistrusted building outside the city wall. Here, where the shacks of beggars and paupers clung with draughty, verminous tenacity to the high stone protection behind them, the words had most potency and moved most swiftly.

'Obit,' the whisper flew, and – the word sweet on tongues more accustomed to bitterness – 'alms'. The following day, four years from his death, Richard Daker's son was to be mourned and prayed for, remembered in the light of candles and, more to the benefit of the poor, in shillings and pence.

Murmurs, had they passing trails like the silent snail, would have been seen entering and emerging from every dwelling in the city; neither the poorest nor the richest immune to the scent of something out of the ordinary.

An obit after four years? When none had been commemorated at his death? No week-mind, no month-mind, no obit at his year-mind had pleaded for the young Daker's soul nor gladdened the hearts of the poor of Salster.

Why now? they asked.

The swollen, hazy sun of several days past was gone, and over the college and its crowds hung a heavy, rumbling sky that allowed no escape to the fetid air of the city and left the citizenry sluggish beneath its oppression.

Rain, Gwyneth reflected, would be welcome.

She remembered John's funeral, four years ago to the day. Though drought had broken hours before the interment, the cathedral gravediggers had been as hard put to it that day as any other of the summer to cleave the soil, so dry had it been baked.

That John was buried in the common site before the cathedral had shocked many. Some had held that the boy's body would certainly be taken to London for burial. Others were sure his father would secure a site for him inside the cathedral, to lie with others of rank.

But Richard had remained true to his beliefs in the equality of every man and had consigned his son's remains to the graveyard where all Salster's residents not high-born or friar were destined – the crowded green.

John's funeral, in the nave, had been the first of three, the other bodies also lying on biers in the great belly of the church. Salster was a thriving city: where so much life took place, one had also to look for death as a daily occurrence.

But not a death like John's, she thought. Death from age

or infirmity was expected; as it was in the perilous venture of childbirth. But a hale young man cut down by a chance movement—

'*Did the cripple have a hand in it?*'

Now, as then, the words slithered into her ear despite her efforts not to hear them. She knew that Toby had not been to blame; she knew also that his presence on the building site had led, inescapably, to John Daker's death.

Gwyneth stood in the rutted street as her masons, each holding a candle, each flame flattened by its holder's grave step, walked around the outside aspect of the college. Three times they had been instructed to circumnavigate the site before halting. Gwyneth, knowing these men, had calculated that on the first pass their embarrassment at this sombre and unaccustomed ritual would preclude the air of solemnity that the occasion demanded. On the second turn, they would begin to achieve a degree of tolerance to the stares of the crowd, as the city's folk watched masons walk in ceremonial silence. On the third circuit, Gwyneth reckoned, their faces would be be properly grave, their movement in procession and the candles that they held beneath the lowering sky drawing them towards a state of readiness for what was to come.

Three times they passed before her – Edwin Gore, Ranulf Bere, Steven Holdere and the rest – three times around the high walls of the outer buildings and the wide arches that beckoned the eye towards the nearly complete Octagon before coming to a halt, each man five paces from his neighbour, around the college's perimeter. Every mason stood, his face towards the crowd, unsmiling now, his candle held at his breast.

These movements were unrehearsed – Gwyneth would

not be accused of gaudy – but she had calculated the linear distance around the college site and measured in her mind the number of paces each mason would need to stand from his neighbour in order that they should be evenly spaced. These instructions had been issued to the masons with their candles. Some had asked what priest would lead them, to conduct the appropriate prayers: Gwyneth had replied simply that there would be no priest.

As they stood, silent before the taut and expectant crowd, a faint, warm breeze began to rise and hands were swiftly raised to cup and nurture easily doused flames. Gwyneth felt her flaming cheeks cool as she stepped forward, took a bundle of clothes from a hand cart that stood between Alysoun and Henry and handed them to her foster-son. He accepted the bundle in silent acknowledgement and made his way to the archway at the northwesternmost corner of the college, where he took up a station before the candlebearers and looked out impassively at the crowd.

Stepping forward as Henry came to rest and taking another bundle, Gwyneth held it out to an approaching figure in sombre black. Piers Mottis bowed his dark-capped head slightly as he received his bundle and made his way wordlessly past Henry and around the college to his allotted post at the southeastern archway. Nicholas Brygge walked forward, in his turn, to take up an identical pile of clothing and finally, lifting that last remaining bundle into her own arms, Gwyneth made her way to the remaining archway. She and Brygge, whose intelligence of the city and its inhabitants was second to none, had together decided which elderly paupers should receive the woollen coats with their blue octagon sewn into the breast. Now, standing with the candlebearers at her back, she called out the four names that she had committed to memory. The crowd murmured as if in agreement with the selection of those to be favoured and made way for the men and women thus summoned as they shuffled forward to stand before Gwyneth, their faces torn between seemly humility and eager expectation, their eyes darting constantly to Gwyneth's face and away again, as if her countenance scorched their eyes and yet they were compelled to fix their gaze on her.

As she looked out at these despised ones of the city, the unfortunates against whose hardships the rest of the populace measured its blessings, Gwyneth felt a contraction within herself as she remembered that even these people had turned away from her boy, had made the hated sign against the evil eye, had muttered and droned against him, against his very life. Abomination. Devil's child. Accursed.

Bile rose in her throat, and for a moment she felt the weight of the coats heavy on her forearms and had the urge to fling the woollen bundle at the row of hopeful faces and knock them to the ground.

Instead, she breathed deeply and concentrated on her purpose.

'This place,' she began abruptly, her voice strong and clear in the still air, 'will, in future times, be called Daker's College, founded and endowed by Richard Daker, vintner of the guild and of the city of London. And here, most unfittingly, died his son, John Daker, ending his father's line and name. Now the name of Daker will live only in this college. To honour the memory of Richard Daker and his son John, these alms are given you. In recognition of this gift, will you promise to pray for the future completion and good governance of this college every day of your life?'

Her eyes, which had played along the line of waiting

recipients, now focused on the figure nearest to her – a thin, elderly man who supported his hunched form on a crutch, one leg twisted under him as if a broken hip had mended awry. He returned Gwyneth's intense glare for no more than two heartbeats before lowering his eyes and bowing his head further.

'I will so pray,' he conceded, as if cowed, jerking his face sideways to see whether his fellow paupers were prepared to do likewise. All joined in the chorus, assenting that they, too, would so pray.

As Gwyneth stepped forward to put the coats into their waiting hands, she barred her ears to the half-muttered questions that rose from the crowd and battered at her. She knew her words had shaken and disturbed them. Prayers for the dead were the usual fee for alms; prayers for the prosperity of a building, for *this* building, raised hackles. 'No priest,' she heard. 'How can she speak of such things? It is a priest's task.'

Well, she had known they would not likely welcome such novelty.

But she realised that three further repetitions of this alms-giving oath by Henry, Piers Mottis and Nicholas Brygge, in turn, might see the crowd's uncertain muttering transformed into the outraged baying of a mob.

Quickly forestalling any move on Henry's part, Gwyneth stepped forward and quieted the half-guarded discontent before her with her still silence.

'Friends,' she began, when the hubbub had abated to let her speak, 'as you have seen alms delivered in kind to the poor and lowly of our city, so you will see also, in due course, alms given to the young.'

She raked the crowd with a long look, drawing them back to her, so that her words could find their mark.

'John Daker was not yet a man when he died but a youth on the threshold of manhood. Such are the young men who his father, Master Richard Daker, hoped would come – from our city of Salster – to his college.' She flung her gaze far and wide, seeking the eyes of the young men who might have been John's companions, had he lived.

'Youths on the threshold of manhood,' she continued. 'Young men who would be better fitted – by their learning here – to make their way in the world, to live justly and honourably so that they, in their turn, might rise to a position from which they could care for the poor amongst us.'

She paused. She had silenced the murmuring but their faces were closed, not yet prepared to accept what she was saying.

'I was close by the day John died, here' – she looked swiftly, involuntarily, over her shoulder in the direction of the lime pits that lay some way off beyond the college –'and on that day he was full of questions about the building.' Her voice dropped slightly, became more confiding as she smiled with the memory, and the crowd strained almost imperceptibly forward to catch her words.

'He asked what each tool was for, how they were kept sharpened.' Gwyneth racked her memory, snatching questions Simon had relayed to her as he went over and over the day in the hours while they waited for John's inevitable death. 'Why did we build this way and not that? Why was the college constructed so, and not as others are – like Wickham's new college at Oxford?'

She let her gaze travel over them again, seeing untied coifends catch the suddenly stirring breeze, a child's ragged skirt plucked at by the borning wind. Letting them absorb the implication that this College, Daker's college, was to be compared to that of William of Wickham, erstwhile chancellor of the realm, she then proceeded, her voice dropping still further into an impassioned, intimate register.

'The reply' – she did not mention Simon's name for fear of agitating them once more – 'was that in Salster there is no need of a high-walled quadrangle for, unlike Wickham's, this college is not to be filled with strangers, studying out of sight and out of mind, privileged beyond the city's own people. This college, Daker's College, is to be *our* college – built for the sons of the city to study in. There will be no need of stout oak doors to defend this college because it is to be a college of the city, a college unlike all others, a college through which *all* are free to walk, to see the labours that proceed within.

'And' – here her voice warmed and swelled as she felt the crowd's mood shift – 'as our city is English, so will our college be English, and only English spoken within.'

Gwyneth paused to let the burst of audible astonishment subside before continuing. 'Master Daker's wish was that boys would not have to turn from their native tongue when they would study law or medicine.' She regarded them so fiercely that those who did not know her would think that she was fighting for a dearly held notion of her own instead of the strange visions of a man she had hardly known and whom she had not always entirely trusted.

'Is law,' she cried, 'carried out in our courts in Latin?' The crowd remained stubbornly silent, so she supplied the answer for them. 'No, nor in French either. We are English and here, in Daker's College, *our* college, our sons will learn and debate and understand in English. For English is as good as any language – as good as Latin, or French. The very clerk to the king's works – Master Geoffrey Chaucer – is a poet who writes his works in English.'

'Does he write bawdy verse?' a voice called from the crowd, to general laughter. It was, Gwyneth knew, the laughter of relief. At last, this wag had made a bridge between her and the crowd and they could receive from her once more. The alms-giving could continue.

'When those in our midst who have reached old age without family to care for them have had their alms,' Gwyneth pronounced, 'there will be fifteen pence distributed at each archway of the college.'

A ragged, unfocused cheer went up at this announcement. As she turned to Henry and signalled him to begin his dole of clothing with the required words, Gwyneth caught a thread of speculation as to how these monetary alms would be allotted. She, Brygge, Mottis and Henry had – after much debate and consideration of accounts – decided that John's obit would be celebrated for a period of ten consecutive years, reasoning that this would sufficiently honour the house of Daker and procure the ongoing good will of the citizenry until such time as they should see the benefits to themselves of the college's existence.

She stepped towards Alysoun to collect the four purses of fifteen pence that would be distributed from each archway – one penny for each year of John's life – and as she did so she heard heard the slow, dull beat of iron-shod hoofs on dusty, stony ground.

Others heard it also and heads began to turn, one by one at first and then – drawn by the attention of others – in dozens and scores, to see the source of the interruption.

Slowly, as the crowd parted before a small band of mounted men, a loud grumbling of discontent arose, carrying within it the name that Gwyneth had dreaded hearing all the while.

'Copley!'

His men at arms watchful behind him, the bishop sat on his tall horse – a fine-bred animal to Gwyneth's eye, no simple hack on which to ride from here to there – and gazed at the scene. The crowd, now mute, regarded him with undisguised hostility. Salster's Priory of St Dernstan had been unpopular for generations with its taxes, its monopolies and its dominance of the life of the city, but this bishop – being more powerful than most – was, consequently, hated more.

Nicholas Brygge, drawn from his post on the south side of the college by news of Copley's arrival, strode to Gwyneth's side. He stood at her shoulder and together they waited for Copley to speak.

While the silence lengthened and Copley glared down at them, Piers Mottis quit his post and joined them, as did Henry. The four standing figures faced the mounted man as the paupers had, not five minutes since, faced Gwyneth to wait for their dole. The bishop, they knew, had no charity to give them.

'What is this mummery that has drawn the town from its walls?' The bishop's hostility made his horse nervous; the animal tossed its head and moved its feet uneasily as if wishing to flee the spot.

'We are here to distribute alms in memory of John Daker,' Gwyneth stated, flatly.

'An obit.'

'If you will.' Gwyneth's tone was implacable.

'And are prayers offered for the dead?'

'No.'

Copley's eyes narrowed. He had not expected such a bold admission.

'If this is an obit, why are there no prayers offered for the deceased?'

'Are we not free to distribute alms as we see fit without making the poor *buy* our charity?' Brygge asked, his tone light and mocking.

'You are not free to scorn the precepts of the Church,' Copley snapped. 'Nor are you free to conduct a service of religion without the presence of a priest!'

'This is not a service of religion—'

'*Do not bandy words with me, grocer!*'

Nicholas Brygge gazed up at Copley, apparently unabashed. At his side, Gwyneth felt her heart knocking her breast as if it would burst and drown her.

Abruptly, Copley kicked his horse forward, dividing Brygge from Mottis and reining the animal in when its shoulder was level with the mayor. Slowly, he leaned down, until his forearm rested along his thigh, the reins held tight and his horse's head pulled back to its chest. 'Do not think,' he said, his voice low and tight, 'that I do not know you for a Lollard. And do not think that your position will save you when the king promulgates a bill condemning Lollard heretics to death.'

Suddenly he turned to Gwyneth and she felt her guts speared by terror as his eyes met hers.

'I know,' he said, in the same tone, 'who buried your twisted mockery of a child. And where. I know that you and your husband – who has had the good sense not to keep himself before me – associate with Lollards if you are not yourselves taken in by that heresy. When the law is promulgated, you, too, will be condemned. And then this college will be pulled down, stone . . . by stone . . . by stone. And,' he added, maliciously, 'whoever you have persuaded to purchase your roofing glass will have to watch while it is smashed, one pane after another, by my men.' He sat up in the saddle once more and swept the college site with disdainful eyes before looking down at Gwyneth and Brygge once more. 'All this . . . will come to naught. And the Church will prevail.'

Gwyneth, finding her voice with her courage countered, 'All will come to naught, finally, my lord. And only God will prevail.'

She saw his jaw clench but was unprepared when he wrenched his horse's head round, causing the animal to knock Brygge from his feet and into her, casting them both to the ground at the horse's feet.

A hissing sound arose, somewhere in the crowd, at this unnecessary act. Swiftly taken up, the sound soon consumed the whole crowd, every mouth a thin line, every breath directed towards Copley in censure, every eye trained on him to see how he would respond to this defiance.

His horse, unnerved by this eerie sound, half-reared. Pulling the animal back almost onto its haunches, Copley turned to his men-at-arms. 'Clear this area! Get all these people back inside the city! There is to be no more of this sham!'

The mounted men-at-arms moved towards the crowd, their swords drawn, making as if to herd the populace back into the city. But the people were not to be baulked of their alms. The crowd parted before the horses but did not turn towards the city gates, simply moving aside and surrounding the men-at-arms who, cut off from each other, became more and more ineffectual, wheeling their horses and waving their swords at people who simply stepped out of the way, laughing.

The bishop, crimson with rage, watched his men being made fools of for no more than a minute before shouting, 'Enough!'

Wheeling his horse around once more and making the poor animal dance on the spot by both holding it in and spurring in frustration, he addressed Brygge.

'Order this assembly to disperse or I will arrest you.'

'On what charge?'

'Heresy.'

'And how have I committed heresy?' Brygge asked, his eyes narrowing.

'That is for me to prove in court, not to argue with you here! Now disperse this crowd back to their business!'

Brygge regarded him impassively. If he was daunted by the bishop, Gwyneth thought, he did not show his fear.

'*The bishop will not touch me and mine unless he wants riots in the streets of his city.*' Gwyneth remembered the mayor's words. Did he intend to display his power by starting a riot now?

Finally, Brygge spoke. 'I am not minded to disperse my fellow citizens without good reason. They will return to their homes and businesses when the almsgiving is done.' He paused and then said, in a slightly louder voice, as if he wished everybody in the crowd to be sure of hearing, 'I suggest that you return home, My Lord, and allow us to conclude our business here.'

'You refuse to put an end to this?'

'I refuse to put an end to lawful business.'

Copley turned his head to his men-at-arms.

'Arrest this man.'

After a brief jerking of heads and shrugging, two men-at-arms dismounted and handed their reins to their fellows. Advancing on Brygge, they made to take hold of him, but Gwyneth was too swift for them. Stepping in front of Brygge she declared, 'No. You shall not take him unless you first take me!'

'So be it!' The bishop's snarl had triumph in it. 'Arrest her also!'

'And me.' Piers Mottis stepped forward, swiftly followed by Henry.

Confused now, the men looked to Copley for guidance. As they did so, Alysoun stepped out of the front rank of the crowd, leaving her handcart, and joined her husband and foster-mother.

'You must take me too.'

Slowly, and then with gathering momentum, the crowd followed Alysoun to the mayor's side as a heap of pebbles will tumble if a crucial one is displaced.

Soon, the men-at-arms were surrounded, as they had been before, by the crowd. But now the people who surrounded them were not laughing and dodging their horses' hoofs, they were pressing in against them, making it impossible to draw their swords, still less to use them. In sudden frustration, one of them lunged with his shoulder to one side, intending to barge his way through the crowd, and was immediately felled as his legs were kicked from beneath him. As he lay on the ground, it looked likely that he would be trampled or smothered, but Brygge called out, 'Stay friends! Let no violence be done here today!'

A few voices were raised in protest, but most acquiesced and the man was offered hands that pulled him, roughly, to his feet.

As Copley's man pushed through the crowd and took the reins of his horse once more, Brygge stated, in a voice audible to everyone in the crowd as well as to the bishop, whom he was facing, 'There will be no arrests here today, My Lord. We, as citizens of the city, will go about our lawful business and conclude what we have begun.'

A rumble of half-wary, half-defiant agreement came from the crowd.

Brygge paused and, stepping back so that he was more visible to the crowd, raised his voice once more.

'Let it be known that this college no longer belongs simply to Richard Daker or to those whom he has endowed. By this act today, this college becomes the care of us all in this city. When it shall be completed, our sons will learn here and our city will be enriched by their learning and wisdom.'

He stopped once more and waited while a few muted cheers rapidly petered out. 'And let it further be known that this college, though founded and endowed by Richard Daker, is henceforth to be called Kineton and Daker College, for it would not have been built but for Simon of Kineton, and both Richard Daker and Simon of Kineton have lost their only sons in its building. As both men were joined in grief, so their names shall be joined – as their efforts have been – in this college.

'So, on this site of Kineton and Daker College, let the almsgiving proceed. Let us all return to our former places.'

And, before he could be made to look more foolish than he already did by being stranded on the receding tide of the crowd, Copley turned his horse and spurred away, followed in disarray by his men-at-arms.

Sixty-three

Salster, present day

Letters in hands by turns flamboyant, assertive and unsteady with age, emails, visually similar but electronically as unique as fingerprints with their names and ISP tags, arrived at the offices of Damia Miller and Ed Norris from the four corners of the globe. The vast majority expressed outrage at Baird's plan, fond reminiscences of Toby, deep gratitude and support for the college. Inevitably, a small, pragmatic proportion wondered whether, in the historical context of an ever-changing Salster college scene, the time wasn't ripe for such a union of ancient and modern.

Some supporters expressed regret at their failure to provide solid financial backing before this and appended gift-aid statements; one elderly gentleman (J.Crowther [matric. 1933], Cranbrook, Kent) apologised for an inability to offer 'more tangible support' but promised daily prayers for the future of the college. Damia, remembering the words of Toby's Obit, took comfort from the thought and wondered at this evidence of unsuspected credulity in herself.

She had arrived at her desk early – barely after eight –

having woken an hour before the alarm to a sense of dread that took a moment or two of wakefulness to resolve itself around the meeting at five o'clock that afternoon. Deep in the pit of her stomach was the knowledge that it was not only the college's future that would be decided that afternoon. Her job prospects, were she to be made redundant by the proposed takeover, would be limited, and Ian Baird had made it very clear that, having rejected his offer to jump ship, there would be no job for her in the new, amalgamated college.

As she thought about the meeting, she tried to ignore the potential consequences of her defiance of Baird: the loss of her little house, an enforced move from Salster, a sudden brake on her accelerating career.

And the loss of Toby. Of its unique foundation, of its history as an independent entity, of its long-lost story. What would Baird make of the emerging story of the Kinetons, what spin would he put on it?

Conference delegates were strolling across to the Octo for lunch when the phone on her desk shrilled.

'Hi, it's me.'

Damia had not spoken to Neil since he had turned up at her house fresh from London and the Public Records Office with his news about Simon's court case and the vanishing endowments.

'Hi.'

'Excellent blog – did it do the trick?'

'You can come and see my desk if you like – awash with letters and email printouts.'

'Good. Are you free for lunch?'

Damia's instinct was to claim a prior engagement, but she stopped herself. They needed to talk.

'Yes,' she answered. 'Free as a bird.'

Worried that she would give in to cowardice and hide behind small talk for the whole of the meal, Damia forced herself to leap straight in to the conversation she knew they must have. As soon as their drinks had arrived and their orders were placed she said, 'So. The baby question.'

'Have you thought about it – having a baby together?'

Damia grinned wryly. 'Yes, I've thought about it a lot.' She snorted a laugh in her nose. 'Literally night and day, actually.'

'And?'

'I'm still thinking.'

'What's stopping you?' His tone was calm but Damia felt the passion beneath his words. She had not anticipated such feelings. She had been so wrapped up in her own doubts and desires that she had not thought to analyse Neil's motives for wishing to become the father of her child beyond assuming, somewhat vaguely, that he wanted to maintain a connection with her.

'Have you thought how complicated it would make things for future partners?' she asked. 'How's any future girl-friend of yours going to feel if you're constantly coming round to my house to see our child, if you have a relation-ship with me from which she's excluded?'

'Would she need to be excluded?'

'That just gets weirder and weirder.' Damia held his gaze. 'And what about when one of us has to move? You're not going to stay at the cathedral for ever – I may be about to lose my job!'

'I'd be prepared to commit to staying in Salster until the child is eighteen,' Neil said, calmly.

Damia stared at him. 'But how can you? You don't know the future!'

'London's commutable – if I can't get some kind of job there I won't be able to get a job anywhere. Or,' he said, as if he'd considered all these options and weighed them up carefully beforehand, 'we could agree to relocate. If one of us was offered a job we just couldn't refuse, maybe the other could try and find a job in the same area and move too.'

She shook her head. 'Neil, this is taking on a life of its own, I need more time to think it through.'

He took in a deep breath. 'Should we go and talk to someone? A professional or something?'

She nodded slowly. 'Yes. Yes, that'd be a good idea. But after all this is decided, OK? I can't decide anything else until I know what's happening with Toby.'

Dear Dr Norris,

Please find enclosed a cheque for five hundred pounds towards the Max-a-Million campaign initiated by Jon Song. I have raised this money by selling my most prized possession – a blade won during the Lent Furlongs in my second year at Toby in 1938. I rowed at 5 and, as you will see from your college records, we were the most improved eight that season. With the help of my great-grandson, Oliver, I put the blade up for sale on eBay with the enclosed success.

Having completed my degree at Toby, I volunteered for the Royal Navy and ended the war as a Lieutenant. My son Tom, born in 1943, was a Tobyite, as was his son James, and now young Oliver wishes to follow in Dad's, Grandpa's

and Great-grandpa's footsteps and come to Toby too,
though he is proposing to break with the family tradition
and study medicine rather than law.

It saddens me beyond all reason to think that he might
not be able to fulfil his wish. The college gave me so much
– a sense of purpose, of perspective, of integrity, and it is
those things that I would like to see Toby continuing to give
to young men – and, of course, young women now, too.
(Hooray!)

My generation of Tobyites seems, I am sad to say, to
have died out by now, but I am still in touch with a few old
lags from Tom's time at the college (tragically, my son died
in his forties) and now that young Oliver has made me
'computer-literate' I shall try to contact more by email.
Quite an exciting thought after all this time! My aim is to
see if we can't get together a legacy club in order to leave
the college a decent bit of money to take its good work into
the next generation.

I shall, in due course, let you know how I fare on that
venture.

Yours very sincerely

Eric Thurley

Back in her office, Damia could settle to nothing but reading
letters and emails of support. Again and again she read the
attachment Julia Todd had sent to all contributing old members and wondered how many – if any – would respond to
her plea.

❖

'Ladies and gentlemen.' Norris discreetly called the murmuring members of the governing body to order. 'I have not pre-pared an agenda for this meeting, as you are all aware that we have only one item to discuss – the formal proposal for the amalgamation of our two colleges by Sir Ian Baird, president of Northgate College.'

Damia, sitting at Norris's side, was aware of a feeling of profound unease around the table. Even those members of the governing body who favoured Baird's proposal must, surely, feel an undercurrent of doubt at the thought of ending six hundred years of Toby independence.

'I hope that nobody here has been influenced by that dis-play of petulance outside.' Charles Northrop's voice was loud in the silence that followed Norris's introduction. 'How on earth did the undergraduates know this meeting was taking place? It's out of term, they shouldn't be here – it's nothing to do with them.'

Damia's heart begin to beat with the frantic pulse of fear and fury.

'I think that comment eloquently sums up the ideological gulf between those who want to become part of Baird plc and those of us who want to maintain Toby's independence,' she snapped back. 'To say that the decision as to whether we amalgamate with another college is nothing to do with this college's undergraduates is insulting!'

'Ah yes, the famous community of learning – taken to the heart of the city but still maintaining global reach and influence,' Northrop mocked. 'That kind of utopian vision unfortunately takes a great deal more money than we cur-rently have or can reasonably aspire to, Miss Miller.' He turned to Norris as the meeting's chairman. 'Can we please begin with some hard facts, Mr Chairman?'

'No, Charles.' Norris folded his hands in front of him and

took in each member of the governing body with his gaze. 'If you don't mind, before we begin with facts of any kind I would like to say this. Speaking personally, I am fundamentally opposed to an amalgamation with Northgate College for reasons you are all well acquainted with. But I am not here in a personal capacity, and no more are any of you.' His eyes moved searchingly from face to face. 'I hope that we can conduct this meeting free from personal bias and selfish desire. That we can genuinely look towards the greater good not only of this college but of the whole federation of colleges here in Salster. We were elected to the governing body – all of us – not just because of our administrative skills but also because of our commitment to this college. I would ask you all to remember that commitment as we debate Ian Baird's proposal.'

When she and Norris had met to collate messages of support during the morning, Damia had not found Norris in buoyant mood. 'I'm afraid the Max-a-Million campaign may just have come too late, Damia,' he had said. 'If we had a million pounds in our bank account tomorrow, we could probably fend off Baird's proposal, even if he does have some backing on the governing body. But it's unlikely that, even if we *do* reach the target, it'll be in time to make any significant impact on our deficit. And don't forget that a good chunk of it is earmarked for the windows anyway.'

He seemed, however, to have managed to put such pessimism to one side before coming to the meeting.

'Ian Baird's proposal,' he said now, all eyes in the conference room on him, 'is, essentially, that we continue much as at present in terms of undergraduate numbers and even graduates but that the teaching staff could be reduced by the resulting scope for economies of scale. Some of the less well represented subjects would no longer be offered here and the Toby administrative staff would, by and large, be made redundant, with just a few being re-employed by the new combined college to reflect the larger numbers involved. All services would be centrally managed, all applications would be to the combined college, with those studying subjects that would be taught here living here, and those whose tutors would be based at what is currently Northgate using existing accommodation on that site.'

As he concluded his summary there was a silence while the governing body digested his words. Then the first person spoke. 'This may sound simplistic but it sounds as if we can't lose – our students stay on, most of the staff stay on—'

His words released a spate of pent-up argument and counter-argument.

When Damia was finally invited to speak, she withdrew a sheaf of papers from the folder in front of her.

'These are all emails, letters and logged phone calls from old members, all supporting Dr Norris, all opposing the merger with Northgate. I'd like to give you a flavour of one or two—'

'Oh, for Christ's sake, this isn't a bloody wedding!' Northrop erupted.

'No, currently, it has more the feeling of a wake, but I'd like to think that's a little premature,' Damia retorted.

'Look.' Northrop's voice dropped to a more conciliatory tone. 'I'm sure all that support' – his eyes pointed to the subject of his sentence – 'is very nice, very touching, but it's too little, too late!'

Damia held up her folder. 'Every single one of these

letters of support came with a donation. Every *single* one! Most of the emails were pledging money too.'

'Yes, yes, yes! The loyalty of Tobyites has never been in question. The nice cosiness of our traditions here – the fact that people *like* them, for Christ's sake! – has never been in question. The *question* – the *only* question – is can we afford to go on like this? And the answer, quite clearly, is No.'

'I don't think that *is* the only question,' Damia countered. 'I think the larger question is "Does Salster need a college like Toby, one prepared to buck the trend, to hold out for values of truth, social justice—"'

'Social justice?' Northrop scoffed. 'How do we uphold values of social justice when we're an elitist institution?'

'You forget that not all the members of Toby are students and teachers. We have a social contract with our admin and domestic staff. Because we're not a profit-making organisation—'

'You can say that again!'

'Because we're not, we can pretty well offer jobs for life to those who want that kind of stability, followed up with a reasonable pension. How many cleaners in this country do you think are offered a pension by their employers, Charles? The angels here are given a good deal, but they also give *us* a good deal – your average contract cleaner isn't going to look after new, vulnerable students who've left home for the first time, they're not going to spot the potential suicides, the sudden changes in routine that signal something wrong. They're not called angels for nothing – they guard our young people.'

'Again, nice, laudable, lovely! But *we can't afford it*. We don't have *the money!*'

Damia ignored his interruption. 'And did you know that

a group of undergraduates have formed a voluntary services committee which has taken a proposal to the city council for summer schools, after-school sports clubs and mentoring facilities for under-achievers? That's social justice, Charles.'

'Where's – the – money – coming – from?'

'In the case of the voluntary services committee, from Salster City Council. And I think, if only more time was granted, you'd see that money would come in, that we would be able to balance the books. For instance, I've already started negotiating rights to the Kinetons' story.'

Before Northrop could respond, Norris held up a hand, his head cocked in the direction of the windows. Thinly at first, but gathering strength quickly, the strains of 'For He's a Jolly Good Fellow' were audible in the Yard below.

Rising to his feet, Norris crossed the room to the window.

'Oh, my word,' Damia heard him say, softly.

What she and the governing body saw, when they joined the Regent Master at the window, was a crowd that filled the Yard, singing lustily and looking up at the conference room window. A large figure in a voluminous floral dress and immaculate chignon, standing on what looked to Damia like the JCR speaker's box, was conducting the singing with theatrical arm movements. Seeing the changing expressions and upward gaze of her singers, she turned on her makeshift podium and bowed low before skipping lightly down and approaching the staircase beneath them.

Toby Blog

[Click here] to see a picture of a real live guardian angel. Her name, for those of you who weren't lucky enough to be her contemporaries at Toby in the mid-Eighties, is Julia

525

Todd. She's now a barrister taking time out to bring up her two children and, as it turns out, to rescue the college.

In response to my desperate round-robin email asking for support for Ed Norris ahead of the extraordinary governing body meeting, Julia came up with a plan. She asked us to forward the following email to all recent donors:

Dear fellow Tobyite and direct debit giver of funds

Chances are you won't know me (Toby 1985–88) but we are all – as the amazingly dynamic Ms Miller would say – members of the worldwide community of Tobyites. As such, I have a plan that will not only give Edmund Norris financial and moral support at this emergency meeting, but might actually give him some breathing space in which to get more money rolling in and sort out some of Toby's problems in a way that spares us the Northgate final solution.

My proposal is this: on Friday, as many of us as are able should turn up at Toby whilst the EGBM is in progress and demand that, as shareholders, we should be consulted before any such decision is taken. For the lawyers amongst you I know it's shaky ground, we're not *technically* shareholders, but I'm sure we can bring some kind of case that there is an implied or implicit contract between us and the college which they are in breach of. At the very least we can throw confusion around with a liberal hand and delay any decision.

If you're with me, turn up in the Toby Yard around five o'clock and we'll take it from there.

Cheers (to all those who know me)
Best wishes (to all those who don't)

Julia Todd.

❖

Julia's appeal brought an astonishing crowd of around almost three hundred old members to the yard where, joining forces with the several dozen undergraduates who had gathered to protest against the meeting, they formed an impromptu choir under Julia's leadership and sang 'For He's a Jolly Good Fellow' until the governing body emerged to investigate.

The subsequent conversation went something like this:

Julia [in full stately galleon mode]: We've all pledged money – many of us in excess of a thousand pounds a year – to this college. We are *stakeholders*. You can't simply decide to amalgamate with Northgate College without conducting a meeting that includes us.

Bursar [regretfully, but firmly]: Unfortunately, I think you'll find that, legally, we can.

Julia [firmly and not in the least regretfully]: Ah, but unfortunately, I think *you'll* find that, when we set in motion civil legal proceedings against you, even though you would probably win, you would be tied up for so long, and at such great cost, that Northgate would no longer be interested.

Charles Northrop (dean) [dismissively, outraged]: Legal proceedings on what grounds?

Julia [promptly]: Breach of contract.

Charles [yet more dismissively]: Don't be ridiculous, there is no contract between us!

Julia [warming to her theme]: I think you'll find that there are grounds for us to assume an implied contract between you, the institution, and us, the donors, which states that you will make a reasonable attempt to restore the college's finances to health in exchange for our money. And we do not consider a measly handful of weeks before caving in to be a reasonable attempt. [Finishes with the full-dentition smile of a shark homing in on an out-of-condition seal.]

There was chaos and confusion for some time after this exchange as various interviewees tried to explain to the media (brought out in force by the undergraduate contingent) what had happened, but eventually an agreement emerged from a decidedly rattled governing body. As a result of Julia's intervention, a general meeting of all interested parties (students, staff admin, domestic and teaching, tenants, old members) will be held in a month's time (i.e. exactly a week after the Fairings) to look once again at Northgate's proposals. See you there?

Sixty-four

Salster, late summer 1398

Late in the afternoon on the day following the celebration of John Daker's strange obit, as the day dimmed towards twilight and the rain eased slightly on the warm edge of the westerly wind, a carter came through the south gate of the city of Salster, his cart loaded with stone.

'I am Halkin Scaff,' he informed the gate-keeper in a burr the man did not recognise and assumed to be from somewhere well to the west of the country, 'bid to bring this stone to the house of Master Mason Henry Ackland. Can you tell me where that might be?'

'Master Ackland lives at the house of Master Mason Kineton, though Master Kineton is not here presently,' the gate-watcher said.

'It is Master Ackland I am bid to,' repeated the carter stolidly, the comings and goings of his betters of no great concern to him.

The gate-keeper told him where Simon and Gwyneth's house was to be found, but then said curiously, 'But should you not be leaving the stone at the college site, friend? For that is where Master Ackland's business is carried on.'

The carter looked dubious. 'I am bid to the house,' he said, uncertainly.

The gate-keeper, obviously deciding that this was not a man used to making his own decisions, suggested that he send a boy to the Kinetons' house to fetch Master Ackland here, or ask for instructions as to the desination of the load. After a moment or two's rumination, the carter agreed that this would likely be the best plan, as he did not relish getting his cart through the city streets, 'nor finding lodging for my horse, neither'.

Henry, having come in person to the gate and supervised the unloading of the stone into the lodge and the disposition of the horse, took the carter by the sodden shoulder and steered him back through the city gate. 'Come friend,' he said, 'I shall see you accommodated for the night beneath my roof.'

As they walked through the streets, the rows and houses still dripping from their thatch and the men's boots splashing mud, Henry looked sidelong at the carter. The man was bent slightly from somewhat above the middle height, as if his sitting stance on his cart had curved his back and set his head thrust forward on his shoulders; a week's growth of grey and brown beard clung to his lined face, but beneath it he looked pale, unlike most of his calling, who were leathery from exposure to all winds and weathers. His head was plainly shorn against lice beneath his cap. No long ends straggled out from beneath the worn and stained leather.

'Do you not have any oiled skins to shield you from the weather, friend?' Henry asked agreeably.

'No, master,' was his reply. 'As you see me, so am I always attired.'

'We must see if we can do better for you for the return journey,' Henry said, 'for the weather looks set to soak us for days yet.'

The carter swung his head suddenly to look at Henry but did not speak, allowing an unspoken question to hang in the air between them as they came to the warmth and dryness of Gwyneth's house.

Leading the carter in and closing the door behind them, Henry burst out laughing.

'By all that's holy, Simon, I wouldn't have known you unless I had expected you! Where on earth did you get Halkin Scaff?'

'He was a carter I knew once,' Simon said in his own voice, straightening his back and wincing. 'I must take these clothes off and put dry on, I am chilled to the marrow.'

Gwyneth, ministering to her husband as he stripped, washed in the warm water she brought him and dressed in fresh linen more fitted to his station, scrutinised Simon narrowly. Even allowing for the absence of his beard his face was thinner and more drawn than she had ever seen it. His hair, revealed as a half-inch growth on his head, was thinning and greying, receding from his high forehead, and Gwyneth, suddenly the tender wife as she regarded him, wondered whether the servants at Kineton were feeding their master properly.

'You do not look well, Simon,' she said, tenderly.

'I have caught a chill on the journey,' he said. 'The rain has fallen on me almost all the way from Kineton and sleeping under the cart proved little protection.'

They had hatched this plan for Simon to return to Salster

weeks before, after Gwyneth's conversation with Piers Mottis. She, Henry and the nursing Alysoun had decided that a belated obit for John Daker, with generous almsgiving to both old and young, would be likely to win the hearts of a good number of those in Salster who might otherwise be persuaded to dance to Copley's tune and aid and abet the college's destruction. The promise of ten years of almsgiving was more than likely to keep them loyal to their benefactors. And the longer the college stood, was peopled, and educated the young men of Salster, the more it would become a city institution, accepted by the populace and taken to their hearts – she hoped – as their own.

Hard on the heels of plans for John Daker's obit, Gwyneth had conceived a passionate desire for a similar ceremony to memorialise Toby. To her surprise, Henry and Alysoun agreed, and the plans were made for Simon's unremarked return to Salster.

Now that the accommodation blocks were finished, complete with their statuary niches, Gwyneth had planned to erect the twin statues of Toby in readiness for his obit.

She could tell what it had cost Simon to be here. Hardship and humiliation were written in his drawn, shaven features, his poor-man's head of greying hair. She could hardly bear to tell him what she must.

'Simon,' she said, slowly, her eyes on him, 'we cannot celebrate Toby's obit this year.'

His head snapped up as if punched from beneath the chin. 'What? Howso?'

Briefly, Gwyneth told him about Copley's intervention at John's obit.

'We cannot risk provoking him further,' she finished. 'I am sorry, Simon, I had thought to soften people's hearts towards us by having John's obit first but I had reckoned without Copley.'

'Did you not know he was in the city?' Simon demanded.

Gwyneth sighed unhappily. 'I did. But I have grown so accustomed to building unhindered that I did not consider how he would see an obit with no priest, how he would react to almsgiving so obviously designed to buy the people's favour.'

Simon stared at her. Gwyneth knew her husband; knew the rage and frustration likely to be rising within him as he contemplated everything he had endured to come here unrecognised only to be told that his son's life would not be celebrated, that his sacrifice must remain unknown, for another year.

It was with the greatest astonishment, therefore, that she watched him sigh gently, heard him say, 'It does not greatly matter. What is of importance is that the college is built, that the images of our son are set in place, that all may see him, body and soul.'

Gwyneth touched his arm tentatively. 'I am sorry, Simon. I have failed you in this.'

He covered her hand with his own and smiled at her, his eyes soft. 'You are forgiven, wife,' he said. Taking a step forward, he put a gentle hand on her shoulder.

Gwyneth's pulse thumped and she responded without a second's thought. Closing the gap between them with one short step she stepped into the circle of his arms and put her mouth to his.

Sixty-five

The helicopter hovered like a throbbing, fat-bellied dragonfly over the sunlit city, its cameras steadily taking in the scene below. On ten million television screens an invisible hand covered the bird's-eye view of Salster city centre in computer-generated squiggles. Fairings rules were being explained and running patterns analysed.

Circles encompassed colleges, arrowed lines were the probable routes from one to another, and the star at the centre of it all was St Thomas' college, final destination of Salster University's Fairings.

One by one, the helicopter's cameras zoomed in on Salster's foundation colleges and, superimposed on an image of main quad or impressive façade, photos of smiling young athletes appeared, their vital statistics, sporting honours and subject of study displayed as the colleges' runners were introduced to the watching nation.

Duncan McTeer (reserve last year), 1m 79cm, 60 kilos, reading Law

Sally Mackle (running for the second year), 1m 70cm,
56 kilos, British universities 800m champion, reading
Classics
Ellen Ballantyne (running for the second year), 1m
61cm, 50.5 kilos, AAA under 18s national champion
1500m, reading Medicine
Sam Kearns (running for the first time), 1m 85, 63
kilos, reading Psychology

Damia turned her face from the sky, to her runners. 'The eye in the sky,' she commented. 'BBC, I expect.' She resumed her pep-talk. 'OK, twenty minutes till we have to be up at the bridge for take-off. Everybody happy?'

The four runners stood before her in their claret and navy running silks, Stephan Kingsley's formulaic logo in bold embroidery on the front, the Kineton and Dacre tun and compasses on the back. Those who had not made the final four were also there, in their training tracksuits, ready to 'scout' for their teammates.

As sponsorship had raised the stakes over the last two decades, 'scouts' had become as vital a part of the race as the actual runners. It was the scouts, with their observations of other teams' running patterns and the position of remaining roses on the trellises, who determined strategy in the latter stages of the race. Meeting the runners at agreed waypoints they would call running-codes that sent the silked-up runners off to their next destination, either confirming or changing the team's predetermined running pattern. It was a system that had remained largely unregulated until the financial rewards available to the Rosebowl winners had lured St Dunstan's College into ensuring the supremacy of their team by equipping scouts and runners with hands-free mobile phones.

The victorious team had been severely censured by the college council and barred from competing in the following year's race.

Now, race-marshals were constantly vigilant and both scouts and runners were searched before and after the race for hidden receivers or wires.

Damia scanned the faces of her runners. Their apprehensiveness was, she knew, entirely of her making. She had formulated a plan for the Fairings that would see the Toby athletes on television screens across the world. 'We've got to get global reach – contact all our old members – hit them with a big message,' she had said. And now, these four young people were going to put their weight behind that message.

Edmund Norris, kept ignorant of Damia's plans for the race on the assumption that he might have reason to value deniability, stood in the Octagon Yard being interviewed by the BBC. Close by, but standing at an angle so as not to appear at his side, was Ian Baird.

'Dr Norris, how does it feel to have been abandoned by your associate college?'

The quirky smile that passed briefly over Ed Norris's features suggested that the question had been predictable enough to make a private bet on. 'Do you know,' he replied, 'any sense of abandonment I might have felt has been totally wiped out by a huge sense of pride in how our worldwide college community has risen to the challenge of supporting our athletes both financially and morally.' He tapped the lapel of his summer-weight jacket, where a small, enamel badge had pride of place. 'The "By, For and With" campaign has proved that it is possible to retain a moral stance on sponsorship and still field a well-financed team.'

'Your coach – Damia Miller – is also the marketing manager at Kineton and Dacre College; I gather she's been the driving force behind this resurrection of the college's identity as an institution that bucks the current trend?'

'I don't think Damia would claim to have done all this single-handed, but she has been a tremendous force in focusing and harnessing the ethos of the college and hopefully redefining it for the twenty-first century and our next six-hundred years of independent service to the city and the nation.'

'Sir Ian.' The interviewer turned through ninety degrees to Ian Baird. 'You're in the process of trying to bring that independence to an end?'

'Good Lord, David,' Baird chuckled, 'you make me sound like some fascist dictator! It's not quite as unilateral as that, I assure you. No, I'm responding to a perceived need within Kineton and Dacre College itself for a bigger, more financially muscular partner to help it meet the ever-growing challenges with which we in higher education are presented. If we are to continue to offer world-class education here at Salster, it's imperative that we develop new, advanced methods of research and scholarship, we cannot afford to operate with a nineteenth-century or even a twentieth-century model of tradition and heritage. We have to be realistic. I think the proposed merger of Kineton and Dacre with my own college, Northgate, will be the first of several such mergers at Salster so as to produce not only *bigger* institutions but also leaner, fitter institutions which can compete with the Yales and Harvards of the world.'

'Dr Norris – a twentieth-century model of tradition and heritage?'

Norris reprised the enigmatic smile. 'Oh no, our

traditions are much older than that! Our college was founded in the late fourteenth century to train young men to think independently, not to take the comfortable or politically expedient line. I think that's a heritage well worth preserving. In fact, I think that in our current age it's not just worth preserving, it's essential to our freedom and democracy that some scholars are prepared to remain independent of business and commerce in order to be able to provide a critique of our society that has integrity.'

'Sir Ian, in ten seconds – would your proposed merger stifle the independent critique that Dr Norris is so concerned to provide?'

'I can assure you in *one* second, David. No, it absolutely will not.'

The Cobbles, like every other road in Salster between eleven o'clock and one o'clock on Fairings Day, was closed to traffic. Only runners and team members were allowed to set foot on the vehicle-free roads, the tens of thousands of noisy, colourful spectators confined to the pavements by crowd-control barriers, stewards and police officers.

Damia and her runners formed a claret and navy platoon within a battalion of silked and tracksuited young people striding confidently along the Cobbles towards the Pilgrims' Gate Bridge. Like athletes at the Olympics' opening ceremony they smiled, waved and showed off their finery, looking into the densely packed supporters and spectators on the pavements for friends and family. Banners in college colours waved with encouraging messages – 'Go Kings!' 'We ♥ Prince E's'. College scarves had been dragged out of wardrobes, merchandised college gear was everywhere, branded and bootlegged. Damia saw a huge claret-coloured silk banner with Stephan Kingsley's logo in navy and waved madly at the students holding it. The crowd around them waved back and chanted 'Toby! Toby! Toby!' to the wide-grinned jubilation of their runners.

The cameras that followed the competitors in procession down the Cobbles – shoulder-mounted to minimise camera-shake on the unforgiving surface – broadcast pictures of a rainbow river of silk; the maroon and gold of the combined King's/Eversholt team, the green and silver of St Thomas' and its associate John Wyclif, Traherne and Dover's purple and cerise, St Dunstan's and its twentieth-century partner Faken-ham in red and black. Prince Edward's college – formerly the only foundation college with no associate – and its silver livery with black piping looked almost ascetic when seen in the company of the rich jewel colours of the other colleges' silks.

Sally looked around suddenly. 'Where's Northgate?' she shouted above the noise of the crowd. Sam took her arm and pointed silently ahead to the Bridge where a knot of runners stood awaiting the multi-coloured marchers. Northgate Col-lege, running under its own name for the first time in its history, had chosen blue and white as their colours.

The colours, Damia thought, of Microsoft and IBM.

'Gamesmanship,' Duncan mouthed. 'Getting there before everybody else as if they're welcoming us.'

'Yes,' Damia agreed, speaking almost into his ear, 'but think how long they've had to stand there getting nervous, waiting for everyone.'

'Nervous is good' – Duncan turned his head to her ear, unwilling to be mollified. 'Gets the adrenalin flowing.'

'Up to a point,' Damia soothed, her hand in the small of his back. 'Only up to a point.'

Damia and the runners had met up at her house early that morning to have breakfast and go over plans for the race one last time. Damia had lain awake for much of the night playing and replaying scenarios in her mind. There would be no greater opportunity than this to send Tobyites the world over a message that called them to action at the unprecedented meeting of the college community in a week's time. If Damia and her runners failed in their task then Kineton and Dacre College, its unique history and place in the world, might be lost.

When Duncan, Sally, Sam, Ellen and the two reserve runners Jim and Ali arrived at eight, Damia had been up for hours. A huge fruit salad stood on the kitchen table, surrounded by plates, bowls and cutlery. On the work surface were teapot and cafetiere, wholegrain cereals of various kinds and bread ready to be toasted.

Having asked Duncan and Sally how the revision for finals was coming along, Damia took a deep breath that silenced the team. 'I just need to ask you all one more time,' she said, 'are you all happy that we do this according to plan? Because it's going to be news – and if we don't win, the news may not be very kind to us.'

The runners, having been asked the question several times before, were nevertheless sobered by her tone and by the proximity of their fifteen minutes of fame or infamy.

'Yeah! Hell, this is Toby's future we're talking about,' Sam burst out finally. 'So what if we end up in the papers?'

Though the day had started fair and fine, by the time the runners were making their way to the Bridge a wind had begun to tug at their silks and dark clouds were crowding over the city from the horizon. Damia handed tracksuit tops to her chilling runners and hoped fervently that it wouldn't rain. Though it would not stop their plans, wet quads and persistent rain could significantly affect their execution.

Precautionary 'By, For and With' umbrellas appeared here and there, as did hooded sweatshirts bearing the logo. The British summer was proving an aid to marketing if nothing else. Damia watched journalists working the crowd and wondered whether any Tobyites in Fairings merchandise would make it on to the television screens. Free advertising would be useful.

As they reached the Bridge where the runners would check in with the marshals, Damia checked her watch for the twentieth time since setting off from Toby. Still more than ten minutes before the first runners were set off. She turned to her athletes. 'OK guys, I'm off to my station. Good luck.' She embraced each of them hard, in turn. 'You're brilliant – all of you – you know that, don't you?' And, with a nod at their embarassment, she set off at a trot back along the Cobbles.

On the final, definitive pip of Greenwich noon, the clock tower at King's College clanged into sonorous voice and the packed pavements of Salster erupted as the mass countdown gave way to cheers, whistles, air-horns and yells at the start of the most exciting event of the Salster year. Damia smiled despite her nerves. Ellen and Sam would be off, their head-turning sprints given extra speed by the crowd's noise and the adrenalin-buzzing sense of occasion.

The purpose of the Toby team's hell-for-leather start was to give the false impression that they were going for the classic first move – the team's fastest runners setting out to take the easy pickings at the nearest colleges – Traherne and St Dunstan's. Traditionally, any team whose first two runners were able to secure both these roses would go on to win the race, as they were then free to tackle two of the remaining three colleges in pairs before combining for the fifth college and heading back to St Thomas' together. The addition of a Northgate rose to the running order had complicated this equation, but all the pundits were still of the opinion that early acquisition of the St Dunstan's and Traherne roses would be the key to victory.

But at the moment when one of them should have shot in through the Traherne gate to sprint across the quad ahead of the other runners in the pack, both Sam and Ellen tore onwards, slowing slightly as they separated, Ellen to continue past St Dunstan's, their bluff played out, Sam to head off through the back streets behind the Cobbles to King's. Ellen turned hard left at the Mummer's Cross with a wave to Damia in the packed and screaming crowd. There was no one in pursuit. All the other runners were intent on earlier colleges either as singletons or – having failed to grab the lowest rose – as pairs.

Exactly one hundred seconds after Ellen and Sam had sprinted away from the Bridge, Duncan and Sally set off at the back of the remaining pack, peeling off along the Cobbles, she to Traherne and he to St Dunstan's, both ignoring frantic yells from the crowd that 'The lower ones are gone – do it together!'

The television cameras in Traherne and St Dunstan's both broadcast images of single runners entering quads long since denuded of roses accessible to the stretching hand. Pairs had removed the next lowest blooms, leaving only those on the higher levels. Puzzled at the entrance of lone runners who should, by rights, have been struggling to reach these higher roses even as a pair, producers instructed their cameras to remain on these two quads and the commentators to voice over what was happening.

'The Kineton and Dacre team are running an inexplicable pattern here – I can't imagine what they're doing. We might have expected Duncan McTeer and Sally Mackle to work as a pair if she was adept at shoulder-stands, but they have separated. And here's Sally Mackle coming into Traherne quad at a full sprint . . . what is she . . . Oh my good Lord . . . she's run straight up the wall . . . let's see that again . . . yes, here she comes, up to the wall, straight up as if she was defying gravity, then that flip, neatly plucking the rose as she went over and now she's off out of the quad . . . I can honestly say that in all my years of watching the Fairings, I've never seen anything like it . . . the hours of practice that must have taken . . .'

Duncan McTeer, less than half a minute later, performed an almost identical stunt at St Dunstan's and then joined Sally to head down the Romangate towards Toby.

The television companies, meanwhile, suddenly became very interested in what Sam and Ellen were doing. Producers in OB vans stared at the images from the magnificent quad at King's, zooming in on the tall, narrow trellis secured to the famous sundial that rose from the dead centre of the quad's immaculate lawn. Sam raced along one of the flagged paths that divided the lawn into four isosceles triangles, slowed just enough to pluck the lowest rose from the sundial's trellis and then speeded up once more to sprint out through the King's cloisters into the college garden.

'No freerunning stunts here at King's, and perhaps that's the point – as the runners are not allowed to touch the trellis, and there was no wall on either side to run up, the only way a single runner could pick this rose would be to make it *here before anybody else. The Kineton and Dacre College plan suddenly becomes a lot clearer. I wonder if Ellen Ballantyne is heading to Prince Edward College for a similar reason?'*

Ellen sprinted over the hospital bridge and up Prince Edward Street, breathing hard but regularly. Leaping up the shallow steps that led into the college's front quad with its sunken lawn she sprinted along the flagstoned terrace at the side of the lawn, and around to the far wall of the quad behind which lay the college library with its famous clock tower. Huge windows admitted as much light as possible and the rose-trellis had been erected between two of these windows, the edges of its frame almost butting up against the glass. Just as at King's, photos from previous years had shown that there would be no scope for freerunning manoeuvres here. Ellen plucked the lowest rose, pulling it free of the virtually headless nail with which its stem was attached to the trellis, and turned to retrace her steps.

As she approached the gate, she heard pounding footsteps and realised that she had only just secured the singleton's rose. Who had got here so quickly?

The answer, in sky blue and white, passed her as she skittered down the low steps. Northgate running as if their lives depended on it. An erstwhile teammate flashed her a grin as he sprinted past; Ellen smiled briefly back and then set off at a more sedate pace up Prince Edward Street towards the Fairway and a rendezvous with the rest of the team at St Thomas'.

Northgate was the unknown quantity. As Damia stood with a Toby scout named Sophie in the packed and chanting crowd aound the Mummer's Cross, she found herself holding her breath as she waited for Duncan and Sally to come into view at the entrance to Popers Lane, one of the streets that gave on to the Fairway, fifty metres away.

They still had not appeared half a minute later when Freddy, another scout, skidded to a halt at her side. 'Northgate's a blow-out. Sam can't get his rose. We need Duncan and Sally up there.' He put his hands on his hips and panted hard.

Damia had already calculated odds, runners who'd gone past, patterns run. She did not need to think. If Sam could not get the Northgate rose their gamble had failed and the decision was already made.

'No,' she said. 'It's plan B.'

The scouts, primed and ready, ran in pursuit of their runners.

By this stage in the race, the television cameras at the Mummer's Cross were reduced to crowd-shots and were winding down, anticipating that all future action would be at St Thomas'. Only the vigilance of the crew high up in the helicopter ensured that the most extraordinary events ever to take place in the Fairings were captured on camera.

Beneath the whirling blades the gimble-mounted camera was angled this way and that, zooming in on scenes that no one but Damia Miller and her runners could possibly have anticipated.

Communicating with the producer in the OB van on the ground, the commentator in the helicopter informed him that as soon as the winning team had plucked its rose at St Thomas' he needed to cut straight to the footage they were getting from the aerial camera. 'This is gold, Nick,' he gabbled to his producer, 'pure bloody gold, mate.'

❖

At fourteen minutes past twelve noon GMT, millions of television screens all over the world abruptly cut from an image of four young people in sky-blue and white silk in ecstatic celebration in the library quad of St Thomas' college to a strange procession on Salster's Romangate. The helicopter crew had captured the scene as eight scouts in Toby tracksuits entered a building on North Lane and emerged, with difficulty, a few moments later bearing between them a kind of stretcher. Once on the pavement they arranged themselves so that two bearers stood at each corner, holding the projecting poles of the stretcher. The four Toby runners who had, in response to the messages of the scouts, gathered around Damia, waited until the stretcher came to a standstill in the middle of the crossroads. Then, led by their coach, they took their positions: Sam in front, Ellen at the rear, Sally and Duncan flanking the stretcher. Damia walked out on to the deserted tarmac of the Romangate and, at a slow, dignified pace led the strange procession south, towards Toby.

The camera zoomed in and the voice of the commentator was heard above the dopper-dopper-dopper of the helicopter's rotors.

'They appear to be carrying some form of bier or platform. We can't see what's on it because it's covered over with a cloth or sheet, but it's obviously heavy as it's taking eight people to carry it.'

Initially, the crowd was confused and wanted to know what was going on. Was this part of the Fairings or what? Questions were shouted, the crowd pushed and shoved more or less good-naturedly, nudging and laughing, trying to climb over the barriers and join in. To Damia's relief, the stewards held firm, as did the police, their faces to the crowd.

Then, suddenly, as the procession started down the Romangate, two uniformed officers, flak-jacketed and armed, closed in at either side. A third, a leashed dog at his side, accompanied them.

'I'm going to have to ask you to put that down and uncover it,' one of them said, while the other spoke inaudibly on his radio.

Damia did not hesitate. Motioning to the bearers to put the bier down she took the officer aside and spoke rapidly to him, her expression tense. Then she turned and freed a corner of the sheet so that he could see what was beneath. The dog was brought forward to sniff, after which more talking ensued. Finally, all three officers fell in behind Ellen and the little procession resumed.

As they made their way at a slow march down the Romangate, a silence moved with them. The crowd, influenced by the closed, still faces of the bearers and runners, gradually fell silent. They watched, waiting for something to happen, for things to become clear.

As the procession neared the lower end of the Romangate and Toby, the sound of an engine broke the silence and heads turned to see the outside broadcast van, accompanied by two police outriders, coming down the road. The passenger door opened and a burly man slid out, a camera on his shoulder, closely followed by two other figures. They hurried after the procession. None of the bearers turned to look in their direction.

Damia was aware that the policemen who had joined their procession were now allowing people to leave the stewarded

547

pavements and follow them down the empty road. She could hear the sound of many feet but little talking. The hush was expectant, the crowd taking its lead from the silent cortege.

When they reached Kineton and Dacre's northeastern arch, the procession stopped. Damia slid her rucksack from her back and extracted four pillar-candles. After checking by the police officers and the sniffer dog, these were distributed amongst the four runners and each lit in turn. Then, shrugging back into the rucksack, Damia led the procession around the perimeter of the college.

Uncertainly, the crowd followed, becoming slightly more vocal, sensing that things were about to come to a head. Damia made an instant decision; she could not afford to let the crowd break the silence too far, she had to act before they turned it into a carnival. As soon as they had circled the college once, arriving back at their starting point, she motioned to the bearers and led the procession in to the Octagon Yard.

The clouds which, earlier, had lain on the horizon were now lining the sky above their heads in marbled lead. The wind gusted and eddied, moving hair across faces, ruffling running silk against muscled torsos, whirling the multi-coloured plastic windmills bought from street vendors by frazzled parents.

Damia looked around, her heart beating furiously with the enormity of what she was about to do.

She waited for the crowd – as great a part of it as possible – to arrange itself in the Yard. At a signal from her, the bearers, who had taken up a stance beneath the empty statuary niche, put down their bier. Four of their number bent to untie the loops that held the cloth securely to the bier. Then, with reverence and the grace of much rehearsal, they lifted the cloth clear of the shape beneath and stood back from the bier. As the murmuring crowd exchanged glances and shook heads, the cloth was folded decorously and put on the ground next to the bier. The remaining four bearers laid hands on the uncovered form and raised it to an upright position. Both actions complete, all eight bearers, in carefully aligned pairs, walked to the steps of the great Octagon, where they stood silently.

The runners, at a signal from Damia, left their honour-guard positions and came to stand before her. Taking the rucksack once again from her shoulders, she unzipped the front pocket and extracted four envelopes. Putting the ruck-sack on the floor behind her she gave one envelope to each runner. Aware of the cameraman's uncertainty as to where he should stand as Sam, Ellen, Duncan and Sally each moved in a different direction, Damia motioned for him to stay where he was, slightly at an angle in front of her.

As the runners took up their positions to the north, south, east and west of the great Octagon, the mighty Great Hall door swung open and four people came down the steps. All four turned as they reached the Yard and took up positions around the Octo.

Damia, aware that all this was taking place, but not look-ing around, waited until she saw the crowd's eyes refocusing on her. As a huge, furry boom-mic was manoeuvred in her direction, she took a deep breath and began to speak the words she had memorised.

'This college, called Kineton and Dacre College – founded by Richard Dacre, vintner of the guild and merchant of the city of London, built by Simon of Kineton, master mason, and Gwyneth of Kineton, master carpenter – will be, as long as it stands and men look upon it, a memorial to Tobias Kine-ton, their son.'

As she said these last words, she put out a hand towards the statue that stood on its bier. She waited until she saw the camera turn towards the statue of a twisted, tortured boy; a boy held upright by a cage that was both his prison and his release.

'Tobias Kineton' – the camera swung back to Damia once more – 'looked upon with scorn, called cursed and abomination, was great of heart. His life wove a pattern of love and forgiveness, where he was shown hatred and neglect. He loved much and he gave much, as much as any of us is able to give, even unto his own life.'

Damia's eyes swept the crowd. They were confused, but held by the power of the words, the sense of a ritual being enacted. Would they understand that this boy, this crippled, imprisoned boy, had given up his life so that the college in whose yard they stood could exist?

She was suddenly overwhelmed with the sense that, though Toby had died, he had also *lived*. He had lived and, far from simply struggling against his deformity, he had attained greatness; attained the maturity to forgive in a way that many five times his age could not; attained an understanding of his place in the scheme of things that allowed him to give the only thing he had, his life, so that his father's ambition could be fulfilled. He could not be an apprentice, could not carve, or shape, or contribute ideas. But he could offer his life. And he had. Damia's voice cracked and then steadied on a breath as she continued.

'For as John Dacre, only son of Richard Dacre, died in this place, cut short before manhood, so Tobias Kineton chose his own death as atonement for that other end. A life for a life, one taken by senseless action, the other given with selfless love.

'And to his memory, and in both their names, this college was completed.

'For each man has his own worth.

'Each man, though he be humble and crippled, is equal before God.

'Each man, though he follow not in his father's footsteps, will have his place in the world.'

Damia felt the tears swell in her eyes and her throat constrict. She swallowed hard and continued.

'And this college stands here to equip men, whoever they be, to take that place, to care for the poor and lowly and to remember love, faithfulness and forgiveness, even unto death.

'Those whose names will now be called, come forward and accept your alms, given in memory of Tobias Kineton, crippled in body, great of heart.'

Sick children over whom Gwyneth of Kineton, like any mother, would have wept, were present, their wasted limbs and downy heads representing the hospice to whose representative Ellen Ballantyne gave her alms. To the words 'You who are given these alms in remembrance of Tobias Kineton, will you pray for the continuance and good governance of this college, all the days of your life?' the hospice's official recipient replied without hesitation, 'I will.'

The elderly residents of the city, many abandoned in a way that would have been unthinkable to those who built the college, were represented by Help the Aged, whose spokesperson, asked by Sally Mackle if she would pray for the continuance and good governance of the college, responded with a heartfelt, 'I *will* so pray!'

Duncan McTeer's alms envelope went to the twenty-first century's outcasts – those homeless individuals who used the facilities of the Gardiner Centre. Damia's erstwhile colleague promised, with a nod of mumbled embarrassment, that the required prayer would be offered.

As she watched the progress of the extraordinary event that she had instigated, Damia wondered how the fifteenth-century crowd had received that first obit for Tobias Kineton. Toby's Obit. Had it changed their minds about the way they saw a crippled boy? Had they believed him capable of giving his own life? Had they held fast to the view of the dean and the bishop that Toby was cursed, a child of ill omen, a demon-possessed soul? Or had they seen what Simon had clearly seen – a person 'great of heart'?

Sam Kearns, when his turn came, gave his alms to a representative of the British Paralympics Committee. The sportsman bowed his head in response to the request for prayer and said simply, '*Yes*.'

Sam's was the last almsgiving and, as Damia watched him, she wondered what this young man would do with his life. He had admitted, during one post-training conversation, that he had chosen to read psychology because he had wanted to go into advertising 'and earn a lot of money', but that since coming to Toby he had changed his mind.

'Maybe marketing's more my thing,' he'd said, with a provocative grin at Damia. 'What d'you reckon?'

As the runners and scouts broke ranks and began to greet people in the Yard, giving the crowd its cue to disperse, the cameraman and his two companions hurried to Damia's side.

'We'd like to do an interview with you—'

'Good. I do have a few things to say.'

Sixty-six

'Sim, let me hold your arm will you?'

Simon Ackland, master mason, held out a muscular fore-arm to the only grandmother he had ever known and smiled down at her proudly. 'You do not need an arm, Gramma, you are as strong as ever.'

'Not quite, Sim, though I have nothing to complain of.' Gwyneth caught her breath, then said, 'I had thought that sawing and planing for so many years might have seized up my joints but I have been fortunate in that as in so many things.' She looked up at him fondly, including him in the tally of her good fortune.

'Yes, Gransha was not so fortunate.'

His grandmother's face registered nothing but calm, resigned to her grief these many years. 'Your grandsire saw his college completed. He saw tutors and scholars within and he saw it accepted in the city. He needed no more.'

'But he did not see Toby's Obit celebrated.'

Gwyneth sighed, remembering how keenly she had felt Simon's absence at her side ten years ago on that first occasion. 'No. He did not. But they were his words we spoke and we will speak the same words today and every time Toby's Obit is held and alms given in his remembrance.'

They walked side by side down the stairs and into the entrance hall. As Simon put his hand on the latch to let them out he turned to his grandmother.

'Gramma?'

'Yes?'

'Henry told me once that Gransha had put the words and duties for Toby's Obit into one of the images of him that stand in the college. Is that really true, or was my little brother teasing, as he does?'

'No, he was not. Simon did do that.'

'Why?' he asked, steadying her hand on his arm as she stepped over a puddle.

'Because he said that a time might come when the truth was lost and nobody knew, any more, who Tobias Kineton had been. He could not bear to think of such a thing.'

'But if the paper is hidden in the statue—'

Gwyneth interrupted before he could finish. 'Hidden only until those who are looking come,' she said. 'Not precisely hidden, even. Put away for safekeeping.'

After the unseasonal rain of the last several days, the college was radiant in the sunshine as they entered through the northeastern arch. Unlike that first obit of John's which had been held outside the still unfinished college, all subsequent obits for him, and afterwards for Toby, had been conducted in the central yard, with the crowd standing around the inner perimeter and alms distributed, as on that first occasion, at each entrance archway.

Crowds were already beginning to gather, drawn by the

rumoured distribution of pennies to craftsmen with no work, as well as to the lame and crippled.

Gwyneth looked up at the octagonal building at the centre of the yard. Though she had hated the college once, when she thought Simon had loved it more than her or their son, she had come to love it as a memorial to Toby. She had been reconciled by the years to Toby's gift of his own life to his father and had come to see, as then she had been unable to, that his life had assumed a significance in that one act that it could never have had if he had simply lived out his days in silence and passivity.

In the teeth of Copley's opposition and Ralph's constant attempts at frustration and delay, the college had been raised. Would she – or even Simon – have persisted against all threats and stays had it not been for Toby and his self-sacrifice?

She knew that she would not, that she would have been too afraid of the consequences; of Copley. No man's vision would have been worth standing against an anointed bishop; but her son's wish that his father should have his college had prevailed with her and she had built the college when Simon could not.

And the lame and crippled of the city blessed Toby's name – and would do, every third year in perpetuity – for giving them the means to live and to be an unaccustomed material blessing to their families. This dole of money and clothing might, Gwyneth often comforted herself, stay a hand that would otherwise smother a child born twisted or malformed. Another Toby.

'Where are your parents?' she asked Sim, looking about her.

'They are meeting with the Regent Master,' he said. 'He has invited you to come within and take some refreshment before the ceremony, if you will.'

She heard his carefully neutral tone and asked, 'Why do you not like him, Sim – our Regent Master?'

'He is a lawyer and a scholar. He deals in words and opinions. I deal in stone and wood and building. We are not likely to be kindred spirits.'

'Weasel words, my boy. Tell me – *why don't you like him*?'

Her grandson smiled. His teeth were white against his browned skin. 'All right Gramma, since you will have it. I don't like the fact that he is Nicholas Brygge's son. Would he have been appointed if he were the son of anybody else?'

Gwyneth sucked her cheeks in and pursed her lips. 'It's true we took a chance to oblige Nicholas,' she admitted, as if, on balance, she could tell him the truth, 'but without him as mayor of the city the college would not be here, Sim. And the chance has turned out in our favour. I think Richard is a good Regent Master.'

She looked at him shrewdly as they made their way to the hall's curving staircase. 'If my Simon had not been watched one day by a sharp-eyed beggar boy, you would not be a master mason living in a fine house with a wife and children. You would most likely be a beggar yourself, or else a labourer, living in the hovels outside the city wall, waiting for a penny here today, like these poor souls.'

He grinned wryly. 'But my father had something to show Simon – a faithful copy of a statue he himself had carved.'

'And young Richard Brygge had something to show too – a shrewd business sense, like his father, and – like him – a determination not to be cowed by any man.' Her tone took on a sharper edge. 'We did not *just* appoint him to make Nicholas happy, we did have some proof that the young man was worthy of the trial.'

Sim nodded. 'Aye, aye, I know.'

As they reached the foot of the stone stairs, a young woman with a small child holding either hand matched her steps to their path. Simon put out an arm and encircled his wife's shoulders, tousling the head of his five-year-old son as he did so. 'Well, my rascally Hal, have you looked after your mother and your little brother, as I said?'

'Yes, father.' The slight, blond boy gazed earnestly up at the powerful frame of his father, looking – to Gwyneth's eyes – for all the world like the young waif who had been Henry Ackland. Harry smiled his grandfather's wide, blue-eyed smile and lit up Gwyneth's heart. 'I can swim now, Gramma Gwyneth!'

'Can you, my chick?' Gwyneth asked, a catch in her voice as she spoke, remembering a little boy, so many years ago, who knew he could not.

Henry Ackland, now well past fifty, had as much silver as gold in the hair which, in despite of fashion, he wore as master masons had done in his youth, long and flowing. Smiling briefly at Gwyneth as they watched the procession of candle-holding scholars parade three times around the college before stopping at intervals around the interior, he stepped forward to intone the words that Simon of Kineton had written in memory of his son.

'This college, called Kineton and Daker College – founded by Richard Daker, vintner of the guild and merchant of the city of London, built by Simon of Kineton, Master Mason, and Gwyneth of Kineton, Master Carpenter – will be, as long as it stands and men look upon it, a memorial to Tobias Kineton, their son.'

Henry swept his gaze around the yard and Gwyneth did likewise. She had not expected so large a crowd this time; ten years before, at Toby's first obit, it had seemed that the whole city had come, out of sheer curiosity to see what the Kinetons would do to memorialise their crippled boy. No fewer had turned out three years later.

Perhaps Simon had been right. 'I think we will not celebrate this every year,' he had said whilst engaged in drafting his ceremony, 'for if a thing is to be commemorated in perpetuity it will become too commonplace if it comes around every year.'

'We could celebrate it every eight years,' Gwyneth suggested quietly, 'remembering that eight years was his span of life.'

He had met her eyes with tenderness and put out a hand to her. 'I think eight is too long,' he said, with his new gentleness. 'People will forget to look forward to it, they will get out of the way of it.'

'Every two years then?' Gwyneth suggested. 'So it does not become too commonplace?'

She remembered Simon staring into nothingness as if contemplating some great matter, or consulting someone who was not there, before replying, 'I think every three years would be fitting. Then all who study here would see it enacted once and once only in their time at the college.'

And so it had been decided. Every three years the citizenry would be invited to gather on the anniversary of Toby's death to commemorate his sacrifice in the giving and receiving of alms.

'Tobias Kineton, looked upon with scorn, called cursed and abomination, was great of heart. His life wove a pattern of love and forgiveness, where he was shown hatred and neglect. He loved much and he gave much, as much as any of us is able to give, even unto his own life.'

Gwyneth's eyes scanned the onlookers' faces. She and Simon had debated endlessly whether he should make it clear that Toby had deliberately sacrificed himself for the college, to pay the debt of John's death.

'They will not believe it!' she had protested. 'They will say he was incapable of such a thing – they will laugh! I could not bear that!'

'Just because they do not believe it does not make it the less true,' Simon had pointed out, evenly, 'and to say anything else is to dishonour Toby's memory and his sacrifice.'

'Yes, but—'

'If we say nothing about his gift of his life for me, then all we do is commemorate a poor boy who was a cripple and who died.'

'And that is not enough?'

'No! Because he was not a poor boy who died. He was a man in his heart, a noble man, a courageous man. And he did not simply die, he gave up his life as men do in battle, for a greater thing than themselves.'

Gwyneth knew that it comforted Simon in some fashion to see their son as having attained some of the attributes of manhood; it helped him to feel that, in some way, Toby had achieved in eight years what some men fell short of in the whole span of a life.

'For as John Daker, only son of Richard Daker, died in this place, cut short before manhood, so Tobias Kineton chose his own death as atonement for that other end. A life for a life, one taken by senseless action, the other given with selfless love.

'And to his memory, and in both their names, this college was completed.

'For each man has his own worth.

'Each man, though he be humble and crippled, is equal before God.

'Each man, though he follow not in his father's footsteps, will have his place in the world.

'And this college stands here to equip men, whoever they be, to take that place, to care for the poor and lowly and to remember love, faithfulness and forgiveness, even unto death.

'Those whose names will now be called, come forward and accept your alms, given in memory of Tobias Kineton, crippled in body, great of heart.'

Gwyneth stepped forward and, as she had done on all previous occasions, read out the lists of those to be given alms at each archway of the college.

And, as before, as each person was given their bundle of clothes and purse of coin, they were asked:

'You who are given these alms in remembrance of Tobias Kineton, will you pray for the continuance and good governance of this college, all the days of your life?'

And all replied, as each was able, 'I will so pray.'

Having given the first bundles and purses at the north-eastern arch, Gwyneth waited quietly for the three other groups of beneficiaries to receive their alms. And as she stood, she thought how different things were now to that day, eighteen years before, when John Daker's first obit had been commemorated in the teeth of Copley's opposition and amidst the curious citizenry.

Now there was no Copley. He had fled the country when Henry Bolingbroke took the throne and deposed the rightful king. Copley had been Richard's man through and through, and he would not wait to see what Bolingbroke, styling himself Henry the Fourth of England, would make of his rival's loyal men.

But Copley's departure had hardly signalled an end to the Church's suspicion of the college and its purposes. The years after Henry's usurpation had been hard for the Lollard cause in England, and Richard Brygge had played a shrewd tactician's game in his presentation of his English-speaking college that put itself outside the Church's jurisdiction. When, two years ago, the law had been promulgated declaring heresy to be contrary to common law as well as canon law, Gwyneth had feared for them all, but Brygge – ever his father's son – had protected his own, saying that teaching in English was not heresy, it was simply contrary to the will of the Church; that since he did not require men whose livings were paid by endowment to come and teach at his college, leaving parishes empty or vicariously filled, he would thank the Church to leave him alone to his business; that there was no chapel connected to his college where heresy could be preached or practised.

That there were those in the Church who thought that teaching in English *was* heretical – that only Latin, connected intimately with the Church as it was, could be orthodox – Gwyneth knew full well. But she trusted in Daker's vision, she trusted in Mottis's choice of masters and she trusted in Brygge – father and son.

And she had, she reflected, been proved right in that trust. For the people of Salster – ever fickle, like all citizenry – had taken the college to their heart. Teachers who joined with them in the work of the religious guilds, whose wives gossiped with them in the market, whose children were educated with theirs by impoverished scholars keeping body

561

and soul together – these men gained acceptance for the college as part of the city as nothing else could have.

It was even remarked upon that, now, when a scuffle broke out – as it did from time to time – between scholars of Kineton and Daker College and those of a hall of residence, the young men of the town were quick to join the fray on the side of 'their' scholars – these young men being easily identified by the absence of clerical gown or first tonsure.

The future of her college, Gwyneth felt confident, was assured by the city's acceptance of it, which would, in time, turn from propriety even to love.

She tried to imagine a similar ceremony of almsgiving in future decades, when she would be long gone. Would the Church still peer suspiciously at her college far into the future, she wondered, as the people of Salster commemorated her Toby?

Would the Church ever come to be benign enough to relax its grip on power, on men's minds? Or would it always see those not born as others were as accursed, as possessed of demons, as an abomination?

Gwyneth looked up at the eastern wall to her left, at Toby in his frame, and suddenly, for the first time, she saw him as Simon had seen him – a prisoner, strapped to a contrivance not of his own devising. But Toby had been freed by the frame, not made prisoner! She knew she had freed her boy with her ash-hoops and oak runners, freed him to stand tall and move about on the earth like other boys.

But his freedom had led to John Daker's death, and his own.

Did freedom, she wondered as she moved back to the central building and her family, always carry with it the seeds of disaster?

Epilogue – seven years later

Salster, the week before Easter

Beneath a furrowed cloud-bank, on flat land where rivers meet, a city spills out like a child's bricks tipped from a box – densest at the middle, more thinly scattered at the edges.

Clouds shrug restlessly across the city and shadows flow over cathedral, castle, colleges, tourist honeypots. A fly's-eye dome of leaded glass, brilliantly illuminated in the windy gloom of a pre-solstice afternoon, glows warm like a beacon of invitation.

The yard in which the glass-domed building stands is crowded with people, gathered, as they gathered three years previously, to see the enactment of a ritual devised in another age.

As at the ritual's first celebration six hundred years ago, the poor are here. Those of the underclass, whose poverty denies them even a roof over their head save that provided by the shabby refuge of the Gardiner Centre, are often seen here in this place of apparent privilege and are welcomed, as they welcome those from this college who visit them as mentors and tutors.

And the lame, they are here too. A small figure, bound by Velcro straps into an electric wheelchair, has come on behalf of the organisation who paid for this, his twenty-first-century version of Tobias Kineton's frame.

The seventy-two final-year undergraduates of Kineton and Dacre College have processed around the outer perimeter of the college and now come to take up their positions within the walls, their fragile candle flames lighting solemn young faces.

At the centre of the ceremony stand representatives of the college community that came together with such determination seven years ago and resisted the predatory intentions of Sir Ian Baird. Together they stand: the Regent Master; the tenants' representative who ousted the belligerent Hadstowe to work closely with Norris; the elected college staff member; a scholar chosen by popular undergraduate acclaim and an old member selected at random from the ever-growing number registering throughout the world. Each is poised, cheque in hand, script committed to memory.

Within the gathering of community members, onlookers and tourists, a little knot of people stands in the gathering dusk.

The women, one dark, her hair in beaded braids, the other fair-skinned, dark-haired with the body of a dancer, stand companionably close. Occasionally, they lean to speak, mouth-to-ear. One wears a baby-carrier on her back; the baby, cheeks pink beneath a blue fleecy hat, sleeps, oblivious to the solemnity around him. The man who stands at the women's side holds the hand of a little girl. She is, possibly, four years old and has unmanageably crinkly hair, stuck with futile but delightful clips. She wears purple wellingtons sprinkled with multicoloured stars, vibrantly pink dungarees and a purple jumper. It is easy to tell, by the way that she frequently strokes the arm of her coat with her free hand, that this garment, brilliant white and ostentatiously fluffy, is her pride and joy. As the Regent Master steps forward to speak she tugs at the man's hand and demands to be lifted up on to his shoulders. The women look on and share a private smile. Their little girl already has her father where she wants him.

'This college,' the Regent Master's voice comes steadily through the PA system, 'called Kineton and Dacre College – founded by Richard Dacre, vintner of the guild and merchant of the city of London, built by Simon of Kineton, Master Mason, and Gwyneth of Kineton, Master Carpenter – will be, as long as it stands and men look upon it, a memorial to Tobias Kineton, their son.'

'Mummy!'

Damia looks up at her daughter, who is bouncing with excitement on her father's shoulders.

'Yes, Evie?'

'Can we go to Daddy's house? I want to see the guinea pig babies!'

Damia raises an eyebrow at the father of her child. 'Guinea pig babies?'

'Look, I know it's not one of my days for having the kids, but Evie's guinea pig – who we all thought was a Henry – has proved to be a Henrietta. Where there was one, as of yesterday there are six.'

'Can we, Mummy?'

Damia turns to her partner, who is easing her shoulders beneath the sleeping weight of her son. 'What do you think, sweetheart?'

Smiling, the love of Damia's life, restored to her by the

miracle of the internet and its social networking sites, looks down at Evie and winks. 'Who can resist guinea pig babies – eh, Evie?'

'Yay!' Evie's heels pound her father's chest, jubilant.

'Can we have tea at your house then, Mr Gordon?' Damia asks playfully.

Neil, who lobbied hard for the unorthodox family to live together in a large, subdivided house before conceding that living in the same street was probably sufficient, says lightly, 'I think we can manage tea, yes.'

'OK,' Damia says, quelling Evie's impatience, 'let's just wait for everyone to put out their candles, then we'll go.'

The ritual blowing out of candles by their bearers at a signal from the Regent Master has come to mark the end of the ceremony in the twenty-first century, and Damia suddenly wonders how the fifteenth century rounded out the almsgiving and sent people on their way.

She feels her eyes being drawn upwards to the west wall where Tobias Kineton stands, strapped to a strut, the prisoner in his liberating cage. And as the light fades on Toby's birthday – the new date set for his obit, the date of his death falling inconveniently in the summer vacation – and the candles, still unsnuffed, burn brightly in the gloom, Damia's inner eye turns to the first-floor hall above them.

In the quiet of the Great Hall a figure stands. He is oblivious to all that proceeds without. No one exists for him, at this moment, nothing but the task before him. Turning from the freshly plastered ashlar wall, he looks around. Eight walls, four almost taken up by windows, surround him. Each wall is new-built, untouched; each has faint lines upon it traced by this man's hand. A Master Mason, he is used to stone –

knows to within a hair's breadth the action of gouge or chisel on the surface of limestone, marble, sandstone or purbeck. But these lines are different. These are not cutting lines, traced from templates; they are guidelines for the story he has determined he must tell. His own hand drew them – a flowing line for vine-tracery, two tall ovals to each wall for the outlines that will frame his tale. But he, who has set mallet and chisel to stone for forty years with never a held breath, fears to begin this venture. He cannot discard a marred effort and throw it away as he could with a poorly cut stone. He cannot chide or chastise another if this work is not done as perfectly as he wishes. This is his task and no other can accomplish it. He, who is famed for his rounded stone images, has taken pains to learn this fluid, flat-work craft. If he has mistaken his lines, his draughtsmanship, he knows he will have to replaster.

Not beginning is better than marring the work he must render perfectly if he is to satisfy himself.

The paint he will use sits in pots at his feet – brown, green, red, yellow, a little black, a smaller amount still of precious blue.

The work will flow once he starts, this much he knows, but still he is reluctant to begin. He turns back and gazes appraisingly at the lines he has drawn in the first oval. Has he allowed just space? Will the whole appear constrained by its border or simply framed as he intends, an image captured? He can see his intention most clearly with his inner eye, but a lifetime's experience of creation tells him that what is produced rarely matches what was envisaged.

Suddenly he turns and strides across the hall, stopping to gaze intently out of the window.

There, across the yard, stands his son, held aloft and

looking upwards, perhaps for a glimpse of the whole boy who is standing on tiptoe on the other side of the great Octagon. Suddenly pierced by a great longing and a yet greater grief, Simon of Kineton strides back to his former position, his fingers working already at his side, grasping at an action that may pluck this nail of pain from his soul.

Stooping, he picks up the bowl of green pigment, stirs at it with his brush, bends once more to make a mark on a crumpled, much-scraped sheet of parchment at his feet and, without more hesitation, sets the brush to the first of his guide marks.